Pelican Watch

Other books by Rose Senehi

Shadows in the Grass

Windfall

Pelican Watch

Rose Senehi

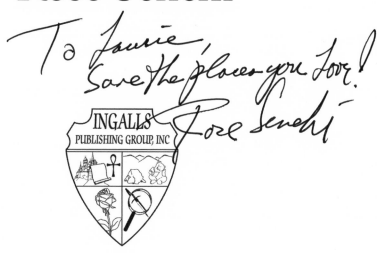

2007

INGALLS PUBLISHING GROUP, INC

197 New Market Center #135

Boone, NC 28607

www.ingallspublishinggroup.com

Cover design by Ann Thompson Nemcosky
Cover photography by Ann Thompson Nemcosky &
Penelope Christensen

Library of Congress Cataloging-in-Publication Data
Senehi, Rose.
     Pelican watch / by Rose Senehi.
         p. cm.
     ISBN-13: 978-1-932158-80-9 (trade pbk. : alk. paper)
     ISBN-10: 1-932158-80-4 (trade pbk. : alk. paper)
  1. Pawleys Island (S.C.)--Fiction. 2. Women artists--Fiction. 3. Murder--Fiction. 4. Habitat (Ecology)--Fiction. 5. Real estate development--Fiction. I. Title.
     PS3619.E659P46 2006
     813'.6--dc22
              2006019857

First Printing: February 2007

For Isaac, Katie & Michael

ACKNOWLEDGMENTS

Judith Geary and Joanne Goldy, for their hours of reading and rereading my manuscript and all their astute suggestions. To Barbara and Bob Ingalls for their committment to good books and to this project. To my friend, Tom Warner, of Litchfield Books, a true bookseller and supporter of the art of writing. To Gene Dickson of Delta Guide Service in Georgetown, SC, who inspired the character of Mac Moultrie. To Genevieve Peterkin of Murrells Inlet who helped me with some of the dialect, and to all the wonderful people I've met since coming to live in South Carolina—especially all my real estate clients and associates whom I now count among my friends, and who have contributed to my understanding and love of the South.

Pelican Watch

Rose Senehi

PROLOGUE

Billy Cleary had spent the better part of his forty years committing nasty crimes and believing it was just a matter of time before a lucky break would change the course of his miserable life. Now, in the middle of the night, in the middle of the marsh, a tantalizing feeling told him this was that time.

He carefully lifted the oars out of the water, then dipped them back into the saltwater creek and tugged until the drifting boat hugged the wall of marsh grass. He looked up and figured by the way the water rippled softly as it moved past the moonlit buoy in the distance the tide was starting to go out. He swiped the sweat trickling down his face with his sleeve, then stared through the curtainless window at the shack's bare light bulb. Damn! That old man had better come out soon or he'd never make it back to his pickup before daybreak.

The moonlight flickering along the subtle waves reminded him of the church he burned to the ground in Greenville; but killing a man at close range was going to be a lot riskier than watching a building go up in flames from a safe distance. He took a couple of deep breaths and switched his thoughts to the money. Ten thousand wasn't bad for one night's work. That is, if everything went as easy as the man at Wendy's said it would. He felt his back pocket to make sure the wad was still there. How could anyone be so stupid as to pay him in advance? Then again, maybe ten thousand wasn't that big of a deal to him.

Billy couldn't shake the memory of the aura of money that had surrounded the man. He had a hunch this was the big chance he'd been waiting for, and if he worked this deal right, his days of hauling the cotton mill's Jockey shorts up and down the interstate were over.

The date on the calendar seemed almost to jump out at Mo Washington as he put his pork chop sandwich into an empty bread bag pulled from a space between the cabinet and refrigerator. But the stained face of the clock over the stove told him it was time to get moving. With the stump that was left of his arm pinning his sandwich to his side, he reached for the string to turn off the light, but then hesitated for a moment and let go. The shrimp were already running, but the darkness outside triggered his life long fear of not returning from the sea. If anything happened to him, his boys had to know what was in his heart. He'd been putting it off for weeks; he couldn't put it off any longer. He pushed back a pile of unopened mail on the scratched enamel table top, picked out a flier and flipped it over.

Thank th' Lord Ma had sent him to the church school for learning. He picked up a ballpoint pen and started the agonizing task of explaining to his two sons why he was skipping their generation and leaving the peninsula to his granddaughter.

He spoke to his wife, absent from this one-room shack for over twenty years, in words laced with the old slave Gullah language.

"I jus got tuh do dis, Martha. We's done broke us backs holdin' on tuh dis place. Dem boys got dey union pension and dey ain' gonna put dere money in taxus tuh hang on tuh dis old slave land."

He looked up at the photographs hanging on the aged cypress wall and stared at the image of his great-grandfather standing in front of the shack he built on the land bought from his former master. An elaborate longhand inscription read: *Moses Washington, Freed Slave, Chertow Island, 1869.*

Tears stung his eyes as he studied the gangly figure. The bulging shoulder muscles testified to years of backbreaking labor in the swampy ricefields of Alston Plantation. Old Moses should see the slave alley now, he said to himself. Same land. Same ole alley. Except now a row of million-dollar homes sat where the shacks used to be.

He spoke his words out loud as he wrote in his slow, arduous script. "Boys, I love yuh. Yuh don' good fuh yourself. Made me too proud." His hand shook as he held the pen. "But yuh neva saw what dis land has stood fuh. Our dignity is here."

He faced the chair across the table as if old Martha were sitting there. "Pains me tah do dis tah yo' boys, Martha. But if'n dey go head and sell, all us from duh old slave down will lose face. We come by it hard, payin' all dem taxus." His shaky hand pressed the point of the pen back on the paper. *So I'se leavin' it tuh Cheryl cause I do know she won't sell out tah no white folk.*

He stared up at his granddaughter's broad dimpled grin in the

10

snapshot tucked into the window casing until he could hear her voice pierce the steamy night air with song as he emptied his shrimp net.

He finished the letter and read it out loud as if he wanted Martha to hear. "It do pain me tah do dis. Specially tah you Little Mo bein de oldest. But I gots to honor dose dat gone before and what dis land meant tah dem. Forgive yuh daddy."

Mo slid into the familiar somber mood that had become a part of his soul as he remembered his millionth humiliation. When he went down to Mt. Pleasant two months earlier to see a lawyer about the will, the receptionist made him wait an hour before she even bothered to let Tommy Warren, Jr. know he'd come on business.

The old fisherman signed his name and carefully folded the paper. He got up, wincing at the pain in his joints, and went over to the calendar with a picture of a pelican that hung from a nail. After checking to make sure the envelope containing the will was still securely taped to its back, he slipped in the letter. Everything would be safe there until Cheryl came to visit.

He glanced once more around the shadowy room he'd been born in, then tucked the Wonder Bread bag under his stump and pulled the string to the light.

Billy crouched behind a wax myrtle overhanging the edge of the dock. He had watched Mo from the creek the day before and grinned when he saw his maimed arm; but the old man's six-foot muscular frame could still be dangerous. Billy planned to whack him from behind before he was on to him. One good thump on the back of the skull, then he'd drop him into the creek—just another drowning of a lone inshore fisherman.

Billy bit his lip. What a dumb-ass thing! Agreeing to look for a will afterward. Especially after the man had the balls to tell him not to leave the place looking ransacked.

Suddenly the light disappeared from the shack. Billy's muscles tightened. An outboard droned on the marsh creek to the south. If it got near, he'd have to make a run for it.

The door creaked open, then shut. The flashlight beam bobbed along the path. Off in the distance the outboard got louder. Mo's labored breaths sounded footsteps away. Billy slowly raised the padded baseball bat and held his breath. Mo's towering bulk blocked the light of the moon and Billy Cleary swung.

The impact tossed Billy onto the fallen giant and he searched the wooly head for a gash that would leave blood. Nothing! He jumped up and dragged the leaden hulk toward the boat, crouching low in case the outboard appeared from out of the marsh. In one gut busting heave he shoved the body into the water.

Billy froze and listened keenly for the outboard. All was quiet again. He rose upright and grasped a dock post until the painful wrenching in his chest subsided. Suddenly, an iron grip latched onto his ankle and flung him into the air. Salt water burned his lungs. The stranglehold on his throat was not enough to block his animal cunning. The old man was strong, but he only had one arm. Billy wedged a knee against his chest, and in one brutal thrust, threw him back. Lunging forward, Billy locked an arm around Mo's head and wrestled him under the water. Just as Billy feared his lungs were about to burst, the old man stopped struggling.

Billy erupted onto the surface, sucking air into his lungs with a painful gasp. His heart pounded in his chest, his throat ached. A hoarse holler jumped out of him as a dark mass surfaced. Mo's wooly head glistened in the moonlight with his face down, his strong gangly arm floating limp.

Billy stared. The cagey old man might be playing possum. Only after what seemed like an eternity was he convinced the body gently bobbing in the water was truly lifeless.

Did he hear the outboard again? His gaze darted around the vast darkness until he was sure there was no one nearby, then he pulled himself out of the water, jumped into his boat and took off.

"*Sh ... it!* If that man wants the damn will, he's going to have to find it *him ... self!*"

🐚 CHAPTER ONE

Nicole Sullivan had always believed that it only took one single pivotal action to change the course of a life, and she had a sneaky feeling something like that had just happened to her. But she was afraid she'd jinx it if she so much as thought about the gallery. This fear kept her from shouting her triumph to everyone sitting on their porches trying to catch a cool breeze off Boston's bay. Subdued smiles and discreet hellos were all anyone was getting.

Her silky summer dress swished around the cumbersome portfolio she was toting the five blocks home from the subway station. Her emotions seesawed from euphoria to despair, as a parade of opportunities squelched by her brother's illness kept interrupting her thoughts.

As usual, she kept enough distance between herself and the neighbors so they wouldn't have a chance to ask, "How's Jack? Doing any better? You poor thing." Did they really care, she wondered, or were these incessant inquiries some subtle way of putting her in her place. One sympathetic encounter could snuff out the hopefulness that embraced her, and she wasn't going to chance it.

An exhilarating stream of possibilities swam around in her head as she contemplated the one-woman show the gallery owners offered her. She couldn't forget the look of confused disbelief on their faces when she told them she needed a couple of days to think it over; but how could she explain her ability to put together a spring show hinged on how many insane episodes her brother was going to come up with.

She shoved her brother's condition out of her mind. Instead, she relived the heady conversation in the gallery and dared to believe the show could happen. After a few giddy moments dreaming about the possibility, she tossed her head and laughed.

Wild ideas popped into her head as she brainstormed. If only she could get away somewhere and draw with no distractions, she could pull together a successful show and wouldn't have to do those tedious textbook illustrations any more. But what was she going to do about Jack and her parents? The chance of a lifetime was staring her in the face; but she couldn't see her way beyond that.

She ignored the stinging blisters on the back of her heels and breezed along, skillfully avoiding eye contact with anyone. She erected an invisible barrier between herself and the inhabitants of this aging middle class Boston suburb of Woburn to ward off more than just talk about her brother. She and her mother were trying hard to protect her father from the indignities of Alzheimer's, and the last thing they wanted was for visiting neighbors to gape at the once-proud hunk of an Irishman staring mindlessly into space.

Twenty-nine Cherry Street came into view beyond the big old maple tree heaving the sidewalk. The small front yard still looked manicured, in spite of Jack's insistence on helping. Nicky carefully inspected the front of the old house, not missing a detail. The fading paint was the least of her troubles. She threw a smile to Mrs. Murphy who was sweeping grass clippings from her driveway, then unlocked the front door and went in.

The familiar smell of corned beef and cabbage, drifting in from the kitchen, mingled with a cool breeze flowing through the open windows in the living room. She carefully closed the front door with its leaded glass window, lovingly placed the portfolio on the floor so it leaned up against the side of the staircase, then slipped out of her heels and placed them neatly next to the bottom step.

She padded through the downstairs to the kitchen where her mother was busy with the meal. She kissed her tenderly on the cheek and looked into the searching eyes still harboring a hint of a sparkle. "Things went well. The gallery took all twelve sketches."

Patricia Sullivan wiped her hands on her apron and caressed Nicky's face with her hands. "I knew they would. They'll sell fast too."

Nicky went over to the sink, ran some water, and blindly felt for a glass in the cupboard while gazing absent-mindedly out the window. She weighed telling her mother about the show.

"I don't know about that, Mom. There are a lot of people out there doing really good stuff."

"Not like you. Your birds look like they're breathing." The mother set the tureen with the night's meal on the kitchen table. "Pour water in the glasses, dear."

Nicky filled a pitcher, shook the dreamy thoughts out of her mind, and advanced to the inevitable question.

14

"Where's Jack?"

"Up in his room. He hasn't been out all day except to help me with your father this morning."

"What about lunch?"

"I took it up to him."

"His medicine?"

The mother's voice fell. "That too."

"Did you watch him take it?"

Mrs. Sullivan scrunched her apron in her hands. "You know how he gets. He took the tray and made me leave the room."

Nicky bit her lip. Every time she left her mother alone with Jack, she was putting her at risk of being tormented by another of the hideous schizophrenic rages filled with filthy language. So far, he'd never raised a hand to either of them, but Nicky still feared it could happen. The part she hated most was when they ended; his pitiful begging for forgiveness broke their hearts all over again.

Tonight, Nicky wanted to give her mother's spirits a boost by sitting down and sharing the thrill over the gallery show. They could plan who they would invite, even what they would wear. Maybe a small get together at the house afterward. It would be just like old times. But the turmoil in the house could keep her from getting enough drawings done in time. Nicky shook her head and decided against mentioning the show. She knew her mother would latch on to any ray of hope with the last bit of optimism she had left, and a cancellation would crush her. She was already filled with guilt about saddling Nicky with all the family's problems.

Right now, things were going pretty smoothly at the house. Why raise everyone's expectations and risk another painful disappointment. So she just went to the refrigerator and dutifully filled a bowl with ice.

The transparent cubes crackled in the red plastic glass as she poured the water. Sensing a presence, her gaze traveled in halting motions across the cross-stitched tablecloth and onto the rumpled slacks, then upward past the tee shirt soaked with perspiration to Jack's flushed and sweaty face. The sandy-blond hair was tousled like she remembered it from when he was a boy, but the beautiful steel-blue eyes peered menacingly from under a deeply wrinkled brow.

She braced herself and waited to discover his mood.

A self-satisfied smile surfaced on Jack's face.

Nicky pulled out a chair and coaxed, "Sit down, Jack. Mom's got dinner ready."

Mrs. Sullivan looked more like the grandmother than the parent of the two at the table. They were born a year apart, sixteen years after her first son, Sean, when she was in her early forties and her husband in his fifties.

Jack served himself, let the ladle sink back into the tureen, and started eating as if he were the only one at the table.

This is good, Nicky thought. He will be calm tonight. In her head, she played the never-ending game of what to say or not say and finally decided on a conversation she was pretty sure wouldn't erupt into an abusive tirade.

"The roses in the back yard are blooming beautifully. You're doing really well with them, Jack."

He dropped his fork on his plate and gave Nicky a menacing stare. The two women's eyes locked.

The veins in Jack's neck bulged. "Roses, schmoses! What are we all doing in this rotten house? What if the damn roof starts to leak? Hell! The water's barely coming out of those corroded pipes. God only knows what kind of chemicals are being pumped through our bodies!"

Nicky's palms grew moist, but she managed to sound relaxed as she pushed a piece of meat around her plate with a fork. "Don't worry about any of that, Jack. Sean will help us out if we get into trouble."

"Sure ... sure ... big, fuckin' Sean. The big fuckin' deal surgeon. He sends us blood money every month." He paused, and nudged his mother. "Get it? Blood money?"

The stoic old woman stared at her plate.

The grin on Jack's face faded. "He's sitting in his big-assed house in Wellesley right now fanning through his stock certificates while we choke down one more corned beef and cabbage dinner!"

"Please, Jack." Nicky glanced sideways toward her mother. "Don't put Mom through this tonight."

"How am I supposed to eat the slop she made with the same hands that changed the old man's shitty diapers? Look! That senile old man's killing her." He leaned over and stuck his face into Nicky's. "You know what I'd like to do?"

Nicky's eyes shot up at him.

"I'd like to put him in the car, drive down to Mexico, and leave him in some damn bus station!"

Nicky's jaw tightened.

"When we're all dead from exhaustion and the old man's here all alone floating in shit, Sean's going to have to do something then!"

Nicky, worried this outburst could ignite into a major scene lasting all night, made her voice sound as soothing as possible. "Jack, he's got two kids and a new practice. He can hardly come here every day and take care of Dad."

Jack jumped up, scraping the chair noisily across the linoleum. "Hell, he couldn't even find the place! He took off for medical school and never looked back! That nosy bitch across the street almost fell off her porch when he pulled up to our curb this winter!"

He paced angrily. "While I'm schlepping the old man's diapers to the garage, he's out sailing in the bay!"

"Jack, it's not like that and you know it. Mary Beth seemed genuinely concerned about us when she dropped by this morning."

"That southern belle he married is good for only one thing. And from the looks of those big, succulent lips I bet she gives ..."

"Jack!" Nicky sprang up, slamming her chair against the stove.

Jack leaned back against the counter and crossed his long legs at the ankles. A shadow of a grin appeared. "You're all wound up tonight, Sis. *I was just making conversation.*"

The grin gave way to a smirk. "Can't stand to think about sex, *can you?*"

Nicky ran her hand through her dark shoulder-length hair, pulling it back off her forehead, and wished he would shut up. She had enough to worry about without dreaming about something that wasn't going to happen.

"You're the one that blew it. Not me," purred Jack. "That candy-assed boyfriend of yours needed more than you were willing to dish out. Richard and I were great friends. If it weren't for our chess games, he never would have waited for you to lift your skirt as long as he did. Those years in the Catholic school really screwed you up."

Memories of that horrible night she found Richard standing thunderstruck in the darkened upstairs hallway sat like a stone on Nicky's heart. He must have come in the front door and rushed upstairs to look for her on the back upstairs porch. There'd been a horrible row in the kitchen with Jack spewing out the usual insane accusations that their father had raped her and molested him. Then a hideous litany of imagined molestations until her father ended the confrontation in the usual way, by throwing his fists.

The room fell silent. Jack reached over and put his hand on Nicky's shoulder. "Don't worry, Sis, you'll find another sucker."

Nicky stood there biting her lip and telling herself once again that losing Richard was probably all for the best. The hardest part was when she ran into him with his family and couldn't help wondering if her babies would have been as adorable.

She pushed these thoughts from her mind, took several deep breaths until her taut muscles started to relax, then switched her attention to her mother. She went over and gently massaged her shoulders. "Mom, you're tired. I'll do the dishes, then help with Dad."

Nicky knew her mother was used to Jack's violent mood swings, but she could see each episode took a toll. A sweet smile appeared on the deeply wrinkled face as she patted Nicky's hand. "I'll get them, darling. You go upstairs now and look after your animals. Jack will help me with your father."

Nicky searched Jack's face.

He waved her off. "Yeah! Yeah! What the hell else am I good for?"

Nicky stood facing the brother she'd taken care of for as long as she could remember. So much unrewarded hope. The twenty-four year old young woman, burdened with a wearisome household, and one step from being totally overwhelmed by it, spoke encouragingly. "Don't talk like that, Jack. I haven't given up on you yet."

He laid a hand on her shoulder. "I'm sorry I said all that crap about Richard. That was a low blow. Go on upstairs. I'll help Mom with Dad." He smiled begrudgingly. "I just hope I can keep from puking."

Nicky hurried through the living room, snatched up her portfolio and heels and raced up the stairs. She knew every step on the oak staircase and enjoyed the cool feel of them under her stockinged feet. All in all, it had been a good day. First the luck with the gallery, and now it looked like they were going to get through another night without one of Jack's maniacal episodes.

Noticing the open door to her father's room, she tiptoed over to the bed. The drawn ashen face with the open toothless mouth made him seem like a stranger. His hair had been white for as long as she had known him, but it was no longer thick and wavy. Fine strands fell haphazardly on the lace-edged pillowcase. Even though her arms were full, she managed to lean over and kiss his forehead, then quietly back out of the room.

She nudged her bedroom door open with a knee, and a cool breeze streaming in from the window greeted her. She quickly changed into shorts and headed for the enclosed porch at the end of the hallway.

As a wildlife rehabilitator, she was now caring for three animals. The rabbit busily munched on lettuce her mother must have brought up. Nicky slipped a finger through the chicken wire and gently stroked its fur. The water and paper had been changed too. She wondered if maybe Jack had done it. She smiled to herself. His disdain for animals was just a pretext. She'd seen him show them kindness dozens of times when he thought she wasn't looking.

A pathetic mew came from the cat she'd brought from the vet last week. The tiger, blinded and battered from being hit by a car, whimpered when lifted from the cage. The vet had found no broken bones, just muscle and ligament damage. Nicky placed it on the porch floor hoping it would walk around some before being put back.

After cleaning the cage, she opened a can of cat food and coaxed the animal to eat by gently rubbing some on its mouth.

The cat purred loudly. Nicky shook her head, wondering if the shelter would ever be able to find it a home. Worse yet, she'd seen how other animals attacked the weak and defenseless of their species and knew it could never be allowed outdoors again. She sat there motionless under a blanket of sadness, struck with just how much Jack resembled the blind cat.

Nicky shook off the thought and turned her mind to the injured thrasher she'd been drawing each night for a week. She put the bird in a small cage and cleaned its coop, then took it to the studio next to her room and placed it on the platform beside the drawing table. She filled the cup near the bird's head with seed and turned on the light.

Satisfied that the slender, long-tailed creature was in the same position as in previous nights and the lighting was right, she pulled back the drafting table's canvas cover and studied the life-sized drawing. Delicate washes in reddish browns revealed a silhouette of the bird with only its head clearly defined by hundreds of pen strokes.

She picked up the fine-pointed tip lying on the paper towel and carefully inserted it into a holder, then opened the India ink bottle. Poised to start, she studied the wings and imagined them thrusting the bird up into the sky. She found each stroke of her pen coming quicker than the last, filling her with exhilaration and lifting her outside herself. Through her drawings, she could soar.

Dr. Sean Sullivan directed the Mercedes SUV off I-95 and made his way to the Wellesley section of Greater Boston. He pulled into the driveway of a massive brick colonial that, after a hundred thousand dollars of sprucing up and an equally hefty sum for decorating, was something he was proud to pull up to.

The sculptured garage door silently slid up and he pulled in. As he started to punch in the security code next to the kitchen entrance, the door swung open.

"Hey, sweet thing!" Mary Beth trilled. "It's about time you got home."

"Where are the kids?"

Mary Beth's voice dripped with soothing southern comfort. "You know I don't like to keep the girls up much past eight. Go on up and take a peek at them while I get your dinner."

Sean ate in the kitchen to the sound of some smiling voice matter-of-factly repeating the day's disasters on *CNN*. Mary Beth emptied the dishwasher for the second time that day. Once the financial news finished, she pulled out a chair and sat down. She reached over and brushed a lock of hair from her husband's forehead. "A rough day?"

"Three operations."

"I had to pick something up at the antique shop on Palmer Street this morning, and thought if I could find the house I'd stop by and visit your parents. We've hardly seen them since we got here."

Sean looked over his glasses as he sopped up the last of the salad dressing with his bread. That heavy, dark place in the back of his mind where he pushed his guilt about ignoring his family started to gnaw at him. He suspected he wasn't going to like where the conversation was heading.

"Sean, I'm afraid the picture we got when they came for our housewarming is far from reality. When I got out of the car, I could hear your brother's awful language through the open windows. The lady working in the yard next door didn't even notice. She's obviously heard it before." She looked directly into his eyes. "Sean, that brother of yours is out of control. I don't know how Nicky's coping. Bless her little heart. God only knows how long this has been goin' on."

Sean kept one eye on his wife while he poured some Perrier into his glass.

"Your mom and I had a cup of coffee in the kitchen and I asked her about Jack. She wouldn't say much, but I finally got her to show me the medicine he's taking. An anti-psychotic. Why wasn't I surprised? And then when I went upstairs to say hello to your dad, he didn't know who I was."

Sean picked up the remote and snapped off the set. He rested his chin on his fist. It had been obvious his father was drifting into senility and something was wrong with Jack, but with the demands of entering the new practice and having to take on the patients of two retiring partners, he had put off getting to the bottom of things until he had more time.

Nicky's evasiveness about Jack not having a job and his mother's excuses for not visiting, suddenly added up. The two women didn't want to burden him with Jack's problem. *Damn!* He'd spent half his life taking care of other people and left those two to fend for themselves.

"After Nicky showed me her drawings and the animals she's taking care of, I tried to get her to answer some questions about Jack, but she clammed right up."

Mary Beth squeezed Sean's arm. Her voice took on the singular mixture of self-assuredness and sweet persuasiveness that he loved so much. "Honey, I know you had it rough working your way through college and med school ... and now the new practice ... but you've got to make time for your folks. Nicky and your mom were so tense I hated to leave them."

Mary Beth got up and took a glass out of the cupboard. After filling it with water, she looked off into space and said, "I just can't get Nicky out of my head. She was so happy to see me. When I watched how tenderly she cared for all those sick animals she keeps, it just about broke my heart. I've always thought of her as a mousy Plain Jane. But she's not. There's so much there, Sean. Her patience with Jack, those incredibly beautiful drawings, her cheerful nature. I kept seeing our Molly."

She turned to her husband. "We've just got to do something. That kid deserves some kind of life."

Sean knew she'd hatched a plan and hoped it was a good one.

Mary Beth sat down at the table. "After lunch, Nicky got dressed to take some of her drawings to that big gallery in Faniel Hall; but before she left she told me about a three-year contract she's got to illustrate a series of textbooks."

Mary Beth twisted the glass in her hand. "Sean, I've been thinking. I'd love to get her to Chertaw Island. She can stay in the beach house my aunt left me for a year or so and get a new start."

"Honey, it's going to be tough walking in there after being gone so long and telling Nicky what to do. I hardly know her."

"Come on, Sean. If we don't do it, who will?"

Mary Beth slid her arm around her husband's shoulder. "Darlin', something has to be done about your dad and your brother. A check on the first of the month isn't gonna cut it. Those people are drowning. You've got to go in there and take charge."

Sean took a deep breath and pulled himself up from the table. "Well, all I can tackle right now is some TV."

Mary Beth's gaze followed him out of the room. She slowly turned and started to clear away the dishes. The droning of the TV coming from the family room made her wish she'd been more persuasive. She should have told him about the dark circles under Nicky's eyes and the way her hands trembled when she picked up her coffee.

On the way to the dishwasher Mary Beth stopped and listened. The house had become silent. She turned and saw Sean putting on his jacket.

He started for the door and said, "I'll be back in a little while."

Nicky glanced up, startled. Nine-thirty. Who could be calling so late? She couldn't stop now. Two more strokes were needed on the bird's neck. The muffled commotion below pulled at her attention, but she pushed it aside. Every stroke had to be perfect.

Footsteps sounded down the hall, then in her father's room. After a few minutes, someone knocked softly on the door. Without taking her eyes from her work, she said, "Come in," her steady hand deliberately defining a feather. Finished, she looked up at the tall figure. Not handsome like Jack, but the wide-shouldered, self-possessed man reeked of quiet authority.

"Sean? What are you doing here so late?"

He pulled up a stool and sat down. Instantly, like a cloak of thick fog, his bedside manner permeated the air.

His words rang with finality. "I took a look at Dad. It'll be better if we put him in a nursing home. I'll arrange for the move tomorrow."

The sudden realization that she and her mother had failed to keep their secret from Mary Beth washed over her. She felt her ears get warm and the tension that held her together melt. She grew strangely aware of the sound of the thrasher pecking at its feed; and except for the bird's jerky movements, all in the room were motionless.

Mercifully, Sean broke the long silence. "Can I see your drawing?"

Nicky looked up at him, dazed, then tilted the Bristol board upward.

"You have a wonderful talent, Nick." Sean reached over and took her hand. "How would you like to leave this place and go live in Mary Beth's beach house in South Carolina and do nothing but draw?"

For a split-second, Nicky felt hopeful, then defeated again. "What are you talking about? I can't leave Jack."

"His problem can be controlled. I'll send him to see Mike Green. He specializes in this kind of case."

South Carolina? She'd never been out of Massachusetts. Jack's problem controlled? That she'd have to see. "Sean, you have no idea what he's like. It's a full-time job keeping him calm. I can't just leave and expect Mom to handle him."

"Listen, Nick. I don't expect her to handle him either. Trust me. There's medicine out there that'll take care of Jack's problem."

"Oh, Sean. If only that were true."

Sean softly patted her hand. "It is, Nick. You'll see for yourself."

Nicky felt herself drifting into a dreamy fog, hardly noticing that her brother had stood up.

"It's about time I took care of things. I want you to concentrate on nothing else but getting yourself to South Carolina."

Nicky felt the fog lift, as if a great weight were lifting from her shoulders.

"Do you have a car?" Sean asked.

"Car?" She looked around confused. "There's Dad's."

"That won't make the trip."

Sean leaned against the door casing, took off his glasses and rubbed his eyes. This was the first time Nicky had seen him looking so vulnerable and it moved her.

He cleaned his glasses with his tie saying, "Mary Beth needs a new car. You can take her Volvo wagon."

Nicky rose and went over to her brother. Her eyes roamed the face she barely knew, searching for some connection. The deep creases and dark arcs under his eyes spoke of years of study and work. She put her arms around him and pressed her cheek against his jacket. Her throat tightened painfully as tears streamed down her face.

He pulled her close to him and squeezed. "It's over, Nicky. It's my turn now."

🐚 CHAPTER TWO

"Nicky!" resonated from downstairs and the two women froze.

Nicky hurriedly pressed the cat's cage into Mary Beth's hands and motioned toward the door. "Don't worry. I'll handle this."

Mary Beth brushed by Jack as he appeared in the doorway, while Nicky, hands on hips, scanned the stripped room.

"Well, little brother, I guess this is it."

"I've got your car packed to the ass!" Jack said breathlessly. "Your bedding's on top of the pile so you can get that set up tonight. You're going to need help getting the drafting table out and reassembled. Then, maybe someone to drown the damn cat!"

Nicky laughed. Jack's "take charge" attitude delighted her. The new medicine had kicked in, and he was obviously basking in all the attention he was getting from Sean, Mary Beth and Dr. Green who'd been seeing him every other day for three weeks.

Nicky giggled with relief once she woke up to the fact that Jack was anxious for her to leave. She gave him a hug. "I'm going to miss you, little brother."

"Like hell you are! You packed like you were running from the cops!"

The family waved Nicky off and the few neighbors who were out early watched the loaded Volvo turn the corner and head for I-95.

About an hour into the drive, the fear that someone was going to whisper in her ear that the whole thing was a hoax subsided, and Nicky relaxed her white knuckle grip on the steering wheel.

For the first time since Sean and Mary Beth had brought the car over, Nicky stole glimpses of its interior. Daring to exert her proprietorship, she fumbled with the controls until the air-conditioner sent out a stream of cool air. Next, she figured out how to zoom all the windows shut, a move that made the cat stop moaning.

After six hours of driving south, she still found it hard to believe that tonight she'd be in a beach house on a South Carolina barrier island. She pulled out a list from her shorts pocket, put it on the dash and tried to remember Mary Beth's last-minute instructions. Johnny Bumps! That's who she said to call if she needed anything. Mary Beth had seen to the phone and electricity, and Johnny was going to have all the shutters open and everything working by the time she got there. The key was in a little bottle tucked in a joist under the front porch.

Nicky picked up the list and quickly glanced at the other name: Trippett Alston. He was an old friend of Mary Beth's who'd spent his summers on Chertaw Island all his life like she had. The way Mary Beth had spoken his name, stretching it into so many syllables with unique melodic intonations, had made Nicky feel uncomfortable, then silly for feeling that way.

Acres of colorless cotton fields outside Richmond gave the first clear indication of the South, then the need to turn up the air-conditioning full blast.

Nicky felt empty. Absent was the ever-present feeling of fear of having to be ready to handle the inevitable terror of Jack's rages. She felt like she'd been severed from a domineering Siamese twin and had to reinvent herself.

Suddenly, guilt flooded in to fill the void. How could she have left her mother all alone with Jack! She hit the brake pedal and tried to swerve off at an exit, but spying a huge tractor-trailer barreling behind her in the rearview mirror, sped up again.

Before she reached the next exit, an opposing guilt sent her reeling. What had she been thinking? She couldn't turn back now. What would her publisher and the gallery say if she changed her plans after all the rushed arrangements had been made to accommodate her so she could overnight her work and receive her checks on the island?

A picture of Jack's newfound smugness settled on her mind and brought her back to equilibrium. She remembered the encouraging expression on her mother's face as she had said, "You go now, child, and make a life for yourself."

What's wrong with me? Nicky asked herself as she took a long, slow breath. Everything's going to be just fine. She ran her hand over the plush leather seat and stole another quick glance around her newly acquired status symbol. I'm just tired. A pit stop! That's what I need.

She pulled off at the next exit and into a gas station. Once the tank was filled, Nicky was curious to get her first taste of the South. She opened the door of the mini-mart and peeked in. The interior was exactly like the ones up north—same array of candy, drinks, even the little felt paper roses in the plastic boxes sitting next to the cash register.

The young man at the counter greeted her with an energetic, "Hey! How you doin' this afternoon, ma'am?" Then, along with her change, "You have a safe trip, ma'am."

Nicky smiled all the way to the car. She put the key in the ignition, stopped for a moment and tried to recall the last time some teenager behind a counter even made eye contact with her.

By the time she hit the South Carolina border with its sign touting *Smiling Faces, Beautiful Places*, the sun was beginning its descent. At the Myrtle Beach exit, a horizon of billboards peddling fireworks, golf courses and amusement parks gave her the distinct impression she was headed for a fun place.

An hour and a half later, Myrtle Beach lit up the twilight sky with miles of neon. Nicky buzzed the window down to let the excitement of being at the beach touch her, but the suffocating hot air, quickly reversed her decision.

Barreling south on Hwy 17, the Volvo left South Carolina's tourist Mecca behind and continued toward Charleston with the fading sunset gently mellowing to a dark orange glow above the forest of tall yellow pines. Her eyes burned and muscles ached from the long drive, but an exciting feeling of discovery kept her acutely alert. Five miles past McClellanville, a blinking yellow light hung across the deserted highway next to a small Chertaw Island sign. She turned onto the asphalted causeway, pitch black beyond the headlight beam, and scrunched forward straining to see.

Off in the distance, moonlight danced on the rippling marsh creek. Eyes back on the road, a stop sign loomed in front of her and she slammed on the brakes. Left! Mary Beth said to take a left at the dead end!

There it was. The mailbox that looked like a shrimp boat. Nicky squinted in an effort to make out the writing. *King's Nest*. This was it! She let the car creep up the sand driveway through an eerie cavern of live oak trees, dwarfed by the ocean's salt spray, and stopped in front of a sun-bleached wood structure.

She left the headlights shining on the porch steps and got out. The air was different than when she had opened the window in Myrtle Beach, with the sweet smell of jasmine afloat the cool ocean breeze.

She gingerly felt along the dark joists under the porch, but she still managed to knock a small bottle onto the sandy ground. She quickly twisted off the rusty lid, bounded up the stairs and opened the door. A gust of ocean air with a hint of mildew wafted out. She fumbled in the dark for the light switch, and became transfixed at the sight in front of her.

Deep golden tones of ancient tongue-in-groove pine planks enfolded the huge room. The kitchen's linoleum-covered counters and porcelain sink and drain board spoke of another era. Her eyes constantly roaming, she crept through the downstairs feeling like she was going back decades in time.

Shutters had been opened in the living room and latched overhead. Nicky's nose rubbed against the screen as she peered out into the darkness, barely making out the large covered porch. The roar of the surf pounding just feet away and moonlight flickering endlessly on the ocean beyond seemed to be telling her something, and she made herself believe it was good.

She wandered through the living room, running a hand over the comfortably worn furniture casually scattered in front of a stone fireplace, then peered into the bedroom, sparsely furnished with an iron bed, dresser and a small wall sink.

After unpacking some essentials, she lay curled up in bed with the cat at her feet, unable to wipe the smile from her face. The sensation of being in a moving car still hung over her, but she felt free—freer than she had felt for as far back as she could remember. She pulled her knees up tight against her chest, hugged her legs and rocked happily, giggling at the squeaking of the ancient metal springs. Tomorrow she was going to do nothing but sketch! Day One at the beach! Yes! Everything she saw, so she'd never forget it!

🐚 CHAPTER THREE

The room was dark, but an urgency in the air, that always seems to exist just before the dawn breaks, excited her. Waves, tumbling with a soft sudsy splash, seemed farther away than the night before, telling her the tide was out.

She sat up and swung her feet onto the floor. The cat, startled by the bouncing springs, leapt onto her lap. Nicky rose. Gently caressing the animal, she swished her face across its fur. Gusts of ocean air blew into the room and a maroon line in the distance announced her first Chertaw Island sunrise.

The screen door sang out a long screech and then banged shut behind her. Nicky leaned against the porch railing and watched the top of the blood-red orb nudge its way toward the sky that was now glowing a dark red. Gently rippling waves, reflecting the russet color in the sky, lay beyond the sandy beach that seemed to stretch toward the ocean for a hundred yards.

A lone figure accompanied by a black Lab ran along the distant shoreline to the south. By the time they passed, the sun had broken away from the horizon and climbed into the cloudless sky.

Eager to explore the beach, Nicky slipped into some clothes and ran barefoot out the door. She skipped three steps down from the porch, ran along the boardwalk that stretched over the dunes, then scampered down a flight of stairs to the beach.

The cool, hard-packed sand was flawless except for occasional shells and jellyfish, and the water bathtub warm, unlike the way she remembered Gloucester in June when you could turn blue after fifteen minutes in the surf. Her back to the ocean, with the breeze swirling her hair into her eyes and mouth, she studied the beachfront—mostly tops of old beach houses peeking from behind enormous dunes.

Next to the King's Nest sat a beautiful two-storied raised house with gracefully columned porches. It reminded her of photos of mansions in Charleston's historic wharf district she'd studied for one of her textbook illustrations.

Distracted by the return of the jogger and his dog, she backed into the water to let them pass.

"Good morning," spoke the friendly, relaxed voice. Again, direct eye contact with a ready smile.

Nicky was struck so hard by the man's handsome looks she failed to blurt out a hello until after he had passed. Her eyes lingered on the tall, athletic figure, when the dog mischievously circled and ran back toward her.

The man agilely turned around, and while jogging backward, laughingly said, "Come on now, Winston. Don't bother the lady."

The dog circled Nicky, and after showing off in the surf, ran back to his master. With another smile and wave, the man turned and jogged off. The two faded into the distance, making an abrupt turn into the dunes.

Nicky watched them disappear, unaccountably lonely, as the man was a stranger. The excitement of being in a new place reemerged and Nicky waded in the direction the man had gone. When a V-shaped contingent of pelicans sailed by and swooped down onto the water, she decided they'd be her lucky charm.

There were five houses before the end of the island. The last one had a sign over the boardwalk reading, *Alston's Hideaway*. Was this where the man had gone? Was he the very Trippett Alston Mary Beth was going to ask to help acquaint her with the island? Yes! She grinned as she told herself, *Nicole Sullivan, you should be ashamed of yourself. Just one day out of Boston and you're already getting ideas.*

She reached down and joyfully swept armfuls of water into the air. Yes! She was going to leave Poor Nicky Sullivan behind forever.

While splashing around in the pool formed by the vast sandbar jutting into the ocean, she noted that the island was separated from the mainland by a golden-green carpet of marsh sliced open by a meandering tidal creek.

Wanting to explore, she followed a path leading to the marsh side and strolled along the dusty roadway. With no ocean breeze, by the time the King's Nest mailbox came into view, she was anxious to get out of the sun. Not even seven, and the temperature already had to be over eighty degrees. She'd unpack, get something to eat, and see if Johnny Bumps would come over and help her set up her drawing board.

Trippett Alston came out of the shower, wrapped a towel around his waist and slapped on some shaving cream. As the razor peeled away the foam, he studied his deeply tanned reflection—something he was doing more and more of these days. The brush-cut almost belied the fact that he had hit forty, but the annoying specks of gray gave him away.

Noting deepening crow's feet at the corner of his eyes, he pawed through his medicine cabinet for the sunscreen Kim Dusenbury had bought him, then put it back. He'd start wearing his sunglasses instead. As he pulled on a pair of khakis his eyes fell on the half of the bed not mussed and a pang of regret shot through him. Why had he been so damn indecisive? He and Kim were a natural: he, one of Charleston's foremost restoration contractors; she, one of the city's top interior decorators. Kim's tall, lithe and beautifully blond looks weren't a handicap either.

Trippett slipped his bare feet into a pair of Dockers, strolled out onto his bedroom balcony and gazed out at the ocean, Kim's words ringing in his mind. "We either announce our engagement as soon as my mother can arrange a party, or call it quits. Five years is plenty of time for any man to make up his mind ... even *you*, Trippett Alston."

That was six months ago. Somehow he hadn't been able to take the plunge. Was there something wrong with him, he wondered? He'd always expected to be struck by a thunderbolt; instead, he and Kim had never really connected.

There'd only been a couple of big arguments, but they'd been pivotal. As polite as Kim was, she'd made it stingingly clear that she thought he was wasting his talents restoring dilapidated old buildings in Charleston's historic district when he could be making easy millions developing oceanfront condos.

Old. That was the key word. How he loved old things. They had a story, a history, and stirred an emotion in him. It was as if he needed to take care of them. When he finished bringing a mansion back to life, he felt connected to the people who first breathed life into it—another caretaker in the building's ancient history. Something a high-rise condominium could never do for him.

From the top of the staircase, his eyes rested on the great room below. With yesterday's announcement of Kim's engagement in the Charleston *Post and Courier*, he could finally get rid of the beachy furniture she'd stuffed the place with. Mostly items salvaged from redecorated condos, he suspected. His mother would be happy to see him finally clearing his old furniture out of her carriage house.

He found his dog, Winston, sprawled lazily on the floor of the screened porch, and crouching down, vigorously massaged behind his ears. "You won't have to worry about her coming back anymore, boy. By next week you'll be able to sleep on pappy's couch again." And he'd get his recliner back, too.

The big black Lab lay with eyes tightly shut enjoying the rub. Rising, Trippett spoke firmly, "Stay around the house, Winston. I don't want the neighbors fussin' about you roaming the island." He checked the screen door to make sure it was unlocked so the dog could come and go, and slid into his black Yukon XL.

As he passed the King's Nest, Trippett glanced down the long dark driveway, catching sight of what he thought was a Massachusetts license plate. Must belong to the girl on the beach this morning. The one Mary Beth phoned him about. With all he had riding on his current projects, he didn't need to have to babysit some forlorn transplant from the North. He'd call Johnny Bumps and make sure she was being looked after.

Sweet memories of the summer before he and Mary Beth went off to college drifted in and out of his mind as he crossed the Cooper River Bridge. When she had called to ask him to befriend her sister-in-law, it had been impossible to turn her down.

Trippett cruised along King Street in Charleston's historic district until he turned into a narrow alley boxed in by brick-clad buildings. He made a sharp right into a small courtyard packed with vans and trucks in front of a massive federal-styled house.

In the expansive entry, workmen fitted balusters into a circular mahogany staircase that climbed seemingly unsupported to the third floor, while a blaring radio tried hard to overreach the cacophony of pounding hammers. Trippett went over to the workbench where the supervising carpenter was examining a blueprint and shouted, "How's everything going?"

"Like clockwork. Savannah Millwork did a beautiful job matching these mahogany spindles. You can't tell the new from the old." Trippett picked one up and tapped it on the palm of his hand, happy for the firm that still had the original knives, skews and gouges used in the 1800's to fashion ornate woodwork throughout Charleston and Savannah.

Trippett put the spindle down and walked past the room he used as an office, cluttered with blueprints and antique architectural remnants. Outside, he studied the progress the workmen were making on the roof and wasn't pleased. They had to move faster if they wanted to get it buttoned down before the relentless rains of the hurricane season started.

He flipped open his cell phone and quickly arranged to meet with the roofer the next morning. He ran up the temporary staircase to the second floor where a workman was pouring plaster into a mold at a bench.

Without looking up from his task, the man said, "We're gittin' there," then moved on to the next form.

Trippett's eyes scanned a run of cornice on the fourteen-foot ceiling, every once in a while spotting a fresh white section of plaster that had been glued on. Two walls where the room in earlier years had been partitioned for apartments had no cornice details remaining.

"When do you think you'll have the work completed on this floor?"

The man put the plaster bucket down, wiped his hands on his apron and thumbed through a notebook. "We'll need to pour over two hundred pieces for those two walls alone. Four more weeks should do it."

Trippett studied the ornate ceiling one more time and cringed at the thought of having it destroyed by rain.

Malcolm Cameron, his partner, appeared at the doorway. "There's some coffee in the office," he announced.

On the way downstairs, Malcolm gave Trippett an update on the East Battery house he was managing, then, once back in the office, flopped into a battered swivel chair, put his feet up on a column lying across the floor and lit a cigarette.

"I thought you quit."

Malcolm ignored the remark, took another drag and examined the cigarette as he said, "I read about Kim's engagement last night." Shaking his head, he added, "I hope you know what you're doing."

Trippett leaned forward, rested his elbows on his knees, and cracked his knuckles. He looked up and gave his partner a broad smile. "It was the toughest indecision I ever made."

Malcolm laughed knowingly and rocked back in his chair. He took a few drags before saying, "Last night I ran into Art Thompson. He does a lot of excavation work for the Deveroux Company. He told me there's a big project coming down on Chertaw Island."

Trippett's gaze shot toward his partner.

"I talked to a couple more guys in the Fish House. They said talk's been on the street for a couple of days now."

With that bomb dropped, Malcolm left.

Trippett thought fast. The Deveroux Company spelled condominiums, and to the best of his recollection nothing in the island's zoning laws prohibited them. Why not! The only thing anyone ever worried about was Winston roaming the island! He tapped his pen on his desk. He'd better call the building permit division and see what was going on.

🐚 CHAPTER FOUR

Mac Moultrie wiped his sweaty face on the shoulder of his soiled tee shirt as he finished mixing the oil and gas for the motor on his Boston Whaler. For someone who had just seen fifty-two, he was fitter than most men at twenty, with thirty years of laboring at commercial fishing to thank for his sculpted muscles. His teeth clenched the stub of an unlit cigar and he had the look of someone who could handle anything ever meant to float on water.

Already halfway through his routine checklist, he finished inspecting all the lines for chinks. He opened the hold and systematically checked the life jackets, first-aid kit and rain gear. He religiously followed this procedure before taking anyone out on a fishing trip. Years on the high seas had taught him that a storm could come from nowhere, and without the proper equipment, lives would be at risk.

He jumped onto the dock and enjoyed instant relief from the blistering rays of the sun under the shelter of the cabana's tin roof. The dead stillness of the hot afternoon was shattered by the creek's waters slapping against the boat and the crisp snap of the tab from his beer can.

He threw his head back and enjoyed a long swallow when something caught his eye. Bobbing above the golden marsh grass in the distance was an image, wavy from the intense heat, of a girl's head with brown hair swirling around a large straw hat. More of her became visible with the rhythm of her gait. Next, the broadly striped shirt, then the white shorts, until she finally appeared full-length at the end of the boardwalk with Trippett Alston's Winston at her side.

Taking another long swig, Mac stared down his nose and watched her haltingly raise her hand and shyly wave.

Figuring it was only polite to acknowledge her, he shouted, "How ya doin', ma'am?"

"Can I take a look at the creek from your dock?" she shouted back.

"Sure. Come on over."

Sitting casually on the railing with his feet resting on his toolbox, the fisherman sipped his beer and sized the girl up. "You the Yankee that's fixin' to spend the summer in the King's Nest?"

Without pulling her eyes off the lazily twisting creek, Nicky answered, "Yes," then turned and looked up at him. "How'd you know?"

"Pretty much know everyone on the island by sight ... but that brogue of yours sure helped."

Nicky nodded her head as she thought the remark over. "What do you do here on the island? Fish?"

"Some. Do guide fishin' too."

"In the ocean?"

"Mostly along the shore in the estuaries."

"What kind of fish do you get?"

"Spottail bass ... mackerel ... flounder. Depends on what's running."

The black Lab pawed at Mac's leg until he relinquished the empty can.

"You know this dog?" she asked.

"We're old pals. He belongs to Trip Alston."

The dog's paws clamped down on the can with a thump.

"There's an ordinance about dogs being on a leash after eight during the summer, but the old devil's been roaming the place for years. Knows the sound of Trip's truck and hightails it back the minute he hears him comin' over the causeway. When they see him racing across the beach, all the folks know Trip's on his way. I reckon he's had to drive a little slower these days to give Winston time to make it back in time."

Nicky laughed, then crouched down and patted the dog's head. "I love animals." She leaned forward on her knees and looked across the marsh at a wading blue heron. "Especially birds."

Mac didn't say anything. Something about this girl was hauntingly familiar. Like she was on the run. He sensed she had a need to connect with another person in this place strange to her and decided he would let her reveal herself in her own time. Something he didn't think came easily.

She squinted from the sun as she looked up at him. "I'd love to go out on the water with you some time."

"You fish?"

"No. I draw."

"Shoot! Johnny Bumps told me that!"

Nicky smiled, pleased to be discussed among her neighbors in a complimentary light for a change.

"Well?" she asked.

"I don't know. I'm taking some folks out fishin' tomorrow, then I'll be shrimpin' every morning from then on?"

"Oh! Can I come?"

Mac reached into the cooler and took out a beer and offered it to her. She thanked him but shook her head. He shrugged his shoulders, snapped the tab and took a long gulp.

"Well?" she asked.

"You Yankees sure are persistent."

"I'm sorry. It's just that I really want to see everything so I can start working on a portfolio of marsh birds." She straightened her back and tried to give her remark a casual tone. "I'm going to have a solo show in Boston next spring."

Mac rolled some beer around in his mouth and gave the girl a long hard look. "You'd have to get up at three or four in the morning ... maybe a bit later. I set out when the tide's comin' in."

"That's no problem."

"Once we go out ... if you're sick or something ... the only way you're getting back before I'm finished is if you swim."

"I'll be all right. My dad used to take me fishing in the ocean out of Gloucester."

"Maybe next week. Check with me Tuesday afternoon. I'll let you know then when I'm setting off."

Nicky glanced down into the water and noticed a small dark mass bobbing around.

"What's that?"

Mac leaned over and peered in. Spying a small snapping turtle with a gash across its shell, he reached for a net and scooped it up.

Nicky caught sight of a flipper moving. "It's still alive. I'll take it to a vet."

"There's no need to do that, girl. I fix 'em all the time. It's from propellers."

He went over to the storage bin in the cabana and got out a box and some rags. The turtle lay still on the dock as Mac wiped it dry, careful not to get within range of its mouth even though it had receded into its shell. Mac took out some supplies and squeezed resin from two tubes, mixed them together and spread it on the turtle's back, then cut a piece of mesh and smoothed it over the shell.

"There. That'll fix him. He'll be all right in a couple of days. Mostly needs food."

"Can I take him?"

Mac gently placed the turtle in a pail and handed it to Nicky. He

35

picked up the toolbox and they started down the boardwalk. The distant roar of a motorcycle drew their eyes toward the sandy path. By the time the cloud of dust came close enough to make out the Harley Davidson Road King, it stopped in front of them.

The driver's attitude made as much of a statement as what she was wearing. The tight shorts and narrow strip of elastic across her ample, firm breasts contrasted with the studded collar around her neck. Her black leather wrist guard jerked as she twisted the grip to rev up the engine.

"Hey, girl. How you gettin' along today?" said Mac in a much thicker accent than Nicky had detected before.

The woman quickly lifted her tanned, muscular leg and swung it around the back; and in one swift motion had the bike up on its kickstand. Mac put his arm around her waist, looked back at Nicky and said, "Tuesday afternoon," as if he had other things on his mind.

Nicky watched them cross the roadway and disappear into the wax myrtle bushes in front of a small beach house she presumed belonged to the fisherman.

Standing on the deserted peninsula in the blistering heat holding the pail, a mantle of loneliness descended upon her until the dog appeared from the marsh watching expectantly for her to lead him somewhere.

The beach held a promise the next morning, as if the world were starting off on a clean slate. The birds were still asleep, giving the stretch of sand on the edge of the ocean the kind of deserted look that's filled with expectation —like someone or something was about to burst onto the scene.

Nicky was hoping that the someone would be Trippett Alston on his morning jog. She had to be careful, however. She didn't want to look as if she were lying in wait.

The sand, still wet from the receding tide, was cool under her feet as she watched the speck on the horizon get larger. Figuring it was the woman who mysteriously appeared on the beach every morning with a cue stick, Nicky decided that today, instead of just nodding, she was going to make a friend. Nicky calculated they would meet just beyond the fisherman's house; however, the woman suddenly turned off toward the dunes, crossing the beach that was vast now that the ocean was at low tide.

Nicky had decided to wait another day for a chance meeting, when she noticed a wide, deep track going from the ocean directly toward the dunes. A giant turtle must have come from the sea! Excited, she ran toward the woman who had lodged her stick in the sand and was now talking on a cell phone.

"I'm in front of Mac Moultrie's place," she spoke into the phone. "I'll wait for you."

The woman was pleased with herself. Somewhere in her mid-fifties, she was attractive enough to make Nicky believe that she had to have been quite a beauty in her younger days.

The woman extended her hand and held her back erect almost as if she were standing at attention. "I'm Uta Foster. I patrol this island for the loggerhead project." She anticipated Nicky's curiosity about her German accent. "I was a stewardess for Pan Am when I met my American husband. He passed away a while back, but I still live on the mainland."

Nicky wanted to tell her that she was a wildlife artist and rehabilitator; but fearing it might sound pompous, just introduced herself.

"Is this a nest?" she asked.

"Yes." The woman bent down and carefully brushed away some sand. "See. Here are the eggs. The mother came in last night, and went right back out to sea after she laid them."

"How many do you think there are?"

"I will tell you exactly, because I'm going to count them. The most we've ever found is a hundred and ninety-seven. Usually there are around a hundred."

The woman marked a circle around the nest with her foot. "If the team thinks it's too close to the water, we'll move it. I patrol this beach every morning from May to October checking the nests and keeping count of the eggs." She sighed. "These guys are a threatened species and the number of females that nest along this coast has been declining for years. Development has destroyed a lot of their nesting beaches, but here on Chertaw Island, especially out on the far end of the peninsula, they're still pretty stable.

"Their birthplace is imprinted on the memories of hatchlings as they follow the moonlight glittering on the waves. Since the peninsula has been untouched, their pattern of reproduction hasn't been disturbed. On developed beaches, it's another story. Bright lights confuse these little creatures and instead of heading for the water, they're found dead in lighted swimming pools and over the dunes in parking lots."

Now Nicky understood why the sign on the porch light switch indicated it could only be used during the winter.

The woman checked her watch, then got down on her knees. "They should be here soon. I better start clearing away the sand and expose all the eggs."

Nicky slid down and asked, "Can I help?"

The woman must have recognized she had a convert, for she

proceeded to get right into Nicky's training. "Yes. Just be careful. When we count them, we take them off in layers, putting them in the same exact position as they were laid. Then we put them back, making sure they're in the right layer. They'll have indentations indicating where they touched another egg. Because the yoke falls to the bottom of the egg and leaves an air pocket on top, if it's turned upside down, the turtle will drown."

"How long does it take for them to hatch?"

"Sixty days. The last batch is usually laid in mid-August, so I patrol 'til around the middle of October. Unfortunately, out of the hundreds that hatch, maybe one makes it to maturity."

Nicky wrinkled her brow. "That's terrible."

Uta made a face and shrugged. "They become fish food. Sea gulls dive for them. Crabs get them as they walk across the sand. I've watched them head for the ocean when they hatch during the day. The waves keep pulling them back to shore. These little guys have to really fight to survive."

Nicky sat back on her heels and listened.

Uta's accent thickened as her tone became angry. "When they're grown they can get trapped in a shrimp or gill net from one of those big factory trawlers. They put up such a fight to get out, they reduce their oxygen supply and shorten the time they've got to reach air." She shook her head. "These nets don't get pulled out of the water soon enough and most trapped turtles drown."

Slamming car doors signaled the arrival of others. Shortly, three men and a woman emerged from a path between the dunes. Nicky quickly rose and stood aside, to stay out of the way of their work. Spotting Winston off in the distance, she said her goodbyes and headed toward the beach house.

🐚 CHAPTER FIVE

Gleeful screams of children at play and the sound of barking dogs drifting in from the beach told Nicky it was Friday. The lucky few North and South Carolinians who owned vacation homes on the island were starting to roll in for the weekend.

She carefully stacked the Underground Railway materials she'd been working on for the textbook company, and put them back in a portfolio along with the two drawings she had done for her Boston show. Winston, who was lying on his side next to the cat, started to stir. He had bonded so solidly with the blind animal that Nicky named the cat Salem.

Nicky's relationship with the dog was routine by now. Moments after Trippett's Yukon whizzed by in the morning, he would appear on the porch and nuzzle the screen door open. In the early evening, he'd suddenly perk up his ears, listen for a moment and then race toward home, leaving the screen door banging behind him.

At first, Nicky was afraid she was taking too much upon herself and infringing upon Trippett's life. But after thinking it over, decided she hadn't overstepped since the dog had adopted her. Besides, hadn't Mary Beth told her that Trippett said he would be happy to befriend her? He was probably just too busy with his construction company right now to come see her.

Nicky snapped the leash she'd bought onto Winston, and he stood up wagging his tail at the clear signal they were going for a walk. The sand burnt Nicky's feet; and just as she was about to sprint to the surf, someone called out from the porch next door.

"Hey, girl! Come on up and have somethin' cool to drink."

Nicky made out a hazy figure of a woman through the screen and enthusiastically replied, "I'd love to!"

Before making her way to the imposing boardwalk, Nicky coaxed Winston to the shade under the porch overhang.

"I've been watching you, girl," said the sweet, delicate voice.

A smiling Dede Morgan held the door open. She was wearing an ankle-length linen shift that didn't fail to reveal the shapely figure underneath. The softly curled blond hair and large dark brown eyes that stood out from the flawless complexion gave her the look of a baby doll. Other than the eyes, everything about her was petite, from the delicately chiseled nose to the slender jeweled and manicured fingers.

While Dede left to get drinks, Nicky tried to relax in a sumptuously cushioned wicker chair. Her gaze moved slowly around the porch, taking in decorator touches that are only snatched up by those for whom cost means nothing. Cool glossy wood floors and the kind of understated elegance that takes thousands of dollars to achieve were also visible through the wall of glass. The closest Nicky had ever gotten to a place like this was flipping through expensive magazines while she sat around waiting in gallery lobbies.

"I'm forgetting my manners. How could I have left you out here so long!" sang Dede as she placed a drink on a monogrammed napkin.

Nicky smiled at the natural politeness ingrained into the Southern character.

In only a few minutes of artfully directed small talk, Dede sketched out a brief outline of her life, including that she was divorced and selling oceanfront real estate for the Deveroux Company. "Love, I understand you're quite an artist."

Nicky marveled at how everyone on the island seemed to perceive her in a positive light.

Dede took the drink from Nicky's hand and placed it on the table. "Come. I want to show you something."

Before entering through the heavy sliding doors, Nicky bent down and brushed the sand off her feet. Looking up, she was dazzled by the ornate Italian antiques and plush overstuffed furniture. Once inside, the fine Persian carpet felt silky under her feet.

"There it is," cooed Dede.

The blank wall revealed nothing.

"Can't you see an Italian pastoral scene? With an antique finish, of course. Something like Leonardo DaVinci would do."

Nicky laughed. "Dede, I'm no Leonardo DaVinci."

Dede patted Nicky's shoulder. "From what my handyman tells me, you're DaVinci enough for me."

The phone rang. Dede's demeanor suddenly changed. The voice was still sweet, but the tone strictly business. "Lloyd, I'm glad you returned my call. I just wanted to tell you that there's a lot of interest in that condo you're looking at. If you want it, I suggest you make an offer as soon as possible."

Dede reached for a pen. "Okay ... let's go for eight hundred and fifty thousand. I'll present it to the listing agent right after we get the contract done."

She doodled on the pad as she listened. "Twenty thousand down will show them you're serious."

The conversation ended with Dede saying she'd meet him in her office in an hour and a half.

Nicky couldn't imagine waiting that long for such a huge sale. "Why don't you run right over there?" she queried.

Dede laughed lightheartedly. "Darling, I never present myself unless everything's perfect. First, I'm going to take a shower and wash my hair. Then I've got to go over my nails. It'll take me twenty minutes just to pick out what I'm going to wear. Another ten minutes for jewelry. There's *no way* I can be ready in less than an hour and a half."

She ushered Nicky to the door saying, "We'll talk about the mural later."

Dede guided her beige Mercedes coupe into her labeled spot in the side lot of the Deveroux Company offices, located a few miles down the coast from the island. Before getting out, she checked herself in the visor mirror. Like she had told Nicky, she spent a great deal of time making sure she looked perfect. In spite of the three hundred thousand plus she earned in commissions each year, she was still nagged by a deep-seated insecurity formed during her impoverished childhood in the mountains of North Carolina.

When Dede bragged about working her way up from the bottom in the condo business, she wasn't exaggerating. The only job a girl of fourteen could get when she hit the beach was cleaning rundown condos on the wrong end of town. When she finally landed a job in a new high-rise, she promised herself that some day someone would be cleaning hers.

The thing that eventually got her that piece of real estate was her uncanny intuition. After overhearing two agents talking about earning fabulous commissions, she wasted no time in getting her license and learning the business the hard way—by selling time shares. But once she had a car, a wardrobe and a taste of more than the pitiful kind of money you get under the table, she started her steady climb to the top of her profession and never looked back.

Once out of her car, Dede carefully smoothed out the bold floral-patterned, ankle-length shift that she'd finally settled on. With each step across the lobby, a tanned leg reached out from one of the deep slits, attracting the eyes of Tommy Warren, Jr., the firm's lawyer.

After gracious hellos, Dede disappeared into her office and Tommy Warren, Jr., strolled down the hall to the corner office where Walter Satterfield was waiting for him.

Tall and thin to the point of looking unhealthy, Walter Satterfield seemed devoid of vigor or emotion, but underneath this lifeless façade was a raging opportunist. He looked up from his desk and said, "Shut the door."

As Tommy sank into an overstuffed chair, Walter tossed his pen on the desk and leaned back in his chair. "Let's have it."

"We're all set with Mo Washington's two sons. They've signed the option contingent upon the Probate Court's final decision to give them the land. Should happen in six months."

"What's wrong? Why are you so edgy?" Walter asked.

Tommy stretched his neck and rubbed under his chin. "It's just ... Well, if that sonofabitchin' will ever shows up ..."

Walter stared at him over his glasses for a moment. "We've already been over that a hundred times. We know the girl doesn't have it or she'd have paid a friendly visit to the county clerk's office by now. Listen. The dump's been gone over with a fine-toothed comb. If the will were ever going to show up, it would have done so by now. My guess is one of the two sons has it ... and we both know they'll never say anything." Walter rocked in his swivel chair. "We've got to keep our eyes on the ball, Tommy. How are you doing with Mac Moultrie?"

"Like I told you, we've known each other since we were kids. He should be a pushover."

"Well, start pushing."

"I don't think it's too wise to pursue this so soon after ... well, you know. Let's wait for the dust to settle before we go charging in."

Walter went to the window and stared out onto the bank of mid-rise condominiums flanking one of the most valuable strips of sand on the East Coast. As president of the Deveroux Company, he had ridden a wave of incredible profits brought about by the baby boomers' rush to the beach. However, this gated community, that boasted a pristine beach and all the amenities the wealthy demanded, was now sold out.

Walter turned. "We don't have time, Tommy. We're shit out of product. If we don't get our hands on that peninsula soon, by this time next year we won't have a damn thing to sell. Christ! I've got the architects working on it right now. I want this done before that damn fisherman gets wind of our plans, otherwise he'll jack up the price."

He continued as if he were thinking out loud. "Everything's all set with the county. They're going to let us put up four mid-rises with forty units each. If we get Mac's land, five." He tossed a site plan on the desk. "Prices on the first floor will start somewhere around four hundred thousand and end up around six on the top floor."

Tommy picked up the plan, but noticing his hand shake, laid it back down.

"As you can see, Tommy, I can't wait much longer for you to cut a deal with Moultrie."

Tommy took out a handkerchief and wiped his brow. "I'll take care of it tomorrow. Mac's taking me and one of my clients fishing."

Tommy looked over at Walter. "Have we heard anything from Trip Alston?"

"What do you mean?"

"Has he got wind of any of this?"

"I don't think so, or he'd be beating down the planning board's door."

Tommy resented Walter's smug confidence. All he had to do was pick up the phone and someone jumped. That is, someone other than Mac Moultrie. With all his power, there were people out there who even Walter couldn't get to roll over.

As absurd as it seemed, Tommy couldn't help wondering if Mo Washington had been one of those people. Old Mo drowned just days after he'd mentioned the will to Walter. Then Tommy got the call. A three percent partnership in their Chertaw Island development if he kept his mouth shut about the will and talked Mo's sons into selling.

Tommy had always marveled at the ability of his wealthy clients to sit back and mull over their next deliciously lucrative move and then expect him to accomplish it for a mere hourly fee. When Walter offered to deal him in on the big money, it only took a heartbeat to justify to himself that Mo's two boys deserved the land more than the granddaughter.

After the funeral, however, he still had bouts of wrestling with his conscience. But, as the days of his silence slipped by, so did his chances of extricating himself. Now that he couldn't turn back, Walter expected him to do whatever it took to get the project going; and delivering Mac's land before Trip could mount any resistance was the next hurdle.

"All that loser cares about is those white elephants he's restoring in Charleston," continued Walter as he railed against Trip. "He had a chance to get on board with us five years ago on the Bates Island project but blew it. If we work fast, this will be a done deal before he knows what's happened."

That's not the only thing Trip blew, thought Tommy. How did he let Kim Dusenbury get away? He couldn't understand people like Trip. With his family connections ... hell, he could have had the coast by the tail by now.

Tommy reached for a copy of the site plan. "Can I have this?"

Walter nodded. "Just don't let it out of your hands."

Back in his car and away from the heady atmosphere of Walter's office, Tommy's confidence started to disintegrate. He pounded a fist on the steering wheel. How could he have gotten in so damn deep so damn fast? He'd worked all his life to get where he was. Heck, his parents couldn't even read or write.

Damn it. He knew exactly why. No matter how hard he tried, he still wasn't in the same bracket as someone like Trippett Alston and his crowd. And when he laid eyes on old Mo Washington when he walked into the law office six months ago, all he could see was ten pristine acres on the Chertaw peninsula. If ever he smelled an opportunity, this was it. He even typed the will himself so his secretary wouldn't know. Now, however, he was knee-deep in a conspiracy. He could lose his license, maybe worse. Gnawing at him even more were lingering suspicions about the old man's drowning.

He floored the accelerator and roared out of the parking lot, his thoughts focused on the fishing trip Mac was taking him and one of his clients out on the next day. Walter, with his Harvard Business School mentality, had no idea how to handle someone like Mac. You can't just call him on the phone and offer him a deal. You have to work it.

To get Mac to leave his bungalow on the peninsula he'd have to put forth a bigger effort than he let on in front of Walter, but he had no choice. Pausing at the stoplight, he noticed the site plan lying on the seat. Since he couldn't turn back, hell, he might as well keep his eye on the ball just like Walter had said and in a few years he'd be in the same league as Trippett Alston. The one question he asked himself, however, was who, if anyone, in Trippett's lineage had been willing to commit a felony to launch the family into the comfortable upper classes?

Tommy spotted his client on the dock with Mac the next morning as he pulled into the parking lot of the McClellanville marina. After handshakes all around, everyone got in the twenty-footer, and Mac, who'd motored up from the island, took off down the creek toward open water.

The ocean was visible on the horizon as they crossed Chertaw Bay. Once on the other side, the boat slipped into a quiet marsh creek, slicing through the mirror-like water. The golden green grasses stretched to the end of the flawless blue horizon on both sides. Mac cut the engine and the boat drifted to a bobbing halt. A pelican sat as still as a statue on a lone sun-bleached post sticking out of the water.

"You boys know the drill," said Mac handing them each a rod. "If you don't like your lure, just let me know and I'll get you a new one."

He pointed to an area thinly covered with marsh grass. "There's a whole mess of li'l ole spottail that hang out over there."

Tommy's client threw his rod back, flicked the line forward, and within a few minutes reeled in a six-pounder. Mac grabbed his camera and took a picture of the proud client holding the beautiful silver fish glistening in the sunshine, this gesture obviously one of his proven marketing tools.

The three men settled down to leisurely casting in the estuary.

"This is a nice business you've got going here," Tommy said to Mac.

"Suits me."

"A lot different than when you and me were kids, aye."

Mac smiled.

"I remember when we would row back down to your pa's property on the peninsula and cook the fish we caught and sit there 'til the sun set."

"Yeah. Just a few folks on the island back then. Old Mo Washington, his two boys and their ma on our end, and the Kings, Alstons and a couple of families on the other."

"Things sure have changed."

"Yep. Haven't spoken to Mo's two sons since I left the island at eighteen."

That's good, thought Tommy.

"I was gone the week old Mo drowned. Missed the funeral and everything."

Tommy decided not to mention he had attended the funeral. Might lead to Mac asking questions. Tommy remembered Trip wasn't at the funeral either and wondered if he and Mac ever spoke. He doubted it. Trip was just a kid when Mac took off, and these days they hardly ran in the same circles.

Mac threw out a long, slow cast. "I'm just counting the days until some realtor's sign goes up on the far end of the peninsula."

Tommy jumped at the opportunity. "Once they start selling lots out there, cars will be driving by your place night and day."

"I know. Won't hardly be the same."

"If you were smart, you'd sell out before that happens."

Tommy expected some kind of response to gauge Mac's interest, but the silence grew.

"I'm a dirt lawyer, Mac, and know a lot of people buying up land. You want me to see if I can get you a good offer? I can save you the commission."

Mac slowly reeled in his line and sent a soft whistle through the air as he cast in the smooth confident motion of a seasoned fisherman. "I don't want to rush into anything. I figure I'll be fixin' to sell out one of these days, but hadn't counted on it being quite so soon." Mac failed to mention that, when he was ready, he was going to make sure he knew to whom he was selling and exactly what they were going to do with his land.

"Hell," said Tommy, "I'd rather be rich when I was still young enough to enjoy it." He waited for that to sink in. "Floating around on a nice catamaran in the Caribbean wouldn't be a bad way to spin out the rest of your time on this earth."

"How much do you think you could get for my five acres?"

"It's hard to say, but a million wouldn't be too far off."

Mac rolled the sum around in his head for a while. "I think I'll be better off if I wait a spell."

"Why do you say that?"

Mac turned to Tommy, squinting from the glare of the sun. "I'm thinkin' I can get more if I subdivide the land and sell it one parcel at a time."

"Sure. But you'd have to get it surveyed, get the place zoned, market it. Hell, you'd have thousands into it before you saw a dime."

Suddenly, Tommy had a big fish on the line, and as he struggled to pull it in, Mac got the same sickening feeling he had whenever he was reminded of why he left commercial fishing.

What triggered that reaction, Mac wondered. Unless it was Tommy's mention of his having to get his land rezoned before he could sell it. Hell, it was already zoned residential. Why was he getting a gut feeling that something was wrong? Maybe it was because, ever since they were kids, Tommy Warren, Jr., always came out on top, and Mac had always wondered how.

Mac had felt this same uneasiness when the government first hatched its plan to encourage investment in big fishing fleets. He didn't know then what was going to happen, just that something *was* going to happen. A wave of regret raced through him as he thought about the disaster to Atlantic fishing that had followed.

By noon, Tommy was pulling out of the marina's parking lot when his phone rang.

Walter didn't bother to stand on formalities. "Well. Do we have a deal?"

Tommy took a deep breath. "Do we really need Mac's property? I mean, won't the Washington's ten acres at the end of the peninsula make the project fly?"

"Are you telling me you don't think he's going to sell?"

"No. I'm not saying that. It's just ... well, I don't think it's going to be as easy as I thought."

Walter put the phone down without saying goodbye. Alone in his office, being Saturday, missing were the usual sounds of ringing phones and voices trailing down the hall. He reached in his pocket and pulled out his wallet. Carefully tucked under one of the flaps was a small piece of paper with a phone number. He fingered it for a moment, methodically folded it, then slipped it back in.

🐚 CHAPTER SIX

The flashlight beam skipped along the sandy path. Up ahead, the light coming from Mac Moultrie's shack caused the swaying sea oats to cast dancing shadows across the dunes. Relieved at this sign of life, Nicole Sullivan ran up the steps to the porch.

The door flung open.

"Hey, gal! Was about to leave without ya!" Mac said as he handed her a pail.

Nicky pointed her light into the bucket over a squirming mass.

"This here mullet will make nice bait for the traps," said Mac.

"Aren't we going shrimping?"

"Shoot! There you go again. You Yankees are always one step ahead of yourselves. Just gonna check my crab traps on the way back."

Nicky noticed the shrimp net lying in the boat as they loaded up. Mac started the motor, flicked on a soft-beamed light, and took off down the creek.

The moon came from behind the clouds, casting deep shadows across Mac's prominent features. His jaw was broad and square and lips little more than a thin line curling up at the corners, making him appear smiling. The thick dark head of hair and long gray sideburns in need of a trim gave him the overall appearance of casual ruggedness. But nothing could be further from the truth. Every move he made was deliberate, almost as if he were wary that potential disaster lay in wait just around the corner and he didn't want to get caught. All the years spent on the high seas with harrowing life and death experiences and narrow escapes had carved out his granite character.

A strong breeze laden with the scent of saltwater announced they had reached the ocean.

"The sun's coming up," Nicky said, pointing to the fine red line across the sky."

The sound of the motor changed as it slipped into idle. Mac lifted the funnel-like net and threw it into the water, grasping the trowel boards. He secured the towropes and increased the speed just enough for the boat to drag the net on the bottom of the ocean.

The two sat quietly for a while as the boat glided along. Mac got out a thermos and poured them both coffee.

"Our first drag's gonna take about an hour," he said. "Right now we can relax, but after we dump the first catch we're gonna be busy."

"Sorting?"

"Uh-huh. We're going to have to pick out the trash. You know. Things we're not going to eat or sell. Then we've got to ice down the shrimp."

Nicky gave Mac a long studied look. "How long have you been fishing?" she asked.

Mac took a sip of coffee and crossed a leg over his knee. "Pretty much all my life. When I left these parts I joined the Service and was assigned to a research ship at the North Pole. After that I tried commercial fishing. Fished from Alaska to New England to the Gulf of Mexico. Also the Pacific and all along the Panama section."

Nicky loved the trace of a drawl in his craggy voice.

"What was your job?"

"Everything ... crewman ... first mate ... captain." Mac reached over and checked the drag rope on the net. "I wasn't one of those guys that came ashore, got drunk and had to be carried back to the ship. I usually stayed behind and got everything ready. Eventually I owned my own boat."

"What kind of fish did you catch?"

"In Alaska we got halibut. In the North Atlantic we got scallops in the summer and flounder in the winter. We went shrimping in Key West and all along the Gulf. Got grouper and snapper off the South Carolina coast."

"Why'd you stop fishing and come back here?"

"It's a long story."

"Go on. I'd like to hear it."

Resting his forearms on his legs, he hunched forward clutching his coffee.

"Well, back in the seventies there was all this controversy about the Russians and Spanish fishing too close to our borders with their big factory ships. Back then there was only a twelve-mile limit. Then the government declared a 200-mile limit for foreign fleets." He turned toward Nicky. "That puts them off the Continental Shelf. There's no sea life after that. Ninety percent of the seafood is in ten percent of the water closest to shore."

"You mean, in the great majority of the ocean, there's nothing?"

"That's right."

They were quiet for a while, then Nicky asked, "Wasn't the two-hundred-mile limit a good thing?"

"Not once the politicians got a hold of it." Mac rubbed his hands in such a way Nicky could tell he was upset. "They said, now that we've pushed the limit to two hundred miles, American fleets can't handle that much ocean, so they made up the National Marine Fisheries Service to help our fishermen get the kind of factory boats they'd need to do the job. They offered investment tax credits to anybody buying these monsters. Then they went one step further by getting together syndicates looking for investment tax credits ... doctors, lawyers, you know, people with money.

"After a while, there was so damn much money chasing these tax credits that these syndicates were buying *anything* that would absorb this capital. They were putting in staterooms, central heat, closed circuit TV, carpeting ... any damn thing that would jack up the cost. Overindulgence in every possible way."

Mac's speech, usually slow and easy, came across so fast Nicky had no doubt this issue struck at his heart.

"The guys running these syndicate ships were all subcontractors since most of the good fisherman already owned their own boats. These inexperienced subs, who didn't need a license or have to take a Coast Guard exam since they weren't hauling passengers for hire, crashed into docks up and down the coast."

Mac got up and checked the towrope again, then poured himself another cup of coffee and continued as if he couldn't stop. "The whole damn Atlantic got overpopulated with boats ... twenty-five men on a trawler ... then super trawlers. That kind of stuff. And it was payback time for all the syndicates that had invested. They weren't demanding a profit, but they sure as hell didn't want to put out more money to keep the fleets afloat.

"These factory boats had to bring in enough fish to meet the monthly payments on the damn ships ... seven-hundred-thousand and up. So many fish were being brought in, it wasn't funny. One packinghouse in Hampton, Virginia, that used to handle fifteen to seventeen boats on a regular basis, started juggling a hundred and forty. They had to put on shoreside managers to handle the refueling and re-icing. It became an ongoing nightmare. And in three years time, things went from plenty of fish in the ocean to absolutely scratching out a living."

"What happened to all those fleets?"

"That was interesting. There's a thing called the insurance valve that seems to blow off like a relief valve just beyond the continental shelf where boats can't be retrieved. It's funny how there's always a friend nearby just as the boat starts taking on water." He shook his head. "The government caused this problem, but the insurance companies took the hit."

Mac stared out at the water, then his voice saddened. "The bigger boats finally caught the last of the codfish. Hell, they would have taken the very last one if it hadn't been for a moratorium. The end of the codfish was the final nail in the coffin for New England fishing."

Mac kept shaking his head. "Flounder's been dragged to death. Other than a limited quota, there's no flounder fishing from North Carolina to Canada." Mac paused. "When baby flounder would come out into the Chesapeake Bay from their birthplace in the estuaries, no local fisherman would catch them ... but those new captains who were driven to make the damn monthly payments on the syndicate boats, would net them less than twelve months old."

Mac looked at Nicky. "We used to get scallops as big as a plate, and in three years they were smaller than three inches and slipping through our nets. When we complained, the government just told us to use two-and-three-quarter-inch nets."

"What's going to happen now?" Nicky asked.

Mac shook his head. "I don't know. The government to this day still refuses to take their licks. It's all strictly politics. There's nobody who's willing to do the right thing. Just a lot of suck-egg crap. Right now there's the gill nets. All kinds of fish and aquatic mammals are getting caught in these monofilament entanglement nets. Invisible under water, they're deadly. Even birds get caught in them when they dive down after the swarming fish."

Mac stood up. "Let's see what we've got."

He slowed down the motor, wrestled the net into the boat and spilled the contents onto the deck, then quickly threw the net back in. Once the boat was back at cruising speed, he picked up a shrimp and waved it at Nicky. "Put these critters in this here basket." He bent down and picked a brown crab with long legs out of the pile and showed it to Nicky. "This here is a spider crab. It's sort of a miniature version of the king crab. You don't see them inshore. Just when you drag in deep water. We'll toss him and any other critters we're not going to eat back in."

Crouched next to the pile, Nicky asked, "How much will this basket hold?"

"Five pecks ... a fifth larger than a bushel."

Nicky smiled. Mac was so specific and methodical. She thought about that for a while and figured it was the only way someone could survive thirty years on the open seas.

With the last shrimp picked out, Mac grinned. "We're gonna have a good day. Three baskets. That's almost two hundred and fifty pounds. Not bad for our first drag."

He handed Nicky a shovel. "Start dumping this trash into the water while I ice down the shrimp."

When they finished the job of clearing all the seaweed, shells and ocean debris from the deck, they sat down next to each other. Mac looked at Nicky and said with a smile, "Hey, girl. I've been shooting my mouth off all morning. Now it's your turn to spill your guts."

Nicky laughed then shook her head. "Mac, the last thing you want to hear about is me."

"What's a matter? You some kind of serial killer?"

Nicky looked off across the water toward the horizon, then quickly back at Mac. "No." She let out a short cynical laugh. "Just Poor Nicky Sullivan."

Mac reached over and lifted Nicky's chin with his big rough hand. "Things can't be that bad."

Nicky locked her hands around a crossed knee and leaned back. "Everything was okay when I was a kid. My mom and dad are really great. It was just that they were kinda old when my brother Jack and I were born, so naturally when we hit our teens they were in their sixties."

Nicky paused as she watched Mac take out a cigar and light it.

"Keep going," he said.

"The problem really is my brother, Jack. He was quiet, but a good kid. That is until he was around twelve or thirteen. After a while we found out he was schizophrenic, but in the beginning we just didn't know what to do. He had temper tantrums, imagined threats. I was afraid to leave him alone."

Nicky brushed away a strand of hair that had flown across her eye. "I've been thinking about it a lot lately. What happened was that I became his nursemaid. Anything to keep him out of trouble and in school. I kept praying he'd get better. I'd always had a lot of friends, played baseball with the neighborhood kids ... that kind of thing. But after a while I didn't have any friends left, since I was always with Jack. If I did try to chum around with anyone, he'd get jealous and things got horribly out of control."

Nicky took a deep breath and slowly let it out. "I always figured that if I could get him through college, he could settle down as an accountant somewhere, and I could get on with my life. But after he lost the second job, my mother and I just couldn't put him through that again."

"Didn't you have any beaus?"

"Once. But he blew me off when he found out what a weird family we were."

Mac's eyes met Nicky's. Nicky wiped away a tear by casually swiping the back of a hand across her face as if she were just pushing her hair back. In a voice coated with irony, she said, "Jack can be likable if you give him half a chance, but he can turn on you in an instant. He's vicious ... as if there's a deep well of hate somewhere inside him."

"Weren't there any other family members to help out? Uncles, friends of the family?"

"At first, it was pride. My dad didn't want anyone to know. I have a brother who's sixteen years older, but he left to go to college and we never really saw much of him after that. He was working two jobs to get through college, then medical school."

Nicky gazed off into the distance and wrung her sweaty hands. "As my parents got older, little by little, things fell on me. In the end I was taking care of the house, my parents, Jack, everything."

"How'd you pull away?"

Nicky's voice cracked. "My other brother just walked in one day and took charge." Nicky looked over the water through squinted lids, and continued as if she were talking to herself, "It's a good thing too. I was just hanging on by my fingernails." She shook her head. "I still can't believe it. Just like that ..." She snapped her fingers and smiled, " ... my big brother and his wife fixed everything."

She stared expectantly. "You probably know my older brother's married to Mary Beth King. It was her idea to send me here." Her tone became hopeful. "They want me to get a new start."

"I've got a new start for you, gal. Why don't you throw in with me and we'll make millions diggin' up pirate treasure. You know Blackbeard used to run in these here waters."

Nicky nudged Mac with her shoulder. "Wouldn't that make your motorcycle mama jealous?"

They both laughed.

"What's her name?"

"I call her Sweetie."

"Surely, she has another name."

"I call all my girls Sweetie. That way I don't accidentally call any of them by the wrong name."

Nicky laughed. "I got a better plan than treasure hunting."

"Don't tell me you're going to buy one of those magnet gadgets and become a beachcomber."

"Fat chance of that! You may not know it, but I'm a pretty good artist."

"Are you now?"

"Uh-huh, and I think I can put together quite a few drawings of wildlife along these tidal creeks for my show in Boston. Something people will respond to." She nudged him again. "I've even got my first commission. Dede's asked me to paint a mural for her."

Mac enjoyed seeing Nicky so animated and happy, her deep dimples and broad smile exuding the openness and innocence of youth. He couldn't resist gently brushing by her freckled nose with his fist in a slow imitation of a punch.

After finishing the last netful, they started toward the estuary where the boat pulled up to a Styrofoam marker bobbing in the water.

"How do you know which traps are yours?"

"My number and color are on them. Same as on my boat."

Mac leaned over and pulled the trap up, yelling for Nicky to hand him a pail. They emptied and restocked a dozen with mullet, before the boat headed back across the bay for McClellanville.

Suddenly, Mac pointed toward the side of the boat and yelled, "Look! We've got three dolphins following us! Parents with their calf!"

Nicky screamed with delight as Mac circled several times with the dolphins leaping into the air and diving. She reached over the side and tried to pet them until they finally swam off.

Mac sped up again and headed for the docks. Nicky held her face to the headwind and inhaled the salt air and knew that she had irretrievably connected with the Chertaw estuary. The vast stretches of marsh grass edging the graceful tidal creeks teeming with wildlife spoke to her in a way that nothing else ever had.

The boat left the bay and chugged along the creek until the McClellanville docks came into view. They pulled up to the packinghouse and a boom swung a bucket out over the hull.

"Okay, gal! Let's fill'er up!"

The shrimp were dumped into a vat of water, then scooped onto a conveyor belt. Inside, after several women finished pinching the heads off, the packing manager gave Mac a slip.

Mac tapped Nicky on the shoulder. "Let's go get our money."

Nicky was quiet on the trip back to the island. Opening up to Mac sucked all the nightmarish memories out of her head. Her life in Boston was now officially behind her and all she could feel was a giddy sort of hopefulness.

Mac, on the other hand, after reliving the death of his life on the high seas for the zillionth time, felt the weight of his loss. The oceans of the world and all the things that swam in them had been the great love of his life and not a day went by that he didn't mourn them.

Nicky, with her fingers dragging along the water off the side of the boat, sat recalling the family of dolphins enjoying their freedom while cavorting in the open bay. These gentle creatures being swooped up and crushed by tons of fish and debris in an enormous net was unthinkable. She'd seen pathetic pictures of turtles with torn limbs and other injured marine life sprawled over the decks of gigantic factory trawlers in one of her wildlife rehabilitation courses.

She turned and looked up at Mac, her hair blowing across her face. They had become a natural team ever since Winston led her to his dock, both trying to make a new beginning. She smiled inwardly and wondered if the dog had known.

Suddenly she wanted to be at her drawing board, the one place where she could truly express herself. She loved these waters; and since being needed was core to her personality, she felt inflamed with a desire to do something to earn her place there.

🐚 CHAPTER SEVEN

The smug faces of the pampered agents made Walter Satterfield fight a cynical impulse to laugh out loud. They had no inkling that this time next year they might very well be hanging on to their Mercedes by their fingernails if the Chertaw Island project fell through. Walter couldn't help feeling that the kind of money they were making by simply touring clients through this oceanfront Mecca he had developed was almost obscene.

While the broker-in-charge who was conducting the weekly sales meeting shifted his motivational skills into high gear, Walter's mind went through his options in the event this did happen, one being looking for a new job. With the success of the Deveroux Company under his belt, he was well positioned to land in the top slot of another development company with a huge chunk of beach property.

He thought about his wife. Things had finally started to go right between them again. She was thrilled with the new oceanfront house, and was finally getting what she felt was due her, including her vision of their retirement. When she wasn't gushing over the new furniture, she was busy planning retirement trips to world-class playgrounds as well as a second home in Santa Fe.

The meeting ended and everyone stood up and prepared to leave. This was the part Walter hated most: having to feign interest when collared by an agent trying to impress him with some deal they were working on. Out of the corner of his eye, he spotted Dede Morgan. The only reason he had reluctantly agreed to go to one of her parties in a couple of weeks was because she wasn't always trying to ingratiate herself like the rest. Besides, his wife was looking forward to it.

A few moments after Walter arrived back in his office, he got word that a hurricane might be headed for South Carolina. It was early in the season for this kind of storm, but orders were given to make preparations.

Walter was putting the phone back into its cradle when his secretary came in and started talking in the annoying constrained whisper she used every time something she couldn't control appeared on her narrow horizon.

"There's a man here to see you."

"Well?"

"He looks a little ... I tried to get rid of him, but he insisted you'll want to see him."

Walter's gaze jumped from his secretary to the man now standing in the doorway, landing on his sardonic grin.

"I'll handle this," he said to his secretary. "Close the door."

In the time it took for Billy Cleary to saunter over to a chair, Walter Satterfield's life plummeted from nearly normal to a living nightmare. Walter's breathing constricted as he waited to hear Billy speak.

"It's nice to see you too," said Billy. He snorted out a half laugh. "Relax Walter. I don't want to get you in no shit."

"Then what in the hell are you doing here?"

Billy whistled softly. "Do a guy a favor and this is what you get." He looked around the room. "I ain't here to cause trouble. I just gotta have a roof over my head since the li'l ole cotton mill's closed. By September, they'll have it goin' again in Juarez with cheap Mexican labor, but they're still goin' to need good drivers."

The smug grin on Billy's face incensed Walter. How did he ever let himself get into this position? Other than the meeting at Wendy's, the six-o'clock news was the closest he'd ever gotten to anyone on the other side of the law.

Billy Cleary tossed his head toward the row of mid-rise condos out the window. "One of those high dollar things might be just what I need."

Walter almost laughed at the absurdity of the suggestion. However, the precariousness of his situation quickly made him take a moment to gather his thoughts. "How did you find me?" he finally asked.

"Findin' a high roller like you ain't hard ... not everybody can live in one of them big ole mansions. Hell, I could make a livin' just mowin' your lower forty." He leaned toward Walter and leered. "That's a right nice lookin' wife you got, too."

In a few hours, Walter would be sitting in the elegant dining room of one of the most prestigious private golf clubs in America, sparring with some of the most influential men in the South—a position he had earned over a lifetime. But at this very moment he found himself rubbing elbows with a moral low life—unfortunately, a position he also deserved.

"Where are you staying?" he asked in a somber tone.

"The Breakers Motel."

"I'll call you tomorrow." Walter gave the man his coldest stare as he rose. "Never come back to this office again. And the next time you step foot near my house, I'll kill you."

Billy stood up. "Don't get your feathers ruffled, Walter. I just reckoned you might be wantin' to help out one of your barnyard dogs ... only 'til September."

Walter glared at him. "I said I'll call you."

Billy left and Walter tried to calm himself by doing some work, but finally gave up and went over to the wet bar, poured himself a couple of fingers of scotch and gulped it down. Life had taught him that most problems could be solved if you throw enough money at them. He stared out the window at the row of condominiums and wondered just how much he would have to throw at this one.

Never one to put off an unpleasant task, Walter called in the maintenance manager whom he knew felt a blind loyalty to the Deveroux Company, due mostly to the fact he had risen to his position without attaining a high school diploma.

"I need a place to stay for someone doing some landscaping for me. What do we have?"

"Not much. There's those two ground floor units we let the agents use for some of their clients."

"No. Nothing here. What about over at the plaza we just bought. Wasn't there a trailer out back?"

"Remember? You told us to get rid of it."

The maintenance manager had to be thinking hard. After all, it wasn't every day he got called into the headman's office and asked for a favor. "There's a small apartment over the Crab House."

Walter mulled that over. Not a good idea. The last thing he needed was to have Billy perched on a bar stool every night. "No. That won't do either."

"How about that old beach house on Chertaw Island that's been boarded up for a couple years now."

Walter had forgotten about the place two or three lots down from Mac's property. When it had gone on the market, he had felt if they ever wanted to develop out on the peninsula, it might come in handy. He thought for a moment. It would do for the couple of weeks it might take to settle with Billy.

"Can you have it ready by tomorrow?"

"I suppose so. I'm sure I can get the water and power turned on and the boards off the windows. It's just the phone."

"Forget that."

Realizing Walter wanted this kept a secret or he would have had his secretary handle it, the maintenance manager smiled reassuringly. "Don't worry. Nobody's going to know about this," he said, and left, confident his job was a notch more secure.

He was paid up for another night, but moments after Walter's call, Billy threw his things into a frayed athletic bag and left the motel. When he turned onto the causeway at the Chertaw Island sign, the peninsula jutting out from the marsh in the distance reminded him of the night he killed the old man.

What a stroke of luck! The money had finally let him dump the pestering old bag he'd been shacking up with and install a trailer on his pa's place in the North Carolina mountains. It didn't have running water or electricity, but being tucked way off in the woods high above the main road was worth the trade off. If the Feds ever came after him, he'd see them in plenty of time to escape.

He made a right at the end of the road and started to look for the place Satterfield had described. He was concentrating so hard he almost hit the girl and dog, but landed in front of the shack as he slammed on the brakes. He glanced in the rearview mirror. She was small, but then she'd be easy to handle. He didn't like the looks of the dog, but that could be taken care of, too.

Hell, what was he thinking! He had to keep that stuff out of his mind and not draw attention to himself. Old Walter was his ticket to the easy life and he wasn't going to blow it on some piece of ass, no matter how tempting it looked.

He pulled a cigarette from his shirt pocket and lit up. His gaze meandered up to the rearview mirror again. Hell, there ain't no harm in just looking, he thought. When the girl disappeared into a cluster of dwarf oaks, he took a satisfying deep drag, then slowing exhaled. One li'l ole murder of a no 'count old nigger and here we was—smack in the middle of the rich man's paradise.

Nicky sat back and studied the sandpiper running across the sparkling white sheet of Bristol board, his determined head down as if he were hell-bent on getting somewhere. She looked hard at the drawing, questioning if she had captured the blurry speed at which these energetic little shore birds moved.

She covered the image and placed it on top of the stack of drawings

59

she was saving for her show, then reached for her sketch pad and flipped through the pages until she found what she was looking for—dolphins in the bay. She took the pencil from behind her ear and quickly sketched an image that had been swirling around in her head for the past half hour.

If Winston hadn't sat up and pricked up his ears, she wouldn't have noticed Johnny Bumps peering through the screen. Nicky closed her sketchpad, slipped the pencil back behind her ear and went to the door.

As usual, Johnny Bumps looked sweaty. Easily fifty pounds overweight, his dark curly hair was pasted in ringlets around his pudgy flushed face.

"Pardon me, Miss Nicky. Didn't want to startle you any by knockin'."

"That's all right, Johnny. Come on in."

"Trip called. I'm supposed to fasten everything down."

Nicky wrinkled her brow. "What are you talking about?"

The corners of Johnny's lips tightened. "Ain't you heard? Hurricane's comin'."

Nicky glanced toward the ocean, puzzled. The sky was a beautiful cobalt blue and the water only kicking up a bit. She looked at him sideways and asked, "Just what are you supposed to do?"

"Fasten the shutters and bring in the porch furniture."

"I can manage that."

"You need me to help you pack?"

"Pack? Pack what?"

"The governor just gave a mandatory evacuation order for all the barrier islands. You've got to leave."

Nicky shifted her weight onto one foot and ran her fingers through her hair. "I can't just pick up and go. I'd have to take everything with me, the animals anyway." She cocked her head and raised an eyebrow. "Do you really think there's going to be a storm?"

Johnny rested his clasped hands on his bulging stomach, twirled his thumbs and grinned broadly, giving Nicky the feeling he was enjoying the effect the news was having on her.

"Don't worry about me," she said. "If the weather gets bad, I'll know enough to leave."

"Whatever you say, Miss Nicky, but I'd turn on the TV if I were you. By the way, the shelters won't let you bring in that li'l ole cat of yours. And if you think you're going to need any water, you better git it while the pump's workin'. They'll be fixin' to turn off the electricity to the island first."

"First?"

"Uh-huh. Once the power company determines we're going to take a hit, they turn off the juice." He leaned forward and looked her square in the eyes. "When water hits hot wires, the sparking causes fires." His eyes wandered over to the phone and he looked as if he wanted to add something, but evidently decided against it. "Gotta go and take care of Trip's house."

He tossed his head toward Winston. "Supposed to take him home with me. Trip's got two houses to board up in Charleston and doesn't think he's gonna make it back to the island before the storm hits."

Nicky quickly fastened the leash onto Winston's collar and handed it to Johnny.

He shuffled out grumbling, "Not even July tenth and we're already getting our first hurricane." He turned, gave her another grin and said, "I wonder if this li'l ole island will still be here next week."

Agitated, yet determined not to let the man get her worked up, Nicky flipped on the Weather Channel and listened for a while before snapping it off. As yet, the storm was only a category two and not expected to hit the coast for a couple more days, somewhere between Florida and North Carolina. She didn't relish the fact that she might have to find a hotel and sneak in Salem and the injured animals she was caring for.

She sat down at her drawing board, brought out the Underground Railway illustration and spent the rest of the day working on it, annoyed she couldn't go over and ask Mac what she should do. He had taken his boat to Beaufort on a fishing trip.

The next morning, the sun was shining like any other day, except the breakers were rolling into shore at a ferocious pace. Nicky padded over to the coffeemaker and was relieved to see the numbers on the clock still lit. She turned on the TV to catch the weather report while the coffee brewed.

Doppler radar showed that the storm, now churning in the Atlantic, was expected to move rapidly along the coast a hundred miles offshore. Experts from various weather services were saying it could make landfall anywhere between Jacksonville and Cape Hatteras, more than a six-hundred-mile window.

Cup in hand, Nicky's eyes took in the choppy sea as she considered her options. Everything was neatly stored in portfolios except for the ten or so stacks she was currently working on. Since she could have everything safely packed in the Volvo in under two hours, she decided to wait until five when they'd be able to predict the storm's course more accurately, and then make up her mind whether or not to leave.

She brought the drawing of the sandpiper back out and taped the corners to her drawing board. On the table next to her, she spread the dozens of sketches she'd made while sitting on the beach. Every stroke was carefully examined while she concentrated on her next move. One feather slightly ruffled by the wind had to be added to give the impression of the speed with which these birds raced across the sand. She hadn't put the finishing touches on the legs yet and decided to draw several possible renditions on a scratch pad to make sure she had it right.

Every once in a while she glanced at the TV and caught a glimpse of some reporter frantically yelling into a mike, hair whipping in the wind with waves breaking furiously in the background. The last ambitious soul enjoying fifteen minutes of fame on network news had been standing on the beach in Fort Lauderdale.

Closer to home and much more frightening were aerial shots showing gridlock on all the roads leading out of Charleston. Some cars had been bogged down in traffic for as long as twelve hours, causing local officials to demand the State designate both lanes of traffic westbound so vehicles could be funneled to I-95 twice as fast. The report of a woman having a baby in the back seat paled in comparison to the details of the man who died of a heart attack and couldn't be extricated from his car for hours.

Other reports said the gridlock on I-95 was just as severe, with people pouring out of Florida and Georgia. Maybe she should just stay put and ride out the storm. No. If there were the remotest chance the hurricane would hit the island, she had to have her drawings safely inland.

She picked up the phone to assure Jack and her mother that she was okay, but changed her mind. They were obviously unaware of the storm, or they would have called her. So why get Jack riled up unnecessarily? Arms folded, she stood deep in thought wondering if her indecisiveness in leaving was a reaction to Johnny Bumps trying to scare her.

By two, hungry, she made a sandwich and wandered out onto the porch. The dark menacing sky seemed close enough to touch. An odd sensation crept up on her, until she realized the house had become silent. She spun around and saw the TV had gone dark. She ran over, picked up the phone and discovered it dead. A picture of Jack screaming profanities at some innocent telephone operator shot into her head.

Trippett Alston threw the last of his file boxes into the Yukon and gave the beach house a somber look. Would he ever see the place again? As someone who had lived through Hugo, the threat of this hurricane filled him with gut-wrenching fear. He had raced back to the island the moment he finished boarding up his projects to retrieve his irreplaceable collection of early Charleston house plans. Now he was anxious to get back to Charleston before the storm hit.

Flying branches and debris whipped up by the violent wind intensified his fear that the plywood on the unfinished sections of the King Street roof might not hold. He'd been so careful with scheduling; but no one could predict a hurricane coming so early. If the roof were lost, with the rains that would follow, he'd pretty much have to start from scratch. The money didn't bother him; that was what insurance was for. What made him sick was the possibility of losing the two years of devotion to detail that had gone into restoring the place.

If his luck held out, there'd be enough time to pick up Winston at Johnny's house on the mainland and get back to Charleston and give his buildings one last check. The SUV plowed down the road toward the causeway and he shot a glance at the King's Nest for reassurance that Johnny Bumps had fastened all the shutters. Damn! He saw clear through the building to the ocean, and the Volvo was sitting in the driveway! He slammed on his brakes and threw the Yukon into reverse, then sped forward again down the driveway, flying out the door before the vehicle came to a stop.

Nicky, packing feverishly, glanced up as Trippett charged through the door, his face flushed with anger.

"I sent Bumps to pack you up and get you out! Why are you still here?" He raced over and started fastening down the shutters hollering, "You've got two minutes to get your stuff together!"

The slamming shutters and Trippett's rage numbed Nicky with embarrassment, yet she stubbornly continued carefully placing her individual stacks of research materials into their portfolios.

Trip's anger surged. "You Yankees come down here and don't know a damn thing about what you're getting into. You ignore all the warnings and instead go surfing for God's sake. No wonder we have to keep pulling you out of the trees after every storm!"

Nicky kept packing at the same cautious speed. Suddenly Trippett towered over her.

"Okay. This is it! Get moving!"

"I've got to get all my work packed."

"Honeychild, you should have thought of that two days ago!"

Nicky slid a large book into its envelope. "I'm not going anywhere without my work." She eyed the stack of finished wildlife drawings she had done for her show and decided that next she would carefully secure them in a portfolio.

Trippett shook his head in disgust. "Lady, you have no idea what trouble you're in."

He marched over to the dresser, pulled out a drawer and started tossing in the stack of drawings.

"Stop!" Nicky shouted. She rushed over and yanked the drawer from Trippett's hands so fast most of the drawings flew across the room. "Oh, my God!" she screamed.

Trippett picked up a drawing left in the drawer and examined it. His gaze shot over to Nicky, then moved across her face as if he were curious about her.

"So you're Nicky?"

She glared at him.

Trip's voice softened. "I'm sorry."

Nicky, tears running down her cheeks, fell to her knees and started picking up the drawings.

Trip touched her shoulder and said, "I'm really sorry. I'll help you pack."

Nicky rose. "I'll get my portfolio."

Trip gathered the drawings and his gaze locked on one of himself jogging on the beach with Winston. He looked over at Nicky, and when he noticed she was busy unzipping a large leather case, carefully tucked the sheet back into the pile and put everything on the desk.

He lifted a stack of folders saying, "I'm going to put these in your car."

Without looking up from her packing, Nicky said, "I want you to know I was getting ready to go before you came." She gave him a quick glance, and with an edge on her voice, added, "And I don't mean surfing."

Trippett rolled his eyes and headed for the door.

By the time Nicky had everything bundled, breakers were crashing violently against the boardwalk. Trippett rushed in from his fourth trip to the car wearing a rain-streaked slicker. Nicky hurriedly handed him the cage with her cat. He grasped her arm firmly, shouting, "We've got to get out now! The causeway's liable to wash away any minute!"

"Wait! I've got to get the others!"

"What others!"

She ran into the bedroom and brought out a carton, the seagull's beady eyes fixed on Trippett.

"His wing's injured!"

"All right! Let's go!"

"No! You've got to get the turtle! He's in a box under ..." Seeing Trippett's face twist into an incredulous expression, she shoved the carton with the bird into his hands and ran back into the bedroom. Rushing out clutching a shoebox, she yelled, "Okay! I'm ready!"

The howling wind whipped the wax myrtles against the ground and almost wrenched the box out of Nicky's hands as she scampered down the stairs. Rain streamed down her face as Trippett yelled for her to open the car door. The screen door banged angrily against the porch railing while he packed the animals.

Suddenly Salem was out of the cage and on Trippett's back. A large piece of tin roofing sailed through the air, and the sopping wet cat leapt onto the porch and into the house.

Nicky started for the stairs. Trippett grabbed her arm, pulled her back and shouted, "Get in the car!"

"I've got to get her!"

"Are you nuts! We've got to get out of here! This place could blow any minute!"

Nicky yanked loose and flew up the stairs. Frantic, she ran through the darkened rooms desperately searching for Salem. Enormous waves crashed against the walkway and shook the house. She could hear Trip's angry shouts as she fell to her knees and looked under her bed. Trip suddenly appeared and started to lift her up.

"Wait! There she is!"

Nicky quickly wiggled under the bed and grabbed the cat cowering against the wall. Trip pulled Nicky from under the bed and they ran out with Trip clutching the hysterical cat with an iron grip. Once it was back in the cage, Nicky slid into the Volvo's front seat, rolled down the window and yelled, "Where should I go?"

"Follow me! I'll take you to the 526 on-ramp in Charleston! You'll be on your own from there! Take it to 26 and go north!"

Waves pounded the causeway railings, now under several inches of water. Terrified, Nicky locked her eyes on the back of the SUV parting the waters in front of her.

For the next half-hour the thumping of the windshield wipers drummed in her brain as their convoy made its way through flooded section after flooded section of Route 17, stopping only once to pick up Winston.

An endless ribbon of red brake lights on the 526 bypass greeted them in Mt. Pleasant. Trippett pulled off the road and ran back to the Volvo head down to shelter his face from the pelting rain.

"This is no good!" he shouted as she buzzed down the window. "His white-knuckle grasp of the window edge exposed blood incrusted cat scratches on the back of his hands. With rain running freely down his face, he looked up and stared thoughtfully at the traffic.

Finally, he stuck his head in the window. "I can't send you into this traffic with all those animals! I'm going to take you to my mother!" He looked her in the eye. "Whatever you do, don't lose me! And pump your brakes every time you pull out of water!"

They crossed the Cooper River Bridge with bumper-to-bumper traffic ominously coming at them from the opposite direction, and parted the waters through the streets of Charleston's deserted historic district until two National Guardsmen signaled Trippett to stop.

Nicky stared beyond the wipers noisily swatting away the rain, catching glimpses of Trip in animated conversation, until they were waved on. The SUV stopped in front of an immense wrought-iron gate, which slowly opened after being commanded from some electronic device. Nicky followed it into a courtyard. Dozens of huge Palmetto palm trees were writhing in front of a massive balconied mansion pockmarked with plywood.

They scurried across the branch-strewn brick plaza and up onto the porch. The door swung open and a tall, patrician-looking woman shepherded them in.

The slamming of the huge door echoed in the massive entrance hall. Dripping wet and holding the cat cage, Nicky felt foolish and out of place in the elegant surroundings until Winston shook himself and his clinking tags broke the silence.

The woman, dressed in a simple black dress, ignored the spray and was surprisingly calm as she spoke in a cultivated Southern accent. "Nell's been holding dinner for you, Son." She turned to Nicky and smiled warmly.

Trippett quickly said, "Mother, this is Nicky ..." He frowned as he groped for her last name.

"Sullivan!" Nicky piped up.

Trippett rubbed the back of his neck and threw his mother a sideways glance. "I've got to check on my projects. Nicky's Mary Beth King's sister-in-law. She's been staying at the King's Nest. Can you ..."

The woman graciously put her arm around Nicky. "Of course. Come with me, child. Let's get you into some dry clothes."

A few steps up the flowing staircase, Elizabeth Alston turned toward Trippett who was going out the door. The housekeeper, holding the cat cage, had Winston by the collar and was coaxing him toward the kitchen.

"Be careful, Son," said Mrs. Alston.

"Don't worry. I'll be back as soon as I can."

Torrents of rain and wind battered the Federal-style mansion, but Elizabeth Alston was too gracious to let that prevent her from engaging her guest in small talk.

Moments earlier Nicky had been able to get through to Boston on the hall phone, and managed to smile at Trippett's mother two rooms away while Jack screamed profanities at her for not calling sooner.

"I love your house," Nicky told Elizabeth Alston who was sitting at the head of the imposing table.

"My great-great-grandfather built it for his bride in 1807."

The housekeeper came in and placed two bowls on the table. She laid a hand on Nicky's shoulder and said, "Girl, this should make you sleep good tonight."

"Maybe it'll help the young lady, Nell," Mrs. Alston said. "But it'll take something a little stronger than Frogmore stew to put me out."

"Don't you be frettin' none about Trippett's houses, ma'am. Trip will be home in a right good little bit. They've been fussin' with them for two days now."

"I know Nell, but he sure has a lot riding on them. Every time I think of Hugo, I shudder."

Nicky, who hadn't had a chance to inquire about the storm up until now, asked Mrs. Alston, "Do they know where it's going to hit?"

"I'm going to let Nell tell you, dear. She's the expert tracker." Leaning toward Nicky with a twinkle in her eye, Elizabeth Alston whispered, "She's got charts and things the newspapers pass out."

Nell, a tall, nicely built middle-aged woman in shorts and a sleeveless top, leaned against the sideboard, put her hands in her apron pockets, and put on the same solemn air of authority as the weather experts on TV.

"Right now they're predicting landfall somewhere between Charleston and Wilmington. She's moving at a hundred and fifteen miles an hour with the target zone being pushed northward all the while. If she keeps up this speed, Myrtle Beach or Wilmington will take the hit. If she slows or veers left, I'm afraid we're going to get it."

"When do they think it'll strike land?"

"Three in the morning ... two, if it comes at us."

All through the meal, Nicky kept hoping Trippett would walk through the door as she listened to Elizabeth Alston's charming patter, obviously intended to mask her concern. Then she wished she'd gotten to know her sister-in-law better, hearing all the intimate stories of Mary Beth as a child at the beach.

"Do you have any children other than Trippett?" asked Nicky.

"Yes, my son, Charles. He's a surgeon in Atlanta."

"One of my brothers ... the one that's married to Mary Beth ... is a surgeon in Boston."

"And the other?"

"My other brother? Ah ... he's in the accounting field."

Nicky had allowed herself to feel like she belonged in this house with this extraordinary woman waiting for Trippett to come home, but having to lie about Jack jarred her back into reality.

After dessert and tea, Nicky felt herself slump into a semi-stupor.

Elizabeth Alston rose. "You're exhausted, dear." She put her arm around Nicky. "Go on up to sleep, precious. I'll wake you if anything happens. But, don't worry. This house has stood for almost two hundred years."

Lying in the four-poster bed with the cherubs peeking at her from the corners of the immense ceiling, the events of the day swirled in Nicky's head. Trippett's and his mother's kindness were in striking contrast to Jack's brutish rantings. This time he'd even managed to call her a slut.

She couldn't ignore the chasm of difference between her background and Trippett's. While his great-great-grandfather was engaging scores of craftsmen to build this house for his bride, hers was likely digging up potatoes on a rented hardscrabble farm in Ireland, wondering if he would ever have enough money to marry.

Just before turning off the light, Nicky's eyes traced the pattern of the Greek motif carved in the mahogany doors, and she tried to imagine what it must have been like to grow up in this house, and how it must have shaped Trippett's personality.

Curled up between the silky sheets and cocooned in the serenity of this great house, the erratic sounds of rain pounding on the roof and palms swishing angrily against the balcony mellowed into a blurred symphony that lulled her to sleep.

🐚 CHAPTER EIGHT

Nicky woke with the knock at the door and managed a sleepy response to Nell's greeting.

"Here are your things, Miss Nicky. I washed and dried them first thing this morning."

Nicky sat upright and hugged her knees. "Nell, what happened with the storm?"

"Thank the Lord, it passed us. But I'm afraid it's givin' poor North Carolina a fit. There's enough rain falling on that place for them to get flooding for the next two weeks." She tossed her head toward the sound of voices drifting up the staircase. "That must be Trip. He wasn't home all night. I've got to get along. He'll probably be aimin' to give me instructions."

Nicky sprang forward. "I hope he's okay!"

"Probably nothin' a little sleep won't fix."

The look in the housekeeper's eyes embarrassed Nicky. For sure, she was wondering what her relationship with Trippett was.

Nicky dressed, gave the sumptuous room a lingering glance and headed downstairs to check on her animals.

Elizabeth Alston, standing in the hall talking with two workmen, saw Nicky and excused herself. "There you are, precious. Did you sleep well?"

Nicky glanced at the waiting workmen over Mrs. Alston's shoulder, and felt awkward. "Yes, I did, thank you. I guess I better be going now."

"You don't have to be rushin' off, dear."

"I'm worried about everything on the island."

"All right then, but not without a proper Charleston breakfast."

Mrs. Alston gently handed Nicky over to Nell who served her shrimp and grits and buttermilk biscuits from the sideboard in the dining room.

Finished, Nicky gathered Salem and the boxes with the turtle and the bird from the kitchen and left her "thank you" with Nell since Trip and Mrs. Alston were nowhere to be found.

Outside in the courtyard, workmen were loading plywood and broken limbs into trucks. Nicky put the cat cage into the car and headed out into Charleston's puddled streets littered with branches and debris. The only sign of the storm outside the city were the ponds flanking the deserted highway, waiting for the evacuees' return.

Nicky reached the causeway and was surprised to see it in good shape, even though there was plenty of evidence of the storm scattered about the island. The air was uncustomarily free of humidity, the sun intense; roof shingles, signs loose from their moorings, and palm fronds were everywhere. Nicky was relieved to see the King's Nest standing undamaged. She waded through ankle-deep puddles to unload the animals and some of her portfolios before setting out to look for injured birds.

All the houses on the beach were boarded up, with no sign of life in either direction. Farther down on the creek side, Mac's boat was gone. Must still be in Beaufort or maybe he's taken it inland, she thought. Nicky had never ventured beyond Mac's place before, but decided to start her rescue mission there.

The sound of a truck rattling across the causeway caught her attention. She recognized the pickup that had almost run her over. Being alone on the island with someone she didn't know in the eerie silence made her feel uneasy, and she wished Winston was at her side as she hiked up the sandy path past Mac's house.

Coming from around a dune, she saw disjointed sections of what once must have been someone's home. An old photograph sticking up from the sand caught her eye. She picked it up and studied the image of a barefoot black woman sitting on a porch heading shrimp. Nicky ran a finger along a crease and imagined that the woman's ankle-length skirt and bandanna were colorful, maybe red and blue. She turned the photograph over and read: *Martha Washington '32.*

She tucked it under the cloth in the basket she'd brought along to put injured animals in, then reached down and lifted a small narrow cabinet lying on its face in the sand. The doors swung open and empty bottles and cans spilled out.

The sun reflected off glass near a heap of boards and drew Nicky's eye. She scanned the debris until she spotted what she thought was a corner of a frame. She gingerly stepped through the jumble, moved a board aside and pulled it out.

The scar across the face of the tall lanky man in the ancient photograph made her shudder. Her breathing accelerated as she read: *Moses Washington, Freed Slave, Chertaw Island, 1869.* Nicky moved things off the pile, until she found an old wood crate to put it in.

The sun was scorching, but her latest find compelled her to keep picking through the debris. When tossing aside a cypress plank, something registered in her mind's eye. At first she ignored a bothersome urge to flip it over, but finally gave in.

She lifted the board and a calendar slipped from a nail and slid to the ground. Nicky picked it up and admired the reproduction of an old Audubon etching of a pelican. The year was 1945, but the ink hadn't faded. Probably because very little light came into the house. Rainwater dripped on her leg from the calendar and she dropped it on the sand.

She didn't find much worth saving except for some post cards and several old bottles and buoys, so she decided to get moving. She bent down and started to pick up the crate when she spotted the old calendar again. She didn't have the heart to leave a picture of a brown pelican to rot, plus she could study the etching's artfully executed lines. She picked it up and tossed it in. The crate was too cumbersome to lug around the beach, so she tucked it behind a cluster of oleanders and continued her search for injured birds.

After hunting to the very tip of the peninsula, all she found was a conch shell swept in by the high waves. She came from behind a dune to the place where she had discovered the fallen down shack and almost ran into a man poking around in the debris.

Startled, she took a step back and couldn't help studying the wiry figure. His plaid shirt was darkened with sweat and his high-top shoes and heavy jeans were out of place for the beach. He moved with the sort of nervous energy seen in a wild animal, and the scar cutting across his upper lip gave him a dangerous appearance even before the predatory grin surfaced.

"Didn't mean to stir your innards, ma'am."

Nicky hugged her basket as he came toward her.

"What ya got in there?"

Nicky braced herself.

"I ain't gonna mess with ya," he said as he reached for the basket. He lifted the cloth and took out the photo of the woman. He held it between two fingers and kept flicking it with his thumb.

Nicky backed away. His eyes roamed her person. Nicky held her breath, put her foot back and dug her toes in the sand.

"I see you been scratchin' around in here yourself. Is this here all you got?"

71

Nicky, convinced that the things she had put in the crate were none of his business, nodded.

Then suddenly, as if he had figured he was wasting his time, he dropped the photograph back in the basket saying, "Didn't mean to hold you up none, ma'am."

The hair on the back of Nicky's neck tingled as she watched him turn and head back down the road. When he was well out of sight, she retrieved the crate she'd hidden behind the bush and hurried back to the beach house. She'd had enough excitement for one day and would save the other half of the island for the morning.

She nursed and fed her injured animals and methodically entered the date and treatments onto a chart. With that done, she reached into the crate and lifted out the wet calendar. She extended her arm to keep it from dripping all over her, glanced around the porch until she found a nail protruding from a beam and hung it up.

The rest of the items she carefully laid on a blanket of paper towels. Nicky studied the picture of the former slave. The deeply creased face told a story of hardship, yet his expression was that of a man of kind spirit. The meanness he must have experienced unsettled her and reminded her of the look in the eyes of the stranger on the beach. She got up and latched the porch door, then locked the one in the kitchen.

🐚 CHAPTER NINE

Nicky sat at her drawing board sipping coffee, every once in a while looking up at the rising sun's reflection dancing on the gently rippling ocean. The sound of a vehicle barreling down the road told her Trip was on his way to work.

The cat stood and stretched as the distant clinking of Winston's tags grew louder. The big Lab nosed the door open and exploded into the room. Nicky vigorously massaged him with one hand, and grabbed the small table holding supplies with the other to keep his wagging tail from tipping it over.

"You've adopted the two of us, haven't you, old boy?" Nicky said as she scratched behind the dog's ears.

Satisfied with his greeting, Winston went over and plopped down next to Salem. The cat, only able to get around the beach house by feeling his way with his whiskers, purred at the return of its companion.

After two more hours of textbook work, Nicky got out the card she was drawing to thank Elizabeth Alston for her hospitality. A droll looking pelican in sandals, wearing a baseball cap turned backward, graced the cover, with Winston sneaking behind a dune in the background. Inside, the mischievous pelican tattled on Winston's unauthorized activities, and a series of finely drawn pen and ink sketches depicted his daily rounds. The tale ended happily with Winston rescuing the bird from a hurricane.

Nicky picked up a brush and finished putting a bright purple tint on the cap. She turned the card over and painted the two small sandals in a heap at the bottom the same color. Penned was © *by Trying to Make It at the Beach Productions.* Tomorrow she'd mail it to Mrs. Alston.

Nicky, wanting to stretch her legs a little before going over to Dede's house to work on her mural, decided to take a walk. The beach was deserted except for two small boys fishing with their father. Nicky strolled with Winston past Mac's place almost to the far end of the peninsula where she sat down next to a dune to rest.

A low guttural growl from Winston made Nicky look over her shoulder. The man with the scarred lip stood above her.

The man slid down the dune—something that no one who lived on the island would do—convincing Nicky he was a complete stranger to the area. From the corner of her eye Nicky watched Winston rise up in a hunched posture and bare his teeth.

The man slowly raised his hands and cautiously stepped backward. "I ain't hankerin' for no trouble now, ma'am."

Nicky gave him a halfhearted smile, then once he'd turned his back and started down the beach, reached in her bag and gave Winston a treat. She waited until the man disappeared behind the dunes, then went to Dede's to finish the mural.

A couple of hours later, Nicky stepped back and gave a final critical look at the scene of a blue heron overlooking a marsh that she'd just finished painting on the wall, when Dede sang out, "Honey, it's a masterpiece!"

"I wouldn't exactly call it that," Nicky said shaking her head and gathering up her supplies.

"Wash up and I'll give you some iced tea."

Finished in the bathroom, Nicky followed Dede's call to her bedroom where she found her rummaging through the closet.

"Here it is!"

The floor-length silk dress was beautiful—dark blue with large creamy white magnolias.

"Try it on!"

"But, why?"

Dede helped Nicky with her tee shirt saying, "You'll need something nice for my party next week."

Nicky slipped on the dress and admired herself in the mirror while Dede kept up the patter. "Don't wear any underpanties with that dress. The elastic will show right through that fine material."

Dede responded to Nicky's incredulous look with a flick of the wrist. "I never wear underpanties. Breaks up the line of the skirt." She stood back and gave Nicky a long look. "Honey, this here party has got to be perfect. Everyone ... I mean everyone's goin' to be there ... my broker, the company president, my syndicate people."

"Is Trippett going to come?"

"Oh, Yes!"

With their age difference, Nicky was sure Dede couldn't have romantic aspirations toward Trip. Her curiosity was satisfied as Dede pawed through her jewelry case.

"Trip doesn't just go anywhere ... but he's comin' to Miss Dede's. His ex-fiancée, Kim Dusenbury is coming with her future husband, too."

"Won't that be a little ..."

"Heavens no, darling. That's been over with for months. Besides, being in the same type of business, they're going to bump into each other all the time anyway." She looked up and smiled. "They might as well get used to it."

Nicky tried to sound casual. "Why did Trip and his fiancée break up?"

"Trip's been avoiding marriage for years. They were a perfect couple though. Both gorgeous ... from old Charleston families and all. But ..." Dede pulled out a long string of beads. "This is what I've been looking for!"

She placed the string around Nicky's neck and exclaimed, "Perfect! You're going to look wonderful."

Nicky looked shyly into Dede's eyes. "I don't know if I'll be right for this party."

"Don't be fussin' now. I'm sure you'll do just fine serving the hors d'oeuvres. And we'll probably need you to help out old Jeb with the drinks, too. Collecting the glasses and that kind of thing."

Nicky slowly took off the necklace, then got out of the dress while Dede got carried away with her party plans. "Getting old Jeb to bartend for me was a real coup. He only does the high-class parties in Charleston. When Jeb Sinclair stands behind your bar in his tux ... that distinguished black face of his and that head of white hair ... girl, you've arrived."

Dede took a white sarong dress out of her closet and spread it across her front. "Not bad for twenty-four-hundred dollars, aye?"

"It'll look great on you, Dede."

"You sound a little down, gal. Don't be frettin', I intend to pay you for helping me out next Saturday." Dede hurriedly draped the blue dress over Nicky's arm and led her toward the door. "Get here by seven so you can help me put the flowers around. The caterers will have everything set up. I just need you to look pretty and help out here and there."

CHAPTER TEN

The face in the mirror had changed. The cheeks were fuller and outrageously dotted with the freckles she hadn't seen in years. The brown hair, now streaked with gold, curled gently around the heart-shaped face and tumbled playfully onto her shoulders.

She slowly turned her head to allow the shadows to roam across her face, searching unsuccessfully for the darkness that had circled her eyes for years. Nicky held her breath, for it was the first time in a long time that she saw an image of a pretty girl reflecting back at her from a mirror.

The ringing phone startled her. She quickly glanced at the clock. It had to be Dede making sure she was coming. She picked up the phone and an almost forgotten tone in Jack's voice jarred her.

"Jack. How are you?"

"I'd be a hell of a lot better if you hadn't ditched us. Here, the old lady wants to talk to you."

The tension in her mother's voice instantly put Nicky back in a time she thought was over.

"Honey, Jack wants me to tell you ..." Her mother paused for a moment, then blurted out, "Nicky, he's sick again!"

Muffled sounds told Nicky they were scuffling for the phone.

"You got the picture, sissy?"

"Jack, are you taking your medicine?"

"Yeah. Are you taking your birth control pills?"

"How can you be so nasty?"

"Hey! I know why you got the hell out of here. You wanted some."

"Jack, you've got to calm down."

"Not until you get back where you belong."

"Put Mom on the phone."

Nicky saw her pained expression in the mirror as she waited for her mother to speak.

"Nicky, darling, don't worry. Everything's going to be all right."

Nicky strained to pick up on her mother's signals.

"Jack's been off his pills for a couple of weeks and it's going to take a few days for them to take effect again."

"Mom, do you think I should come home?"

"No! Mary Beth and Sean are taking care of everything. As long as he takes his pills we'll be just fine."

"Are you sure?"

"Yes, sweetheart."

Nicky's concern was deepening. "How's Dad?"

"The same. We go see him twice a week, but ..." Her voice became a whisper. "Jack's got to wait in the car."

Nicky rolled her eyes. "What happened?"

"Your brother ... you know how he gets. When the nurse came in with your father's medicine ..." Her voice became rushed. "Oh, Lord, it was horrible. Jack accused her of poisoning Dad. They got into an argument and he went berserk." Her voice kept trailing off as if she were struggling to hold onto the phone. "The orderlies dragged your poor brother down the hall ... the head nurse called Sean."

Another muffled struggle and Jack was back on the phone. "Never fear, Sister dear, the big deal surgeon is going to fix everything. One snap of his bloody fingers and I'm back in. That Gestapo isn't going to keep me out!"

Nicky's eyes froze on the clock. Dede wanted her there by seven. She recalled that Jack had sounded agitated the week before. Why hadn't she picked up on it? Only away for six weeks and the ability to recognize every nuance of his moods was already beginning to fade.

"Jack, please be good. I'll get back home as soon as possible, but you've got to promise me you'll take your pills."

"How long is it going to take to get your ass back up here?"

"Three days. Maybe four."

Nicky's promise calmed Jack, and she hung up.

The cat's soulful cry told her it was hungry, but she stood motionless with tears trickling down her warm cheeks as the animal rubbed against her leg. Her eyes drifted over to the drawing of the pelican on the calendar she'd picked out of the sand, then her dolphin drawings. She closed her eyes and felt her throat tightening as she recalled the cool rush of sea air against her face when the boat raced ahead with the playful family darting in and out of the water.

The phone rang again. She eyed the clock. Seven-fifteen! This time it had to be Dede. She wiped her nose with the back of her hand and picked up the receiver. "Hello?"

"Nick, it's me, Sean. Mom just called. Listen to me, kid. You're to stay right where you are. You can't let Jack play you like a yo-yo. We've got him back on his medicine and everything's going to be fine."

"But he's expecting me to come home."

"Don't worry. I'll take care of that. Right now, the girls want to talk to you."

Giggling voices of small children sounded in the background.

"Hi, Aunt Nicky. It's Molly. I love the book you made for me. I keep it in my treasure box."

Nicky wiped the tears from her face and laughed and cried at the same time. "I'll make you another one, darling."

When the only distinguishable word coming from the two-year-old was *dolphin*, Nicky laughed with joy.

The phone call finished, she rushed into the bedroom and hurriedly fixed her face, then poured some food in Salem's dish, and slipped out the door. She ran toward the sound of the musicians warming up, feeling like a thief in the night. She forced herself to block out Jack's call, for she knew some irrevocable event had occurred. She'd been cut loose, maybe even locked out from a place that had imprisoned her for most of her life.

However, something—maybe her soul—warned her to find some happiness soon or it would disappear somewhere deep inside her and die.

Nicky slipped in through the porch past the musicians to the tables where a huge fish lay on a plate as if it were swimming. A woman, busy arranging fresh sprigs of rosemary around the platter, looked up.

"What kind of fish is that?" asked Nicky.

"Poached pink salmon, caught offshore this morning."

"How do you eat it?"

"Well, honey, you just flake some off with this here fork and put this mustard-dill sauce on it. Mark my words; this will be picked clean to the bone by the end of the night."

Nicky's eyes roamed over the tiers of platters laden with hors d'oeuvres. With arms folded behind her back, she meandered over to a table where a white-smocked man was setting up a table. Their eyes met and he smiled.

"What are you serving?"

"Clam cakes and roast beef."

She pointed to something that looked like a flaky cream pie.

"What's that?"

"Brie cheese. We coat it with brown sugar and wrap it in phyllo. The sugar caramelizes when it's baked and makes it sweet."

Nicky's attention shifted to the kitchen where Dede talked with the chef, her anxiety apparent in her animated gestures. She looked spectacular with her shapely leg provocatively sticking out from her beaded sarong skirt.

Noticing Nicky, Dede motioned for her to come over. "Land's sake, you look good, girl."

Nicky was amused. Dede was obviously preoccupied, yet went through the motions of the friendly greeting her Southern upbringing had taught her was indispensable.

"I've been waitin' on you, darling. Old Jeb Sinclair's been taken ill. You're going to have to tend bar." Dede tossed her head toward a table. "That young man over there is going to help."

"Dede, I've never mixed a drink in my life!"

Dede raised her ring-laden hand to her forehead, pinky outstretched. Her large eyes pleaded. "I don't know what else to do."

Nicky turned to the chef who hunched his shoulders and threw up his hands. Nicky grimaced resignedly and said, "Okay, Dede. We'll handle it."

Dede scurried into the kitchen like a sandpiper, shuffled through a drawer and returned with a drink recipe book. Nicky took it to the bar where the young man had already lined up the liquor bottles and was engaged in setting up the glasses.

"Do you know how to do any of this?" Nicky said under her breath.

"I've helped out before, but I'm no Jeb Sinclair." He smiled and poured her a large glass of sauterne. "Here, knock this down."

The room filled quickly with everything going smoothly, until someone told the young man that the chef needed help. Nicky was studying the pamphlet with determination, when she noticed Trippett Alston in a tux towering over her. She slapped the booklet on the table.

"You're a girl of many talents."

She responded dryly, "Wait until nine. That's when I do my stand-up comedy."

He chuckled.

"What can I get you?"

The creases at the corners of Trippett's eyes deepened as a slow, dazzling smile emerged. "Dewar's on ice."

Nicky's eyes skipped along the army of bottles searching for the label, when a woman sauntered up to the bar.

"Well, I declare. Trippett Alston, you're handsomer than ever."

Nicky was grateful for the respite and hell-bent on not letting Dede down, at least not in front of Trippett Alston. She quickly put ice into the glass and poured the Dewar's. When she handed it to Trippett, she was struck with how the cuff of his white shirt contrasted with his rugged, deeply tanned hand.

The way in which the woman leaned against Trippett made Nicky suspect that there was more warmth in the South than the sun and the smiles. Good Lord, what would Father O'Leary say if he saw her do that! There certainly was a sharp contrast between the stiff formality of the Northeast and the laid-back atmosphere of South Carolina! Trippett's complicity in the woman's playful sparring didn't escape Nicky, either.

"I understand your old flame's gonna' be here," the woman teased.

A man suddenly put his arm around the woman from behind. "Which one?" he asked.

She looked accusingly at Trippett. "You heartbreaker, you." She glanced over her shoulder. "And, Malcolm Cameron, you're not much better." The woman looked at Nicky. "Darling, please give me a vodka gimlet." Looking back at Trippett, she loaded her voice with a plaintive Southern accent, "I'm gonna need it."

Nicky nervously thumbed through the booklet, but when she felt Trippett standing next to her, stood erect and confidently slid a napkin toward the woman as he prepared the drink.

"Well, I declare. I'm honored, Trippett. Havin' li'l ole you wait on me like this."

"My pleasure, darlin'."

The woman scanned the guests and when she saw Dede talking with a cluster near the sliding glass door that led to the porch, tossed an enthusiastic wave. Everyone's attention turned to Dede, who turned to come toward them. Someone must have closed the door on the hem of her skirt, and she walked right out of it, leaving her stark naked from the waist down.

The woman covered her mouth with her hand to stifle a scream. Trip's lids lowered and he shook his head. The silence grew. Nicky only caught a fleeting glimpse of Dede through the crowd before a guest took off his jacket, wrapped it around her and led her, ashen and wobbly, out of the room. Slowly a soft murmur rose, and everything quickly became normal again with people chatting and laughing.

The woman clutched Trip's arm saying, "She'll be all right in a few moments. Heck, who in this room hasn't seen her like that before anyway?"

"Let's not be catty now, darling," sang out Malcolm.

After a few minutes of small talk, the woman drifted off with Malcolm. Trippett turned to Nicky with an amused smile.

Nicky apologized with, "I'd go in and help her, but I think I better stay here."

"Don't worry. She's got plenty of people in there with her." He swirled the ice around in his glass like he was searching for something to say so the conversation wouldn't end. "Have you ever made a drink before this party?"

Nicky shook her head.

"How do you manage to get yourself in these jams?"

"Stick around a little longer and I'm sure you'll find out."

Trippett grinned. He took a sip of his drink and waited for her to continue, but she was embarrassed for Dede and could think of nothing to say.

Finally he asked, "How are all your little patients doing?"

She looked up at him and smiled, relieved to be on familiar ground. "Everyone's all better." She almost added that she was caring for two new birds but gave it a second thought.

"Maybe you should take a look at my Winston. He hasn't been eating much these days."

He appeared amused with her wide-eyed guilty look.

"My mother showed me your card. I hope Winston's not bothering you. He can be a pest."

"No! Oh, no. He's good company. Especially when I go for walks."

Nicky wanted to add how he had helped her with the stranger on the beach that day, but decided she didn't know Trip well enough to get so personal.

"My mother was delighted with the card. In fact, she wants me to have it framed for her. She thinks you're extraordinarily talented."

Trippett took a swallow of his drink, and looked around. "How did you ever get roped into this? I thought you were supposed to be an artist."

"You should see how creative I get with some of these drinks."

He chuckled, then pointed to the wall mural with his glass. "Did you do that?"

"Uh-huh." She didn't know whether to be modest or proud.

His gaze roamed over her face. "I need a wall painting in one of my Charleston houses touched up, but can't find anyone who can do it before we have to start refinishing the floors. Would you be willing to take a stab at it?"

Anxious to be regarded as more than a servant, Nicky answered haughtily, "I've got deadlines to meet, but I might be able to fit it in," and was immediately embarrassed by her pompous tone.

Trippett threw his head back and laughed. "I promise it'll only take you away from your pressing engagements a couple of days."

Just then, he caught a glimpse of Dede laughing and hugging a guest. He tossed his head and said, "See. Didn't I tell you?"

Nicky stood on her tiptoes to see over the crowd. Then, feeling relieved, filled her wineglass again.

Trippett wiped his hands on a cloth. "Call me tomorrow and I'll set up a time to show you the painting." He leaned toward her with a devilish grin. "If you haven't had anything to eat ..." He raised a brow and eyed her glass. "... I'd go easy on that if I were you."

As Trippett walked away, he glanced over his shoulder at the small figure with the freckled face and deeply dimpled smile and couldn't figure out what had changed. He didn't remember her as being pretty.

Looking around the room, he spotted Kim's bronze, statuesque figure in a clingy white gown that covered her just enough to keep her from getting arrested. She was talking with Walter Satterfield's wife, and he recognized the pasted on smile she mustered for listening to lucrative clients' banal comments. The back of Kim's long neck and sleek bare back stirred him—until he caught sight of Walter Satterfield.

Malcolm slid up next to him, drink in hand. Noting Trip's glare at Satterfield, he said, "Did you find out what that no-count bastard's up to?"

Trip twisted his glass in his hand. "He's got it all sewed up."

"What do you mean? They're not building on Chertaw Island, are they?"

"I talked to Skeeter Nash, my friend on the county planning board. The island's in his district. He says it's pretty much a done deal. The board is going to recommend to the County Council that the south end of the island be rezoned for a Planned Unit Development."

"How in the hell can they build out there? They don't have the infrastructure."

"They're putting in their own sewer treatment plant, underground wiring. The works."

"Whoa! What kind of a project are they talking about?"

"He couldn't give me the details. The Deveroux Company knows Skeeter isn't going to play ball with them, so he's not on the inside track on this, but from what he hears from the other board members, they're putting up four mid-rises."

"Shoot! That's going to change the whole character of the island. Heck. They're even going to have to widen the damn causeway."

Up until now Trip had been able to disguise his anguish, but hearing himself talk about five stories of cement and steel on the peninsula made him shift his weight and turn toward the wall as he struggled to hide his emotions.

Malcolm put his hand on Trip's shoulder. "Can't you fight this?"

Trip swirled the ice around in his drink. "I'm afraid we were asleep at the wheel. We should have covered this in our zoning regulations when we incorporated as a town six years ago, but all anyone seemed to worry about back then was Winston prowling around the island." He clenched a fist. "Who would ever have thought that anyone would want to put up a damn condominium?"

He reflected for a moment. "I never dreamed the Washington boys would let that land go. The way that family has hung on to it for generations. Shit! Mo's got to be turning over in his grave." He shook his head. "Damn! I should have gotten to his funeral and talked with the boys."

"Don't beat yourself up over that. You were on a fishing trip for Pete's sake." Malcolm searched for something to say. "Can't you get the Planning Board and County Council to go up against this?"

"It's all politics. Deveroux controls so much property along this coast, they can dangle something in front of every one of those folks. Evidently they've leveraged all kinds of deals to get everyone solidly behind this project."

"When's the start-up?"

Trip took a drink. "Skeeter said there's a snag holding everything up. Mo didn't leave a will so Deveroux's going to have to wait until his estate clears probate before moving dirt. They're keeping everything under wraps as long as they can, so this won't turn into a tar baby. Near the end of the summer the planning board's going to hold a token public hearing then recommend it to the council."

Malcolm drifted toward the bar, and Trippett onto the porch. The scent of the blooms on the tea olive bushes that grew on the edge of the dunes lingered in the air. Golden-red reflections from the setting sun bounced off the gentle waves and the foamy surf quietly floated over the dry sand as the tide crept toward shore. God! How he loved this island!

Ever since his father died, he assumed the protectorship of this sacred place, and now he'd let everyone down—his dad, Mo, old Martha who would treat him to a pork chop sandwich every time he passed their shack when he was a kid. He gritted his teeth. All the folks that were dead and gone couldn't be hurt, but the beauty of this island was about to be stolen from those yet to come. Someday he was going to have children, and he regretted letting them down most of all. Why hadn't he been more vigilant?

Kim's long, lithe arm touched his as she gently gripped the railing. "Trippett Alston, I've been lookin' for you."

He turned and his eyes ate up her flawless features. "Congratulations," he said as he turned back toward the ocean.

She put her hand on his. "Trip, I wanted to tell you about the engagement myself, but every time I picked up the phone, I just broke down and cried."

"Consider yourself lucky. You're getting a great guy."

"I know that. It's just ... like somethin' died."

He was glad it had grown dark, for tears swam around in his eyes. Why was it that all the Alston men cried? He remembered when old Blue died, watching his father bawl unabashedly as he dug the dog's grave. Even though he never loved Kim enough to ask her to be his life's partner, he wanted to hold her in his arms and let the overwhelming sadness drain out of him.

"I imagine you've already heard about what they're planning to do to the island," she said.

"Yep."

They stared out at the advancing water, then Kim spoke. "That's the trouble with you, Trip. You don't like change. And, honey, it's only goin' to hurt you." Her tone turned bitter. "We had so much going for us. Especially you. It should be you developing these condominiums. At least, then you'd be able to control everything. Now, all you've got is a bunch of regrets."

"I've got regrets, Kim. But not because someone else is developing those monstrosities. I should have bought that property from Mo's boys myself."

"What are you talkin' about, Trip. You know you don't have the kind of money to just have it sittin' there?"

She was right. He could never tie up a million dollars in the peninsula.

"Trip, honey, you've got to be more forward lookin'." She put her arm around his waist and squeezed. "Bob's goin' to be huntin' for me." She started to go inside, then stopped and looked back. "You comin' to the wedding?"

"Sho 'nough, sweet pea. You gonna' save a dance for me?"

"Damn you, Trippett Alston! You're adorable!"

🐚 CHAPTER ELEVEN

Mac put the pail of mullets in the stern of the Boston Whaler, wiped his forehead with a bandanna, then wrapped it around his neck to sop up the sweat he knew the heat would draw out. His ragged khaki shorts and faded red tee shirt, that had pulled him through many a summer, contrasted with Nicky's crisp white shorts and navy top. They both got settled into the boat with Winston, who by now was a regular fixture on their trips to check the crab traps.

The tide was still coming in and the heavy alluvial smell of the muddy oyster beds on the banks of the channel permeated the air as the boat wove its way toward the bay. Fresh bright-green shoots of spartina were pushing their way up through the aging marsh grass that had turned varied shades of gray at the waterline. A mullet fish leapt free of the water, leaving delicate dimples on its blue sunlit surface.

Nicky adjusted her big straw hat, for even though it wasn't yet nine, the sun was already scorching. Exiting the creek onto open water, the boat sped up and skipped bumpily over the waves as it raced across the bay with Nicky holding onto her hat with one hand and Winston's collar with the other.

When the boat reached the winding creek that sliced through the endless sea of marsh grass on the other side of the bay, Mac cut the engine. With the boat bobbing in the water, he reached over and tapped Nicky on the shoulder. She turned and he handed her a cap like the one he was wearing.

"Put it on, girl. It's about time I made you my First Mate."

Nicky pulled off her straw hat and examined the gift. It looked like a baseball cap, except the visor was longer with a dark underside and a flap that shaded her neck.

Mac took it from her and adjusted it snug on her head. "There. Now you look like a genuine offshore fisherman." He started up his trolling engine and took off for the traps. In a voice loud enough to be heard over the hum of the engine, he said, "The New England swordfishermen designed this hat for when they went out harpooning off Nantucket."

Nicky smiled, for she knew Mac was about to tell her the history of the hat. He may not have gotten a college degree, but his inquiring mind had absorbed a lot of knowledge while kicking around the oceans and ports of the American hemispheres.

"They'd have a lookout who sat in the pulpit at the end of the bowsprit. You know. That long beam that projected out from the front of the boat. He'd have a harpoon with him. Those were the days before Polaroid glasses when they needed the long visor to block out the sun. See how it has a low crown and runs smooth around the head? That's so the wind out on the ocean rolls over it. The dark underside helps with the rays reflecting off the water. The whalers picked up on it and now they call them whale watcher's caps. Here in the South, we brought the old tech up to date by putting a flap on the back so the sun doesn't burn our necks. We call them flap hats."

The two friends easily slid into their routine, with Mac pulling up a trap and retrieving the crabs and Nicky refilling it with mullet while he got positioned to steer the boat to the next destination.

Nicky was delighted when Mac announced that he was going to catch a few spottail before heading back, since she had so much to tell him.

She followed his gaze and listened for the whistle of the line. Mac chomped on the stub of an unlit cigar and cast into an open area barely sprinkled with grass. "You watch. I'll have us one in a minute."

"Here she comes," Mac uttered between his teeth as he reeled in a beautiful silver fish. He put it in a cooler and said, "Gal, you ready for a beer?" Nicky shook her head.

He laid his cigar on the tackle box, then opened a can. "Sounded like someone on the island was having a little soirée last night."

"It was Dede. I went to it."

"What's a little gal like you doin' at one of Dede's big shindigs?"

Nicky bit her lip. "She needed me to help."

Mac studied her face for a moment, his eyes peering out from his sun-toughened face. "Did you have a good time?"

"I was pretty much in over my head tending bar ..." Her uneasiness faded and a slow grin spread itself across her face. "Trippett helped me out a bit, though."

Mac lifted an eyebrow and studied her for a moment. Then he pulled off his cap and ran his gnarly fingers through his flattened hair.

He slapped the cap on his knee and readjusted it over his thick wavy head of hair. After taking a moment to let his eyes roam across the lush marsh, he took a long drink, then leaned forward on his forearms and slowly rolled the can between his two huge hands. Winston jumped next to him from the bow, causing the boat to rock and the water to slap up against the sides in a relaxing monotonous rhythm.

Mac's stalling told Nicky that her news of the party made him uneasy. She gazed at him steadily, waiting to hear what he had to say.

Mac drained the last of the beer and gave the can to Winston. Reaching into the chest for another, he finally spoke. "You're not gettin' sweet on Trip, are you?"

Nicky felt her cheeks redden as she glanced haltingly at Mac and then away.

"You don't want to be settin' yourself up for a fall, gal. I'm warnin' ya. His crowd don't take too well to outsiders."

"My brother married a girl from Charleston."

Mac crossed a leg over his knee, reached for his cigar and lit up. Fingering the stub, he said, "It was easy enough for Mary Beth to *leave* that li'l ole social circle, but it's next to impossible for someone like you *to get in.*"

His comment reminded Nicky of how hard Dede had worked to impress her guests. Even she had been worried about fitting in. Nicky took a deep breath to bolster her confidence. "Elizabeth Alston was very nice to me when I stayed with them." She looked down at her sketchpad and spoke breezily as she made a few strokes on the figure of a fisherman casting his line. "She likes my drawings, too."

Mac rose and expertly cast a line back to the same spot where he had snagged the first spottail. His wanderings throughout the fisheries of the hemispheres had never allowed him to deeply connect with women the way men do in a marriage. For him, it had been mostly one-nighters. However, he did know enough about them to recognize when one had made up her mind.

Nicky looked up and tilted the brim of her hat so the sun wouldn't shine in her eyes. "Jack called last night and wanted me to come home, but my brother Sean told me to stay put." She looked out over the water. "It's so hard to understand. Jack was doing so well on his medication, then two weeks without it, and bam!—he's right back where he started. It makes me nervous. You just can't completely relax and say it's fixed."

She sat back and recalled the eternal draining tension of her days in Massachusetts. "Sean says he'll be all right in a couple of days, but it tears me apart to think what my mother must be going through." She looked up at Mac. "Jack can be so vicious and disruptive."

As was their custom on these long, tranquil trips, Mac would be silent until the young woman said all that was on her mind.

Nicky carefully closed her sketchpad, put the pencil behind her ear and leaned back, balancing herself by hugging a knee. "I got to talk with my two nieces." She slowly rocked back and forth. Lately, she had pictured herself with children of her own and it surprised her, for she had never had such presumptions before. No room for such dreams in Boston, just a head full of fears and desperate strategies. Her mind settled on Trippett's handsome face and his strong, tanned hand. She wasn't the least bit disconcerted by his constant appearance in her thoughts, because she knew that the spirit that had been awakened in her was on a mission.

"My little nieces liked the books I made for them." She laughed. "I sent one to my editor. It was about a dolphin family and a young girl that comes to the bay. The baby dolphin goes out to sea for the first time with his parents and they all get caught in a net. The baby's able to escape but tears his flipper. He makes his way back to the bay and the girl nurses him back to health."

Nicky stopped rocking and looked up at Mac. "My editor really liked it. She tried to get her boss to publish it, but he turned it down, so she sent it to a friend of hers who has a small publishing company right here in Columbia. I've got my fingers crossed."

Nicky looked up at him, squinting in the sunlight. "I've got another book idea, Mac. I've been thinking about it ever since I met Uta Foster and she told me about the loggerheads. You know who she is, don't you?"

"*Oh, yeah!*"

Nicky's eyes shot up and she stared at the back of his head, suspecting a story lay behind the remark.

Mac reeled in another spottail.

"Is it true that the peninsula is one of the loggerheads' major South Carolina nesting spots?" asked Nicky.

Mac put the fish in the cooler. "It's been like that as long as I can remember."

Her eyes swept over to him. "Uta's a nice looking woman. She'd be a good catch for you."

"Catch? It'd be more like a surrender!"

"Oh, Mac! You need a good woman. You're not getting any younger, you know."

He examined her drawing, hoping to change the subject.

"You're not going to be putting any of these here drawings of me in a book, are you?"

88

Nicky patted her sketchpad. "I don't know Mac. I might just have something like that in mind. Think of it." She reached out toward the sky and looked off into space with a wistful expression. "*The Fisherman and the Turtle Lady ... A Saga of Love on the Dunes.*"

He put a hand around her throat. "How about *Murder on the Marsh?*"

She laughed out loud at the look on his face. For once she was on the other side of a friendly joke. She turned up her nose and said with a cocky manner, "I think I'll take you up on that beer now."

Patricia Sullivan finished the rosary, kissed the beads and tucked them into her pocket. The cross sticking out of the small rip in the corner revealed it was time for a new apron, but she was too close-fisted to consider buying anything for herself, especially if she could possibly mend it. She glanced up at the black plastic cat with the tail wagging off the seconds that hung over the stove. The hands on its stomach read two-thirty. She always waited until off-peak hours to place long distance calls, but this one time she would break her rule and ring up Nicky so they could have a chat over afternoon tea, just like old times.

She put on the kettle and retrieved the frame with her daughter's picture that she kept on the living room mantle. She hugged the picture of the five year old and remembered how happy she'd been in those days. Two more beautiful children after all hope was lost. She had been sure it was all the novenas and rosaries; and since they had finally got their hands on a house in a safe neighborhood, she determined to do right by them and not work night and day to get ahead like she had with Sean.

Why hadn't she listened to her husband's urgings for her to relax about money and quit her job at the grocery store while their Sean was growing up? After all, her husband made union wages and had a pension to look forward to. But the fear of becoming destitute, drilled into her by parents who had witnessed abject poverty in Ireland, had driven her into a frenzy of work and saving.

She searched her brain for some intimate detail of Sean's teenage years, but all she could come up with was images of him running off to after-school jobs or slipping out the door early in the morning to deliver papers. She blinked back tears when she remembered that after he went off to college down south, they rarely saw him, and when they did, he always seemed to apologize for intruding. Thank God, at least her husband had always stayed close to his Seaney Boy, while she gave most of her attention to her pigeon pair, Nicky and Jack.

Sometimes she believed what happened to Jack was God's way of punishing her for indulging her two last born after demanding so much of the first.

She dunked the tea bag until the water in her cup turned a golden brown then hung it from a nail over the sink so she could use it again in the morning. Her gnarled fingers lovingly stroked the picture. If it weren't for her beloved Nicky taking on most of the burden of Jack, she never would have recovered from her nervous collapse. She looked up at the picture of the Sacred Heart and prayed that everything would be all right now that Sean had come home. "Please, God," she whispered, "let my darling little girl have a life." Then she picked up the phone and dialed.

The unexpected call from her mother delighted Nicky and reassured her that everything was fine at home. Then a call from the publisher in Columbia, asking to see more of her work, sent her into euphoria. She worked contentedly the rest of the afternoon on her textbook drawings. And since everything seemed to be going her way that day, decided that instead of phoning Trip about the painting she'd go by his house after dinner.

Impulsively, she went into the bedroom and searched through the closet for the linen sheath Mary Beth had given her as a gift before she left for Chertaw Island. Holding it up to herself, she appraised the image in the mirror. The bright blue brought out the color of her eyes and set off her new tan. She slowly nodded her head in approval. Yes, she'd take a shower, wash her hair and put this number on before she went over to see him.

The day's work carefully put away, she checked her schedule, and feeling comfortable that she would easily meet her monthly deadline with her publisher, got out her book of reptiles.

She thumbed through the pages until she found the turtles. Kemp's Ridley, Hawksbill, Leatherback ... there! Loggerhead! She quickly noted their genus as Caretta Caretta and the name Loretta Caretta instantly popped into her head.

Her imagination in full gear, she began reading. They're named for their large head ... adults weight two hundred to three hundred and fifty pounds and measure about three feet in length ... hatchlings are two inches long and are from light to dark brown ... adults, reddish brown with a medium yellow under-shell.

She kept glancing back at the biological drawing as she recreated the image on her sketchpad. *Loretta Caretta's mother came lumbering out of the sea, her heavy body dragging across the sand.* It took several tries to get the tracks to look the way she recalled. What had Uta said? Now

90

she remembered. They count the hatched eggs to make sure they're all there. If not, they search in the sand for the ones that are missing. A look of discovery flashed in Nicky's eyes. Loretta Caretta would be missing and the two little girls, who would find the egg the next morning while digging in the sand, would be named after her two nieces!

She was so engrossed in her drawing, the phone startled her. The man introduced himself as Malcolm Cameron, Trip Alston's partner.

"Trip wants me to show you the wall painting on our King Street project. Do you think you can get here tomorrow?"

Finished with the call, Nicky picked up the pad she had scribbled the directions on and tapped it against the palm of her hand as disappointment descended on her like a wet blanket.

Walter Satterfield folded the *Wall Street Journal* and stared off into space as he thought about the article he'd just read—one of the country's major executives indicted for grand larceny. He laughed bitterly to himself. What would they say to murder? He couldn't believe it was he, Walter Satterfield, having these thoughts. All his life he'd grasped at every opportunity; and one could say he even created quite a few opportunities to grasp at. But he'd never done a thing he could be arrested for. Why on earth had he stepped over the line!

Walter was reflecting on his life a lot these days. Not only was the securing of the ten acres at the end of the Chertaw Island peninsula going to lock him solidly into a financial bracket he'd strived to be in his whole life, but, because of the way he'd secured it, locked him just as solidly into the criminal class. He felt none of the jubilation one would expect from reaching a lifetime goal, because he hadn't actually wanted the goal as much as he wanted to know that it was he who had achieved it.

Unfortunately, the prize he cheated to win could never be truly enjoyed. But worse than not being able to savor a victory, was that he now hated himself, for the prize was paid for with another man's life.

The annoying voice of his secretary shook Walter from his thoughts. "That man's calling again."

Walter's arm stiffened as he picked up the phone. "What do you want, Billy?" By now Walter registered no indignation or anger in his voice. The situation had gone way beyond that. Walter was now firmly in the teeth-gritting stage.

"That was quite a party over here on the island the other night. Saw you with all your high-toned friends."

Walter closed his eyes and drew a deep breath.

"Yep. You folks sure know how to have a good time. That wife of yours looked right beautiful, Walter. Heck, she's got to be at least ten years younger than you."

"Billy, you've got two seconds to tell me what you want."

"Dang it, Walter. Just when I think we're gettin' on real good, you go and spoil it. It's only because of all your frettin' about my goin' to Mexico that I'm callin' you in the first place. I figured you'd want to know 'bout my transmission."

Walter felt the blood drum in his head to the rhythm of his heartbeat. "How much?"

"There's a li'l ole shop on the highway ..."

"I said, how much."

"A thousand would get my front tie-rods fixed too. No tellin' when ..."

Walter interrupted him dryly. "Meet me at the usual place at midnight." Then he dropped the phone into its cradle.

Walter went over to the window and gazed past the shaded veranda to the flawless blue sky. He had stoically come to the realization that Billy was never going to disappear completely. Walter could live with that as long as he had plenty of money, but he couldn't tolerate the bastard crashing in on his life.

Why in hell had he taken Billy's phone number from his operations manager at the last company he had presided over? *If you ever want anything burned down, this is the guy to call.* That was five years ago. He had been surprised when Billy answered the phone. The meeting at Wendy's had been brief. All he had said was to get rid of Mo and bring back the will. It had seemed so neat and simple then. What had possessed him?

Walter took a deep breath and steeled himself. Somehow he was going to have to strike a bargain with Billy and then get him the hell out of town. But he had to be careful. He couldn't look too anxious. It was going to take all the cunning he'd acquired in a lifetime of deal making to get Billy Cleary under control.

The pickup coasted to the side of the gravel road. The marsh and ocean beyond stood out against the clear blue sky on one side, and an old plantation house nestled amidst a grove of live oaks on the other. Billy turned off the engine, leaned back and thought about his conversation with Walter Satterfield. He was more naive than Billy had imagined. How could Satterfield believe that he had any intention of ever stepping foot south of the border again?

Scheming being second nature to Billy, his thoughts solidly locked onto how he was going to get in on the new condo project. Billy had no education to speak of, but his mind was keen. And why shouldn't it be? All his life he'd relied on animal cunning to get what he wanted. And since he had never had a sense of guilt or feeling of compassion for any human or animal, he had naturally fallen into committing the kind of crimes that the ordinary felon had no taste for.

With the way the FBI was fanning out all over the South, Billy figured he had no choice but to try his hand at white-collar crime. But before he could give Walter his full attention, he had to get back to North Carolina and thumb his nose at the FBI one last time. When he called the woman he'd been living with, she told him someone was looking for him. He knew the guy. Wanted him to take care of an abortion clinic. They were in the same category as black churches as far as Billy was concerned, and he wasn't going to miss the pleasure of blowing one up.

Billy rolled down his window, rested an arm on the edge and took a long drag. His eyes slowly roamed the scenery and landed on the high rises peaking out from the horizon down the shore. Woo wee! he shouted as he slapped the steering wheel. I got them rich boys by the balls!

From the moment he arrived at the beach he had smelled money; and like always, being around those that had more than he did, made him feel inferior. Especially Walter, who never paid him the respect of looking him in the eye.

"Ha!" Billy threw his head back and laughed. Now *he* was in command. But he had to be careful. This was a chance of a lifetime and it was going to take all the cunning he had acquired in years of scheming to work this for all it was worth.

Malcolm Cameron sat down at his desk, now that he was finished checking with all the subs working on the house. The thick, humid air was stifling, but nowhere near as suffocating as it would be by noon. Malcolm's lanky birdlike physique was casually dressed in his usual tee shirt, shorts and sandals. The halo of brittle blond hair shook as he wiped the sweat from his forehead with his sleeve and chugged down the last of the soda.

Someone at the door caught his notice. His gaze quickly jumped from the bibbed shorts to the nicely shaped tanned legs. The girl was small but solidly built. She was wholesome-looking with a glowing, if somewhat freckled, complexion and wore not a trace of makeup. Her firmly placed feet and broad dimpled grin reflected a youthful bravado. He smiled.

"Something tells me you're Nicky."

"Yes. I made your drinks at the party the other night."

He glanced at his watch. "You sho 'nough believe in getting an early start."

"Do you want me to come back later?"

"No. This will do fine. Let me show you the painting."

Noises from workmen upstairs drifted down the staircase and mingled with the echoing of Malcolm's sandaled footsteps as the two walked down the cavernous hall to the front entry. An image of a man standing on a wharf with tall ships sailing in the bay in the background towered above them. At least eight feet in height, the painting appeared fragile, yet intact, except for a small section covered with crusty water stains at the top.

"If it were up to me, I'd just get rid of it. It was painted on canvas and glued onto the wall in the late eighteen nineties. We had some preservationists take a look at it. At first they wanted to peel it off, remove the glue, and restore it. But, in the end, they figured it would disintegrate if they touched it."

"Who's the man in the painting?"

"The husband of the daughter of the original owner. He was a Yankee from a Boston shipping family who came down here after the war. When his wife inherited the house, she had this stuck up there. Probably to remind anyone who walked through that door who her husband was." Malcolm laughed to himself thinking how that marriage must have gone over with all the ladies in her social circle.

Nicky examined the painting, while Malcolm talked.

"It's disintegrating, but Trip's insisting we get someone in here to make it presentable." Malcolm shrugged his shoulders. "He just can't find it in his heart to destroy anything old."

"Oh, Malcolm. I'm with Trip. This is wonderful. It would be a crime to tear it down."

"So you're going to give it a shot?"

Nicky's voice suddenly sounded less self-assured. "First of all, Malcolm, I don't like altering another artist's work. Secondly, this is really a beautiful painting and I don't know if I can do it justice. Can't you get someone else with more experience?"

"Oh shoot. Everyone says the same dang thing. We've got to get this place ready and we're plumb out of time. I don't know why we're fussin' over it. If we can't get you to fix it, I'm going to get the plasterer in here tomorrow and have him take it down."

"Don't! I'll fix it!"

A slight smile appeared on Malcolm's face.

Nicky ran her hand along a scratch. "This should be repaired too." She stepped back, put her hands on her hips and studied the painting. "Removing the water stains will be a little tricky." She thought for a moment. "... and the tones won't be easy either since it's so old." She turned to Malcolm. "Can you get some scaffolding up?"

"Sure. When are you coming back?"

"I'm going to start on it right now."

"Now?"

"Yes. I'll get my supplies from the car and see if I've got all the paints."

Malcolm covered his grin with a hand as she efficiently pulled out a list from her pocket and studied it. His ploy had worked.

"There are a couple of places nearby that should carry anything I don't have. I phoned them yesterday."

Just then, Sonny Barnes, the foreman, appeared. Malcolm introduced him and asked Nicky to tell him what she needed. The minute Nicky's Yankee brogue pierced the air, Sonny's back stiffened. Anxious to dodge any snide remarks about the North, Malcolm quickly excused himself and disappeared into his office. Fifteen minutes later, on his way out, he was relieved to see the two setting up a workstation with sawhorses and planks and apparently getting along.

Returning to his office for a blueprint later that morning, Malcolm ran into the foreman coming out of the building and asked how Nicky was doing.

"She got right to it," then added somewhat vexed, "Y'all don't have to fret none about that li'l ole gal being too shy to ask for anything."

Malcolm looked apprehensive.

"She had me fetchin' water. Then had me set up a fan." He shook his head. "At least when a Southern gal asks you for somethin' she puts a little sugar on it; but this one's *strictly* business."

"Do you know what she's doing about lunch?"

"Oh yeah! She said she didn't want to take the time to eat 'cause she had to finish today." The foreman tossed up his hands. "I can't figure out why those Yankees are always in such a dang hurry."

Malcolm was greeted by an odor of chemicals as he entered the building through the back door. A fan was humming atop the scaffolding and Nicky was bent over the workbench busily arranging her supplies. He quickly retrieved his blueprint and slipped out before she noticed him.

At the Fish House, Malcolm spotted Trip beyond the throng of noisy tourists. He was sitting at the bar digging into a plate of clams. Malcolm

95

made his way over and ordered a beer and a cup of she-crab soup.

As usual, their projects were casually discussed as they ate. Eventually, the condominium project on the island came up.

"The chairman of the county planning board told me I was free to take my case to the rest of the members, but didn't feel anyone's mind was going to be changed. Damn it, Malcolm. I can't get this thing out of my head."

"Can't your mother help you? Doesn't she know a lot of these people?"

"I'm going to talk to her tonight."

Malcolm ordered a piece of pecan pie, and with an amused look on his face, said, "That gal showed up at seven-thirty this morning to fix the painting."

"How's she doing?"

"She works fast. Heck, it only took her two minutes to get Sonny all riled up." Malcolm signaled for another beer. "I got a kick out of her. She was a little overwhelmed by the painting, but when I made noise about ripping it off, she stepped up to the plate. For such a little thing, she sure is steely."

"What was she doing when you left?"

"She hadn't started painting yet, but she's got the mess from the roof leak cleaned up. She's planning on finishing by the end of the day."

"Good. Now we can line up getting the floors refinished."

"How old do you think she is?"

"Who? Nicky?"

"Yeah."

"I don't know. Twenty-six, twenty-seven. Somewhere around there."

Malcolm leaned forward and studied Trip's face. "She's kind of cute. You ever go out with her?"

Trip dipped the clam at the end of his fork into butter and said, "Don't even go there. She's just a kid, and we've got *nothin'* in common."

"I thought you said your mother liked her?"

"That's right, Malcolm. My mother. And I'm not even going to get into this thing she's got for animals." He tossed his head. "You wouldn't believe the menagerie we had to cart out of there when the hurricane hit. And, as if she doesn't have enough, I've been told she troops all over the island with Winston. Hell, when I pull out in the morning, I can see him between buildings running on the beach towards her house."

Malcolm chugged down the last of his beer, grabbed his check and said, "You know what they say ... first the dog, and then the ..."

"Give me a break, Malcolm."

Malcolm reached into his pocket and tossed a tip on the counter. "I won't be getting back there today. If you get a chance, stop by and check things out before you go home. I don't think Sonny's going to get her out of that building 'til she's finished."

"You're not worried about her, are you?"

"That tough little Yankee? *Nah!* Sonny's the one we've got to look out for."

Trip pulled into the King Street parking lot at six and spotted the foreman's pickup with its tattered Confederate flag hanging limply from the antenna next to Nicky's Volvo. Concerned, he rushed in to find them chatting amiably while Nicky packed. After greeting everyone, Trip thanked the foreman for staying over and told him he'd finish helping Nicky get her supplies to her car and then lock up.

"I'll put this in your wagon, Miss Nicky," said Sonny, picking up a box. "And the next time you come down, I'll give you that grand tour."

The huge space became quiet except for the foreman's pickup starting up and rolling out on the crushed stone. Muffled street noises sounded from beyond the massive mahogany door.

Nicky finished putting away her oils. Trip strolled around with his arms folded, at first studying the painting, then her. A beam of late afternoon light swimming with dust particles poured in through a Palladium window, making the soft curls in her wet hair glisten. She turned her flushed face toward him and he was struck by the brilliance of her blue eyes.

"I'm ready."

She looked like a Tomboy in the bib overall shorts, and the paint stains on her arms and legs added to her disheveled appearance. Sweaty enough to have anything she rubbed against stick to her, Nicky wiped her face against the sleeve of her tee shirt.

Noticing Trip's eyes taking her in, Nicky self-consciously took hold of her shirt at the neck and flapped it in an effort to cool herself.

"The heat near the ceiling was a killer," she said.

Trip studied her for a moment, then said, "You want me to show you around now?"

Her face lit up. "Oh, yes!"

Trip's eyes narrowed. "Where *do you* get all that energy?"

"Darn. There I go again."

"You're doing just fine. Heck, you've got to be doin' something right if you won Sonny over."

"Oh, he's just happy he can get started on the floor." She gave him a conspiratorial wink. "At first I didn't know what he was talking about when he kept mentioning 'the war,' and when I asked him 'what war?' I thought he was going to explode." She chuckled. "But once I got the picture, I kept my mouth shut and everything went fine."

Trip let out a knowing laugh, then glanced over toward the painting. "It looks good. I'm really pleased."

"It was tricky, but I ran into some luck. Once I cleaned off the crust, it wasn't really in that bad shape. Mostly discolored. It took a while to get the technique down ... making it look aged and all." She looked up at him. "I hated to touch that painting. I only did it because Malcolm said he was going to take it down if I didn't."

Trip smiled inwardly. "Here's hoping it'll last a few more years."

Trip strolled over to the staircase with his arms still folded. Nicky marveled at how cool he looked. She smiled when she noticed he wasn't wearing socks with his loafers. The short-sleeved knit shirt showed off his tanned muscular arms and the casually draped linen slacks his lean waist.

She, on the other hand, was a mess. Nicky self-consciously glanced down at her rumpled shorts and winced when she spotted a glob of paint on the big toe peeping out from one of her sandals. She quickly pulled a tissue from her pocket, bent down and wiped it off as Trip spoke.

"Isn't this staircase a masterpiece?" he said, not expecting a response. "Some nights after work when everyone's gone and it's quiet I come down here and picture all the original craftsmen working on this place just as if I were there." He looked over at Nicky. "That li'l ole staircase is a real engineering feat. It has no support other than what you see."

Nicky came and stood at his side with her hands behind her back. Her eyes traced the wide mahogany structure as it gracefully wound its way to the floors above.

Trip started toward the circular room across from the staircase. "Come, I'll show you the rest. This was the downstairs parlor the family used. Guests were ushered upstairs to the grand drawing room that stretches across the front of the house. My mother told me my great-grandmother's diary mentions this house a lot. It was quite a place back then."

"What are you going to do with it once it's finished?"

"I'm leasing it to a law firm a couple of my friends started. They've got to be out of their temporary space in less than thirty days. That's why I was anxious about the painting."

He tapped her shoulder. "Come see what we did in the back."

Striding ahead of her, Trip's voice echoed throughout the empty rooms. "They built the kitchens outside away from the house for fear of fire." He stopped and waited for her to catch up. "We found this old door that matches the rest." He opened it. "And used it to hide the elevator we installed on the back of the house."

Nicky ran her hand across it appreciatively.

"You want a ride up?"

"No, thank you."

He looked puzzled.

A mischievous grin spread across her face. "I've been eyeing that staircase all day." She abruptly turned and ran back to the hall, bubbling with laughter.

Trip followed her to the foot of the massive staircase and enjoyed the lines of her youthful body bounding gracefully upward.

At the top of the stairs, Nicky found the front parlor large, dark and cool with shuttered windows on three sides. She walked around tracing all the architectural details with her fingers until she came to the fireplace with a Greek scene in bas-relief applied to the front of the mantel. She looked up at Trip who was coming into the room.

"How charming!"

"It took an artist a month working with a dental pick to remove nine layers of paint."

"Oh! It was worth it!"

Trip, who by now had unlatched one of the inside shutters, leisurely sat on the sill, his long legs crossed at the ankles and arms folded across his chest. He looked up at the ceiling. "A lot of the cornice details were missing, so we had to make them from a mold and reapply them."

Nicky leaned against the mahogany paneling next to the fireplace and slowly slid down to the heart pine floor, hugging her knees and listening to Trip. She studied his face—almost as if he were one of the cherished animals she liked to draw. The dark brown eyes that he was in the habit of turning into slits were hard to read. That, and the creases on his handsome face, gave him an intense look. He held his head confidently, but his eyes revealed a hint of skepticism, as if he knew enough to keep looking over his shoulder. The smile was easy, but not overly broad, giving the impression that he was holding back a little. Even though his brush-cut was dotted with gray, he seemed boyish to her.

"It must be quite a challenge restoring a place like this," said Nicky.

"Finding channels to install air and heat was like writing a murder mystery. We had to hide ductwork in between floors, behind staircases, in the walls. Malcolm's a genius at it."

"When I walked in this morning I felt like I was going back in time."

"That's the way I want it. Preserving priceless craftsmanship really does something for me. Sometimes we spend more time and effort on a detail than makes any sense, like that fireplace mantle for instance, but when it's all said and done, we're glad we did. There are some things you can't put a price tag on."

A horn from an irate motorist on King Street shattered the mood. Trip glanced around the room one final time, then slapped his legs and stood up. "We better be going."

As she drove back to the island, Nicky felt guilty about taking a day away from her projects. She'd already put aside her textbook work for over a week to finish her story about Loretta Caretta, then spent another two days finishing up the one about Winston and the pelican with purple sandals, an idea she'd gotten from the card she made for Elizabeth Alston.

At a stoplight, she glanced at herself in the rearview mirror. Drat! She had a blue paint smudge on her cheek! Funny. None of that seemed to have bothered Trip. She thought about the things he had said to her and then tried to remember the last time any man spoke to her about his deep feelings. Only her father as they sat evenings on the upstairs back porch with her injured animals, and Mac Moultrie.

She mused about Mac. The disaster to the world's fisheries had left an indelible mark on him. He was kind and cheerful, but nevertheless bore the scars of someone who had witnessed a horrific slaughter. That sort of resigned bitterness was missing in Trip, but it worried her that the only thing he seemed to be intense about was his work. She recalled the beautiful Kim Dusenbury and what the young man who was helping at the bar had said. "*How could anybody walk away from that?*"

🐚 CHAPTER TWELVE

Elizabeth Alston lingered at the door after she waved Trippett off. The familiar smells coming from the harbor on this hot, humid evening mingled with the fragrance from the ancient magnolia tree in the garden. Her son's concerns about his beloved island seemed like a natural continuation of the struggles she'd seen the men in her family face in their endless pursuit to preserve the intricately Southern way of life. Tomorrow she would call around and see if she could be of any help.

She closed the door and went upstairs, annoyed at how stiff she'd become. She decided to read a spell in the small comfortable parlor on the house's east side and enjoy the ocean breezes before retiring.

She never tired of the diaries and letters of her great-grandmother for whom she was named. Since her heart needed soothing, she decided to read a few pages written before the war when the family was in its prime.

Tonight she read of Edward Alston, her namesake's eldest son and this Elizabeth Alston's favorite ancestor. He graduated from Harvard in 1842 with high honors; and, after receiving his law degree from Columbia, was given a graduation present of a two-year Grand Tour of Europe.

In high spirits, he wrote his mother about being met in Le Havre by his uncle, and their picturesque trip down the Seine to Paris. Elizabeth smiled to herself as she read of his excitement in visiting the Louvre and his lamentations that he'd never be able to see all the art in the great museum, no matter how many trips he took.

She shuffled through the letters searching for her favorite—about one of Edward's thrilling evenings at the home of an acquaintance he'd made in England. The description of this dinner with Ralph Waldo Emerson and Charles Dickens as honored guests was still spellbinding, even though she had read the account hundreds of times before. He told that Dickens was generally quiet during the dinner and a good

101

listener, however when the discussions turned to America he came alive telling of his reception in Boston and New York. He seemed genuinely touched by the way the crowds lined the streets when he went out, and cheered him when he went to the theatre.

Elizabeth Alston's hand started to quiver, so she let it rest in her lap and sank back in her chair as her mind strolled through the generations of Alstons who had lived in South Carolina's lowcountry since establishing their first rice plantation in 1730. The Alstons had associated with the most respected members of society on the East Coast as well as abroad for over a hundred years before the Civil War. They'd been on cordial terms with Presidents, New York financiers, and the Newport society with whom they mingled during their summers in Rhode Island where they went to escape the unbearable Charleston heat.

Her gaze traced the details of the small room as she thought about her ancestors who had managed to hang on to their homes through two wars. Union soldiers had occupied this one after the Civil War, and the British their first house on the fringe of the Battery during the Revolutionary War.

As she put the letter down, another caught her attention—one that always disturbed her; but she couldn't resist picking it up. She began to read and was deeply saddened by her great-grandmother's bitterness and her contempt for the freedmen who had been slaves. "*There must be a change, such an administration cannot continue. An inferior race cannot have the supremacy over a superior, more intelligent and cultured people.*"

Elizabeth went on to the next, which had been sent by her great-grandmother's son who was struggling to restart one of their rice plantations after the war, and spoke of Union regulations set up for freed slaves. "*The negroes who remain are to receive for able bodied men $9 per month, women $7, children $3.50 and others in proportion to their capabilities ... A more abominable and infamous set of regulations were never concocted, and the desire seems most evidently to ruin the planter and place the Negro upon a near equality with the White man.*"

A letter the ancestral Elizabeth had written to one of her daughters described the plundering of their homes and plantations by unruly freedmen and Union soldiers. She went on to lament the crushing property taxes laid upon all land owners by the Union occupation forces that were driving the formerly wealthy of the Carolinas, who were already financially ruined and living in abject poverty, to sell off their cherished lands. Of this frustrating predicament she wrote "*... I do not feel this horrible chagrin because our slaves have been emancipated ... were that act alone the consequences of the War, I would have no complaints. Also, I do not feel thus because three of my most noble sons have been laid in* *the grave; these things I consider direct events from a Divine Providence ... but I feel so because a heartless, mercenary people, after a victory has been gained, try maliciously to crush the unfortunate victims who lie helpless under their power. Would Lee or Jackson have placed their foot upon a prostrate foe?"*

Elizabeth placed the letter back on the stack and leaned back in the chair. She stared at the cherubs on the ceiling medallion circling the chandelier, and oddly, the fresh face of Nicole Sullivan entered her mind. The child had said her family came to Massachusetts in the early 1900s—two hundred years after the Alstons had laid claim to their Low Country estates. How fortunate the young woman was, she thought. Her family had the enviable luxury of wiping the slate clean when they left Ireland.

Tommy Warren caught a glimpse of the solidly built, leather clad woman through billows of dust and exhaust as she whizzed by his BMW on her Harley. He smiled recalling that, even in their high school days, Mac had always gone for that type.

The familiar smells of saltwater breezes, bait buckets and fishnets drying in the sun hit Tommy as he climbed the sun-bleached steps onto Mac's deck. Ten steps and he was out of breath.

Just as he was about to knock, the door swung open. Mac stood barefoot in a pair of shorts, his shirt baring thick tufts of curly gray hair at the neck.

"Come on in and have a beer," Mac bellowed, as he strolled over to the refrigerator and got one out. Handing it to Tommy, his thin lips split his face in a broad line curled up at the ends. "To what do I owe this honor?"

Tommy surveyed the room. Everything was arranged in an orderly fashion, with the bed in the room beyond, which must have taken considerable use the night before, already neatly made. The only items resembling décor were a colorful string of buoys draped along the ocean side window, and a huge blue marlin mounted over the bedroom door. A few bills and an open checkbook lay on the table next to a pair of glasses—the cheap kind that people buy in the drugstore.

Tommy sat down, snapped back the tab on the can, and took a long pull. "I figure by now you've gotten wind of Deveroux's plans to put up condos on old Mo's ten acres."

Mac pulled out a chair, put a bare foot up on it, and leaned toward Tommy. He had a beer in one hand and a cigar in the other. He looked Tommy over. His old friend's face was puffier than usual. A roll of flab circled his waist tugging dangerously at the buttons of his shirt. Tommy still peered out from narrow almond-shaped eyes like when he was a kid, but they seemed more cunning today. They had always held the sort of intensity that one sees in hunters getting ready for a kill; and the way they were focusing on Mac today gave him an eerie feeling that this morning he was the prey. He rolled the cigar between two fingers and said, "I guess that makes me one rich son of a bitch."

They both laughed.

Tommy waved a finger at him. "But you ain't gonna be rich 'til you sell."

Mac's eyes locked on his old playmate. He hadn't left his plush air-conditioned office and hacked to the beach just for a casual chat.

"The Deveroux Company would sure as hell like to own everything south of the causeway," said Tommy. And before Mac could squeeze in a word, Tommy rubbed his chin and added, "There's something that's been gnawing at me for a long time, Mac."

Mac threw his head back to finish off his beer.

"I always thought it was strange the way li'l ole Lucinda Johnson disappeared right before graduation and then her body washed ashore two days later. Remember that?"

Mac stopped gulping and his gaze shot past the beer toward Tommy. He slowly lowered the can, walked over to the window and stared out at the ocean.

"You took off right after that, didn't you?"

Except for the roar of the surf, the room was quiet until Tommy spoke again. "The last time I saw her she was right excited about you taking her fishin'. Nobody ever asked me, so I never said nothin'."

Tommy stood up, scraping the chair noisily on the wood floor. His tone was somber. "I can get you a million and a half for your property. Think about it."

Mac didn't stir. He just listened to the screen door squeak open and slam shut, then the car engine start up and slowly fade. A horrible, hollow splash sounded in his brain like it had a million times before. His temples throbbed as he remembered crying out Lucinda's name and desperately searching for his flashlight. He swam and dove for hours but she was gone. Finally, at daybreak, he had poured what was left of the whisky he'd snuck from his father's cabinet into the ocean and threw the bottle out to sea. Nearly forty years ago, and it was as if it had happened last night.

The rising sun streaked the billowy clouds with a rich fuchsia that pulled Nicky's gaze so forcefully she could hardly take her eyes from them. On the beach since before sunup, she impatiently scanned the horizon for Uta.

Nicky didn't want to wander so far that she'd miss Trip on his morning run, but eventually found herself next to Mac's place on the south end of the island. For an instant, she was tempted to run up and rouse him out of bed and tell him about the book, but she remembered seeing the motorcycle on the road the night before. Thoughts of what he and his girlfriend might be doing at that very moment lingered in her mind. Whenever she saw him after he'd been with the woman, it would take a few minutes before she could look him in the eye.

Uta appeared on the distant path between the dunes with cue stick in hand. Nicky ran shouting toward her, but the rolling high tide and the choppy surf drowned out her calls. Out of breath from slogging through the deep sand at the edge of the dunes, Nicky stopped short at the side of the woman who was now on her knees examining a nest.

"I don't like the looks of this, young lady."

"What's wrong, Uta?" wheezed Nicky who was trying to catch her breath.

"This chicken wire's been disturbed."

Nicky slid down onto her knees. "How can you tell?"

"I can tell." Her words were crisp. "I'll be back in a minute. I'm going to get my records from the car."

Nicky sat back on her haunches and waited. The salty ocean breeze brushed past her face and through her hair. Now that the sun had risen high, the glowing pink clouds floated across a vivid blue sky. Nicky took a deep breath, exhilarated by the spectacular display that mirrored her feelings of hopefulness.

"I've got it!" yelled Uta as she emerged from behind the dunes waving her notebook.

With an air of authority, no doubt for the benefit of her audience, the woman took off the chicken wire dome covering the nest and began removing the sand. "Don't just sit there, girl! Help me."

"What are we going to do?"

"Count them, of course."

"You don't think any of them are missing, do you?"

Uta's accent thickened as her indignation rose.

"Why else vould I be doing this?"

The surf was whipping up and the tide at its highest—now only a dozen feet from the nest. Uta's short blond hair fluttered in the strong breeze as she carefully lifted off the egg layers and studiously placed them in the sand next to her in the exact position they lay in the nest.

Once all the eggs were removed and carefully counted, Uta checked her notes. "Just as I thought! Eight are missing!"

Nicky was worried, but after thinking it through, decided it couldn't be Winston. He came directly to her every morning and never left her sight all day.

"Why would anyone take them?"

"To eat, of course!"

Nicky's mouth fell open.

"They're quite a delicacy. People dig them up, take a small bite out of their leathery skin and suck out the insides." She shook her head. "It's a shame. Probably only one of these will produce a mature loggerhead." She made a face. "And then they go and do that!"

Nicky happened to look up at the north end of the beach and spied Winston racing toward her house. Just as she had thought. Trip had skipped his morning run. She got up and brushed off the sand. "Uta, please come and have some coffee after you finish your patrol. I've got something to tell you."

Later, over a cup of coffee, Uta was adamant. "We've got to stop whoever it is from raiding that nest or we could lose most of the hatchlings before the end of the incubation period!" Her face twisted into a questioning grimace. "Have you seen anyone suspicious walking the beach?"

"As a matter of fact, I have. I think he's staying in the shack down from Mac's place."

"In that lean-to that's been boarded up?"

"Uh-huh."

Uta stroked her chin. "I noticed a truck parked behind it. We'll watch him." Her diction was perfect, but a trace of her German accent still lingered. "We've got to protect those eggs. If the horrible rumors are true, this might be one of the last nests of loggerheads to hatch on the island."

Nicky's immediate concern made her stop refilling Uta's cup. "What are you talking about?"

Uta waved her hand in disgust. "It's so terrible I don't even want to think about it."

"What?"

"That Deveroux Company is planning on building condominiums on the south peninsula. They'll tear the whole place up with their nasty bulldozers before they even start building."

"Come now. There's got to be some coastal overseeing agency that doesn't allow them to destroy the dunes."

"Sure! But the nasty bastards will go ahead anyway." Uta was implacable. "They'll just chalk up the fine they'll get to the cost of construction!"

Nicky sat down and stared at Uta in amazement.

"And in future years, if any loggerheads do return to lay eggs, both the mothers and the babies will be totally confused by the lights in all the condos."

Uta wrung her hands, visibly distraught.

"Oh, Uta. Surely something can be done. Can't we petition the planning board?"

Uta threw a hand up, a disgusted smirk on her face. "Oh! Girl! How can you be so naïve? Those politicians are all bought and paid for! They'll just say the turtles should go somewhere else."

Uta reached across the table and squeezed Nicky's hand. Her voice was full of self-reproach. "Vat am I doing! I'm getting you all vorried. What was it you wanted to tell me?"

Nicky wouldn't have mentioned her triumph if her book wasn't about the very thing Uta was worrying about. "It's almost like déjà vu. I was going to tell you that a small firm in Columbia is publishing a book I illustrated about a loggerhead. It's for middle-school children. The turtle's born on a barrier island, goes out to sea, and runs into all kinds of difficulties including barely escaping from a trawler net. When she comes back years later to lay her eggs, she finds the dunes disturbed and a row of condominiums facing her. She's totally disoriented and gets lost trying to find the ocean again."

"Oh! That's so sad!"

Nicky put her hand on Uta's arm, "Everything turns out okay when the lady who patrols the island comes to her rescue."

"Oh! Much better!"

Nicky went to her desk, picked up one of her turtle sketches and handed it to Uta. She felt all tensed up as she folded her arms and paced the room. "I don't know why, Uta, but when I went to Columbia yesterday, something about the way the two women who own the publishing company responded to the plight of a helpless turtle made me think there are others out there who would feel the same."

"These condos will already be under construction by the time your book's in print," said Uta.

"Maybe not. It's a small independent firm and the two women were definitely decisive. They even had me sign a contract before I left. I believe they'll help our cause, if they can."

Nicky found herself getting excited as she sat down on the edge of her chair. "They were great, Uta. Somewhere in their late thirties, maybe early forties. Very professional; yet, they had that easy Southern friendliness that makes you feel like they've known you all your life. First, I showed them the finished drawings for my book about a dolphin family, then my illustrations for a story about Winston and a pelican with ridiculous purple sandals. Oh Uta, I could tell right away they liked them by the way they oohed and aahed."

Nicky, responding to the intensity in Uta's face, let herself get carried away in the moment. "But when I spread out the pages of *Loretta Caretta* there wasn't a peep out of them, and it really worried me." Nicky thought it would help the effect if she snatched the drawing from Uta's hand and mimed the moment. "One of the partners picked up an illustration, studied it for a moment, then turned to me with a serious expression on her face. I held my breath, waiting for the usual polite rejection. But then, *lo and behold*, she said they'd been looking for something exactly like it! A conservation cause dealing with the ocean! Something they could put out in paperback!" Nicky couldn't suppress a triumphant grin. "They especially liked it because of the loggerhead being South Carolina's State reptile.

"The other partner, a heavy-set girl with a beautiful doll-like face, said this is exactly the kind of thing the State's Education Department is interested in, and added that she was going to give them a call right away."

Uta jumped up and hugged Nicky. "I knew, the minute I saw you, we were going to be a team! We're getting a group together to fight this thing. I want you to come to the meeting at my house next Tuesday at seven. Maybe you can bring a design for our posters." Uta sat down and rested her chin on her fist. "We're hoping to get Trippett Alston involved. He's got to be just as upset about this as we are." She nudged Nicky. "God forbid someone puts up something like that on his island."

Uta stroked her chin as if she were carefully calculating something. Finally she said, "And vhy don't you bring that friend of yours? Mac. He's got a stake in this island, too."

Uta rushed down the beach toward the place where she entered through the dunes. She always used that opening because it was the closest to Mac's place. Every time she saw the Harley parked there she cursed under her breath, then she promised herself she'd start using the north entrance instead. But the next morning, just as sure as the sun would rise, when she crossed the causeway onto the island, she turned south.

She'd stooped to every trick she knew to start up a relationship with Mac. But the last time she took him a casserole, he opened the door, took it from her hands and turned his back as the screen door slammed in her face.

Ever since her husband died, she'd missed sex and she missed being Mrs. Somebody; but most of all she missed curling up in bed at night and holding on to someone until all the anguish of the day dissolved.

Growing old had been harder for her than for most people. She'd always been a beauty and had turned heads wherever she went for as long as she could remember. She noticed something was different in her mid-forties. Instead of clerks rushing up to greet her when she went into a store, she was being treated with the same indifference as everyone else. And now, in her mid-fifties, everyone looked through her or past her as if she were invisible.

Uta considered the situation carefully. A bachelor like Mac Moultrie probably wouldn't appear in these parts again in her lifetime. There was that girl on the motorcycle, but really, just how much longer could he carry on with a woman half his age! She raced along the beach, keeping her balance by digging her cue stick into the sand. She had no time to waste! She had to browse through her cookbooks for the perfect thing to serve Mac at next Tuesday's meeting.

After Uta left, Nicky started to feel guilty about being excited over the meeting mostly because Trippett was coming. She couldn't wait for Mac to see that she was actually doing something to help the creatures he cared so much for! Maybe a victory on the island would heal some of his hurt. She marched over to the table she was using as a desk, took the pencil from behind her ear and circled the following Tuesday.

The phone rang, and she found one of the publishing house owners on the line.

"I just wanted to get back to you. We're going ahead with *Loretta Caretta* and we'll overnight proofs to you next week. In fact, your drawings are being scanned and the type set as we speak."

"That's wonderful!"

"The Department of Education has all kinds of grant money chasing this kind of thing and told us to start our production cycle right away. They're getting back to us with an order by the end of next week. There's also a strong interest in the dolphin book."

"Do you think you can get it published right away?"

Nicky wanted to kick herself. Being pushy was exactly the kind of thing she was learning turned Southerners off, but she couldn't hold back. "I'm sorry. It's just that we have a real problem here at the beach. We're trying to stop someone from putting up condos on the turtle nesting grounds here on the island, and this book might help."

"Let me think on it. The book will run exactly thirty-two pages, and it's paperback. ... I'll ask our printer to see if he can turn it around in a month."

Nicky crossed her fingers.

"By the way, the State's got a weekly show on public TV, and I'm pretty sure we can get them to feature your book. We can nail down a date next week when we've got a better idea of our production schedule. Is that all right with you?"

"Of course!"

Nicky put the phone down and vigorously tousled Winston's head. The dog pranced and wagged his tail as if he knew something exciting was happening. Nicky seized the cat that had jumped up on the couch, and twirled around, almost tripping over Winston who was trying to get in on the action.

Winded, Nicky sank back down on a chair and brushed her cheek across Salem's fur. In her wildest dreams she'd never thought things could go so well. If only they could get the book published quickly.

Suddenly, Winston stopped nudging her to be petted and stood listening. A muffled roar of a motorcycle sounded in the distance. Nicky put the cat down and made a dash for the door. "Come on, boy," she commanded.

They ran along the wet hard-packed sand toward the south end of the island until Nicky, spotting Mac on his deck, started hollering and waving.

Breathless by the time she reached the top step, she slumped down on a bench as Mac continued diligently repairing a net.

"You're goin' to get yourself all hot and bothered runnin' like that."

"Oh, Mac! Wait 'til you hear!"

"What'd you go do? Find a crippled giant albatross or somethin'."

Nicky laughed. "Oh, Mac, they're going to publish my turtle book."

He stopped knotting and looked up at her. "The one you told me about in the boat last week?"

"Yes! Yes! Yes!"

Mac shook his head and chuckled. "You Yankees sure do get excited."

Nicky smiled to herself. It struck her odd that *Yankee* had somehow become a term of endearment for Mac.

"This morning I ran into Uta." Suddenly she wasn't at all sure of herself. This news could upset him. "Well," she said haltingly, "I don't know if you've heard, but she said some development company's planning on building condominiums right out here on the peninsula. Her group's going to try to stop it, because they're sure it'll ruin the loggerhead's nesting grounds."

Mac continued repairing the net as if he hadn't heard her, confirming Nicky's fears.

"Next Tuesday, they're meeting at her house, and I said I'd get you to come along."

Mac stopped and looked up. Nicky lost her breath when she saw the expression on his face.

"I wish you hadn't gone and done that, gal."

Nicky was confused. She had been sure Mac would be anxious to help.

Mac got up and carefully folded the net. "I won't be goin' out today. I've got some paperwork I got to tend to."

Nicky hung around for a while, but then snapped her fingers for Winston to follow and the two ran down the stairs and onto the beach. She glanced over her shoulder, but Mac had disappeared into his house. Midway down the beach, she picked up a piece of driftwood and threw it in the water for Winston to retrieve, while she tried to figure out what had just happened.

🐚 CHAPTER THIRTEEN

Trip put the phone down, unaware he had snapped the pencil in two. Malcolm rocked in a swivel chair across from him.

"Shoot, Trip. You're gettin' yourself all tensed up."

Trip tossed the pencil on the desk. "That was Jeff Roberts. He does most of the electrical work around the island and heads up a group that patrols the beaches for turtle nests. They're having a fit over these condos and want me to come to their next meeting."

"There you go, pal!"

"Hell, Malcolm. There's nothing these people can do in spite of all their good intentions." He laughed bitterly to himself as he wondered how a handful of naturalists who went around counting eggs could ever stop the Deveroux Company.

Trip rose and started to pace. "My buddy on the planning board said there're a couple members we might be able to put pressure on." He had also told Trip that if the board did end up recommending the zoning change, it would still take a two-thirds vote from the County Council for the rezoning to take effect.

"My mother's going to call the Turnbulls. They've had a place on the island for almost as long as we have, and one of their daughters is married to a member of the County Council that has the power to override any decision the planning board makes."

Trip handed Malcolm a sheet of paper. "Look over this list and see if you know anyone else on that council, or anyone who might know them."

Malcolm scrolled through the names, then stood up to leave. "I've got a friend on the State Education Committee. Maybe someone on the board or council is looking for a new school or something."

If the project were in the city of Charleston, they both were well connected, but Charleston County was another matter. At the doorway,

Malcolm looked back at Trip who was standing at the window. Malcolm finally knew what made his partner tick. Restoration wasn't just a business for him; this guy didn't like change.

When Nicky's maroon Volvo pulled out of the driveway ahead of him, Trip was reminded that Winston had hardly touched his dish all week. How many injured animals were holed up in that beach house of hers by now, he wondered. As he followed her car across the causeway he was annoyed with himself for hoping she was on her way to the meeting. And when she turned right onto Uta's road, he was even more vexed to find he was wishing he'd changed into one of the colorful tropical shirts he'd just bought.

He pulled to the side of the dusty road so he could watch Nicky get out of her car, and wondered, as he was doing more and more often, what had brought her to the island in the first place. Why had Mary Beth been so anxious for everyone to help this self-reliant creature? For a moment he thought she might be recovering from a failed romance, but when she bounced out of her car, he dismissed the idea entirely. In fact, the thought came to him, as unlikely as it seemed, that she was still a virgin.

She bent over and reached into the back seat. He couldn't take his eyes off the pleasing line of her shorts and the nicely sculpted thigh muscles that the strain of leaning forward revealed. His eyes traced past her calves, then down to the white sneakers with pink trim. He smiled at the matching pink anklets. Starting to get aroused, he quickly jumped out of the car and headed for the house.

Out of the corner of his vision, he saw Nicky approaching. He threw her a wave and wished her a good evening and enjoyed her bright response. He opened the door and faced her and allowed his gaze to roam across the pink-and-white-striped tee with a scooped neckline that held a discreet promise. When his eyes met hers, he noted how undaunted she looked. No phony show of shyness. Not a trace of manipulation. She welcomed his inspection.

Stirred by the straightforward invitation he had gleaned from her dazzling blue eyes, he followed her inside, close enough to pick up the perfumed scent of shampoo drifting up from her soft dark curls.

Jeff Roberts welcomed Trip, while Uta came charging out of her kitchen toward Nicky.

"There she is!"

Uta put an arm around Nicky, glanced over her shoulder and whispered impatiently, "Where is he?"

Nicky looked at her questioningly. "Who?"

Uta's eyes rolled toward the ceiling. "Mac, of course!"

Nicky took a deep breath. "Oh. Mac."

By now, the two stood aside in a small hall.

"He couldn't come tonight."

Uta raised an eyebrow and traced her lips with her tongue, obviously readjusting her thoughts. She shepherded Nicky to a chair. "We'll talk later."

Trip looked around at the faces in the room and listened intently to a detailed explanation of the planning board and county council rezoning regulations, followed by a lengthy profile of all the members. He was amazed at the volume of information the group had pulled together. More than he and Malcolm could, at any rate. The groundswell of compassion they obviously felt for the loggerhead touched him. He thought it a unique moment in the history of the island that this small band had so earnestly committed itself to protect the animal's ancient nesting places. For an instant he let himself believe they could make a difference.

Maybe he imagined it, but during the presentation, he continuously felt Nicky's eyes on him and had to overcome the constant urge to look at her. However, when Jeff Roberts asked Nicky to talk about her book, Trip grabbed the opportunity to study her small but nicely put together figure. He liked the way sunlight beaming in from the window cast a pleasantly reddish haze on her hair. When he landed on the dimpled grin he suddenly realized what had changed. A bouncy cheerfulness now permeated the once sad-faced girl he passed on the beach that first morning.

He found himself barely breathing as she presented her clear thoughts in an unembellished, yet appealingly feminine way. This, coming from someone so young, made Trip wonder what challenges she'd overcome that made her so coolly confident.

Nicky receded from his thoughts once the subject of Mac's five acres came up. Jeff speculated that the Deveroux Company was going to make Mac an offer, if they hadn't already. Someone even suggested that was why he didn't show up.

"Nonsense!" Uta admonished. She turned to Nicky. "Go on. Tell them why he's not here."

Nicky put all her experience lying about Jack to use, and invented a story to protect Mac. "He has to retire early since he's taking someone out in the morning." She brandished a beaming smile, but felt like a louse for lying; but she didn't want anyone to get the wrong idea about Mac, and prayed she didn't have the wrong idea about Mac, either.

By the time refreshments were served, plans had been formulated to aggressively woo all the legislators.

Standing at the buffet table chatting with some of the women, Nicky felt Trip's presence at her side.

The deep gravelly voice of one of the older women sounded from across the table. "We're all right excited about your li'l ole book! I'm going to call that publishing company and order up some myself to hand out."

Nicky smiled, then let her gaze roam the approving faces until they landed on Trip. "I'm getting proofs sometime this week. Do you want to come over and take a look at them?"

Trip choked.

Nicky dismissed his reaction and said, "I'll call you when they arrive."

A boisterous cluster encircled Nicky before Trip could respond. He stood there somewhat dazed, for it was now clear to him that he was in the crosshairs of the determined little girl from Massachusetts.

Trip decided to go for a run. It was late, but he found himself unable to concentrate on a spreadsheet for a new project he had in mind. He put Winston on his chain, since he didn't want to take the chance of his running up on Nicky's porch and getting her hopes up—not that she needed any encouragement.

The salty ocean breeze rushed by his face, and he started to relax. He ran along the beach, guided by the full moon that glistened on the edge of the surf. For as far back as he could remember, he had been one with the rhythm of the tides. They were as familiar to him as his own heartbeat. It was impossible to imagine himself living anywhere else.

He ran past Mac's place and noticed lights on. Mac was awake, contradicting Nicky's explanation for his not coming to the meeting. Trip increased his pace, pounding out visions of what might happen to the island if Mac sold out, until he finally reached the tip of the peninsula and had to turn back.

As his pace settled into an easy cadence, memories of island life overtook him. He and his brother must have run to the stars and back in their teens. The moonlight bouncing on the water in front of him reminded him of the night he made love to Mary Beth King the year they graduated.

It was the first time for the both of them. He'd thought about Mary Beth over the years, as their lives drifted into separate channels. Mary Beth worked summers in the city to help with college expenses; but she always joined the King clan who assembled at their beach house for the annual island oyster roast in late September when the oyster beds were open. He and Mary Beth would always talk, and even though the romance had dissipated, a bond that had been forged that night on the beach would always be there.

He'd seen very little of her in recent years. Maybe it was due to her spinster aunt inheriting the place. Once, when Mary Beth came for a weekend, they ran into each other on the beach. Now that he thought about it, her little girl had the same brilliant blue eyes as her aunt.

He felt an overwhelming guilt for lusting after Nicky. She was too serious for a casual affair. The invitation in those remarkable eyes was uncomplicated and innocent. No. He wasn't going to take her up on it. She was too trusting, too willing to take a chance on him. Let someone have her who would keep her. When she called him about her proofs, he'd be ever so gentle; however, let her know he wasn't the one.

Suddenly, he caught sight of a lone small object moving across the sand. He stopped and watched the tiny creature determinedly crawl toward the enormous ocean and walk straight in. When a wave tossed it back to shore, the creature struggled to right itself, then swam feverishly into the water in an effort to beat the next wave. Desperately trying to realize its destiny, it was washed ashore three more times before finally making its getaway into the deep darkness of the ocean. Trip shrugged off the feeling that the appearance of a turtle on this particular night was some sort of sign.

Malcolm walked in just as Trip was hanging up from yet another call with Jeff Roberts. They'd spoken off and on all day, but this afternoon, Jeff had no commitments to report.

Malcolm tossed some blueprints on the desk and sank into a chair. "You're spending a lot of time on this island deal," he said.

Trip handed him a newspaper. "Look at the article in today's *Post*."

Malcolm leaned back and read while Trip continued working. "Says here that Miss Nicky's got a book comin' out."

Trip didn't look up. "Yep."

Malcolm put the paper down. "You better watch out. That little gal has an eye out for you."

Trip continued writing. "What makes you say that?" Not getting a response, he looked up and stared at his partner. "You dog, you. You asked her out. Didn't you?"

Malcolm casually threw his hands in the air. "Hey. All's fair in love and war, buddy."

Trip tossed his pen on the desk and leaned back in his chair. "Well?"

"Well what?"

"What'd she say?"

Malcolm examined his nails. "Evidently she has you in her sights, old boy."

Trip looked Malcolm square in the eye.

"Yep. She says she can't go out with me since you're so interested in her."

Trip pulled his head back in indignation. "You're shittin' me! *She said that?*"

"*Uh-huh.*"

"Well, I'm going to have to straighten her out right quick."

"You sure you want to?"

"We've gone into this already, Malcolm. Let's get some work done."

Trip got his mail from the box at the end of the driveway, then tucked his SUV under the beach house. He'd already worked out what he was going to tell Nicky and planned to get it over with that night. How many people had she gone around and told he was interested in her? All his life he'd been trained in the South's polite code of never confronting, never offending, but this had to be nipped in the bud. That's it. Polite, but firm. Hell, wasn't she always direct? As a Yankee, she'd be able to take it.

He ran up the steps and unlocked the door, thinking it strange Winston hadn't made it back by now.

He dropped the mail on the hall table as he stepped out of his loafers. On the way to the porch he hit the start button on his CD player and unbuttoned his shirt. Winston wasn't there either, and he was starting to get irritated. The screen door slammed behind him as he walked out onto the boardwalk. He leaned against the railing and looked down the beach toward Nicky's house. When he spotted Winston racing home, he made up his mind that this was another thing that had to stop. Tomorrow he'd put him on his chain.

Trip's annoyance dissolved as he watched the big old Lab charge down the beach it had known since it was a pup. The dog's shiny black coat glistened as its rippling muscles worked in tandem with its well-constructed frame. Each time the front paws leapt forward, the strong hindquarters overreached them, dug into the sand and thrust the dog forward in a beautiful athletic rhythm.

Winston was a gift to his father the summer old Blue died, but when Trip came to live at the beach house year round, it was decided the pup would remain with him. That was twelve years and hundreds of beach runs ago.

The dog slowed down just enough to make the turn and gracefully vault up the steps. A plastic baggie bobbing from his collar caught Trip's eye and he untied it as the dog friskily greeted him. Inside was a small card with a turtle drawn in pen and ink on the cover.

Trip self-consciously glanced toward Nicky's place to see if she was watching, then he went into the house, tossed the card on the counter in the kitchen and made himself a small pitcher of Manhattans. He had a strong feeling he was going to need it.

He reached for a can of dog food, but noticing what he had left out that morning untouched, flipped the cupboard door closed. He poured himself a drink, went over to his father's old leather chair and enjoyed the cigar scent that wafted up as he sank in.

The combination of the smooth Manhattan and mellow sounds of Billie Holiday sent a relaxing wave through him as he petted the furry head resting on his leg. In the corner of his mind he could see the card sitting on the counter. That would be the first step out of the quagmire he found himself in. Ignore every effort she made to rope him in. Her plan was totally transparent. First, she'd seduce him, then guilt trip him into a marriage. Uh-uh. She had to be a simpleton to believe that plan would work. Maybe in one of Boston's close-knit Irish Catholic neighborhoods, where the parish priest would make a call on the family of a transgressing son, but not in the real world. No way. He was going to straighten her out tonight. And that included getting his dog back! How long was she going to hang around at the beach anyway? Labor Day was just a week away.

Winston pawed at Trip's leg to get petted again. Trip ran his hand over the short silky fur with visions of Nicky pouring back at him. The way she had held the whole evacuation up to retrieve her cat should have told him she was trouble. Who on earth would risk their life for a blind cat?

He looked into the dog's dark eyes. "You like her, don't you boy?" He got up, poured himself another drink and grudgingly retrieved the card, then sank back down in the chair and took a long sip before opening it.

"Okay, boy, she's got me. Let's see what she's cooked up."

The way the turtle's flippers were drawn digging into the sand made it look as if it were crawling across the oatmeal paper. Trip started to look inside but the intensity in the reptile's watery eyes mesmerized him, telling a story of dignity in need. He studied the fine pen lines with wonder. Not one line too many, or too few.

He turned to the inside of the card. *You are cordially invited to meet Loretta Caretta*, it read. *Just give me a call.* Her number sat on a line by itself. On the back was a miniature drawing of Winston sniffing the words: © *by Trying to Make It at the Beach Productions.*

He'd give her a call all right! After he had another drink!

When she didn't pick up the phone after three rings, he worried that she might be on her way over. Finally, she answered. By the sound of her voice, he knew she was smiling, and the slight scratchy noise told him she had a pencil behind her ear.

"Can you come over tonight?" spoke the sweet voice. "I've got my proofs."

Even though he knew she was on a mission, the beguiling innocence in her tone disarmed him just enough for the politeness that was ingrained into his very bones to take over. "No, I'm sorry I can't make it tonight."

"How about tomorrow?"

"I'd love to, but I've got plans." He pounded his forehead with the palm of his hand. Why did he go and say he'd love to?

"That's okay. Friday will work out much better. They've said I can keep the proofs since they came out perfectly. That's a good omen—it doesn't happen often."

"Friday's out."

"Can we make it Saturday at six, then?"

Trip couldn't find it in him to break her spirit. He pictured the compelling eyes that had spoken to him that night at Uta's. They told him that she had saved herself to give some man untold delights. Then the image of her bending over the back seat aroused him. Like being struck by a thunderbolt, in that one split second he realized that he wanted this woman more than any he'd ever known.

"Saturday at six?"

"Uh-huh. I'll make you dinner."

🐚 CHAPTER FOURTEEN

Nicky's hands were sweaty, just like when Jack got out of control. She was almost to Mac's place, trudging along the creek side so she could check to make sure the woman's bike wasn't there. Every time she passed an opening in the dunes, Winston ran toward the beach, then doubled back when he saw her go on.

Judging by Mac's reaction when she mentioned the meeting, Nicky decided she wasn't going to say anything about the book or the condominiums unless he brought it up first. And she hoped he wouldn't, for if he did, he'd read her mind and know she was worried about his selling out to Deveroux.

She'd only known him for two months, but for the first time in her life, felt the kind of connection that one can only have with a kindred spirit. Her love for nature's creatures had dominated her actions for as long as she could remember, and even though everyone accepted it, she knew they thought it strange. Mac was different. He was of the same breed—someone who felt he'd been put on this earth to protect the innocent creatures of the world.

She didn't think she could live unless their relationship was back to the comfortable way it had been. Looking down the path, she spotted a carefree grin on Mac's face as he came toward her, and the feeling of foreboding that had taken hold of her dissipated.

"How's life treating you, gal?"

"Oh, Mac! I'm so glad you're still here!"

"Was waitin' up for you."

She grabbed the pail of mullet out of his hand and followed him with Winston to the dock. The boat chugged along the creek toward the bay, and Nicky started to relax. What had she been worried about? Everything was fine.

"You planning to do some fishing today?" she asked. She fidgeted with her hair, saying "Trip's coming over tonight to see my drawings, and I'd like to make him some chowder."

"Chowder? What's wrong with you, gal? This isn't Boston! That there fella you got your eyes on is used to gracious Southern hospitality. You're gonna have to do a lot better than chowder to reel that big catch in."

"Well, I didn't say I was going to give him the chowder ungraciously."

Mac chomped on his cigar. "I'm going to have to think on this."

Once across the bay and into the marsh, they started pulling in the crab traps. Nicky waited with the mullet while Mac opened a trap. She enjoyed their practiced teamwork.

He stopped and looked up at her. "You can start off with some of my pickled oysters. I got a couple jars left."

Nicky's eyes opened wide.

"Don't look at me like that, gal. They're delicacies," he said, as he dumped the crabs into his bucket. "Stick in some toothpicks and offer them with a drink when he comes in."

Nicky efficiently restocked the trap and listened.

"Now if you'd gone and told me about this yesterday, we'd of gone out shrimpin' this morning and I'd of shown you my stuffed shrimp recipe."

He lifted the last trap out of the water. "There, we've got plenty for the crab cakes."

"Don't you think we should do a casserole?"

"Good lord, gal! That's the last thing you want to be doing. Around these parts, the first thing one of them widow ladies does when a bachelor appears is run over with a casserole. Heck, I can't count how many I've gotten." He started the trolling motor and moved the boat along the creek. "Yep. You know what they say when an unattached man drifts in, don't you?"

Nicky cocked her head.

Mac hunched forward and whispered knowingly, "*You don't want to be one phone call or one casserole too late.*"

Nicky slapped her thighs and laughed.

He maneuvered the boat into a deep channel and dropped the anchor.

Nicky queried cautiously, "Has Uta brought over a casserole?"

"Yep. And they were pretty darn good," Mac said, seemingly, too preoccupied with the menu to notice that Nicky was trying to engage him in a conversation about Uta. "I'm goin' to get you a couple of nice li'l ole flounder." He dug around in the mullet bucket and pulled out a mud minnow and waved it at Nicky. "They love these. Yep, gets 'em every time." He fastened the minnow onto the hook, saying, "Where would you be if I had a fishin' trip lined up this morning?"

He expertly cast into the deepest part of the channel. "Get your pencil and paper out and make a list." He slowly reeled the line in. "You'll need some dry white wine, onions, Swiss cheese." He took his eyes off the water for a moment and glanced over at her. "You got flour, butter, eggs ... that sort of thing?"

Nicky nodded.

His next cast sent a sweet whistle through the air. "Get some nice crackers and fixins' for a salad."

Mac reeled in a flat, oval-shaped fish. "Here's the first one! Open up the chest."

He laid the fish on the ice. "What do you think of that?" he asked as he pointed to the two eyes on one side of its head.

He moved his hand in a rolling motion. "They swim on their side like this, with those two eyes facing upward. They've got a mouthful of teeth too." He closed the lid of the cooler. "But as far as I'm concerned, this is the best tastin' fish in the ocean."

"Are you going to show me how to cook this feast?"

He gave her a big wink. "Don't you fret none. I believe a condemned man deserves a good meal."

Johnny Bumps read the neatly printed note, then ripped it off the door and went inside. Instead of going straight to repairing the leak under the sink, he laid down his pipe wrench and lumbered over to the huge dining room table Nicky was using for a desk. Nosing around other people's things was a habit he'd cultivated since he was a kid when his father would drag him along on handyman jobs or his mother to the rich people's houses she cleaned.

In fact, all his life he'd studied the wealthy from the sidelines. He'd been in their bedrooms, inspected the contents of their refrigerators and helped them get ready for their lavish parties. When he was young, there had been a yearning to be included in this world, but over the years he had come to accept the fact that he would never be a part of this pampered circle. But he did get a certain satisfaction out of the realization that a lot of these folks would be helpless if it weren't for the likes of him.

He found Nicky interesting. The letter from her publisher in Columbia caught his eye. The first printing would be two thousand. Was that very much, he wondered? From previous trips, he'd already gleaned that she received a check every month from a textbook company.

He carefully laid the paper down exactly as he had found it, then lifted the canvas cover of her drawing board. An eyebrow shot up at the sketch of Trippett Alston running on the beach with Winston. A slow grin spread across his broad sweaty face. Just as he thought—she wasn't as innocent as she put on. Evidently, she had more on her mind that just those animals she cared for.

His curiosity now piqued, he strolled into her bedroom. Usually neat, it looked almost ransacked. A dress lay across the bed, jewelry was strewn on the dresser, garments were haphazardly spilling out from open drawers. He ran his hand over a silky chemise and figured she had a reason for being even more ornery than usual when she called him that morning, pinning him to a promise to fix the leak before noon.

When the phone rang, he didn't think there was any harm in picking it up and saying hello.

"Is Nicky Sullivan there?"

"Nope."

"Who's this?"

"Johnny Bumps. Who's this?"

"Johnny! It's Mary Beth. How are you?"

"Jus' fine, Miss Mary. Here fixin' the pipe under the sink."

"Good, Johnny. Good. Has Jack shown up?"

"Jack?"

"Nicky's brother."

There had been no suitcase in the other room. No trace of someone visiting. "He's not here," Johnny said with certainty. "Not yet, anyways."

"Thanks, Johnny. I've got to run. Please do me a favor and don't mention this call to Nicky."

All the drain needed was some tightening of the clamps, and with that done, Johnny struggled to get his bulk back on his feet. He leaned against the sink taking a moment to catch his breath and eyed some wine and a bottle of Dewar's on the counter. Yessiree, the little girl had plans for tonight.

Nicky returned from the store to find Mac working in the kitchen.

"I've been waitin' on you, gal," he shouted over his shoulder. "You got the crackers?"

Nicky let the bags slide onto the counter and noticed a bowl of crabmeat Mac had already prepared, sitting in the sink.

"Make me two cups of cracker crumbs. Roll 'em up fine. We've got to get these crab cake fixins' together and let it set for a spell in the fridge." He motioned to a beer sitting on the counter. "Y'all don't mind my helpin' myself to that, do you?"

"I bought it just in case you ever honored me with a visit."

He raised the can in a toast. "Consider yourself honored."

Nicky laughed.

"I put a pail of mullet on the porch for your pelican," said Mac as he deftly prepared a sauce.

"He looks good, doesn't he?"

"Yep. You're a regular Florence Nightingale."

As he prepared the crab cakes, Mac studied the clock. "You say he's coming over at six?"

Nicky nodded.

"Okay, that gives us two and a half hours. Plenty of time." He took a long gulp of his beer. "We'll let that chill while we fix the fish."

Nicky folded her arms, leaned against a wall and watched Mac carefully clean the counter, then methodically arrange the ingredients for the flounder stuffing. On his bicep, the solitary tattoo of a heart with a banner fluttering across it with the word *Mother* made her think about how lonely he must have been, leaving his home and family at eighteen.

Mac waved a knife at her. "Don't just stand there starin' at me, gal. Chop up an onion."

Now standing at his elbow, Nicky asked, "Where'd you ever learn to cook like this?"

"When you're out on the high seas for ten days or more, you can get awfully bored if you don't have some kind of hobby. Some of the guys did whittling ... you know, figure carving. We all did macramé." He looked at her directly. "Knot tying." He brought a platter of flounder fillets from the refrigerator and artfully sliced them in strips. "In the days before TV we used to sit around for hours tying knots. There was no end to the macramé patterns. The *Ashley Book of Knots* was our *Bible*."

He nudged Nicky. "Put a spoonful of this crab concoction on these strips and roll them up like this while I make the sauce." He deftly inserted a toothpick to keep the roll from unraveling.

"When Trip arrives, pour this sauce over the fish and put it in the oven at four hundred degrees. After twenty-five minutes, sprinkle on this grated cheese and put it back in for ten more." He gave her a big wink. "Got that?"

Nicky grinned broadly and saluted. "Aye, aye, Captain. Twenty-five ... four hundred ... ten ... *got it!*"

Mac laughed and ruffled Nicky's hair. She brushed a strand from her face and he noticed her hands shake. His eyes shot up to the clock. "We've got a while before Trip gets here. Let's take a break."

The ocean breeze streamed through Nicky's hair as she sat on a step next to Mac. They both sipped beer and listened to the muffled roar of the ocean as they watched the waves break against the beachhead, then reluctantly pull away again.

"You're a really good cook, Mac."

"I never held a candle to this I-talian guy that crewed for me. He'd pick out conch from the catch and put them on ice 'til he got three or four. Then he'd chop up the meat real fine and put it in spaghetti sauce. You never tasted anything like it. Sometimes he'd gather up dozens of puffers ... sea squab. They've got no spinal system, just two wiggle muscles on either side about the size of my finger. He'd peel them off of at least fifty squabs and then broil them. An *el primo* delicacy."

Nicky hadn't mentioned the condominiums all day, but the thought of them had been there between them just the same. In spite of all the promises she had made herself, she now saw no choice but to face it head on.

"What upset you the other day, Mac?"

He rolled the can between his two enormous hands and gazed ahead at the ocean as if searching for words. Finally he spoke. "When I was a kid, if you told me I'd leave this place and join the Navy right after graduation, I wouldn't have believed you. Shrimping fever was in my blood."

Nicky was silent. Mac was working up to something and was going about it in such a way that she dreaded the conclusion.

"Back then, there were times when so many loggerheads came out of the ocean to lay their eggs you could see their fresh tracks all along the shore. In those days turtle eggs were a favorite food of some of the locals, especially since they made delicious cakes. When these crawls were sighted, word was passed that the chickens were laying and poachers would gather up eggs and sell them to restaurants that specialized in turtle egg cakes. Sometimes they'd even butcher a turtle for its meat."

Mac crushed the now empty can with one hand. "Even though I was just a kid and the words *conservation* and *environment* weren't used much back then, I knew we were interfering with the natural order of things. Disturbing something we had no business messin' with."

He stopped short and looked out on the water. Nicky said nothing for fear of saying the wrong thing.

Finally he cleared his throat and continued. "By the time I was a senior in high school, I had worked three summers shrimpin' and was pretty excited about the new boats being put on line. They were being equipped for long trips and day and night fishing, so we could follow the shrimp seasons along the whole East Coast and into the Gulf of Mexico. We'd be able to haul in as much shrimp in two hours as we could with a smaller boat workin' all day."

Mac looked at Nicky. "They were going to let me captain one of those boats right after graduation."

What he was saying didn't make sense to Nicky. Why would he go off and join the Navy if they were going to give him his own boat?

He slowly shook his head and looked blankly at the ocean, as if he had given up on trying to explain things.

Nicky urged him on with, "Keep going. We've got time."

He gave her a gentle nudge. "We better get a move on. You set up the table, then go make yourself pretty while I do the rice and crab cakes."

Mac, tell me what's wrong, Nicky screamed in her head as she rose to go into the house.

Mac had never intended to tell Nicky tonight why he left the island at eighteen. It just started to unfold by itself, but luckily he stopped before he'd gone too far. But he had to do it before too long. If things didn't go well with Tommy, he didn't want her to find out about his connection to the drowned girl by reading it in the papers.

But no matter what, he wasn't going to let Tommy get away with extortion. Every time he remembered Lucinda Johnson, and there were plenty of times alone on the ocean when he did, he'd think everything through, especially as he grew older and wiser, and come to the conclusion that everyone was better off if it was left in the past.

After her body washed ashore, the autopsy showed that she drowned, and since there was no sign of a violent death, everyone figured she'd been on someone's boat partying in the bay, like half the kids in the school were doing at the time, and just fell off. And that wasn't far from the truth. Why dredge up the sad story after all those years? But if it had to be dredged up to hold on to his land, he was ready to face it. He failed to rescue Lucinda, and there was nothing he could have done to save the fisheries of the oceans, but he sure as hell wasn't going to stand by and let someone destroy the loggerheads' ancient nesting grounds on his piece of the coast.

Mac fried the crab cakes while Nicky showered.

When she ran out onto the porch in her robe to feed the two birds she was keeping, Mac yelled out, "We're goin' to have to let that pelican go in a couple of days. He looks just fine."

Nicky slipped into the blue dress that had been lying on the bed and quickly straightened the room. She only glanced at the deeply tanned freckled face in the mirror for a moment before deciding to forego makeup. She ran the comb through her hair and fluffed it up a bit. It would be dry by the time Trip arrived. She gave the room one quick glance as she slipped into a pair of sandals. Spotting a pair of sneakers on the floor, she quickly nudged them under the bed with her foot.

She stood silent in the kitchen until Mac looked up from his sweeping.

"Girl, I've never seen eyes like yours in my whole life." He leaned on the broom. "They're the same color as that dress."

Nicky blushed. "Mary Beth gave it to me."

They stood looking into each other's eyes for a moment, then Nicky's brow raised as she asked, "Mac, do you think Trip likes me?"

Mac shook his head. "He'd be a fool not to. Hell, if I was ten years younger, I'd come after you myself."

Nicky's stare was intense, as if she wanted to pour her heart out. Mac's was equally intense, as if he wanted her to know it wasn't necessary. He put his arm around the small figure and squeezed. "Don't you fret, sweet thing. Everything's going to be just fine."

Nicky looked at the clock. "He should be coming across the causeway any minute."

A knock on the door startled Nicky. Her eyes wide open, she looked up questioningly at Mac. "That can't be Trip. Winston's still here."

Mac followed Nicky as she rushed toward the door. Jack stood in the threshold like a scarecrow, his clothes crumpled, face flushed.

"Jack! What on earth are you doing here?"

"Thanks for the big welcome. Next to the asshole mechanic telling me I owed him fifty bucks for a new distributor cap, that's the nicest thing I've heard all day."

"Oh, I'm sorry, Jack. Does Mom know you're here?"

"Hell. She spends so much time fawning over Sean's two brats, she wouldn't notice if I dropped dead."

Nicky wrung her hands and turned to Mac. "This is my friend, Mac Moultrie." She nervously eyed the clock.

Mac, who had been massaging his jaw while sizing up the situation, didn't need any other inducement. He offered Jack his hand and coaxed, "Can I welcome you to the island, son, by taking you out for a boat ride?"

Nicky looked hopeful and grasped Jack's arm. "Wouldn't you like that, Jack?"

An indignant grimace appeared on Jack's face as he shook himself free. "What's going on here? Why the bum's rush?"

Nicky looked helplessly into Mac's eyes.

"The little lady's expecting company. That's all, Jack. You've got to be bushed from your long drive. Let me take you over to my place and get you a cold beer, then we'll go into town for somethin' to eat."

"Is this guy some kind of queer!" Jack shouted.

Mac took him by the arm. "Come on, son. Nothing's gonna happen to you. We've got to leave this lady be for tonight."

Mac winked at Nicky. "We'll play some darts at the Mole Hole and I'll have him home by midnight." Mac tapped her on the shoulder, saluted and hauled Jack off.

Nicky's head ached; she took a deep breath and started to calm down. She marveled at the way Mac handled Jack. Was it the sound of his voice or his muscular physique that made Jack submissive?

Just then the phone rang.

"Oh, Sean! He walked in five minutes ago!"

"Okay, Nick. Just give me the phone number of a local pharmacy, and I'll phone in a prescription. In a couple of days you should be able to put him on a plane and send him back."

The pages stuck to Nicky's sweaty hands as she feverishly thumbed through the phone book. "Here's the number! It's in the plaza on the way into Charleston."

The slamming of the screen door and thumping sound of Winston loping across the boardwalk made Nicky look up. Oh my God! Trip's back!

"Nicky, you sound upset. Do you want me to arrange for someone in Charleston to come get Jack?"

"He's my brother. I'll take care of him." She took a deep breath and slowly exhaled. "Just phone in the prescription."

Nicky put down the phone and walked resolutely into the bedroom, slowly ran the comb through her hair and gazed at the woman in the mirror. She forced Jack and the strange concern she felt over Mac out of her thoughts and locked onto a vision of Trippett Alston. The lifetime of frustration and yearnings that were balled up inside her were taking over.

CHAPTER FIFTEEN

Trip emptied his drink and slapped on shaving cream before studying his face in the mirror. His sideburns were almost white, but, hell, he didn't look forty. Damn! Why am I always thinking about my age? he asked himself. Instantly reflecting on Nicky, he winked devilishly at himself in the mirror. Evidently she didn't think him old.

Trip quickly put on a fresh shirt and a pair of khakis, then brushed his navy blazer before putting it on. Pleased at the way the white shirt and dark jacket set off his bronzed complexion, he hurriedly ran a brush through his hair. Winston's tail thumped against the door. "Well, old boy," he said as he adjusted the open collar, "I guess that Yankee gal's got me runnin' over there just like you."

Trip walked along the packed wet sand just beyond where the receding waves cautiously licked the shore. As usually happens this time of day when the sun starts to set, the sky above the horizon had turned a light pink, blending imperceptibly into the blue overhead.

Sea oats glowed a luminescent rose-gold and the blue shadows from the high dunes crawled across the now pinkish-looking sand. These familiar tones excited Trip, for this was his favorite time—when the day slowly becomes part of the past, and the promise of the night starts to creep in.

Desire grabbed him as he recalled the invitation in Nicky's eyes. He couldn't believe he was falling under the spell of this creature from the North. She was nothing like the sophisticated women he'd always been attracted to, looking for a good match or a comfortable social connection. Oh, no. This one had something else in mind. *Like a house full of kids!* Trip rolled his eyes. Good Lord, what am I walking into?

He reached the King's Nest and Nicky appeared from the kitchen, her eyes settling on the man standing in her doorway.

"I'm looking for *Trying to Make It at the Beach Productions*."

She laughed shyly; he wished her a good evening. She glowed at the friendly greeting.

Suddenly she blurted out, "I'll have your drink in a minute," spun around and retreated to the kitchen.

She fell back against the refrigerator and closed her eyes tight. I've got to calm down, she told herself. As long as I get Trip out of here before Jack shows up, everything's going to work out fine. She spilled the sauce on the flounder and shoved it into the oven, wiped her sweaty hands on a towel and started to take in the Dewar's on ice. Her hand shook enough to spill half the drink on the floor, so she poured in some more, put it on a tray and held on tight.

Trip stood examining some of the drawings pinned on the wall. When he turned and looked at her, she was struck dumb by his dark handsomeness and blushed.

He took the tray and placed it aside on a table, then put an arm around her shoulder and pulled her close to him whispering in her ear, "Take it easy. Everything's going to be just fine."

Nicky gently pulled away, took a deep breath and slowly let it out. She avoided looking him in the eye, saying, "I'll get the hors d'oeuvres."

She returned to see Trip cross the room, crouch down next to where Winston and Salem lay curled together in the corner. Winston spotted Trip's glance, cast his eyes down and licked his paw. Trip rubbed his head. "That's okay, boy."

Trip stood up, swirling the ice around in his drink. When Nicky offered the pickled oysters, he helped himself and winked approvingly.

"Where is she?" he queried as he strolled around the room.

"Who?"

Trip looked back at Nicky with an incredulous, yet amused expression on his face.

"*Loretta.*"

Nicky's hands flew up in the air. "Oh! Of course! Loretta!"

Nicky went to the table and opened a portfolio. A moment later she felt Trip standing next to her.

He grasped one of her trembling hands. "Why don't you go get yourself a drink?"

Nicky rubbed her palms on her dress, a habit she fell into when they got sweaty. "Yes, I think I'll do that."

Back in the kitchen, Nicky dropped against the refrigerator again and ran her fingers through her hair. I've got to get a grip! Why did Jack have to show up tonight of all nights! All he needs is one look at Trip

130

and he'll make a scene! She eyed the screen door and wanted to make a run for it. She had wanted Trip to like her, but now he was coming on so strong she didn't know if she could handle it. What had she been thinking? How could she, an inexperienced girl from a traditional Irish Catholic neighborhood, fit in with Trip's obviously more experienced and worldly life style. Then the picture of him, standing in her doorway with the confident look of someone who had come for something and was sure he was going to get it, gripped her with a surge of lust. Feelings of guilt washed over her. She closed her eyes tight and said to herself, "Holy Mother of God, pray for me." Hastily, she put ice in a glass, poured in some Dewar's and took a gulp. Mercifully, on her empty stomach, it started to take effect before she left the kitchen.

Trip was examining a proof when Nicky returned. She braved standing at his side as he studied the pages.

"The publishers will have the book out in a few weeks and I'm scheduled for a TV show then. I want Jeff Roberts to go on with me and talk about what's happening to the turtles here on the island."

Trip turned away from a page and looked down at her. "You're really into this, aren't you?"

"Yes, I am." She fingered her necklace. "I don't know why, but I've got a feeling that I've been brought to this island for some crazy reason. One of the first birds I saw when I got here was a pelican, and I felt that somehow we were going to be connected. But I guess it's the loggerhead that needs me."

Trip put the proofs down, folded his arms and leaned against the table. "So you're available for any li'l ole thing that's in trouble?"

She nodded matter-of-factly.

"Why don't you show me what you've got?"

She led him onto the porch, knelt down and opened a cage. Her small hand reached in and expertly folded around a tiny titmouse. She carefully pulled it out and lovingly ran a finger across its back. She held it up for Trip to see and noticed his squint-eyed appraising look. She rose, holding the bird close to her.

"Winston found it. When I couldn't get him to come out of that cluster of dwarf oaks in front of the beach house, I scooted down underneath there and found this little fella. There's nothing really wrong. It just hasn't learned to fly yet. If left, some feral cat would've gotten it for sure."

They were quiet for a moment, then Trip gently ran a finger down the bird's back. After it was returned to its cage, he said, "What's that in there?" and pointed to a large caged-in area in the corner.

"That's where I keep Peter Pelican."

He crossed the room, crouched down and peered in.

"I found him on the beach the other day. He had a big fishing lure stuck in his beak and hadn't eaten for days. A fish must have swallowed the lure, been cut loose and thrown overboard, only to have the pelican scoop him up."

Nicky crouched down a breath away from Trip and said, "I've drawn it. Do you want to see?"

He nodded with an almost imperceptible smile on his face, making Nicky wonder what he was thinking.

He followed her back into the living room where she retrieved a large sketchpad. She carefully turned the pages until she came to a pen-and-ink drawing. Trip's narrowed-eyed look roamed the page.

"How long have you been drawing these birds?"

"Practically all my life."

Nicky half-sat on the back of the couch, hugged the sketchpad and faced Trip. "I studied art at Boston College, but I'd been dragging my dad to this little shop around the corner from our house and begging him to buy me art supplies since I was a kid in elementary school."

The timer went off in the kitchen. Nicky jumped up. A few minutes later she came back with a steaming dish and set it on the table.

"Can I help?" he asked.

"Yes. Please pour the wine," she called back over her shoulder as she went to fetch the crab cakes and salad.

"You got any beach music?" he casually asked as he filled the glasses.

Her voice sang out from the kitchen. "Just the radio."

After a few moments she heard the music of the Four Tops singing *Can't Help Myself.* She returned with two platters.

Trip snapped his fingers, and gave her a quick wink. "There we go. Shaggin' music. *Perfect.*"

Once settled at the table, he raised his glass. "Here's to Loretta."

"To Loretta Caretta," Nicky toasted as she beamed at Trip. Nicky started to relax as she served Trip's plate with flounder. "What's shagging music?" she asked.

"It's a dance we do here in the Carolinas. It evolved in the fifties when they slowed the jitterbug down to a kind of rhythm-and-blues beat. Every September when the oyster season starts we rig up a dance floor for shaggin' and hold the island's annual roast. Heck, everyone comes down for it."

He sipped some wine. "Since we're fixin' to hold it next Saturday, I'd better teach you a few steps tonight." He winked. "And if you're any good at it, I'll take you over to the Red Barn in Charleston when Doug Clark and the Hot Nuts are in town."

132

"I don't know about that, Trip. I've never learned to dance."

He scooped up some flounder. "Heck, girl. Where you been all your life?"

She almost blurted out, *waiting for you!* Then it struck her how different they were. He obviously knew how to enjoy himself. How was she ever going to catch up?

Nicky's eyes wandered around the room looking for something to talk about. "After the hurricane, I found pieces of a shattered house at the far end of the island. I saved some pictures and things but I don't know who they belong to."

Lines of concentration deepened along his brows. "Can I see them?"

She got up, pulled out a bureau drawer and proudly brought back the frame with the cracked glass.

"Shoot! That's the picture of the first Moses Washington."

Trip leaned back in his chair and pored over the picture. "I haven't laid eyes on this since I was a kid."

Trip looked up at Nicky. "What else you got?"

"Not much." She handed him another photograph. "Just this."

"Dang! It's old Martha, Mo's wife."

"Who's Mo?"

"He lived his whole life on the peninsula. I don't know if his granddaughter, Cheryl, will be coming down again, but if she does, I'd like to give these to her. Would that be all right?"

"Of course. Does she come often?"

Trip put the photo down and dug into a crab cake. "Pretty much every summer to visit her granddaddy. But I don't know if she'll show up again since Mo's not around any more."

"What happened to him?"

"Drowned."

"Is that why the peninsula's being sold?"

He nodded.

She noticed his expression had turned pensive, and she wanted to steer the conversation away from the condominiums. Something she feared was getting to be a habit. "How do you like the flounder?"

Trip gave her an easy smile and said, "Where did you learn how to cook Lowcountry?"

"Mac Moultrie."

"I understand you two have become great friends."

Nicky grinned an acknowledgment.

Trip pushed some food around his plate with his fork. "He hasn't said anything to you about his five acres, has he?"

How could Trip say something like that? Nicky thought. Was Trip uncertain about him too?

"No. Why would he?" asked Nicky.

"You don't really think the Deveroux Company's going to stop at Mo's land, do you? After all, his property abuts to what they've already got their hands on."

"I can't imagine he'd ever do that."

"Then why didn't he come to the meeting at Uta's?"

"I already said he had to go to bed early."

"Then why were his lights on when I ran by his place late that night?"

Nicky put her fork down. He either knew she was lying or thought Mac lied to her. There had to be some reason she lied at all that night. Maybe it was because she wanted to protect Mac from any accusation about selling out; or maybe, somewhere in the back of her mind she, too, believed he might sell out, and the only thing that would erase these doubts was lying. Be that as it may, she wasn't going to lie any more. "I don't know why his lights were on, but I do know Mac. He would never sell his land if it were going to hurt any living thing."

"Not even for a million dollars?"

"I don't think so, Trip. Not Mac. You don't know him the way I do."

Nicky suppressed her anger at Trip for jumping to the wrong conclusion. But that was her fault. What else could he think when he saw Mac's lights on? She slowly picked up her fork and felt a wave of anxiety. Could this be what was bothering Mac? What was he trying to tell her out on the steps?

She glanced up at the clock and remembered his last remark: *I'll have him back by midnight.* Jack would insist on coming back much sooner than that.

She pushed all the spiraling fears from her mind the only way she knew how: by tucking them all away in neat little compartments. That was how she had been able to keep her sanity for all those years in Boston. This ability was now triggered by her strong belief that the man sitting across the table from her was searching for a life just as desperately as she was, and that was the only compartment she was going to open.

Trip reached across the table and put his hand over hers. "I've upset you, haven't I?" He squeezed her hand. "I'm sorry. I'm sure you're right about Mac. I need to get to know him better. He went off to sea when I was just a kid, and since he's come back, our paths never really cross other than to smile and say hello."

"Maybe you can go fishing together," she said.

They started back on their meal and quietly ate, every once in a while looking up, sometimes their eyes meeting. The volume on the radio was low enough to hear the waves gently break and softly splash on the beach.

Trip poured them both more wine and gave her a reassuring wink. She smiled and said, "It's your turn now."

"My turn?"

"Uh-huh. I've told you about my drawing. Now I want you to tell me how you got into the restoration business?"

He remarked offhandedly, "Just like you, it bit me when I was a kid." He peeked under the breadbasket napkin. "Where's the biscuits?"

"Biscuits?"

"*Oh, yeah!* With this meal, you serve warm biscuits right out of the oven."

"Oh, that's in 'Lesson Two.' *Next time* you get biscuits."

She watched him laugh. She liked the playful way he spoke to her with a slight squint. Her eyes slowly roamed the appealing face. The fine lines at the corner of his eyes showed signs of aging and foretold he would always be handsome with lean and leathery features.

When their eyes met, she quickly turned away and reached for a platter saying, "Trip, you're skirting my question."

He put his fork down and took a long sip of wine. "You don't give up, do you?"

She shook her head.

"I think it was a fixation I was born with. When I was just a youngster, I used to peer through the iron gates at some of the houses on the Battery that were starting to deteriorate. I'd study them and go over in my mind just how I would go about fixin' them up. Sometimes I wouldn't even be able to get to sleep at night, frettin' over how I could repair them."

He took another sip and looked at her as if he were asking permission to continue.

"Go on."

He tossed his head. "Summers, when I was in college, I worked for a restoration contractor. It was pretty exciting back then. Everyone had finally woken up to the fact that these wonderful old buildings were treasures. So when I finished at USC I hightailed it right back home from Columbia and bought one."

He started back on his meal.

"My father wasn't too keen on it at first. He was just getting over my older brother enrolling in medical school instead of studying law. But I reckon after seeing me come home to the beach every night covered in plaster dust, he couldn't have been all that surprised I wasn't going into law either."

"How about your mom?"

"What can I say? I bought that first building with a loan from the Elizabeth Alston Bank of Charleston. My mother's family had always been in commerce ... shipping, mercantile ... and I guess she felt perfectly at ease settin' me up."

"Trip, do you really think they'll put condos on the peninsula?"

"The only way we're going to stop them is if we put a heck of a lot of pressure on those council members."

"Maybe they'd listen if we mount some kind of huge outcry."

His expression changed. "Sweetheart, this is the South. We're more laid back than you Yankees. These politicians will only dig in their heels if they see somethin' like that comin' at them."

Trip's tone warned Nicky to stop from telling him he was dead wrong. During the long pause that followed, she tracked what he must have been thinking. No, this Southern gentleman wasn't going to engage in anything that smacked of being pushy. Polite pressure from the old boys' club was his only weapon. That would hardly work against a force like the Deveroux Company. Hadn't Trip noticed the miles of condos along the South's eastern shores? She recalled Dede's luxurious house and lavish party. There was big money in this condo business, and she had a hunch these people would play a lot dirtier than Trippett was capable of doing.

Nicky tried to sound encouraging. "Uta told me they were getting a big response from the article that appeared in the paper."

"Jeff Roberts said the same thing."

"She's going to take my books around to all the schools and work with their librarians to put on some kind of presentation." She smiled coyly. "You don't think it too bold educating children, do you?"

Trip looked up. "You one of them women libbers?"

"Uh-huh." She gave him a wink. "*We all are.*"

As he ate, Trip kept glancing at her with a shadow of a smile.

"It's funny, Trip," Nicky said as she buttered her bread. "We both want the same thing for the island, but for different reasons. I want to save the turtle's nesting grounds, and you just want everything to stay the same."

Nicky had no way of knowing how much Trippett Alston loved the huge lumbering animals he'd known all his life. To him they were intrinsic to the island and he had sadly watched their numbers wane on other parts of the coast.

She waited for him to respond, but when he didn't, said, "Trip, tell me, why haven't you ever gotten married?"

He looked her in the eye for a long moment then tossed the question aside with a laugh.

"*Well?*"

"Watch out, Missy, I could ask you the very same thing."

"Oh, no. That's not going to happen." She punctuated her words with her fork. "You are never going to ask, even if you're dying from curiosity." She leaned across the table and looked up at him. "Your Southern manners are never going to let you confront me with that."

"Don't you be countin' on it, young lady. I just might surprise you."

Nicky watched him fiddle with his fork and hoped he would open up to her.

Finally, Trip said, "About not getting married, I'm kind of a misfit that way."

Nicky put her elbow on the table, rested her chin on her fist and listened intently. "How so?"

"I guess I'm kinda mixed up. Socially, that is. I've got one foot in the past and one in the present. But to me it's all one thing."

Nicky wrinkled her brow questioningly.

"For generations we Alstons have engaged in gentlemanly endeavors ... mostly law ... and now look at me. Messin' with a bunch of old buildings. But to me, they are the South. When I rescue one, I feel like I'm saving something important."

He started back on his meal. "Seems like every girl I ever got serious about was hell-bent on reinventing me into some kind of executive." He glanced up and gave her a wink. "I guess I threw them over for the rundown old gals of Charleston."

"Was that what happened with Kim Dusenbury?"

"I guess in a way, yeah. She was always after me to put up condos."

Trip scooped up the last of the flounder and hesitated for a moment. "Did you want any of this?"

"No. I've had plenty. You go ahead."

Finished eating, he pushed his plate forward and rested his arms on the table. "I don't want you to get the wrong impression, Nicky. Kim was really nice. We had some great times together."

"How nice could she be if she didn't appreciate what you were doing on the Battery?"

Nicky wanted to bite her tongue. Trip threw his head back and laughed forgivingly at her show of jealousy. She sat staring down at her plate feeling the heat in her cheeks rise. He reached across the table and squeezed her hand.

Things weren't going as well as she had wanted. All her emotions seemed to be colliding. She had forced Mac and Jack out of her mind for most of the evening, but the misstep she just made caused snippets of the sort of hideous scene her brother could create flash in her brain.

She'd better get Trip out of there before anything else went wrong.

Maybe she should just tell Trip about Jack. Suddenly the huge chasm between Charleston's genteel lifestyle and the nightmare she'd been living in Boston loomed in her mind. She studied Trip's face—confident the way only someone who'd had everything go their way could look. Could he love Poor Nicky Sullivan, or just feel sorry for her? She swore to herself that he never would.

Trip kept her hand in his. The intense look in his eyes made Nicky gulp. She slowly pulled her hand away and told him she had to clear the dishes. He obligingly stood up, hung his jacket on the back of a chair and followed her into the kitchen with two plates.

Maybellene bounced out of the radio and the sounds of the night birds drifted into the kitchen windows from the creek. Their arms touched as they stacked the dishes in the sink. In the tightness of the room her senses picked up the manly scent of aftershave lotion and body heat.

She turned quickly and bumped into him, a solid wall of muscle. His hands froze in mid-air, as if he didn't know what to do with them. Finally, he gently gripped her shoulders, bent down and kissed her.

She leaned against the sink and held him at bay with her hand. "Trip, didn't you say you were going to teach me a few shag steps."

He laughed and slowly shook his head, then took her hand and led her back into the living room. "Okay, darlin.' But just the basic step. Then I want you to go out, get a pair of penny loafers and practice until you can do it in your sleep."

He held her right hand with his left, an arms distance away. "Don't step. Just slide like this." His sockless loafer-clad feet glided with short steps and his long lithe body gracefully moved to the rhythm of the Dominoes' *Sixty Minute Man* playing on the radio. "You've got to pick up the beat. There's a lot of footwork with this dance. A sort of slowed down jitterbug with smooth shuffling moves."

She peeked over his shoulder at the clock and noticed it was past nine.

"Do the same thing I'm doing, just opposite," he continued.

After dozens of missteps and false starts, Nicky finally felt the gut-level rhythm-and-blues music pulsating through her body. They never really touched, except for his holding her hand and putting his arm around her waist.

The music finished and the two faced each other, as someone on the radio tried to sell them an automobile. Trip reached over and flicked the radio off. Nicky wiped the sweat trickling from her forehead with the back of her hand. He carefully put his hands on her waist, lifted her up and sat her on the chest of drawers. At first, he just slowly brushed his lips across her face; then his kisses traveled up and down her neck and nuzzled her ears. She felt his hands discovering her. Eyeing the clock again, she gently tried to push him away.

"Trip, my brother will be here any minute."

He strained his head back, a pained expression on his face.

"I've been meaning to tell you all night. He's here visiting me. Mac took him out so we could be alone."

Trip slapped his hand on the bureau. *"Dang!* I knew something was wrong the minute I walked in that door. You've been edgy all night."

"I think it's better if you leave before they get back."

His laugh was easy and playful. "What's the big deal? Does he have two heads or somethin'?"

Nicky heard a car door slam and clasped Trip's arms. "That's him! You've got to go!"

His eyes were inches from hers. "Only if you promise to come over once he goes to bed."

"Trip! Please!"

"Not 'til you promise."

Her consent was barely audible as she slid off the chest. She swiftly grabbed his jacket, pressed it into his hands, and frantically led him toward the door, snapping her fingers for Winston to follow.

She scurried down the porch steps pulling Trip along. She heard the bang of the kitchen door and spun around to go back. Trip grabbed her and pulled her tight against the firmness in his loins. She pulled away and blinked back tears.

"Trip, I can't come over tonight. Please understand. We can't get together again until my brother leaves."

When she reached the top of the stairs and looked back, the faint light cast by the living room lamps revealed a bewildered expression on Trip's face as he threw his jacket over his broad shoulder. Disappointed, but relieved, she ran into the house.

❧ CHAPTER SIXTEEN

Nicky opened the screen door and felt the fresh ocean breeze, a welcome relief after the hot, sticky ride to the pharmacy. On her way through the house, she looked into the room where her brother slept. A broken lamp lay strewn across the floor, his pants draped off the side of the bed. She dropped the prescription bag on the kitchen table and followed the breeze to the ocean-side porch.

She couldn't see Winston anywhere on the beach. Since it was Sunday, Trip must have stayed home. Thank God, she got him out before Mac dragged Jack in and wrestled him into bed.

She ran water in the sink, then dampened a washcloth. The coolness felt good as she wiped the sweat off her face and strolled around the room, dreamily recounting the dinner with Trip.

She spent most of the morning washing dishes and clearing the room of the clutter from the night before, and took great care not to make any noise and waken Jack, including taking the phone off the hook.

By two, Nicky sat finishing an illustration when the distant muffled sound of a toilet flushing made her perk up her ears.

Jack's mussed hair gave him a deceptively boyish look as he stood in the doorway gripping the back of his neck. He crossed the room and dropped his six-foot frame onto a couch. Nicky quickly rose and went into the kitchen for a glass of water and his pills.

Jack held out an open hand before she even got near and took them willingly. Nicky sank onto the couch next to him.

"Sis, I'm sorry about last night."

"Jack, you've got to keep taking your medicine."

"I know. It's just that I was feeling so good. I didn't think I needed it any more."

"That's what you said the last time, Jack."

140

"Well, I'll tell ya." His voice began to rise. "If Ma cared for me half as much as Sean's two rotten kids, maybe I would!"

He stood up and paced. Nicky's hands began to sweat.

"You know, I think she wants to get rid of me. I'm so afraid she's going to poison me, I can't eat a damn thing she cooks." He slammed a fist on the table. "Peanut butter and jelly! Goddamned peanut butter and jelly is all I've eaten for the past two weeks."

Nicky wasn't going to make the mistake of contradicting him.

"She wants to put me away like Dad!" The veins on his neck bulged grotesquely. "You don't give a shit about me either, or you would be home where you belong!" A broad ugly sneer appeared. "You haven't got an ounce of decency left. You stood by and let that damn hillbilly drag me out of here last night just so you could get screwed!"

He moved close to her. "That crappy joint he took me to was filled with weirdoes right out of *Deliverance*, for Christ's sake!"

Now near enough for her to see the red streaks in his eyes, and smell the stale smoke and beer he exuded, he shouted, "Go on! Say something!"

She pushed him away, rose and went toward the kitchen. "I'll make you lunch."

Nicky ignored her brother's rantings and kept pushing him away as she warmed up leftover crab cakes from the night before and brought them to the table. Jack's attention immediately switched to the food, which he devoured in minutes. He gulped down his milk and slammed the glass on the table. Worn out, he slumped into his chair.

Nicky wanted to do the same, but instead went over and massaged his shoulders. "You want to go for a walk on the beach?"

He ran his hands through his sweat-matted hair. "Hell, no. I'm beat. I've got to go back to sleep."

She helped him up and into the bedroom. He lay there on his stomach hugging a pillow while she sat on the edge of the bed gently rubbing his back.

The room was still. Just the sound of the surf, and every once in a while, the call of a gull.

"Oh boy, that feels good," Jack said, groggy. "You remember all the times you took care of me, Nicky? Nobody ever cared about me the way you did."

Nicky threw her head back and blinked back tears. Just when she wanted to kill him, he would say something that broke her heart. Her fingers pressed gently into his flesh as she slowly moved back and forth to a relaxing rhythm.

"Nicky, you can screw your head off for all I care."

A cynical laugh escaped as she wiped a cheek on her sleeve without interrupting her motion. She would save her words for right now. Suspecting he was skipping his medicine just for attention, she was planning on having a long talk with him in the morning.

His muscles slackened and his breathing deepened. She slowly drew her hands from his sweaty shirt and leaned back. Sean and Mary Beth may have come to their rescue, but this recurring nightmare would continue as long as Jack felt, that by not taking his pills, he could avoid taking responsibility for his actions. Before he left, she had to drum it into his head that she was finished taking care of him, and he had to start building a life.

She rose slowly so as not to make the metal springs sound, tiptoed toward the door and carefully closed it shut.

For the first time in her life, she had a clear vision of where she stood and it filled her with exhilaration. Then a smile crossed her face as she remembered the look in Trip's eyes. She started back on her drawing, but after only a moment stopped and chomped down on the end of her pen as she thought. A giggle emerged. Loafers! He wanted her to buy penny loafers and practice the dance step 'til she could do it in her sleep!

Her ears perked up. She turned and saw Mac through the screen at the kitchen door. She sprang up and slipped out.

"He's asleep," Nicky whispered.

Mac scratched behind his ear. "I'd have come over sooner but I had a fishing trip this morning. How's the little bastard doing?"

Nicky snorted a reprimand. "I started him on his medicine. We should see some improvement in a couple of days."

"I can't figure out how a little gal like you could handle that palooka. Sorry I couldn't keep him out longer, but that bugger managed to insult everyone in the Mole Hole. Hell, we were lucky to get out of there alive."

"I barely got Trip out in time."

"I made as much noise as I could. Got a little help from Mr. Charm." He leaned toward her. "Are you sure you don't want me to take him out on the boat and deep six him?" He jerked a thumb toward the dusty car sitting in the driveway. "I could get rid of that in a heartbeat."

Nicky shook her head. "Mac, you wait. He's not half bad once his medicine kicks in."

Mac pulled a cigar from his tee shirt pocket, leaned back against the railing and lit up. "Well. How'd it go?"

Nicky put her hands behind her back and leaned against the wall. "Oh, Mac, he likes me. I know it." She didn't dare tell him he wanted her to come over last night.

"Well, if you want him to keep liking you ..." He tossed his head toward the door. "... don't let him get a load of that guy." He handed her a pail. "Here's some mullet for your critters." Gripping the cigar between his teeth, he asked, "Are you going to need any help with your brother tonight?"

"No. He'll sleep right through."

Mac left and Nicky got two leftover crab cakes out of the refrigerator and had a snack before starting back on her drawing. She worked steadily through the afternoon, getting up just once to feed the animals and give Jack another pill, which he took without opening his eyes. Every time she passed the phone, she was tempted to call Trip, but couldn't take a chance on waking Jack.

The light from outside was failing when she rinsed the pen and carefully dried it with a cloth, then listened to the far off song of a whippoorwill. Acutely aware of her breasts rising and falling underneath her low-cut sleeveless tee, she hugged herself and remembered Trip caressing them. All afternoon she'd been able to ignore the tingling between her legs, even though it was never far from her consciousness. She had never felt this way about Richard; but Richard had never had that look in his eye either —like he wasn't going to leave until he got what he came for.

Barefoot, she tiptoed over to Jack's door, opened it a crack and peeked in, then turned back to the ocean-side door. Salem mewed plaintively, so she picked the cat up and walked out onto the porch. The whooshing of the wind and smell of the salt air mixed with the tea olive blooms almost made her heart stop. God! How she loved this place they called "the beach."

Trip threw the pencil on the desk, leaned back and rocked on the chair's back legs. He found it impossible to fine-tune the costs for his new project with his thoughts constantly drifting back to the little girl who took care of animals. He smiled to himself when remembering her asking, *Is it too bold educating children?*

He loved the way she had scratched out the compelling plight of Loretta Caretta in crisp black lines that came together with a naturalness that made the drawing seem real.

He stopped rocking. His life was spiraling inextricably toward Nicky's, but this no longer bothered him, for the night before, as he stood on the porch watching the poignant way she cared for her injured animals, he realized he loved her.

He sat for a moment savoring those memories, then his brow furrowed as his thoughts jumped to the brother. What was it about him that made her so anxious? Was he an over-protective psychopath, a burned-out hippy? No matter, he'd be gone in a few days. He suddenly slapped his leg and laughed to himself. Then, for dang sure, he was going to take up where he left off!

He got out a beer and started toward the porch, when a montage of photographs on the wall caught his eye. They were as familiar as wallpaper, yet it was surprising how easily they could put him back in those distant times. A picture of his father, sitting lazily on a beach chair in the surf, made him recall the old man laughingly tell him not to waste film on the likes of him.

The picture of two tall, skinny boys proudly posing with newly caught fish, their hair swirling in the breeze, saddened him. His brother looked like a typical kid, but he'd been different from the very beginning. Right after med school, he moved to Savannah to spare their parents from coming face to face with his carefully hidden lifestyle; and in all these years not one member of the family ever spoke of his brother's homosexuality.

His gaze lingered on the one of his mother and dad standing as if they were lined up before a firing squad—uncomfortable but still holding hands. It occurred to him that one of the reasons their union had been so successful was that they both came from the same background. Could he have the same sort of bond with someone like Nicky?

Dang! Now she's got me thinking about marriage! He needed a good hard run on the beach if he was ever going to get any sleep. Winston got up to follow him, but Trip thought better of it. He'd be sure to run up on Nicky's porch. "Not tonight, old fella," he said as he latched the chain to the dog's collar.

Trip, in swim trunks and a tee shirt, flew along the beach until he reached the end of the peninsula, then turned around and ran back, tracing his footprints in the sand. At the sight of a second set, he broke stride and gradually came to a dead stop. His eyes riveted on a glistening surf-sprayed figure in the water.

Nicky came toward him, slowly sloshing through the rippling waves with deliberate steps. A gentle breeze blew a strand of hair across her face and the soft moonlight spilled across the firm curves of her breasts at the edge of her shirt. The invitation was profound. He put his arms around her and pulled her to him. Then his hands traveled down her back to her buttocks, and he drew her tight to his loins.

He bent down and kissed her. The touch of her feverish lips made his passion escalate to an intolerable level. He threw his head back and closed his eyes for a moment, then looked down and carefully studied the intense look on her face.

"Nicky, are you sure you want this?"

"Trip, I'll die if you don't."

He stood transfixed as she slowly peeled off her clothes. She stood silent and still. He undressed, his eyes devouring her.

The warm, sultry ocean breeze that brushed past the two motionless figures at the edge of the shore connected them as a web. He took her in his arms and traced the outline of her face, his fingertips barely skimming across her lips and down her neck. When he reached her breast, she melted in his arms. They dropped to their knees and he slowly lowered her to the cool hard-packed sand where the sudsy surf licked their feet. His hand followed the curve of her body to the place where the heat and moistness made him cry out her name.

She felt a fleeting pain, then the power of his thrust urgently repeating to a primeval rhythm. She was filled with him and with the pleasure of knowing she was the object of his desire. She lustily gave back what she was given, throwing herself into a dark stratosphere of desire until she felt his motion freeze, then his muscles relax, and she knew he'd been satisfied.

They lay in each other's arms until the warm surf crept up on them. Silently, they rose and kissed and slowly sank into the warm water to rinse their bodies. He picked her up and started down the beach.

He carried her through his house and up the stairs in the dark as if she belonged to him. Unfamiliar smells and sounds sharpened her senses, and her whole body seemed to be filled with wanting. He gently let her feet slip to the floor of the bathroom and led her into the shower. The warm water splashed against them as he slowly rubbed the soap over her body. She held on to him and when their eyes met, he tenderly kissed her, then whispered, "Baby, I'm sorry I went so fast on the beach. I just couldn't hold back."

She looked up at the water-streaked face, and gave him a trace of a smile that said she wanted him again. They stood apart with her breasts barely touching his chest. He reached for her hand and led it along his body, helping her discover his manhood.

She barely breathed as he slowly dried her off. His mouth covered hers, then traveled down her neck. He took a breast in his hand and hungrily kissed it. She buried her face in his chest and pleaded, "Please, Trip. Please."

The urgency with which he carried her to the bed thrilled her and she yielded to him eagerly. The two bodies, now one, rocked in unison. Her fingers dug into his back and her pleading moans filled the room. The rhythm of his thrusts became slower and more deliberate, and instinctively she gave herself to him with an openness that took her to a height of emotion she never knew was possible, until suddenly she was gripped by incredibly fulfilling spasms. She lay there, his sweaty face next to hers, listening to his deep breathing as he slowly receded from her body. He sank back onto the bed, pulled her close to him and kissed her tenderly, whispering, "I love you, Nicky," before they both drifted into a dreamless sleep.

The sun edged over the horizon, casting ghostly shadows in the unfamiliar room. Nicky gently lifted Trip's arm from around her waist and slipped out of bed so as not to waken him. She tiptoed into the bathroom and caught sight of her reflection in the mirror. A kaleidoscope of emotions, especially triumph, descended upon her. She quickly put on a pair of trunks and a tee shirt she found in a drawer and silently crept down the stairs.

The cavernous living room was dark but she could see Winston's nose pressed against the screen door. She opened it carefully so it wouldn't squeak, and finding him on a chain, bent down on one knee and gave him a good rubbing.

She sprinted down the steps and along the beach, anxious to get back before Uta started her turtle watch or her brother woke. Their clothes from the night before lay at the edge of the high water mark, and without breaking her stride, she scooped them into her arms and scrambled up the stairs to the King's Nest boardwalk. Before slipping into the shower, she peeked into Jack's room. He was still asleep.

Later, at the table sipping coffee in her robe, she heard Trippett's truck barreling past the house. Simultaneously, Winston appeared at her door with an envelope bobbing from his collar. Her fingers skimmed over the three words written on ledger paper. Recalling Trip whispering them in her ear the night before, she lovingly tucked the note in her sketchpad.

Jack woke and ate a big breakfast, then napped and woke again for lunch. Nicky showed him *Loretta Caretta*'s proofs and told him about her the efforts to save the loggerhead's island nesting grounds, hoping he would begin to understand that she was building a new life for herself. She was satisfied with his response and delighted when he decided to go for a walk, leaving her alone with her memories of the night before.

Billy pulled into the Mole Hole's parking lot. The drive from North Carolina had been tricky. He'd driven fast enough to get back in time to scope out the local gossip at the Mole Hole, yet not so fast he'd get a cop on his tail.

He found a stool at the dark end of the bar, ordered his usual one beer and latched on to the thread of conversation from down the bar. Billy could see enough of the man's back to tell he was a monster.

The man waved his fist. "I would have pounded the hell out of that Yankee bastard if you hadn't held me back!"

"Come on, Eddie. You're already in enough shit," said the bartender as he rinsed glasses in the sink. He leaned toward Eddie and said, "Tell me now. What do you think your probation officer would do if you got yourself caught up in another fight?"

Eddie slammed his fist on the bar. "If I see that guy again, so help me, I'll kill him."

The bar cleared and Eddie looked around for someone to shoot off his mouth to. He made eye contact with Billy and looked him over.

"Give the man another beer," Billy told the barkeep.

Eddie took the beer in his big paw, turned around with a broad grin and waved the bottle at the others in the room, then got up and swaggered over to the stool next to Billy.

Billy looked straight ahead, speaking under his breath. "I hate them damn Yankees, too. What did he do to get you so hot and bothered?"

"He came in here and talked like some kind of nut. I tell you, I wanted to crush his brains out with my own two hands. This used to be a right nice place before all them Yankees and Realtors arrived. I hope he doesn't show up for the oyster roast." He looked over at Billy. "Hey. I'm helping the guy that's doin' the roast over on the island. He needs another guy. You want to help? He'll give you fifty, plus all the oysters you can eat."

Billy figured he was finally getting somewhere, and wondered if Walter would be there. "Yeah! I'll do it."

Billy let the tale of the fight run its predictable course, then asked, "Besides the invasion from the North, what else happens in this joint?"

Eddie tipped his beer to show it was empty.

Billy signaled for another.

Eddie took a long swallow and slammed the bottle on the bar. "Nothin' much is goin' on here, except the rich are gettin' richer."

"That's how it is all over," laughed the bartender.

"Except here, they do it by building them there *con do miniums*. He looked at Billy. "Deveroux's putting up a whole bunch of 'em right out there on the peninsula. On the old nigger's land." His mouth curved downward in an ugly frown. "Them two boys of his sure fell into a shitload of money."

The bartender stretched his arms and gripped the bar. "I guess we won't be seeing that granddaughter of Mo's again."

Eddie dropped his chin to his chest, raised an eyebrow and glowered up at the bartender. "*Gee ... I'm really goin' to miss her. We don't have enough smart-assed Yankees around here.*"

The bartender leaned back against a counter, getting in the last dig for the night. "All them tree huggers that came down here to the beach are right riled up over this thing. Hell, if Mac sells his five acres next to Old Mo's place that li'l ole paradise of theirs is gonna look just like that complex down the road."

By the time Billy got back to the beach house he'd figured out why Walter Satterfield wanted the old man killed, and rapidly came to the conclusion that the extra thirty thousand he'd squeezed out of him was chickenfeed. The old fisherman probably refused to sell, and Satterfield knew the two sons would jump at the money. Satterfield wanting that will so bad, though, didn't add up. Why would he need it? From what he had gleaned from the talk at the bar, the two boys were all the old man had. But then, there was the granddaughter. She must have come down a lot, since everyone seemed to know her. Maybe, just maybe, she was the missing piece to this puzzle.

A welcome silence hung over the beach, since most of the owners had packed up their kids and taken off Sunday night. Billy watched the pallid man trudging along the sand. His clothes and the pasty white feet marked him as likely one of those hated Yankees—maybe even the one Eddie talked about the night before. The way he slumped down onto the sand, as if he were giving out, gave Billy a hunch he could be vulnerable, so he sauntered over.

The broad, non-threatening grin he had mastered spread across Billy's face. "You new around these parts?"

Jack shaded his eyes with a hand and looked up.

Billy studied the scowling face. This had to be the guy they were talking about at the bar. He had the beaten attitude of someone who made a habit of feeling sorry for himself, signaling to Billy to play the part of a victim. "They didn't take too kindly to me at the Mole Hole last night. I guess they don't like strangers around these parts," he said.

The menacing look faded from Jack's face, encouraging Billy.

"Some people just don't know how to treat folks. Anybody from outside this joint scares the hell out of 'em."

"They're friggin' assholes," spat out Jack.

Billy smiled inwardly at the remark. He had run into guys like this before. Nut cases that had to be handled with kid gloves. No problem. This guy would be easy to manipulate; but first, he had to find out if he had any useful information. "They were all excited about them puttin' up condos here on the island. Everyone expects to cash in on it."

"Like hell they will! My sister's putting out a book on some damn turtle that'll get hurt if they put them up."

Billy knew which turtles the man was talking about. More than once he'd invaded a nest of eggs on the beach and sucked out the sweet insides of a half-dozen or so. "Do you think a li'l ole turtle can get in the way of somethin' this big?"

"You never know. She's going on TV to talk about it."

"Your sister's some kind of an artist, isn't she?"

Jack barely nodded.

"I've seen her around the island with that dog. They spend a lot of time with that fisherman who lives out on the peninsula."

"That mutt belongs to some guy who lives on the north end of the island."

Billy mulled over all the new information for a moment, then said, "Last night they were all talkin' about the big doins' Saturday here on the island. You goin'?"

"I don't know a damn thing about it."

"Guess everyone here 'bouts goes to it. Some kind of an oyster roast."

When Jack abruptly stood up and brushed the sand off his pants, Billy feared he'd aroused his suspicions with too many questions.

"I gotta run," said Jack.

"Don't let me hold you up none. It was nice talkin' with a gentleman like you. It gets a little lonely around here and I guess I get runnin' off at the mouth when I come across someone decent. Hope to see you around."

"Don't count on it. I'm getting the hell out of here as soon as I can get my carburetor fixed. This place is for the birds. If I want to sweat my ass off, I'll go to a sauna."

Billy looked down at the ground and kicked some sand with his foot. "If you want, I'll take a look at your car. I'm right handy with engines."

Jack's face lit up. With no mechanical abilities of his own, he found this offer appealing. "Yeah. That would be good. I'm tired now, but maybe in a couple of days."

🐚 CHAPTER SEVENTEEN

Nicky took advantage of Jack's walk and got out Trip's note. She flattened it on her drawing board and studied every letter. The strokes were strong with a bold slant. Interestingly, he had included his last name in his signature, as if his image of himself was irrevocably entwined with his family name.

She smiled to herself and patted the note softly as she thought things through. Yes. His declaration of love made everything official.

She placed a fresh sheet of paper on the board and selected a pen. First, *Nicole Alston* was casually jotted and scrutinized, then *Mrs. Trippett Alston*. She sat erect, folded her hands in her lap and examined the signatures, a self-satisfied smile on her face. Then she reached for another sheet. *I can't come over tonight ... but hopefully I can tomorrow. All my love, Nicky*. She fanned through one of her small sketchpads until she came across the page covered with drawings of Trip and Winston running on the beach. She cut one out in the shape of a heart and put it in a baggie with her note.

Winston's head rose and his ears perked up at Jack's approach. Nicky buried everything under a sketchpad and glanced over at the clock to see if he was due for more pills. Hearing his footsteps shuffle across the walkway, she rose to get the medicine. Jack took it readily and went straight to bed. Nicky retrieved the baggie with the note, tied it to Winston's collar and pointed him homeward.

Walter Satterfield had thought he had said his final *adios* to Billy with the payment of the extra thirty thousand, but here he was again, waiting at the end of a tiring day for him to show up. Parked on a dusty road, Walter impatiently drummed his fingers on the steering wheel. He checked his watch for the umpteenth time, then took off his suit jacket and slung it over his briefcase on the back seat. The car kept cool for all of two minutes before the window had to be buzzed down. Mercifully, every once in a while a hint of a breeze floated in on the deadly warm and humid summer air.

The gray moss draping from the live oaks in the ancient grove gave the canopy a smoky, sultry look. Off in the distance, the lowering sun glistened off the water in a creek where a lone blue heron stood motionless. Walter checked his watch again and loosened his tie.

Suddenly, Billy's new truck, ensconced in a cloud of dust, appeared in the rearview mirror. The big grin on Billy's face as he skidded to a stop made Walter grit his teeth, and when he ran in front of the car in flashy new clothes, Walter wanted to run him down.

Walter had given Billy his cell phone number so he wouldn't call the office, but that was a month ago. He never expected to see him again, or at least, he had hoped he wouldn't.

The raptorial grin on the face of the man now sitting next to him gave Walter the nauseating feeling that the rest of his life would be painfully dotted with a never-ending series of final payoffs.

"What the hell are you doing at the beach? You got your money."

"Walter, how are we ever going to be friends if you talk like that?"

Walter slammed the steering wheel with an open hand and gazed out the window. His temples throbbed.

Billy lit a cigarette, took a long drag and blew the smoke upward.

Walter turned and glared at him. "Put that damn thing out."

Billy pulled open the ashtray only to have Walter slam it shut.

"Use the window!"

Billy complied, then leaned back and nervously tapped the fingers of one hand on his leg. After a short pause he said, "We've got some unfinished business, Walter."

Walter expected a remark like this. Billy Cleary was the kind of guy that once he gets a hold of someone, adheres to them like gum on the bottom of their shoe. No matter how many times it's scraped off, it still sticks to the pavement every time a step is taken.

"The way I see it, Walter, I've been shortchanged. You're going to make millions off that condo deal, and if it weren't for me, it wouldn't be happening."

Walter laughed out loud. "I don't know where you're going with this, but the well is dry."

"Come on, Walter, we both know that's bullshit!" Billy took a moment to compose himself. "It wasn't easy to kill that man. I never did that kind of thing before. I've had nightmares ever since."

Walter caught his laugh by pursing his lips. He didn't want to risk getting Billy any angrier.

Billy knew this path of argument was going nowhere. He also knew he had never felt a pang of guilt for any of the misdeeds he'd committed in his entire life. At six, he got locked in a chicken coop for a day after throwing kerosene on the rooster and setting it aflame. Instead of repenting, he just swore to himself that he'd never get caught at anything ever again.

"You got plenty of money for your trouble," Satterfield said.

"That's the way it looks to you, Walter. But look at it from my angle. While I'm behind the wheel of a semi hauling Jockey shorts all over the country, you'll be making millions on those condos on the peninsula."

Walter quickly realized that the payoff was about to be ratcheted up to the next painful level. He would have to part with enough money to set Billy up somewhere too good to leave.

"I'm getting too old for that crap. Besides, I need some respect. Maybe if I had a business. A convenience store or somethin' like that."

Walter's voice screamed in his head. How did he ever get mixed up with this lunatic!

Billy brushed off his slacks. "Look what a few duds did for me. I'm startin' to look like I got some class."

Walter closed his eyes and moaned to himself. How was he going to get rid of this bloodsucker? He took a deep breath and said, "Let me think this over. Right now, I want you to clear out of that beach house and go back to Mexico. Call me on my cell phone in a week."

"Not so fast, Walter. I'm fixin' to stay right smack where I am. And Walter, you shouldn't be so quick to git rid of your barnyard dog. You jus' might be needin' me again."

Walter slowly turned his head toward Billy.

"Don't worry. It's not going to cost you any more. I'll be protectin' my interest. Insurance, you could say."

"What the hell are you talking about?"

"You might be wantin' me to take care of the fisherman who's got the rest of the island. Or, that there gal with the turtle book I read about."

Walter instantly pictured the newspaper clipping with the photo of the young woman who lived on the island smiling from behind her drawing board. How could he have allowed this maniac to move into the beach house! Walter felt his heart beat in his throat, but told himself not to panic. He had already made too many mistakes.

"First of all, Billy, thank your lucky stars you even got all that extra money. And keep in mind, if I go down, I'm taking you with me. And as far as laying a hand on anyone else, don't even dream of it. We'll be lucky if we ... uh, you get away with the first one."

Walter's forcefulness surprised Billy. He thought for a moment and then his mind latched on to the one piece of the puzzle he hadn't been able to figure out, but his crafty intuition told him was the key. "I ain't got plans to put you and me in any shit, Walter. I just want my fair share. You wouldn't want me to go to Mexico and mail the police a copy of the will, would you? Might start them thinkin'. What do they call it, Walter? Conspiracy?"

"You bastard!" Walter started to grab Billy by the neck, but fell back in his seat and pounded the steering wheel. "Where is it?"

"Don't worry. I've got it in a safe place."

Billy's self-serving conversation droned on, as Walter's mind desperately ran through a worst case scenario. He had enough money in his investment portfolio for him and his wife to live comfortably in Europe for the rest of their lives. Not as comfortably as he had hoped, but a lot better than in a ten by six cell. Maybe he could even swing an upscale time-share on one of the Caribbean islands for winter vacations. It might be prudent to start transferring money and securities out of the country as soon as possible.

Unfortunately, he had too much tied up in the new house. At least a million and a half. He could probably have one of his agents manage a quick sale, furniture and all. At any rate, he'd have to make sure his and his wife's passports were up to date. He winced at the idea of having to tell her what he had done. He thought for a moment and wondered if she'd leave him.

The long silence woke Walter out of his thoughts. He looked at Billy searchingly.

"Well? How about it, Walter?"

Walter looked confused. "How about what?"

"The job, Walter. The job."

The thought of giving Billy a job made Walter laugh bitterly to himself. It would be insane to draw him in any closer. He already knew too much. Then again, maybe it would place him somewhere where he could be watched.

Walter turned the key to the ignition and started the engine. "Call me in a week."

Billy got back in his truck and kept from laughing long enough for Walter to get well out of sight. He couldn't believe the bluff about the will worked so well. Yes indeed, white-collar crime was the way to go.

Through the shadowy dawn, Nicky could just make out the tall, strong figure on the beach, lithely striding toward her with Winston at his side. Nicky stood smiling to herself as they neared. She flew into Trip's arms, and he lifted her up and swung her around as they kissed.

Trip let her down, cupped her face in his hands and planted kisses all over her face. "God, I've missed you!"

She coyly pushed him. "I don't see why. You certainly had enough of me the other night."

He threw his head back and laughed, then bent down and looked her directly in the eye. "You haven't seen anything yet, lady."

She threw her arms around his neck. "Oh, Trip. I love you."

He put his hands on her waist and gently pushed her far enough away to study her face. "Listen, the island's oyster roast is tomorrow night. Bring your brother so we can show him some good ole Southern hospitality. My mother's coming and she's looking forward to seeing you and meeting him. And, I won't take no for an answer."

"I don't know, Trip. My brother's not feeling all that well."

He searched her face. "What's wrong, darlin'?"

She gave him a big hug. "Nothing! Except I'm madly in love with you!"

She remembered his scent and the feel of him as his mouth spread kisses all over her face and his hands reached up under her shirt and rediscovered her.

"I won't be able to sleep 'til I've got you back in bed with me."

Eyeing movement at the far end of the beach, Nicky pulled Trip's hand from under her shirt. "I've got to go back in. Uta's coming and my brother might be getting up."

"How many more days do I have to be tortured like this?"

"He'll be gone by Tuesday."

He swooped her up in his arms. "Too long, sweetheart."

"Trip, put me down," she laughed. "I'll try to get away tonight."

He gave her a quick kiss. "Sorry, my love, you had your big chance last night. My mother'll be here with her sister."

Trip put her down and took her hand. "Just promise me you'll come to the oyster roast."

"I'll see what I can do."

Trip held onto her shoulders and shook his head. "If you don't show up, I'll just have to come and get you."

Nicky turned and ran toward the house, then stopped and looked back. "You be careful, Trippett Alston. You come and get me and I'll never leave."

He stood there, arms crossed, a boyish grin on his face as if that were his exact intention.

Billy ran the comb through his fine blond hair and looked in the cracked mirror at the scar on his lip. That li'l ole Shelby had figured she got her revenge, he thought, but every time he saw it he got the pleasure of pinning her down and getting his way with her all over again. She had teased him as she sped past him in her convertible; and he couldn't believe his luck when he drove around the curve and spotted her, long legs and all, standing on the side of the road. Girl, he had said to himself, you never want to run out of gas on a deserted back mountain road. Unfortunately, he had been so busy getting what he wanted, he didn't notice her reach for the broken bottle laying on the ground. His pa was mad as hell for all the blood in the truck, but Shelby knew what was good for her and kept her mouth shut.

Now, he couldn't believe his luck at being invited by the dumb Yankee to the beach house where his sister lived. If he could get inside he'd be able to scope out the place and see what kind of locks were on the doors. Not that he was planning on doing anything. He was sitting too pretty to get into trouble. But if his deal with Walter went sour, he wouldn't mind paying the artist a little visit before taking off.

By the time he got to their house and parked behind the old Buick that sat with its hood up, he was already sweaty. He smoothed his hair back as he climbed the steps, then peered in through the screen for a moment before knocking. The lock on the door handle caught his eye. He could have that open in a few seconds.

Jack appeared at the door, puzzlement on his face.

"Came to fix your car."

Jack's expression changed. "Yeah! Great! Let me get some shoes on."

Damn Yankee, thought Billy. Doesn't know enough to invite me in. Leavin' me standing here like some damn fool.

A low guttural growl came from behind the screen. Winston stood like a rock at the door. Suddenly Nicky, who'd just come in from the beach, appeared.

"Hi there, ma'am. Didn't mean to bother your dog none. Here to help fix your brother's carburetor. He seems mighty disturbed 'bout it."

Nicky hesitated for a moment, then reluctantly opened the screen door. "Do come in."

Billy was pleased. This was a smart move, he thought. She's let her guard down. Even the dog seemed at ease. He kept one eye on Nicky and the other on the way the place was laid out. Same kind of lock on the oceanside door. Nothing but screens on all the window openings with shutters hooked overhead. Everything could be handled with a penknife.

Jack hobbled in from a bedroom trying to get a foot in his shoe.

"This is my sister, Nicky. Sorry I didn't get your name."

"Billy. Billy Cleary."

Obviously anxious to get started on his car, Jack shepherded Billy toward the door. "I'd like you to check my whole car out if you can. I don't want to get ripped off by any more of those sons of bitches lying in wait in all these damn crappy towns along I-95."

Nicky hurried along the beach toward Mac's house with Winston, content that she had seen Trip before he left for work and thankful Jack was getting his car fixed instead of going out with her and Mac to collect oysters. She was also relieved to discover that the man who lived between her and Mac wasn't as treacherous as he first appeared. It was probably the scar that had made her wary.

Mac was on his deck organizing his gear. Nicky put on the boots he handed her, picked up a stack of baskets and followed Mac, who was lugging an ice chest, down to the boat.

Although warm, the breeze still felt good as they motored down the creek. Instead of turning into the open waters of the bay, they made a right and kept going deeper into the marsh creek until Mac pulled up to a dock. A stagnant alluvial smell rose from the muddy bank covered with oysters.

"Johnny's out at his oyster bed with a couple of the islanders, but I figure it won't hurt none bringing in our quota," said Mac as he tied up the boat.

A sign on the dock informed the public that this was a South Carolina recreational bed and they could pick two bushels per household twice a week from September 15 through May 1.

Nicky shielded her eyes from the sun as Mac helped her out of the boat. A sweaty patch already blotted the front of his tee shirt.

"Watch out. These shells are right sharp," he said as he handed her a pair of gloves and a small pickaxe. "Use the sharp end of that there axe to break a cluster free, then hammer them loose with the other end."

In the time it took for Nicky to fill one bushel basket, Mac had three. "There. We got our limit. Let's ice 'em down."

Mac tended to the oysters, then opened a beer and sat down. The way he crossed a leg over a knee and leaned back, she knew he was about to tell her a tale.

"When we were kids, we used to get a couple of pails of oysters ... you know you only harvest them during months with an r?"

Nicky nodded.

"We'd go to the beach and build a fire using driftwood. We had a hood from an old Studebaker hidden behind the dunes. It had a hump going right down the center of it. When we put it wrong side up over hot coals the hump made a dish that could hold the oysters. We'd soak an old army blanket in the ocean, lay it over 'em and wait for the oysters to steam open."

"Sounds like you had a lot of fun as a kid."

Mac took a partially smoked cigar out of his toolbox and lit up. He shook his head as if he'd remembered something sad. Then, as if he were trying to cheer himself up with some good news, he asked, "Well, gal, what's new in the romance department?"

Nicky glanced up, not quite able to suppress a smile.

Mac laughed slow and deep. "So that's the way it is, aye?"

Nicky looked down and blushed.

He reached over and grasped her chin. "Don't you go feeling all shy and embarrassed, gal. It's about time you stepped out."

He took a long gulp of beer. "Just keep that brother of yours out of Trip's sight. When's he leaving anyway?"

"Probably next week some time."

"Is he in good enough shape to drive?"

"He should be by then. I can see a change in him already."

"Where did he get all that hate bottled up inside him?"

"I don't know. It just comes on him."

"Well, just make sure it doesn't come on him when Trip's around."

Nicky slumped forward with her elbows on her knees and sighed.

"Somethin' botherin' you?" asked Mac.

"Trip's insisting I bring Jack to the oyster roast."

"I wouldn't be doin' that, girl."

She looked at Mac pleadingly. "Couldn't you keep an eye on him?"

"I'll be too busy helpin' Johnny with the oysters."

Nicky ran her hands through her hair. "I don't know how I'm going to get out of this, Mac. Trip said his mother was looking forward to meeting him."

Mac thought for a moment. "The other day you said your other brother could get someone from Charleston to take him."

"It's too late for that. Plus, won't everyone think it strange if I show up without him?"

"Not half as strange as if you show up with him." Mac rubbed his chin and thought. "You say he's getting better?"

"Oh, yes! Much!"

"Good! You can send him off in the morning."

"Oh, Mac. I can't just kick him out. He needs more rest. With all the drugs and him being so tired and all, something could happen." She put a hand on Mac's shoulder. "I can't give up on him now. Once he realizes that I've got a life of my own, he's going to buck up and straighten right out. I know it. Actually, I haven't been this hopeful in years. I just know it's all going to be worth it."

"All right. Bring him over to me after you introduce him around and I'll keep an eye on him."

Mac raised an eyebrow. "We didn't exactly hit it off the other night. Do you think he'll stay with me?"

"Don't worry. I'll have a good long talk with him. After I tell him how important this is to me, he'll cooperate."

Mac started up the engine, and keeping it in low gear, slowly motored back along the creek. "I wouldn't count on him cooperating past an hour if I were you."

"Don't worry. I won't."

🐚 Chapter Eighteen

No one on the island thought of Trippett Alston as having a flamboyant nature. They all regarded him as being somewhat reserved with an eye for the ladies as well as the finer things in life, and so the zeal with which he set about organizing this year's oyster roast came as a surprise.

Wearing a faded pair of shorts and a USC tee shirt that must have been a holdover from his college days, he enthusiastically pitched in with Johnny Bumps and one of his helpers to set up the dance floor between the dunes and the high-water mark. As plywood forms were taken from a shed behind his house and carted to the beach, he shouted to those passing by that the festivities would start around six when the tide was out.

Onlookers, great expectation on their faces, stood around in their bathing suits watching Johnny drag oyster tables from his pickup and set them up near the huge portable gas stove that he'd towed to the beach. He efficiently positioned trashcans underneath the plate-sized holes cut out of the tabletops to catch the shells, and then laid boards across sawhorses to accommodate drinks, relishes and the covered dishes everyone would bring.

While Johnny and Trip set up amplifiers near the dance floor, Mrs. Alston made her appearance in a summery yellow shift. Her snow-white hair and white beaded choker set against her tan gave her a dazzling cool look. Trip acknowledged her with a wink.

His enthusiastic involvement in the annual event tickled his mother, and she decided to keep her news until later that night so as not to spoil his evening. As she listened to the friendly banter between Trip and those standing near, she searched her brain for the last time she saw him so high-spirited. Something was definitely new and different, and she began to suspect he was in love. And when he kept glancing up at the King's Nest, she was pretty sure with whom. She nodded to herself approvingly. Now maybe she'd finally have some grandchildren.

The crooning of the Four Aces drifted out of the speakers as Johnny tested the sound system. A little girl toddled onto the platform. Trip tried to coax her to dance, but she turned and ran into her mother's arms, making everyone laugh. Trip motioned to Johnny to keep the music going, found his mother and led her onto the dance floor. The elegant Elizabeth Alston, gracefully doing the shag with her son who so closely resembled his handsome father, brought murmurs from the crowd of islanders who had been connected to each other, one way or another, for generations.

For the umpteenth time, Nicky got up from her drawing board and paced the porch, nervously surveying all the activity. The shouting and sound of trucks being unloaded, mixed with the screams of children at play, had been drifting up to the house since early morning. She spotted Trip throwing Winston a Frisbee and felt a tinge of pride when the dog catapulted upward and caught it in mid-air.

Nicky tried to make out the woman in a bikini who stood watching; but with the broad-rimmed hat and sunglasses she couldn't be sure it was Kim Dusenbury. Now that she thought about it, Trip had mentioned Kim's fiancé's family had a place on the island.

When Trip glanced toward the house, Nicky quickly backed into the shadows. She didn't want him to come get her before she had a chance to talk with Jack.

She dutifully fed all her patients and then made a pot of coffee, hoping the aroma would stir her brother. Just like her wild animals, she tamed him with food. Deep in thought, she ran her finger along the rim of her cup. Suddenly her shoulders were gripped from behind. She looked up and saw a friendly grin on Jack's face—a good sign.

The activity on the beach caught his eye, and she followed his glance to the porch.

He nodded toward the ocean. "What's going on?"

Nicky rose. "I'll tell you about it while you eat your breakfast."

Jack was already perspiring heavily in spite of a strong breeze sailing in from the ocean. As usual, he wolfed down the food put in front of him, but he was different this morning. His muscles were relaxed and the scowl gone. Hope jumped into Nicky's heart.

She refilled both their cups with coffee and pulled out a chair. "Jack, we need to talk." She reached across the table and clutched his hand. "There's going to be a little island event tonight, and the folks around here have invited us to come. An oyster roast."

Instead of firing back a nasty remark, Jack relaxed in his chair and folded his arms across his chest—another good sign.

"Jack, do you think you can handle it?"

He stood up, walked to the door and surveyed the activity on the beach. Nicky's gaze traced his motions, trying to read his every gesture.

Finally, he turned and spoke. "You think I'm going to screw everything up for you, don't you?"

"No, Jack. It's just ..."

"Come on, Nicky. I know you're trying to get established here. What do you think? That I'm some kind of monster!"

Nicky dropped back in her chair and blew out a breath. What was she thinking? This wasn't going to work. She entertained the thought of getting Jack in the car and going for a very long ride, when the music drifting in from the beach made her yearn for Trip. She sat up ramrod straight. "No, Jack. You're not a monster, but you've got to learn to take responsibility for your actions. Sean's done his part by hooking you up with Dr. Green, now it's your turn to follow through with the medicine. You were a wreck when you showed up here last week. This has got to stop."

Jack walked over and collapsed into a chair. "I know the medicine's good for me. Hell, I'm already feeling better. When I went off the pills, all the weird fears came back." He dropped his head into his hands. "Christ, Nicky, like I told Dr. Green, I've always been afraid of everything. When I heard a knock at the door, I was terrified some maniac behind it was going to grab me and tear me apart. I couldn't even pick up a phone. I was sure someone was going to threaten me. All my life I've expected some hideous disaster to explode in my face."

"Thank God, there's finally something that can help you. That's why you have to keep taking it."

He punched his open palm. *"Damn!* I was feeling so good. I don't know what possessed me to stop. I promise this will be the last time I put you and Mom through this."

"Jack, do you think you can handle the oyster roast tonight?"

"I don't know. Do I have to stay long?"

"No. We'll go down to the beach around six-thirty and be back in an hour." She squeezed his hand. "I'm going to introduce you to Trippett Alston and his mother, and it's real important to me that everything goes all right with that."

He rolled his eyes. "Don't worry. I get the picture. I'm not going to screw up your life. Just don't count on me to make nice for more than an hour. Then I'm closing the Donnie and Marie show and coming back and hitting the sack."

"After you meet the Alstons I want you to sit with Mac until we come up."

"What is it with this guy? You got a thing for him or something?"

"He's a good friend, Jack. And I want him to be your friend, too. Promise?"

"Okay. But I won't be able to stomach it for very long."

"Don't worry. I promise you, we won't stay for more than an hour."

Nicky got up and tidied the kitchen before going back to her drawing. Jack read for a while, then after setting up a chessboard and making a few moves, strolled around examining the King family's collection of knickknacks and shells. Nicky looked up and saw him bend down and pet the cat.

"I saw that, Jack."

"Hey, I'm not all bad."

"Just enough to be a big pain in the butt."

"Well, this pain in the butt's going to be out of here in a couple of days. I love you, Nick, but there's nothing to do around here but sweat." He picked up a figurine of a rotund woman in a bathing suit and rolled it around in his palm. "I've been working on organizing my tape collection ... that was when I was feeling better ... so I've got to go home and finish that." He put the figurine back and strolled around the room. "And mom and I were getting all the junk out of the attic. I want to have a big garage sale."

Nicky looked up in disbelief. "A garage sale? You?"

"Yeah, me. What's wrong with that? I've been going to a lot of them lately. Hell, I can make some decent money on all the crap we've got stashed up there."

Nicky put down her pen, perched her chin on her fist and listened.

"Mom and I have been thinking it might be time to sell the house and get into something smaller. Maybe somewhere in the country."

"That's a great idea, Jack."

Suddenly a whole new image of Jack took shape in Nicky's head. Evidently, he had begun to take charge of his life before this relapse.

Nicky went back to work and Jack played a few games of chess with himself before finally deciding to take a nap. In the intense heat of the afternoon, things started quieting down on the beach. Nicky stayed hard at work on her drawing until Winston nosed open the door and sent things flying with his tail.

Nicky saw a note on his collar and anxiously unfastened it. Again, the urgent slanted print. *Mom and Aunt Helen and "yours truly" are all looking forward to seeing you and your brother tonight. The party starts at six! Don't forget your loafers! I love you, Trip Alston. P.S. Malcolm's here too but you're my date.* She affectionately ran her finger over his crude drawing of a man and woman holding hands with a dog at their side.

She went to the phone and started to dial, then placed the receiver back in its cradle. It would be awkward if someone other than Trip answered. She quickly wrote a note saying she'd be down at six-thirty with her brother, tied it onto Winston's collar and led him out onto the porch.

"Go home, boy," she said as she scooted him down the steps. "Go on. Take this to Trip."

The dog obediently headed to the beach, but a stray Frisbee distracted him and he started nosing it around on the sand. Nicky ran down the steps and urged him on. A whistle sounded, and the dog stopped his play and looked up at the lone figure at the end of the Alston walkway, then galloped across the sand toward home. Nicky waved to Trip, then turned and ran back into the house.

Nicky woke Jack at six with a cold glass of freshly made lemonade. She wiped her hands, moist from the cool glass, on her terry robe and readjusted the towel wrapped around her wet hair. His freshly washed and ironed clothes lay on the bed next to him.

She brushed a shock of hair from his sweaty forehead. "We've got to get ready. Take a shower. I left a razor on the sink for you."

Nicky quickly dressed, anxiously glancing past the living room to Jack's bedroom every once in a while to make sure he was getting ready. When he finally emerged, his tall, blond good looks gave the outward appearance of health and vitality. If only they don't ask him too many questions, Nicky prayed.

"Jack," Nicky said, "I told Mrs. Alston you were in accounting." She said sheepishly, "You don't mind that little white lie, do you?"

Jack smirked. "You did better than Mom. At least you gave me a career I'm qualified to lie about. She told the nosy bitch across the street I was writing a book."

Nicky ran her hand down the side of his face. "Don't worry, Jack. I know one of these days you're going to make Mom and me really proud of you."

The two went out onto the porch and stood for a moment mustering their courage. Golden highlights ricocheted off the ocean surface with its endless muffled roar of rising and falling surf. They walked down the stairs toward the crowd sitting on lawn chairs chatting. Freshly scrubbed children played in the sand, and a crowd clustered around the waist-high tables eating oysters. Nicky saw Trip advancing and spoke under her breath, "Here he comes, Jack. Please be nice."

Trip wore a boldly colored tropical shirt neatly tucked in at the waist of his crisp linen slacks. The shirt rippled in the breeze as he extended his hand

and gave Jack a warm, friendly welcome. Nicky marveled at the easy way Southerners smiled. It seemed to come to them as naturally as breathing.

"Well, Jack, she sure has been keeping you to herself."

"I was tired from my long drive."

"Soon as the beer arrives, I'll get you something to drink."

Nicky avoided Trip's eyes. With memories of the night they spent together swirling in her mind, she felt like a hypocrite standing on formality. "Where's your mother?" she said as casually as she could.

Trip turned and faced the beach. "Here she comes now with Aunt Helen."

Elizabeth Alston and her sister smiled broadly as they neared. The Alstons elevated introductions to an art form. "Bless your heart, you're more darlin' than ever," Mrs. Alston chirped as she gave Nicky a hug.

Nicky barely breathed while listening to her brother chat about how lucky Mrs. Alston was to live in the beautiful city of Charleston. That's it, Jack! I knew you'd come through! His knowledgeable tidbits about the city's historic past and links with Boston were Nicky's payoff for years of lugging books home from the library to entertain him.

Nicky enjoyed the lyrical sound of Trip's mother's voice as she laughingly conversed with Jack. She had a trace more of an accent than her son, with the ends of some of her words charmingly lowering in tone.

Eventually, a bevy of old friends enveloped Mrs. Alston and her sister and drew them away. Trip stood with his hands on his hips and a grin of satisfaction on his face. "I'll start you two on the oysters while I get the music going ... and then, darlin', we're going to do some dancin'."

Nicky and Jack followed him to one of the tables. Trip reached into a pot and pulled out a mud-colored oyster with its craggy, rough shell, then picked up a small knife lying on the table. "Just pry them open ..." He dug out the insides with a fork and tossed the shell into a hole in the table. "... and dip them into this here." He offered the morsel drenched in cocktail sauce to Nicky. She slid it off the fork with her mouth and hummed approval.

Jack had already found a place at the table and was busy eating when Mac appeared with another pot, hollering, "How ya doin', Jack!"

Nicky threw Jack a sideways glance. When their eyes met, he shrugged and waved at Mac before gulping down an oyster.

Trip slipped his arm around Nicky's waist and whispered in her ear, "I don't know how I'm going to keep my hands off you tonight."

Malcolm yelled over, and Trip shouted back that he'd get the music going. He managed a discrete kiss on Nicky's cheek and promised he'd be back in a few minutes. As Nicky watched him go, she caught sight of the man who fixed Jack's carburetor. He was helping Johnny Bumps pour water into the pots.

Jack looked in the same direction, but his eyes locked onto another man unloading oysters from the back of Johnny's truck—the same one he had scrambled with at the Mole Hole.

Uta drifted over. While they chatted, Nicky noticed Uta smiling at Mac whenever she could catch his attention, and teased, "Why, Uta, you're flirting with him."

"You're not the only one who's after a man," Uta whispered.

Nicky straightened her back. "Uta!"

Uta nudged Nicky and winked. "I saw the way Trip ran up to greet you." She barely tossed her head toward a cluster of women. "And so did Miss America over there."

Nicky's eyes swept over the crowd and caught Kim staring at her. Nicky smiled awkwardly and returned her gaze to Uta. When Uta finally ran off, Nicky turned to Jack and asked him how he was doing.

"I got introduced like you wanted, now can I get the hell out of here?"

"Is something wrong, Jack?"

"No. I'm just sick of being nice."

Nicky felt uneasy, but it would look odd if they left so soon. "It's still too early, Jack. Please, hang on a little longer." She took him by the arm and walked him over to Mac who was standing at the stove behind a row of oyster pots.

"Okay, boys," Mac shouted to Eddie and Billy. "They're ready. Take 'em away. Bring back the empties." When Mac noticed Jack glaring at Eddie Tuck, he pulled Nicky aside and whispered, "I need to talk to you ..."

Suddenly, Trip came up from behind and clutched Nicky's shoulders. "She's all mine now, fellas!"

Trip led Nicky toward the dance floor. She looked back at Mac and her brother. The expression on their faces gave her a sickening sensation that something was terribly wrong. But the feeling quickly evaporated when Trip briskly sprinted onto the platform and pulled her up.

Elizabeth Alston and a cluster of her friends chatted and watched as Trip skillfully shuffled to the rhythm-and-blues music with Nicky comfortably falling in with the beat. The look on Mrs. Alston's face made Nicky wonder if she knew about her and Trip.

Nicky looked over the crowd until she spotted her brother standing compliantly with his arms folded next to Mac, who was busy shoveling oysters into a pot. So far, everything was running smoothly, but she didn't want to push her luck. After this dance she'd get Jack, thank Mrs. Alston and Trip for their hospitality, and leave with the excuse her brother was tired and she had to finish a drawing.

Nicky looked over at Mrs. Alston. Kim Dusenbury stood next to her, eyes fixed on Trip. Nicky didn't know why, maybe it was the woman's beauty, but her showing up at the party was worrisome.

A lot of the women were wearing the same type of ankle length casually chic dress as Kim. Nicky was wishing she'd put something on other than shorts and a tee shirt, when Trip gave her a playful wink and smoothly twirled her around, a look of confidence mixed with pride on his handsome face.

"You big show off!" she laughed. Thank God, Jack would be gone by Tuesday!

Malcolm appeared and whispered something in Trip's ear. Trip stopped dancing and guided Nicky to the side. "We've got to go get the beer and ice from the house. Malcolm was going to bring everything down in the wagon, but the golf cart won't start."

"Do you need my help?"

"No. I'll take as many of the guys as I can round up so we can get it all in one trip. Why don't you go talk with my mother and Aunt Helen? I'll be right back."

As Nicky wove through the crowd, Dede took her by the arm. "Did I see what I thought I saw? You ... *and Trippett Alston?*"

Nicky blushed.

Dede hugged her. "*You go, girl!*"

Nicky made her way over to Mrs. Alston and easily joined into conversation with the cluster of women. She filled with pride when Elizabeth Alston slipped her arm around Nicky's waist and pulled her close. She now firmly believed that Mrs. Alston knew about her relationship with Trip, and approved.

Kim Dusenbury spoke with a smile, but still, somewhere beneath all the friendliness, Nicky sensed the woman resented the way the Alstons had accepted her. That didn't matter, Nicky told herself. All she cared about was how Trip and his mother felt.

At first no one noticed the commotion near the truck. But little by little people stopped dancing until all were motionless, with The Dominos playing to a paralyzed audience.

You fuckin' redneck! pierced the air. Nicky recognized Jack's angry voice. Her ears burned. The crowd looked shocked and grim. The hushed children had expectation etched on their faces. Nicky's gaze searched desperately for Mac. She saw him off in the distance carrying a pail on his way to the ocean. She could see a scuffle over the heads of the crowd and quickly pushed her way into an open circle. Jack sat on the ground wiping blood from his lip with the back of his hand. She rushed to his aid, but the man who had been helping Johnny Bumps pushed her aside with such force she landed face down on the sand. A cry rose from the crowd.

A woman with a small child straddling her hip helped Nicky up. "My husband's gone for the beer. Let me see if I can get us some help."

Two young boys ran up to her. "We'll go get Dad!"

An old man stepped forward, saying with authority, "Here now, Eddie. Let's stop this." He put his hand on Eddie Tuck's shoulder and was thrown back onto a beach chair, collapsing it. Cries of outrage rose from those standing by. Eddie turned to Jack, grabbed him by the neck of his shirt and punched him.

Nicky, searching the throng of women and children for someone strong enough to help, thought she caught a fleeting glimpse of Billy skulking at the back of the crowd. For a split-second her eyes froze on the concerned expression on Elizabeth Alston's face, but the dreadful sound of another punch made her snap her head toward her brother. Desperation seized her. She ran and jumped on Eddie Tuck's massive back, wrapped her feet around him and pounded him with her fists. He grabbed her by her tee shirt and smacked her to the ground.

Determination was etched on Uta's features as she ran up and splashed a pitcher of lemonade in Eddie's face. Momentarily stunned, he stood dazed until Jack yanked one of his legs from under him and tossed him to the ground.

Nicky, still on the ground, thrust herself forward on her knees and tried to pull the two men apart. Suddenly, Jack rolled over her, pinning her to the ground. Nicky wriggled free and frantically tried to loosen the man's hands from around Jack's neck. Failing, she grasped his arm with both hands and dug her teeth in. He roared, grabbed her arm and flung her with such viciousness, the crowd gasped. He turned and started back on Jack.

Mrs. Alston, her face ashen, helped Nicky scramble up. Nicky raced toward the ocean screaming for Mac. He dropped his bucket and came running back. Meanwhile, Trip, Malcolm and the other men made their way to the middle of the throng. Malcolm held Jack back, as Eddie Tuck, clutching his bleeding arm, reluctantly made his way through the crowd and ran off toward the dunes.

Jack, struggling to get free from Malcolm's grip, jammed him in the ribs with his elbow, then broke loose and punched Trip in the nose. In a reflex motion, Trip threw a punch and knocked Jack to the ground.

Mac and Nicky pushed their way through the crowd. A hush fell. Kim stepped forward and tried to stop Trip's nosebleed with a beach towel. He took the towel from her, motioned her aside and hovered over Jack.

Trip's voice was stern. "That's enough. You get off this island and back to Boston where you belong. We've got enough Yankees around here."

Nicky ran up and dropped to her knees at her brother's side and anxiously examined his grotesquely swollen face. Her eyes blazed at Trip in disbelief. "How could you have hit him? He was already licked."

Trip was silent. All Nicky could see beyond the towel were his tightly narrowed eyes glaring back at her.

Kim tugged at Trip, but he was unmoved. Jack sat up and angrily blurted out, "You think you can push me around just because you're banging my sister!"

"Jack!" Nicky screamed.

"Now that you've got into her pants, we're nothin' but Yankees! She was a virgin before you got your cotton pickin' hands on her. If you have any decency you'll marry her!"

Nicky clutched her mouth with her fists and swallowed a scream. Mac pulled Jack up. "That's enough, fella. I'm taking you home."

Kim, with a shadow of a smile on her face, put her arm in Trip's as he looked around at the horror-stricken faces in the crowd.

Mrs. Alston took Trip's other arm and said, "Come, Son. We better be gettin' home."

As the three parted the crowd, Mrs. Alston looked over her shoulder at Nicky. The two women's eyes met briefly. Mrs. Alston lowered her lids and turned her head. Uta and a few others assisted the old man who had been tangled in the chair as he hobbled after Trip.

Nicky watched their backs and stoically listened to the muted comments of the slowly disbursing crowd.

"Rude Yankees," one man said. "If they don't like us, why don't they just go home and leave us be."

A woman bent down and gently put her hand on Nicky's shoulder. "You going to be okay, dear?"

Nicky looked up at Trip's Aunt Helen. "Yes, thank you."

The woman put her arm around Nicky's waist and helped her up. She examined Nicky's bleeding knees. "Bless your heart. There's no tellin' what could have happened if you hadn't fought so valiantly for your brother."

Mac, with one of Jack's arms slung around his shoulder, struggled to hold him up as he started toward the house. He paused and looked over at Nicky. "You comin'?"

Trip's aunt steadied Nicky as they trudged through the sand after Mac. When they reached the stairs, Nicky stopped. Avoiding the woman's eyes, she gripped the handrail and said, "Thank you very much. I think I can make it the rest of the way."

"Well, I better be getting back. They're probably fixin' to take Trip to the hospital."

Nicky wrinkled her brow. "Do you think he's badly hurt?"

"Don't worry, child. It'll take more than a broken nose to mar that handsome face."

By the time Nicky entered the house, Mac was putting his thirty years of experience patching up drunken sailors to work on Jack. Nicky stalked zombie-like to the bathroom and took a shower. When she came back into the living room in a pair of shorty pajamas, her wet hair slicked back, Mac handed her a shot of Dewar's and told her to drink it straight down.

"You want me to put somethin' on those knees?"

"No. I'll be all right."

"I could kick myself. I should never have let you bring your brother to the party."

"Oh, it's not your fault, Mac. I'm the guilty one."

"Don't you be goin' and sayin' things like that."

Nicky flopped down on the couch. "I shouldn't have left Boston 'til Jack got his life in order. It was selfish of me."

"Good gracious, gal! That's the whole trouble with you! You don't have a selfish bone in your body. You should have thought some about yourself years ago."

She leaned forward with her elbows on her knees and held her head at the temples. "You're right, Mac. All those times, I was just giving him a crutch. It's probably my fault he's the way ..." She fell into sobs.

Mac bent down, put his hand under her chin and lifted her head. "Look at me. Nothing's your fault. Things are just the way they are, and we do the best we can." He helped her up and into the bedroom. "Right now, you need some sleep."

He sat at the foot of the bed and patted her leg as she cried softly, then pulled the bandana off his neck and handed it to her. The kindness in the gesture made her break down.

"Oh, Mac. I'll never forget the way Trip looked at me."

"Don't worry, gal. He'll come round tomorrow."

A worrisome thought struck Mac. He wasn't at all certain things would be the same again. The kind of scene that had just occurred could easily be more than folks like the Alstons could take, especially Trip.

Anger tightened Mac's throat. Not at Trip or Jack. Not even at the lout from the Mole Hole who beat him up. It was the other one he was going to get even with. The one named Billy. He had heard him egging Jack on, and then when he went to the truck for more oysters, he heard him egging Eddie Tuck on behind Jack's back. He'd run across this type before. They called them well poisoners. Something was missing in their character—that little voice that tells you not to do something bad. Totally devoid of compassion, the only emotional high they get is when they hurt someone or something.

For weeks, Mac had been wondering what this guy was doing shacked up in the Deveroux Company's property. And now, he had a pricey new truck. Where was the money coming from? In the back of his mind Mac figured it had something to do with the new condo project, but for the life of him, couldn't figure out what.

He didn't know how long he sat there, but finally decided it wasn't a good idea to leave these two alone for the night. He went into the living room, sank into an overstuffed chair and fell asleep.

In the middle of the night, a male tree frog that must have been stuck on the porch gave out a series of loud nasal hollers. Mac stirred but drifted off again.

Nicky lay wide-awake in bed, tears tracing their way down her cheeks. She took care not to blow her nose too loudly and wake Jack. She rose and tiptoed into the living room. The sight of Mac asleep in a chair with his sneakers still on startled her. His ankles were thin for such a strong, broad-shouldered man. His legs from his knobby knees up to the frayed edge of his shorts were lean, muscular and leathery. He'd taken his cap off, and she could see his hair was still thick on top with dark ringlets sprinkled with gray. She kissed the top of his head and turned off the light.

She drifted out onto the porch and sank into a chair. Salem rubbed against her leg, and she drew the animal up onto her lap and gently stroked its fur. Ugly images of the fight shot into her brain and filled her with a burning shame until resentment took over. All she could see was the familiarity with which Kim held on to Trip as he turned his back and left her kneeling on the sand. What had she been thinking? Mac was right. How could she have believed she'd ever fit in with Trip and his crowd?

Nicky put the cat down and went into Jack's room to make sure he was breathing and caught a glimpse of his wide-open eyes and swollen face in the moonlight.

"Did I wake you, Jack?" she whispered.

He folded an arm underneath his head. "No. It was the damn frog."

Nicky sank down on the edge of the bed.

"I really screwed everything up for you tonight, didn't I?" said Jack.

Nicky blinked back tears.

"I knew that gorilla was going to come after me. I should have gotten the hell out of there."

"Is that why you wanted to leave early?"

"Yeah. He was the one I got into an argument with at the Mole Hole. I said some pretty rotten things to him that night. He's one of those damn rednecks who's still fighting the war, and like an asshole, I needled him."

A strong gust of ocean air fluttered Nicky's hair. She could tell by the smell and the sound of the waves that the ocean was at high tide and creeping up against the porch steps. Sending Jack out in the condition he was in the night he arrived, was a bad idea. She'd done it to get Trip, and that would be the very thing that was going to make her lose him.

"Do you hate me, Nicky?"

"No. I can't hate you, Jack."

In spite of her runny nose and tear-streaked face, she laughed dryly. "But, I could kill you."

"Thanks for sticking up for me tonight. It was just like old times when the public school kids would gang up on us. You were a little rusty, but I've got to hand it to you, you really gave that thug a run for his money."

Nicky wiped her face with her sleeve and sniffed in her runny nose. "But we're not in grade school any more, Jack."

"You're mad at me, aren't you?"

She ran her hand gently down his swollen face. "No. It just broke my heart to see someone hurting you." She took both his hands and clutched them. "Jack, you've got to absolutely promise me you're going to take your medicine. The next time I might not be around to take care of you."

"I promise. And I'm getting out of your hair tomorrow."

"You can't leave now. Your face is a mess."

"That boyfriend of yours was right. I don't belong here. And besides, Mom needs me. Believe it or not, before I stopped taking my pills I was a big help to her."

"I know. She told me. Jack, it made her so happy when you got well. I only wish Dad could have seen it."

"I love you, Sis."

She squeezed his hands. "I love you too, Jack. Now go to sleep."

She crept back to her room and got into bed, careful not to jangle the springs. She lay there in the darkness as Trip's words echoed in her brain: *You get off this island and back to Boston where you belong. We've got enough Yankees around here.* She squeezed her eyes shut and shook the image of Trip's squinty stare from her mind. Slowly, she began to feel separated from her body as she listened to the tide come in. The low, soft rumble of a new wave gradually grew until it peaked and crashed. In her mind's eye, she pictured the next wave slowly climb up, crash and spill casually over itself, creating a sudsy meandering edge of surf licking the sand. Again, and again, and again, the soft rustling roar slowly growing in intensity before breaking and splashing down. Mesmerized by this eternal rhythm, her tense muscles finally gave out, and she was lulled into a deep sleep.

🐚 CHAPTER NINETEEN

Malcolm leaned back in his chair, put his feet up on the desk and read the *Post*. When Trip walked in, he reached for his coffee and took a sip. "It's about time you showed up."

Trip dropped his briefcase on the desk, went over to the window and watched the landscape crew install a row of Indian Hawthorns. The clippity clop of a horse-drawn wagon full of tourists sounded on the street.

"I just stopped by to see if you were okay," said Malcolm. He folded the paper and tossed it on the desk. "You should have taken the week off."

Trip turned around. "How do I look?"

Malcolm studied his face. "I wouldn't get my picture taken any time soon."

"Thanks."

"You're lucky it's not broken. The swelling's almost gone. In a couple of days you'll be the same handsome old dog." Malcolm looked around at the stacks of boxes piled along the walls. "You want me to throw some of these in my truck and take them over to the new place?"

Trip didn't relish having to move all his files every time he completed a house, but since he preferred operating from his projects rather than some remote office, he had no choice.

"No. Thanks. Sonny's having everything hauled out of here this afternoon. I just came in to meet with the decorator."

"That wouldn't be the beautiful Kim Dusenbury by any chance, would it?"

Trip ignored the question, but his mind drifted to the tender way she wiped his face after the fight on the beach. It was good she had offered to show him the decorating plans for his friend's new offices. This way, maybe he'd be able to incorporate some of his design ideas into the building.

"Didn't you think it odd her showing up without her fiancé?"

173

"Don't go there, Malcolm."

Trip sank into his chair, swiveled around, and casually looked out at the activity in the yard.

The men were quiet for a moment. Finally, Malcolm spoke. "Have you talked to her yet?"

Trip shifted uncomfortably in his chair. For the past three nights he had started to phone Nicky a hundred times, but something kept stopping him. It wasn't just anger over the swollen nose, although it hurt like hell. He hated the way the ugly outbreak sealed the end of the island's genteel tradition and heralded in a new, menacing character. Then there was Dr. Elliot having to treat Charlie Nash's leg that was torn up by the beach chair. At least the old man hadn't had another heart attack. That night, tended by the doctor who delivered him and surrounded by people he'd known for most of his life, Trip felt strangely distanced from Nicky. She came from another world, and he could see now that this was never going to work.

The pathetic image of her flushed, sweaty face with its mesmerizing blue eyes pleading for him to acknowledge her gnawed at him. He hated himself for turning his back on her, but somehow at that moment she had represented everything he detested.

"Well, did you?"

Trip swung around and reluctantly shook his head.

Malcolm rose. "I know it's none of my business, but that girl's the best thing that ever happened to you. Trip, it's about time you got yourself a life. For Pete's sake, you're forty."

"Thanks, again."

"So, she's got a nutty brother. So what! You heard what your mother said; she fought for him like a tiger."

"Sure. We'd make a great team. Every time I have a beef with a contractor, I could sic her on 'em."

"She's exactly the kind of girl you need. Hell, man, I've never seen you so crazy about anyone."

Malcolm crossed the room to the door and suddenly stopped. He slapped the casing and swung around to face Trip. "Damn it! I know you. This is the perfect excuse not to make a commitment. You're just going to let this thing fester until she slips away like all the rest." He shook his head. "Buddy, this is one heart I hate to see you break. I'd go after her myself, but the funny thing is, I'm not what she's looking for. I'm not pathetic enough!"

Trip listened to Malcolm's truck door slam and the wheels spin out on the soft stones. Malcolm's apparent feelings for Nicky troubled him, but nowhere near as much as the melee on the beach that night. Maintaining the dignity of his family name had always been important. It came with a price, but in the end it was worth it. When he walked into a room and looked someone in the eye, he did it with an unshakeable confidence that could spring only from being the end product of generations of honor. How could he merge his family with the likes of Nicky's?

Yet, he couldn't remember ever feeling as right about anyone. But now the feeling was gone. Still, he should never have left her on the beach the way he did. He admitted to himself that there was more dishonor in his abandoning her than in Jack's ugly words.

The more he thought about it, the more he hated himself. He didn't want to face Kim in the frame of mind he was in, so he decided to call her office and leave a message with her secretary that he couldn't make their meeting. And then he was going to put Nicky out of his mind and concentrate on the island.

He may have struck out with all the women in his life, but he wasn't licked yet on this condo deal. He picked up the phone and started to dial. Suddenly a sickening feeling descended upon him. That morning after studying his face, in a moment of anger, he went downstairs and put Winston on his chain.

Nicky took two aspirins from the bottle and washed them down with a glass of water. Hopefully they would help with the cramps from her period. Past noon and still in her pajamas, she went over and curled up on the sofa. The light blue chintz fabric dotted with small red and yellow flowers testified to its gracing an elegant room at one time; but now, it was an aged workhorse, its tattered arms the victim of hundreds of children's soiled hands. She stared aimlessly out at the ocean and kept running her fingers along the leash draped around her neck.

An unfinished illustration lay ignored on the drawing board and Salem stood mewing at an empty dish. Unnoticed, he sat down, made himself comfortable and waited patiently. The room was quiet except for the distant roar of the ocean and the sound of the animals on the porch scratching around their cages for tidbits of food.

"Yoo-hoo!"

Uta's nose suddenly rubbed against the screen.

"Found you!"

Nicky buried her swollen, tear-soaked face in her hands and moaned.

Uta boldly opened the door, marched over to Nicky and stood over her with her hands on her hips. "Oh no you don't. I haven't seen you on the

175

beach for two days. You've spent enough time sulking."

She marched off to the kitchen and started making coffee. When Nicky appeared in the doorway blowing her nose, Uta popped in the filter and said, "So has he called?"

"Who?"

Uta's tone was mockingly scornful as she poured two heaping spoonfuls of grounds into the filter and slapped it into the coffeemaker. "You know who. Did he?"

Nicky hugged herself and shook her head.

Uta took two cups from the dish drain and put them on a tray firmly enough to make a statement. "That man's more stubborn than Mac, and he's a snob to boot." She took Nicky by the arm. "Come, dear. Let's go sit down."

Uta purposely spoke loud enough for Jack to hear. "Where's the big troublemaker?"

Nicky sat down, brought her legs up and hugged them, then curled her toes around the edge of the seat. "He's out filling the car with gas and getting the oil checked."

"Good! So he's going."

"Tomorrow."

"That awful Eddie Tuck. Something should be done about him. You look at him sideways and he's liable to kill you. Your brother started a fight with the wrong guy."

"Wait a minute, Uta. What makes you think my brother started the fight?"

Uta shrugged.

Nicky frowned and said tersely, "Is that what everybody thinks?"

Uta dismissed the question with a brisk wave of her hand. "Ach! It doesn't matter. Once your brother's out of here it'll all blow over." She tossed her hand in the air as if she were shushing away all the problems. "Look at Dede the other night. You'd think she wouldn't have the nerve to come to the oyster roast after what happened at her party. But apparently it's just water over the dam to her and everyone else."

Uta got up to fetch the coffee, her voice trailing from the kitchen. "Right now, we've got to concentrate on the public hearing Thursday. When we all went back to Trip's house, Mrs. Alston told us the county council has already given the Deveroux Company a verbal approval for the condos no matter what the planning board recommends."

When she returned with the coffee and saw Nicky quietly sobbing, she put the tray down and pulled a chair up next to her. In a voice thick with sympathy, she said, "I don't know what made you think Trippett

176

Alston could get serious about a girl like you. That family thinks they're better than everyone else."

Nicky blew her nose. "Oh, Uta, that's not true. Mrs. Alston has been wonderful to me. And Trip's not like that at all. He said he loved me."

Uta threw her hands in the air and cried, "Ooh! Do you have any idea of all the women he's loved and left! You've only been here for a couple of months. I've watched them come and go through that revolving door in his bedroom for the past fifteen years!"

A long tearful moan tightened Nicky's throat. Uta reached over and patted her head. "Yours isn't the first heart he's broken." She pursed her lips. "And I'm sure it won't be the last."

Nicky held back a cry as she furrowed her forehead.

Uta squeezed her hand. "Listen, child. You've got to forget that Romeo. In the first place, he's too old for you." She got up and coaxed Nicky from her chair. "Come. I'll help you clean the cages."

Nicky stood up and blew her nose again. Uta slipped the leash from around Nicky's neck and jiggled it around in her hand. "So the bastard didn't let Winston come over today, did he?"

Nicky buried her head in her hands and quietly sobbed. Uta put an arm around her shoulder and led her out onto the porch. "Don't vorry. Trip's never been able to keep that dog at home where it belongs." She rolled her eyes. "Ask anyone on the island."

Trip drove north quite a way past the Chertaw Island turn off in order to catch Skeeter Nash in his office. It was located in a house on the only street in McClellanville that could in any way be described as a business district. In fact, three fish packing houses on the creek, a small grocery store and a couple of shops were the only commercial activity in this remote fishing village other than Skeeter's law practice.

Trip pulled onto a lawn that someone had sprinkled with a light layer of gravel in a half-hearted attempt to make it look like a parking lot. Skeeter's red '75 Chevy Malibu with its license plate imprinted with *Law One* sat under the shade of a live oak next to the house. Black mold covered the porch and the narrow front hall reeked with the smell of age, mildew and neglect.

The paralegal, who everyone knew did most of Skeeter's work, sat behind stacks of folders that would have been neatly filed away if only there had been enough cabinets. She looked the same as she had the last time Trip saw her—upper arms bulging like giant sausages from her cheap sleeveless top, and broad hips spilling out over her chair. She had an air of quiet resignation about her, necessary for a job where one does all the work and gets none of the credit.

She gave Trip a friendly but fleeting smile as she picked up the phone and notified Skeeter of his arrival, then gracefully shifted her heavy bulk in her chair as she processed the papers on her desk.

The room was quiet except for the whooshing of the ceiling fan. The reception area was devoid of anything that remotely resembled décor. The walls were bare and cardboard filing cartons sat on the floor. If it weren't for the thick layer of dust on everything, one would get the impression that they had just moved in. A door opened at the end of the hallway and Skeeter, wearing shorts, a tee shirt and sandals, welcomed his old friend with a languid wave.

Skeeter had good reason not to be rushed. As the recipient of an enormous inheritance, he felt obligated to take the time to enjoy all the pleasures he deemed worthwhile.

He lived in the same house he was born in next to the creek overlooking the marsh and ocean, and tried to arrive at work every day promptly at three-thirty in the afternoon to officiate at any closings or appointments his paralegal had set up for him. Other than that, his days were filled with fishing, sailing and reading the *Wall Street Journal*. The only reason he was willing to take time to serve on the county's planning board, was to have a hand in preserving what was left of the South he loved.

It was a good thing Skeeter liked living in McClellandville, for he'd never make it in the capitols of the New South where there was little room left for the eccentricities of a laid-back good ole boy who expected to have everything go his way simply by virtue of his high birth. But be that as it may, he was generally kindly and easy to do business with.

Trip declined the chair Skeeter offered with a gesture. "How can the council go ahead and make this sort of agreement before getting the planning board's recommendation?"

Skeeter was one of three lawyers on the county's seven-member planning board. He answered knowledgeably. "A development agreement is allowed by state law. It's a device intended to give developers protection from changing local regulations in exchange for public benefits. And it's the council's job to negotiate them."

Trip ran a hand back from his forehead. "What public benefits?"

"Deveroux's donating twenty acres of land they own along the Cooper River to the county for a park in exchange for rezoning the peninsula from residential to planned unit development."

"Is the planning board willing to allow Chertaw Island to be destroyed for that?"

"That li'l ole park will be enjoyed by thousands of voters, as opposed to the privileged handful that own property on your island. You gotta face the facts, boy; the board is lined up solid behind this deal. Basically, the zoning change and the development agreement are following parallel courses. The only thing I can suggest is that you make a compelling case at our public hearing this Thursday. Maybe you can sway them. But even if you do, the council can turn right around and ignore our recommendation and approve the plan. And it looks like that's exactly where this here thing's headed."

A small air-conditioning unit in the window hummed incessantly in a futile effort to cool the room, while Trip looked around searching for some reason why all this was happening.

Skeeter quietly drummed the eraser end of a pencil on his desk. "Maybe I can stall this whole thing another month by making a motion that the planning board ask the Regional Council of Governments to review Deveroux's plans. If I can get it passed, you could use that time to come up with something."

"Please do that."

Trip thanked Skeeter and started for the door. He turned and asked, "By the way, how are you coming on the island's new zoning laws?"

"We've got letters going out to every owner notifying them of a public hearing at the church on the mainland. I'm afraid we're closing the barn doors after the horses are gone, but at least we can make sure these condos will be the last to go up."

Trip headed out of town encouraged. For the first time since he awakened, he was able to suppress the gnawing fears for the island. However, as he swung onto Highway 17, they were replaced by guilt as he allowed the person he had pushed out of his mind all day to edge back into his consciousness.

He noted Nicky's brother's car was gone when he passed the King's Nest, and fought off the urge to swing into the driveway. As he pulled up to his house, Winston strained on his chain. Trip got out of the truck, vigorously rubbed him down, then unfastened the chain. But instead of Winston following Trip up the steps to the front door, he stood with brows furrowed staring up at him.

"Come on, boy," Trip coaxed from the top of the landing. Winston pranced impatiently. Trip shifted his weight, looked out over the dunes at the ocean for a moment, then tossed his head and said, "Okay, boy. I give up. Go on over there."

After watching the dog sprint down the beach, he opened the door, threw his keys on the counter and brought out the vermouth. He got out a pitcher and mixed some Manhattans, his eyes continuously drawn to the heart-shaped drawing pinned to the wall. He poured himself a drink, snatched up the *Post* and padded into the living room.

The old furniture with its fond memories fit comfortably in the enormous room. Much better than Kim's purple sofas. He strolled into the study. His eyes roamed the sparsely furnished space and calculated Nicky's drafting table would easily fit. He shook his head and decided he must be crazy for having such an insane thought and returned to the living room.

The headline in the local news section read: *Turtle's Plight Could Hold Up Island Development*. He had read every word at the office but savored the article again. When his eyes landed on *Nicole Sullivan*, he stopped and gazed at the words, but all he could see were vivid blue eyes, and ringlets, soft from sweat, framing a face with an impish smile.

He'd only known her as a tenderhearted caretaker of injured animals, and would have found a story of her attacking Eddie Tuck hard to believe if he hadn't seen it for himself. He couldn't erase the image of her frazzled appearance and the unwaveringly determination on her face as she made her way through the crowd to help her brother. A deep longing took hold of him, and it wasn't until he gulped down his second drink that he was able to overcome the urge to run over to her house like Winston.

The stones crunched softly below the tires of the red BMW roadster as it rolled to a stop in front of Trip's King Street project. Kim saw Trip watching her through the window. She got out and reached in the back for her illustration boards, mindful that her short skirt crept up as she bent over.

Trip greeted her with an open door and a familiar smile as she ran up the steps. The clicking of her high heels echoed in the downstairs parlor, empty except for an old table. She breezed in and put her sketches down. Her light blue suit, tight at the waist, defined her figure, as did the shapely legs earned over a lifetime of playing tennis.

The first few moments were uncomfortable. Both of them knew they were there for more than just looking over some plans.

Kim gently grasped Trip's jaw and examined his face. "It's not that bad, sweetheart. Does it hurt?"

"Only when I laugh."

Kim moved to get the business part over with first and presented her proposal. Trip commented from time to time, but mostly his eyes traced her neck and stunning features.

He couldn't help thinking how cool she looked and kept comparing her silky blond hair with the sweaty ringlets that always seemed to circle Nicky's flushed face.

Finished, Kim put her boards down and sat on the edge of the table. "Well, darlin'? What do you think?"

He took a lock of her hair in his hand and looked her in the eye and told her he'd never forget her scent, and she laughed the way he remembered she did. She kicked off her heels and lay back on the table. Without taking her eyes off him, she slowly unbuttoned her jacket exposing her lacey bra.

She inhaled deeply and drew her shoulders toward him. "You'd like it right here in your li'l ole house, wouldn't you, darlin'?"

He gripped her thigh and reached under her jacket for a bra strap and had to catch his breath when he peeled it back and saw her perfect rounded breast. She wriggled out of her panties with a good deal of help from Trip. But then he suddenly paused and looked past her as if she weren't there, and slowly scrunched the small silky piece of lingerie in his hands.

Kim propped herself up on her elbows, her long hair tumbling over her shoulders. "What's the matter, sugar?"

Trip fingered the panties absentmindedly, then went over to the window and stared out onto King Street.

Kim sat up. "Dang! It's that no count little Yankee." She jumped off the table and lunged toward him, her shoulders coiling like a snake ready to strike. "It's her, *isn't it?*"

Trip stared out the window, motionless.

"Trippett Alston, I can't believe it! I just can't believe it! She's as common as dirt! You're going to disgrace your family. *Your mother. Your father.*"

She grabbed Trip by the shoulder with such force he spun around. Her beautiful face was hideously contorted. Even in their worst fights, he'd never seen her like that.

"Look at me, Trip! I declare, that Yankee's in high cotton latchin' on to an Alston!"

Trip glowered at her.

His look signaled to Kim that she was going too far. She flicked back her hair and now spoke in a soft melodic, if somewhat shaky, tone as she ran her hands down his chest. "Trip, honey, her kind would never fit in with the likes of us. She wouldn't know how to act. Face it, darlin', she doesn't even know how to dress ... and never will. And think of that horrible, disgusting family of hers."

His cold dispassionate look sent her into another rage.

"How can you insult me like this? I waited around for you for *five whole years*. Everyone's goin' to know you passed me over for that pathetic little Yankee *sslllut!*"

Trip bit his lip and grimaced. "Don't call her that."

With the hand that was known in tennis circles to lob a crushing serve, she slapped his face. "*I'll call her what I like!*"

Trip covered his nose with his hand and winced in pain. But his tortured moans failed to elicit an ounce of pity. Instead, Kim lunged at him and pounded on his chest, sobbing hysterically, until he grasped her by the shoulders and held her at arm's length.

He took a long look at her, but rather than a red splotchy face, what registered on his consciousness was a vision of the graceful Kim Dusenbury regally descending her father's grand staircase for their first date. He blinked back tears and cupped her head in his hand and pulled her close to him.

"Kimmy, you go on back to that fiancé of yours. He's a much better catch than I am." He closed his eyes. "And never mind about Nicky; I don't think I'll ever get her back."

She pulled away and threw her hand back to give him another slap he wouldn't forget, but he caught it in midair. She wriggled her wrist loose and let out an anguished scream. She went over to the table and put on a shoe, hopping around on one foot trying to keep her balance.

She paused for a moment, gave him a measured look, then hobbled over and yanked her panties out of his hand. Once back to the table, she found the other shoe and shoved her foot in. She swished her hair from her face and with jerky motions buttoned her jacket, grabbed her drawings and started out of the room.

Suddenly she stopped and turned with a somewhat amused expression on her face. "Mister, you're never going to amount to *nothin'.*" Her smile broadened as she said, "You know why? *I'll tell you why.*" She planted a hand on her hip and sneered. "You've blown every God-given opportunity you ever had." She looked him up and down. "And another thing, darlin', you're *too old* for that girl."

Jeff Roberts' truck whizzed past the flat countryside dotted with fields of cotton and sweet potatoes on the way to the TV studio in Columbia. Except for occasional pleasantries with his passenger, Nicole Sullivan, Jeff remained quiet as he turned over in his mind everything he could say to help the loggerhead, for he was a man more of action than words.

Raised along the creek, he had an abiding love for the creatures of the ocean. Apart from his small electrical business, he spent most of his time coordinating his cadre of volunteers who kept watch over the sea turtles nesting along the South Carolina coast. Everyone had been surprised when he and his wife of thirty years broke up. However they remained friends and displayed no animosity toward each other, leaving everyone to believe she was just plain tired of playing second fiddle to the turtles.

Jeff had been working to save the turtles before anyone in South Carolina even noticed there were any. And as much as he loved these sea creatures, he loved his dedicated team of volunteers even more. Like him, they were driven by a deep conviction that the earth belonged as much to the turtles as to humans, and that by walking the beaches every day in all sorts of weather counting and protecting their nests, they could make a difference in the very survival of the species.

The two arrived at Channel 13 and waited in a lounge until they were ushered into the studio during a station break. Someone attached mikes to their clothing while the host, a man is his forties, gave them a brief coaching, ending with a slightly cynical warning to avoid looking at the dozens of monitors all over the room when the camera was on them, lest they get struck dumb with fear.

Suddenly they were on camera with the host smiling and commenting on an e-mail he'd received about a prior program.

"This sounds like this guy's got some kind of ultra-liberal environmental agenda going here."

The comment made Nicky's hands sweat.

He introduced his two guests and rushed Nicky through her story of coming to the beach and discovering the plight of the loggerhead as if it were extraneous information. Every time she tried to explain herself, he cut her off with a comment that never failed to label her as a transplant from outside the state. It wasn't until a drawing of Loretta Caretta appeared on the screen that she noticed him smile for the first time. When he switched his attention to Jeff, Nicky had to take several long breaths before she could refocus on the show.

A picture of Jeff repeated over and over again on dozens of screens in the darkened room. He methodically sketched out the efforts of his volunteers and the condominium threat. The host kept interrupting in an obvious effort to engage him in a debate, but Jeff doggedly plodded along, telling the story of the loggerhead in detail.

Nicky studied Jeff on a screen. He looked so pallid and his voice so drone-like, she realized he was too nervous to stop talking. She could see by the expression on the host's face that he was concerned about losing his audience.

"Sure. I feel sorry for the turtles," the host interjected. "But who's worrying about the fishermen! The government's got them so regulated they can hardly make a living. Tell me, what's important here?"

Nicky spoke up before she knew what she was doing. She had one eye on the host and another on a screen with a blow-up of her face. "If we don't regulate our over-fished waters now, there won't be anything left for their grandchildren to catch!"

A broad smile appeared on the host's face as he addressed his audience. "Well, well now. It looks like the lady from the North thinks we need her to tell us what to do?" He gathered the papers in front of him and drummed them into a neat stack in a triumphant manner. *"I guess they don't have any problems up there to tend to?"*

"Sir, this is a universal cause that's getting attention from people all over the world. Volunteers number in the hundreds and they're patrolling nesting grounds from the Carolinas to Florida. Right now these turtles are endangered, and if we don't help, it's possible that two hundred million years of their evolution can be snuffed out in a couple of generations."

Nicky sat up straight and attempted to get the emotion out of her voice, but found it impossible. "When you think of what's happened to the fisheries along our coast in our very lifetime, it won't take too much of a stretch of the imagination to figure out what we can do to something as precious as Loretta Caretta."

The host's response surprised her. "Let's put up one of the young lady's drawings."

Nicky glanced over at a screen showing one of her turtle drawings.

The host continued in a softened tone. "I've fished these coastal waters all my life, and neither I nor anyone else in South Carolina would like to see these ancient animals disappear."

His words calmed Nicky and she began to speak more easily. "No one wants all the condominiums to disappear either. But there has to be a balance. There's room enough for everyone if we use proper planning."

Nicky could see by the large clock on the wall that their time was nearly up, and that the next guest was standing to the side.

While Jeff's cell phone number flashed on the screen, the host asked anyone who wanted to join in their effort to call. A station break cut in, and the mikes were taken off and the next guest seated.

The two were quiet on the drive back, for the confrontational nature of the interview had dampened their spirits. Jeff kept reproaching himself for being so nervous that he didn't even hear the host's questions, and Nicky regretted she'd been baited into being as aggressive as the host.

Just before they reached the island, Jeff's phone rang. After a few moments, his expression changed to elation and he gave Nicky an enthusiastic thumbs-up. Several members of the influential Charleston County League of Women Voters had seen the show and decided to get behind their cause.

"I can answer the damn phone," Walter Satterfield shouted. "For Christ's sake. I'm paying you to screen my calls!" Walter sat down heavily in his chair. His secretary anxiously straightened the files on his desk, then scurried out as Tommy Warren, Jr., walked in and took a chair.

"What's going on, Walter?"

He waved a finger at the door. "If she puts one more nature freak through to me, her ass is out of here! It's about time our PR department started earning their keep!"

Tommy knew what had gotten to Satterfield. Ever since the TV show, he began meeting with resistance from the planning board. For the first time, they were asking about the turtles' habitat instead of what they were going to get from Deveroux. He wasn't looking forward to the public meeting tonight, especially after reading the morning paper.

He tossed a copy of the *Post* to Walter. "Have you seen this?"

Walter leaned back in his chair and impatiently tapped his fingers on the desk. "Lay it on me."

"The League of Women Voters has come out against us."

"It's that damn TV program!" He gathered his thoughts. "I want you to get a tape of it. If those two said anything that wasn't true ... I mean *anything*, I want you to sue their ass off! They need to be taught a lesson!" Walter stood up, walked to the window and looked out at the sunny day that seemed to be laughing at him. "I'll have our PR department put pressure on that newspaper too. Shit! We spend thousands with them!"

Tommy didn't mind change. He welcomed it. But not mindless change that sacrificed more than it was worth. Walter Satterfield's arrogance in believing he could buy anything rankled Tommy and personified the attitude that was eating away at the South. Tommy knew he'd live to regret it, but he couldn't help himself from saying, "This turtle issue strikes at everyone's heart, Walter. There are some things money can't buy."

Walter's fist came down on the desk with a thud. "You watch me! Get that damn land from Mac and I'll show you what money can buy!"

Tommy didn't know that Walter was just as sick of the whole mess as he was. The Deveroux board of directors was pushing him hard. So hard, his doctor had set up an appointment for a stress test.

Walter's cell phone rang. Only two people had the number, and he knew the call wasn't from his wife. He took the phone from his breast pocket and gave Tommy a look that told him to leave.

Tommy rose. "Okay, Walter. I'll give Mac a full-court press this week."

Walter asked him to close the door behind him. Satisfied that no one could hear, he flipped open his cell phone and frowned as he listened to the insidious voice.

"Well, did you find me a job yet?"

For the past few days Walter had vacillated between the two unappealing options of either throwing a big enough chunk of money at Billy to keep him away for a couple of months, or setting him up in a job so he could keep an eye on him. He finally made up his mind.

"Actually, I do have something for you. We're going to need security once our project starts up on the island. Someone to open the gate in the morning, check vehicles during the day and lock up again at night."

Walter listened intently for a response.

"Can I stay at the beach house?"

"I suppose so. That way you can make periodic checks during the night."

Walter smiled to himself. Now he was getting somewhere. He'd have the beach house razed once the project was finished.

"Can I carry a gun?"

Walter, figuring he could get the contractor to hire Cleary and also deal with the gun issue, agreed.

"That's more like it, Walter. When am I goin' to start?"

"Sit tight until we get the go ahead from the county and close on the land. Maybe a month."

Walter snapped his phone closed, placed it on his desk and smiled for the first time in weeks. That's the ticket! This idiot wants power and thinks he's going to get it with some crappy gatekeeper job. Slowly, the smile started to fade. It began to dawn on Walter that Billy might have something else in mind.

🐚 *Chapter Twenty*

Cheryl Washington's sense of herself had been shaped by her family's American journey, the beginnings of which now lay scattered on the sand. She spotted an old rocker jutting out from underneath a heap of battered wood and could hear her grandfather as he rocked back and forth. "The front porch is fuh listenin' and the back porch fuh washin'."

She heard him bragging about his father who everyone said had a voice so clear you could hear him from creekside to the river as he taught the children history with his songs. *When the Big Ship Went Down* was one of her grandfather's favorites, and she loved hearing him sing the story of the sinking of the Titanic he remembered from his childhood.

To see this tradition end in a heap on the sand distressed her, but how could she blame her father and uncle? Segregation had been more than enough reason to turn their backs on South Carolina. And after all it took to pull themselves up from nothing, raise kids and put them through college, she could hardly begrudge them the comfort of joining the ranks of the well off. She bent down, moved some planks and tugged at the rocker.

The moment Billy had spotted the self-possessed black woman trudging toward the peninsula, something about the confident way she planted her feet in the sand made him suspect it was she who was supposed to get the place, and she had come to look for the will. That was the only reason why Satterfield could have wanted it so badly. Convinced as he was it was nowhere to be found since he'd gone through the place twice before it blew down, her combing through the debris threatened him just the same.

"Girl! Whatcha doin' there?"

Cheryl let go of a plank and slowly rose. She was tall and slim with high cheekbones and fine features. Sweat had seeped through her tee shirt, putting a dark blot across the Ohio State emblem.

"What I'm doin' here is none of your business."

"I'm security around here and I ain't takin' no crap from no nigger."

"Don't you talk to her like that!" Nicky shouted. She had come up the path just in time to hear. Winston strained on his leash.

The two turned and stared at Nicky.

The young black woman smiled as she put her hands on her hips and sashayed toward Billy. "My family still owns this whole end of the island and if you don't leave right now I'm gonna go to the cops."

Billy held his ground. "I'm workin' for the Deveroux Company and was checkin' to make sure you had a right to be here."

"They don't own it yet," Nicky said. "So why don't you just leave."

Billy glared at her. "You sho like to come to folk'es rescue, don't you?" He grinned vilely and threw up his hands. "You're not gonna bite me, are ya?"

Nicky glared back at him. Remembering what Mac had told her about him egging Jack on, her voice filled with bitter resentment. "You heard what she said." She took a step forward. "Now leave!"

A low, rolling guttural sound came from Winston as he bared his teeth.

Billy's eyes landed on the dog and then Nicky. He gave her a lingering nasty look and slowly turned and walked off.

Nicky faced the young woman. "I'm sorry he talked to you like that."

She tossed her head in Billy's direction. "It's people like him that made my dad leave this place."

"He gives me the creeps," said Nicky.

"You're not from around here, are you?"

"No. I'm just staying at my sister-in-law's place."

"Take my advice. You don't want to be messin' with that kind of dude. Just blow him off."

The girl bent down and picked up an old wooden spoon and tapped it on the palm of her hand.

Nicky said, "You're Cheryl Washington, aren't you?"

"Yeah. I came to clean some stuff out of the cabin, but ..." She looked around and shrugged her shoulders.

"I picked up some things after the hurricane."

Cheryl's gaze shot over to Nicky. "Really? What?"

"Come over to my place and I'll show you."

Cheryl bent down and started tugging at the rocker. "Can you help me get this out first?"

They struggled with planks entangled in wire but finally released the chair. Nicky smiled to herself for the first time in days as she helped drag it to Cheryl's pickup. Someone who could go through a confrontation with someone like Billy with mellow confidence was just the friend she needed right now. After they put the chair in the back of the truck and Winston jumped in, Cheryl pulled off the sand drive and Nicky directed her to the King's Nest. When they passed Billy on the way, Nicky glanced at the side view mirror and saw him angrily waving his middle finger at them, and decided it would be wise to heed Cheryl's advice.

Cheryl said the truck was an old four-wheel drive that one of her brothers used to clear snow off the driveway in the winter and haul things to the dump in the summer. A small New York Giants helmet swung from the rear view mirror, and snack food wrappers lay on the seat along with a scattering of music tapes. Nicky squeezed her legs into a space next to a large duffel bag sitting on the floor.

Nicky had been fighting off a desperate yearning to go back home ever since the oyster roast. Helping Cheryl gather up her family memories just might give her reason to stay.

At the King's Nest, Nicky went directly to the bureau, brought out the pictures and delivered them into Cheryl's hands. She went to the kitchen for lemonade and cookies, and returned to find Cheryl rocking back and forth on the worn couch, caressing the picture of the slave.

Nicky sat down beside her. "I wish someone had let you know the house was gone."

Cheryl nodded.

"How long were you planning on staying?"

"A couple of weeks. I borrowed my brother's truck so I could bring some things home, but it looks like I'll be heading back tomorrow."

"Why don't you stay with me? There's plenty of room and I'd enjoy some company." Nicky searched her brain for something more compelling. "And we can dig through that pile for more of your family's things. There's got to be a lot of stuff underneath those boards."

The girl looked calculatingly at Nicky for a long while. Nicky nudged the plate of cookies toward her and said she made them with double the chocolate morsels. The girl laughed like she knew she'd been had, and agreed to stay.

Later in the afternoon, Cheryl unpacked while Nicky started dinner. The screen door slammed. Nicky looked up from the kitchen and caught sight of Winston running across the walkway on his way home. She tossed the sliced tomatoes into the salad and started peeling a cucumber. Trip would be hitting the house in a few minutes, and until Winston returned in the morning, she would hold her breath waiting to see if he would come see her. Thank God, Cheryl had shown up before she lost her mind. Six nights had passed without Trip coming over or calling, and all she'd been doing was vacillating from questioning his intentions to remembering his and his mother's tenderness to her. Malcolm's glib remark about all his girl friends when they were at Dede's party was burning a hole in her brain. And every time she recalled Uta's description of his bedroom having a revolving door she collapsed into a hopeless tear-jag.

Her face had been too puffy for her to go to the meeting the night before. When Uta showed up to tell her the planning board had recommended that the council turn down Deveroux's application, all enthusiasm had drained from her friend's face when she saw her.

Halfway through dinner, Nicky's voice trailed off in the middle of a sentence. She strained to hear the far off clinking of Winston's tags. Cheryl, whose chair was facing the door, didn't take any notice until she heard the sound of footsteps on the walkway. She looked up, and then leaned toward Nicky and whispered, "I think it's Trippett Alston out there."

Nicky rose. "I'll be right back."

She brushed by Trip on the walkway without speaking, and sat down on the steps. He sat down next to her and wrung his hands. Twice, he took a deep breath as if he were going to say something, but fell silent.

"I was quite a louse the other night, wasn't I?"

"I think my brother would agree with you."

He cracked his knuckles. "I don't know what got into me. I just ..."

"You don't have to explain, Trip. I understand." The hurt over losing her boyfriend in Massachusetts after he witnessed one of Jack's episodes flooded back to her. "It's not the first time something like this has happened to me."

He put his arm around her. She pulled away.

"I think we should cool it until we get to know each other better. We were pretty reckless the other night. I could have gotten pregnant."

Their eyes met and her look told him she wasn't. Her glance fell to her lap and his swept toward the ocean.

He rested his forearms on his legs and sank forward. "I suppose you've heard about the meeting last night."

Nicky's eyes riveted on the long lean back that ended with broad shoulders. Her throat tightened painfully as she remembered clutching him as he made love to her. She swallowed hard and said, "Uta came over this morning."

"You should have been there. Standing room only." He laughed bitterly. "In the middle of my density presentation someone yelled out, 'what about the turtles,' and Jeff had to take over. I guess I was really wrong about what moved people." He put a hand on her leg. "Nicky ..."

She stood up and leaned against the railing. "Cheryl Washington's here. She's going to stay with me for a while. I gave her the photos."

Trip rose and put his arms around her. She shook him off. "No, Trip! I mean it! I just want to be friends for now." She started up the stairs. "Come say hello to Cheryl."

He shook his head. "Tell her I'll drop by some other time." He turned abruptly and headed for the hard-packed sand at the edge of the surf. He broke into a run. Nicky was glad when Winston raced across the sand after him. She watched until they were specs on the horizon, then turned and went back into the house.

Cheryl looked up from clearing the dishes. "Hey, girl. Looks like you and Trip are getting it on."

Nicky sank into an overstuffed chair, tears running freely down her cheeks. "We were."

Nicky covered her face with her hands and fell into a fit of crying. Cheryl put the plates down and rushed over. After some comforting, Nicky told her about Trip and the fight on the beach and poured her heart out like only a woman can to another.

"Land's sakes, girl. I can't imagine you biting anyone."

Nicky nodded glumly and got up to get a tissue.

"No lie, girl, did your brother really say that stuff about Trip marrying you in front of everybody?"

Nicky blew her nose and let out a moan.

Cheryl threw her head back and gleefully clapped her hands. "Oh, Lord. I'd of paid to be there." Her gaze shot back at Nicky, and for the first time, her amused tone registered resentment. "That must have put a crimp in that little party of theirs." She paused for a moment. "I can't believe, after all that, he came to see you tonight. I know that man. He's proud."

Nicky sat on the edge of the couch and dabbed her cheeks with the tissue. "I've got some pride too, Cheryl. When he turned his back on me in front of everyone and went off with that Kim Dusenbury, I wanted to die." She blew her nose again.

Nicky stood up and paced erratically. "Everything's so messed up in my head right now. I should have told Trip about my brother before the party, but I wanted him so badly, I was willing to do anything to get him. So, how can I blame him for acting the way he did? What a way to find out about my brother!"

She leaned back against a wall and hugged herself. "But still, no matter how hard I try, I can't forget the things he said. And that look ... *that horrible look!*"

"Girl, why didn't you just send your brother packing the minute he showed up?"

Nicky took a long breath and slowly exhaled. "Oh, I couldn't do that, Cheryl. My brother and I have been on a long painful journey together." She thought for a moment. "But I know someday it's going to be worth it. *I just know it.*"

Suddenly exhausted, Nicky plopped back down on the couch, causing a burst of air to release from the cushion. "My brother's illness just about killed my mother. He got so bad when he was sixteen, she had a nervous breakdown." Her voice started to crack. "And that sweet old lady never stopped loving him or believing he'd get better." She threw her head back and closed her eyes tightly. "Oh, Cheryl. All the rosaries, masses, novenas. I can't begin to tell you. I don't know if the reason I never gave up on Jack was because I loved him, or because I couldn't stand to see him break my mother's heart."

She slumped forward. "The whole thing was too much for my dad. He couldn't understand any of it. We had to keep them apart or Dad would have killed Jack."

Tears streamed down her burning cheeks. "When people felt sorry for me, it never really mattered that much. I had my hands so full with Jack, I was happy to survive. But Trip's different ... I never wanted him ..." She squeaked out the words. "... wonderful, beautiful, once-in-a-lifetime Trip ... I never wanted him to meet pathetic Poor Nicky Sullivan." Her words trailed into sobs. "Cheryl, you have no idea what it's been like."

Cheryl's heart went out to Nicky, but it wasn't in her nature to wallow in pity or let anyone else do it for that matter. She put one hand on her hip, cocked her head to the side and lifted an eyebrow. "Girl, I not only *know* what it's like ... *I live it!* Every time I meet someone, my guts churn and I wonder what kind of a whitey I'm lookin' at. Some are color-blind, like you. Others, that's *all* they see and they hate me for it. When I took that shortcut across Georgia, every time I stopped in one of those gas stations on the edge of town, I got that feeling. Just like that dude on the beach. He had so much contempt in his eyes, it made me sick."

Nicky reached over and took Cheryl's hand. "I'm so sorry that happened."

Cheryl waved the comment away. "I don't let that kind of shit bother me. Right now, girl, you need to make some decisions." She squeezed Nicky's hand. "What are you going to do about Trip?"

"I don't really know."

"I don't see this thing going anywhere but breaking your heart. They'll be talking about what happened on the beach for years. You don't know these people like I do. They're not like us Yankees. Heck. We have fights like that every time we have a family picnic. But down here among these folks, being polite is like a religion to them. They may stab you in the back the minute you leave, but honey, they'll be polite to your face if it kills them."

Cheryl solemnly shook her head. "If you don't like being called 'Poor Nicky Sullivan,' how does 'The Yankee Biter' grab you?"

Billy opened the door to the Mole Hole and inhaled the rancid smell of cigarettes, beer and fish—typical of a beach joint. He slid onto the first stool he came to and signaled for a beer. Loretta Lynn was singing her heart out on the radio to the usual crowd scattered around the place; and except for the fishnets, oars and buoys strung around, the bar wasn't much different from the mountain hangouts he was used to.

Billy hadn't come looking for companionship. He was on the verge of seizing the kind of power he'd always craved. That guard job of Satterfield's is only the beginning, he said to himself. As head of security for the Deveroux Company, he'd soon be able to slip in and out of rich people's places whenever he pleased.

Eddie Tuck, who had been waiting for Billy, came over and sat down. By now, Eddie knew that the only reason the man ever came was his keen interest in the local gossip, and that beer would flow as long as he could throw tidbits of information on the table. He hunched over saying, "You heard about the meetin' last night?"

Billy took a sip of his beer.

Eddie spoke just above a whisper to make it sound like it was some kind of secret. "The planning board couldn't stand up to the crowd and they caved right in. They ain't gonna recommend that project of Deveroux's."

Billy reached in his shirt pocket for his pack and lit up.

Eddie kept spinning out the yarn. "Doesn't mean the deal's dead. It goes to the council next. They can say aye or nay. Most people think Deveroux's not going to let them kill it, but that Yankee gal's got everyone right riled up with her book." He shrugged his shoulders. "I don't know why? Hell. It's just some li'l ole baby book."

He gulped down the last of the beer and slammed the bottle down. Billy waved for another.

The bartender reached for the empty as Eddie blurted out, "Damn her! I'd like to take care of that bitch!"

"What bitch you talkin' about now, Eddie?" queried the bartender with a grin.

Eddie rubbed his bandaged arm and stammered, "That ... that artist over on the island."

The bartender looked over Eddie's shoulder at the crowd sitting at tables. "Hey! Eddie ain't gotten beat up enough from that li'l ole turtle gal. He wants to go git some more."

Someone shouted, "How's your bite, Eddie?" sending up another wave of laughter and hoots. While the room filled with laughter, Billy stood up, tossed a tip on the counter, and slipped out the door.

The man sitting in the dark corner wasn't laughing. Mac Moultrie squeezed his drink so hard he could have broken the glass. In all his years of living in close quarters with men, he had formed a keen ability to judge character, and Billy Cleary triggered a major warning signal. Why was this menacing individual so interested in what was happening on the island? Why would Deveroux install someone like him in their beach house? Nothing fit. He didn't like the idea of Nicky being a subject of interest either. With his comfort zone seriously invaded, Mac decided to get her off the island until he got some answers.

Billy returned to the causeway on foot. The only houses he saw lit were the four occupied by permanent residents. Billy knew each place better than he should. Nothing of value at Trip's except a couple of gold watches and a clock that would be easy enough to lift. All the artist and the fisherman had were small amounts of money lying around. The blond with the Mercedes was another story. It could take half a day to haul off everything she had.

He reached the end of the road, and instead of turning right, he crouched next to the bushes and made his way to the King's Nest. Sounds of girlish laughter coming from the living room on the ocean side drifted out of the open window as he crept along the pitch-black driveway. Suddenly a voice startled him.

"You want some popcorn?"

The kitchen light went on, shooting a beam across the driveway. Billy slipped into the bushes. He looked up through the branches and saw Nicky slam the microwave shut, then open the refrigerator and bustle around the kitchen until the popcorn finished. The strap of her nightgown slipped off her shoulder, revealing the edge of her firm breast.

194

He waited until the light disappeared, then crept underneath the raised beach house to the porch on the ocean side. He slowly climbed the steps, hovering low so they couldn't see him. He kept looking over his shoulder for anyone walking the beach as he listened intently.

Good! The black bitch was leaving in two weeks. No mention of the will. Why would she? Hardly knows the Yankee.

When they started talking about Trippett Alston, Billy became intrigued enough to lift his head to catch sight of Nicky. He slowly perused her body, not missing a curve.

Walter Satterfield tipped his office chair back, nestled the phone between his shoulder and jaw, and listened to his doctor tell him the stress test warranted an angiogram. Walter couldn't afford to sit in a hospital for a couple of days right now. The procedure would have to wait until the council approved the project. The medicine would just have to bring down his blood pressure.

He finished talking and went down the hall into the conference room used exclusively for board meetings, every expensive detail tastefully reflecting the stratosphere of the wealthy board members gathered for the day's meeting.

Tommy Warren, Jr., there as the corporate attorney, was rifling through his briefcase as he talked on his cell phone. He looked up when Walter entered, ended his call and leaned back in the thickly padded leather chair as if he were about to watch a drama.

The firm's public relations director, Rebecca Albright, had a pinched look on her face as she introduced the two consultants she had hired the minute she realized she was out of her league with the turtle debate. The closest she'd ever come to an environmental issue was the syrupy prose some copywriter dreamt up for their slick brochures.

The efficient and icy Rebecca Albright wasn't at all used to operating on the defensive. She hated the way her serene and somewhat aloof demeanor degenerated to an almost servile deportment when fielding irate calls. Up half the night polishing her resume and downing bourbon, her hands shook.

The consultant, who in another life had been with the Army Corps of Engineers, spoke. "If you can get your hands on the extra five acres, make it forever wild and throw in public beach access, we believe the council will give you a go ahead. In fact, turning this much oceanfront into public lands will probably garner a recommendation by the agency."

Tommy was impressed that Walter had gotten this far with his plan.

"Do you think the public outrage might be too strong right now to be overcome by a couple hundred feet of beach? After all, we'll be gobbling up the whole peninsula."

The consultant remained confident. "Public beach access is a big issue. Handled right, this could make the council look very good. I'd say, with the five acres, we should be able to get some major politicians to come out for this plan."

With this good news, the public relations director regained her footing. "I'll get our advertising agency on this right away."

Walter got up and signaled for Tommy to follow him into the hall. Once out of earshot of the board members, he said, "I don't want any more excuses from you. Go over there and get those damn five acres!"

The drive to Mac's took fifteen minutes. Plenty of time for Tommy to think. He'd taken off his suit jacket before getting into the car, and now loosened his tie and opened his shirt at the neck.

He glanced across the marsh and swallowed hard when he spotted Mac's boat. Soon, he would be facing his old friend as an adversary. Being a lawyer, this wasn't anything new; yet, it wasn't as if he were dispassionately representing a client either.

In the time it took him to reach Mac's, he spun out several scenarios, the most fortunate being Mac taking the deal; the least being the both of them ending up in jail—Mac for murder and him for extortion. Somewhere in between was the option of his keeping Mac's connection to the drowned girl a secret.

He pulled up next to Mac's truck and sat there for a moment recalling the days they spent as kids fishing, crabbing and swimming. Back then, he loved Mac more than any friend he'd ever had, and if anyone had told him he would threaten him the way he had, he wouldn't have believed it. When Lucinda Johnson's body washed ashore, he knew something terrible had happened; and he had been just as certain that whatever it was, Mac wasn't to blame. But a lot had transpired since those days, including his expensive beachfront home and two kids in college.

He got out, grabbed his jacket and went up the steps. The door flung open and Mac stood towering over him in the doorway. Tommy brushed by, threw his jacket over the back of a chair and sat down. Mac drew up a chair, put a foot up, and lit a cigar.

Tommy steeled himself. "Let's not cock around," he said as he got some papers from his jacket and spread them on the table. He handed Mac a pen and said dryly, "Start signing. The day the probate is finished you'll be a rich man."

Mac stared impassively at his cigar as he slowly rolled it between his finger and thumb.

Tommy was getting a horrible feeling that this was the scenario he had dreaded. "Mac, take the million and a half. Keep the house. Get yourself a lot somewhere and move it." He impatiently waved the pen in the air for Mac to take.

Mac tossed his head toward the door. "Get out."

Tommy's face contorted. "Listen, boy. Don't force me to get ugly. It wouldn't take jack shit to open up the Lucinda Johnson case—an anonymous letter to the DA, a copy to her still-grieving parents. You can pretty much imagine how it'll all work."

Mac took a puff of the cigar and slowly blew the smoke out, forming a ring. "The ugly part's gonna go down a lot easier knowing I killed your condo deal."

"What do you mean?"

"You wouldn't have hauled your high-priced ass over here, if you didn't need my five acres real bad, now would you?"

Tommy took out a handkerchief and wiped the sweat dripping down his face.

Mac, who was now slowly pacing the room, stopped and faced him. "I smelled something fishy from the git go."

Tommy's gaze darted up at him. "You mean when Mo drowned?"

That was it! Suddenly everything started to make sense to Mac, but his face revealed nothing. Mo's drowning was the connection! A macabre picture was starting to form in his head. Billy Cleary had aroused his curiosity from the moment he stepped foot on the island, but now it was evident to Mac how he got there.

Mac decided to see how deep Tommy was involved in this deal. "I wonder if the DA would be just as curious about the man who Deveroux installed in their beach house right after Mo's little slip in the creek?"

Tommy stopped wiping his face and looked up. His gaze bored into Mac's. "What the hell are you talking about?"

"Ask your friends at the Deveroux Company."

Mac crossed his arms and leaned against the sink. "You just might be getting into more shit than extortion."

The bewildered expression on Tommy's face convinced Mac that Tommy had nothing to do with Billy; but he knew his old friend wasn't completely innocent either. Why else would he stoop to his threat of dredging up Lucinda Johnson's drowning?

Tommy must have realized he made a huge tactical error in

mentioning Mo's drowning. He didn't say another word. Just scooped up his papers, grabbed his jacket, and left.

The minute his BMW was on the road, he dialed Walter Satterfield and impatiently cut off the secretary's greeting. "Put him on!"

Walter got on the phone.

"Who in the hell is living in your beach house on the island!"

"We're going to need somebody for security once the project starts."

"Don't hand me that shit, Walter! You better get whoever the hell it is out of town! Mac's on to you!" Tommy's breathing came in rapid bursts. "And kiss your five acres goodbye!" With that, he flipped the phone off.

Not another word! He was already in too deep. He weighed his options. He was still okay. As long as the will with his signature as witness didn't show up, there was no evidence against him.

🐚 CHAPTER TWENTY-ONE

Nicky clutched a cup of coffee as she glanced over at a dejected pile of odds and ends Cheryl had salvaged. A section of an ornate iron bed leaning against the wall that had taken the two of them to carry, prodded her to walk down to the peninsula and see if her new friend needed any help. The days were cooler now, causing Mac's guide tour business to pick up, and Nicky's frequent jaunts with him to end.

The ocean breeze rippled through her hair as she stood on the boardwalk with Winston, surveying the ocean before getting started. Suddenly, Dede's voice sang out from her doorway.

"You gonna' come over and say hello, or not?"

Nicky lowered her lids and moaned. Facing Dede for the first time after the fight on the beach was going to be painful. She trudged over, even though she wasn't in the best of moods.

"Land's sake, gal. How much weight have you lost?" said Dede after hugging her. Dede steered Nicky to a chair saying, "Tell me everything."

"There's nothing to tell. Trip and I are cooling it for a while. I think we should get to know each other better before we go any further."

"And just how far *have* you gone?"

Nicky raised an eyebrow and gave her a sideways glance.

Dede nonchalantly picked some lint from her dress. "So what your brother said was true. I must admit I'm surprised. Never thought Trip had it in him to look beyond those high-born types."

"Neither did Mac. And he warned me about bringing my brother to the party." Nicky glanced around the ceiling as if she were considering her words. "But you know, Dede, I'm glad I did. At least now I don't have to keep his problem a secret from Trip any more. I gave that a shot and look where it got me. So my brother's sick. If these people don't like it, I'm afraid it's their problem, not mine."

"Honey, stop talking like it's all over. Listen to me. Trip wouldn't be chasin' after you the way he has if there weren't somethin' real strong there. But if you push him away now, you could lose him. Especially with Kim's doings."

"What are you talking about?"

Dede gave Nicky a conspiratorial look. "That girl's used to getting what she wants; and you can bet she wouldn't be breaking off her engagement, unless she was cookin' somethin' up."

Nicky was afraid she might run screaming from the house if she heard one more word. Every time she recalled Kim with her drop-dead looks tugging at Trip to leave her on the beach with her brother, she wanted to tear out her hair. Her voice became a little shaky, but she still had the presence of mind to move on to a different subject before she fell into another hopeless crying jag. "If this condo deal falls through, are you going to be in trouble?"

"Don't worry about me, darling. Dede can always land a job selling real estate. You're the one who needs a little help right now."

Dede brushed a lock of hair from Nicky's forehead and studied her like she hadn't really looked at her before. "I can't get over how a little girl like you could cause so much trouble for a big company like Deveroux. Now that this turtle issue has been blown up so big, they've been fussin' all week about gettin' their hands on Mac's place. It's what's going to make or break their deal with the Council." She shook a manicured finger. "And I want to warn you, it might happen."

Nicky's voice rose. "What are you talking about?"

Dede looked her in the eyes, then away again. "I shouldn't be telling you this, but the plans for the new project were lying on my boss's desk, and when he turned his back I saw Mac's property identified as a public area."

Nicky gripped the chair as a wave of nausea hit her. She stood up and said she remembered something and had to leave. Dede jumped up and ran to the door after her; but Nicky, who didn't want her to see that she was crying, went bounding down the boardwalk steps and across the sand with Winston at her heels.

Clouds blanketing the sky, making the ocean look dark and threatening, warned Dede of cooler days to come. She watched the girl and the dog disappear down the beach until her eyes went from being watery to blinking back tears, then she sank into a plush overstuffed chair.

The room, worth over a hundred thousand in furniture alone, did nothing to comfort the woman who had worked like a fiend to own it. In fact, she felt more like she was in an overdone model waiting for a client to show up, rather than in her own home. On the coffee table, the small box from the Philippines made of bone costing nearly three hundred dollars was something that didn't reflect her taste any more than the tall antique olive pots in the corner of the room.

Dede got up, went over to the bank of glass doors and looked out at the ocean. Her mind wandered back to the night of her party and the demeaning sneer on Kim Dusenbury's face when she witnessed her humiliation. And later that night, Kim's cocky grin as she covered her mouth with her hand and whispered to a friend. It hadn't taken much to figure out who she was talking about when the friend started giggling while she looked Dede square in the eye.

Nicky getting thrown over for the likes of Kim was a travesty Dede didn't want to see happen. There was something to be said about such a wisp of a girl taking on a brute like Eddie Tuck to defend her brother. Dede laughed at the thought of it, then tapped her manicured nails on the shiny mahogany table while she wondered what in the world she could do to help.

Nicky left Dede's, and took a walk to clear her head. She made it to the far end of the peninsula and then doubled back to check on Cheryl who had already stacked another pile. Nicky took what she could carry and promised to come back later for more.

She heard the phone when she neared the house, dropped everything, and ran up the steps to find Jack on the other end, happy and excited. She imagined her mother standing nearby trying to listen.

"We went out and did it! There's a mother of a 'For Sale' sign on the front lawn and the real estate lady thinks she's already got it sold!"

"You're being nice to her, aren't you, Jack?"

"Sure. Sure. Every time I help her into her Cadillac I give her a pat on the ass. Mom and I have been driving over to New Hampshire looking at places. There's a small house out in the country we like, and Sean's trying to get it for us."

"That sounds great, Jack."

"It's practically new, and there's a small building I can use as a shop. You would really like it, Nick. There's a woods nearby crawling with animals. I'm sure you can find a couple of sick ones in there."

He paused, and Nicky knew what was coming next.

"Nicky, I don't know if I can make this move by myself. If you could just come back 'til we get set up. All the crap in this house has to be sorted and boxed up. Mary Beth says she'll help, but it won't be the same."

Nicky realized she was at a crucial point. She had already promised herself that she wouldn't be a crutch for him any more. Where had it gotten either of them? Yet, a little help from her right now might be just the thing needed to get him established into a permanently productive life, the answer to all her and her mother's prayers.

"Put Mom on."

Nicky pictured her mother's sweet smile and yearned for her. "Do you like the house, Mom?"

"Oh, yes, sweetheart. It's all on one floor. It'll be easy to keep."

"Jack wants me to come and help. Should I?"

Just as Nicky thought. Her mother hedged just enough to make Nicky believe she might be needed for the move.

"Mom, let me talk to Jack."

Nicky ended the call by telling her brother she'd think about going home. She put the phone back in its cradle, and hearing a tap at the door, looked up. Mac poked his head in. "Brought some food for the critters."

Nicky got him a beer from the refrigerator and they both pulled out a chair and sat down.

"You look tired, Mac."

He took a long thirsty drink. "We've been catching some really big reds ... thirty to forty pounds. They're about done with their spawning, so they'll probably be harder to find after this coming full moon cycle."

"Can you keep them?"

"No. The big ones have to go back. But the men like the sport of catching them just the same."

"Did you get my note about the planning board and Cheryl?"

"Yep." He looked around. "Where is she?"

"Oh, Mac. It's so sad. She goes over there every day and digs around looking for stuff. I don't know how she's going to get it all in her truck."

Mac leaned back in his chair and twirled the beer on the table. Fearful he was about to tell her he was selling his land, Nicky kept talking so he wouldn't be able to utter it.

"I got a call from Jack today. He and my mom are going to move out to the country, and Jack's afraid he can't handle it alone. They want me to come home for a while."

"That might be a good idea."

His response stunned her. "Do you really think so?"

"This place can get pretty cold when the temperature dips to thirty or below."

"But Mary Beth said the propane heater does a good job."

"You'd still have to close off the bedrooms during December and January and sleep in the living room. You don't want to be drawing with your fingers all cold. This way, when you come back in April, it'll be warm again. And don't forget your show in Boston in March."

She knew it! He was going to sell and couldn't stand to have her witness the betrayal. She looked past him and batted back tears.

"What's the matter?"

Nicky searched for a response. Her throat tightened painfully.

"Has Trip been around again?"

She closed her lids tight.

"I figured he would."

It was obvious to Nicky that Mac had no idea what was on her mind.

"Gal, the last thing you want to be doin' is stayin' with him this winter. It wouldn't be right. He's going to have to make up his mind if he wants you or not. You don't want him stringin' you along like all the rest."

Like all the rest. Nicky reached across the table and laid a hand on Mac's. "You're right." She looked at him for a long moment hoping he would just come out with it.

Instead, he slapped his legs and gave her a cheerful smile. "Well, I don't want you goin' without a proper send off. Come Friday after next, I'll take you out and show you the Cape Romaine lighthouse. We'll make a day of it. We'll take Cheryl if she's still here."

He got up to leave. Nicky rose and grasped his arm.

"Mac, didn't you want to tell me anything?"

"No. Just wanted to do some catchin' up. Somethin' wrong?"

"No. It's just that everything's so up in the air. The zoning deal, the turtles, my brother ..." She scrunched up her face. "Trip."

He grasped her shoulders firmly. "Gal, I saw the way he turned his back on you. You can't be chasin' after him. As for this zoning mess, you've done more than your share." He ruffled her hair. "And don't worry. I've got a hunch it's all going to work out for the turtles, and you'll be back at the beach before they lay again."

As he got into his truck, Mac felt guilty as hell for not being forthright with Nicky. He didn't like manipulating anyone, but she'd never leave if he let on what he was thinking.

Interfering was another thing he never did and it suddenly worried him that by separating her from Trip right now, he might be dangerously tampering with her future; but he was still willing to take the chance. No one was ever going to hurt that girl if he could do anything about it.

The idea of her not being on the island made him fight off an impulse to drive over to Billy's shack and punch the truth out of him. No. That could backfire. He had to be more prudent. He'd wait until Nicky was safely off the island, and then find out what was going on. And, besides, if his bluff with Tommy didn't work and blew up in his face, it was better that she wasn't around to see them haul him off in handcuffs.

The new house was in the stage Trip hated most. Last night, he'd forgotten to close the door to the room he was using as an office and now it would need a good cleaning before he could make any attempt at paperwork.

He picked up a set of plans and slapped them against his leg, sending up a cloud of demolition dust. Next, he cleared everything off his desk. While he pawed through a box on the floor for a rag, his cell phone sounded. Dang! It was buried somewhere in the pile. He quickly patted down the papers on the floor and retrieved it just before hearing the last bars of Rosini's *William Tell Overture*. He was sick of the tune, but knew every note and it helped him gauge how much time he had to answer.

Hearing Skeeter's voice on the other end so early in the morning surprised him.

"I just got word from someone on the county planning board. A member of the council notified them at a meeting this morning that Deveroux officially withdrew their application for a zoning change on the island. The letter was hand-delivered late yesterday afternoon."

Trip sank down onto the edge of his desk.

"If we can get our new zoning ordinance passed in the next couple of weeks you won't ever have to worry about condos going up on the island again."

"Did he tell you how all this happened?"

"Evidently the council's been in heavy negotiations with Deveroux. To counter the backlash over the turtles, they wanted them to kick in another five acres of oceanfront with beach access."

"That's Mac's place."

"Yeah. But he wouldn't sell. And without the extra green space, the whole deal went up in smoke."

The phone call ended and Trip sat stunned. A barrage of emotions rushed at him, but all he could see in his mind's eye was Nicky. He remembered how yielding she had been, and then how aloof last week, and wished to God he hadn't turned his back on her. And then he remembered what his mother had said once they were alone the night of the roast. "At least she brought her brother to the party. That's more than anyone can say about us." That reference was the very first time she'd ever acknowledged the secret everyone kept about his brother.

Cheryl went out on the porch to see if the old quilt she'd found under the rubble was dry enough to pack. She lifted it from the railing and buried her face in its softness, then looked out over the ocean at the fading glow of the setting sun. There had been plenty of evenings like this one in the old homeplace. Her grandmother would sit and rock and tell stories, while Cheryl lay listening on her small cot, tracing the designs in the quilt with her finger.

She always felt safe in the old place, like she belonged there. Much more than in the spanking new development up North. On the island, she knew who she was and where she came from. Back home she always felt she had to prove herself, just like her parents. They always had the cleanest house, the nicest clothes and the best manners. But in that two-room shack way out on the isolated peninsula, she was surrounded by a tranquility that came from knowing who you were and that you were loved for it.

Frayed and faded, the old quilt was the only treasure she'd found that made her break down and cry. This tangible link to all those long-gone family members who had been warmed and comforted by it served as a reminder of the calm dignity that was her heritage.

She stood, yearning to connect to all the emotions it had witnessed, when Nicky meandered onto the porch. The animals responded to her presence with a frenzy of pecking and scratching as she listlessly slipped down into a chair.

Nicky's decision to go back home had put a pall on the beach house and neither girl talked about it much. Ever since Dede had come over to the house and talked with her, Cheryl tried to start up a conversation about the possibility of Nicky staying on, only to have Nicky stubbornly stick to her story of having responsibilities in Massachusetts. At first, Cheryl had thought Nicky was better off back home, but Dede changed all that and now she was afraid her meddling was going to cause her friend to make the wrong move. If only Trip would try one more time, Cheryl prayed.

The far off sound of Winston's clinking tags made Nicky jump up and run from the porch into the house. Cheryl hung on to her, but she pulled away, saying she didn't want to talk to Trip and not to let him in the house or let him know she was leaving.

Trip skipped up the steps and found the screen door ajar with Cheryl leaning against the jam. Winston, ignoring the barrier, squeezed past and ran into the house to his dish.

Trip greeted Cheryl warmly and engaged in friendly conversation;

however his good spirits started to wane once it became evident he wasn't going to be invited in. He did get the feeling, though, that Cheryl didn't want him to leave. Finally, he folded his arms across his chest and in a forthright manner said, "Can I please speak to Nicky?"

Cheryl shifted her weight. This was exactly what she had been hoping for; but Nicky's mood had sunk so low she feared it might be too late. Cheryl told Trip she'd be right back, made him promise he wouldn't go away, and disappeared into the house.

Nicky lay in bed on her stomach with her face in a pillow.

"He wants to talk to you."

Nicky lifted her head. "Tell him I'm asleep."

"He knows you're not."

She pounded her fist on the bed. "I don't care what you tell him, I'm not going out there."

Cheryl sat down, put her hand on Nicky's shoulder and tugged. "He loves you or he wouldn't be over here. Why don't you give him another chance?"

"I just can't get the way he looked at me on the beach that night out of my head. Mac's right. I need to go home."

Cheryl sat up ramrod straight and impatiently tapped her hands on her thighs. "Oh, girl, I wish you wouldn't do this."

"Please. Leave me alone."

Cheryl went back to the porch, and was surprised to find Trip in the house. Instead of the usual confident narrowed-eye look she was used to, he met her with wide-eyed anticipation.

She shook her head. "I'm sorry."

His lips curved into a thoughtful frown. His gaze went beyond Cheryl to Nicky's bedroom door, but he only said, "I'm going to Savannah on business for a couple of days and just wanted to ask her if she'd watch Winston. That's all."

Fearing that if she didn't engage him somehow he might never come back, Cheryl asked, "Are you sure that's all, Trip?"

He fell back against the wall, arms folded. "Heck, I don't blame her for being upset. I was a real jerk."

Determined to keep the conversation going, Cheryl slapped her leg and laughed. "I'd of paid anything to have been there! Man alive, it must have been somethin'! I believe it's the most exciting thing that's happened on this sleepy ole island in years."

"It was exciting all right."

"Trip, a lot of this is nobody's fault. You're two dudes from totally different worlds that just happen to be right for each other."

Cheryl could tell she was getting somewhere when Trip's eyes again widened. The slight smile emerging at the corners of his mouth gave him away.

She touched his arm. "The kid's been hurt a lot. Maybe that's why she spends half her time taking care of all these helpless critters." Cheryl put her hands on her hips, and in a way that came natural to her, lightened the mood with, "Heck, the first day I was here and saw them all I thought she was nuts."

He put his head back and stared at the ceiling, smiling as if he knew exactly what she was talking about.

Cheryl decided it was time to make a move. "I'm leaving on Monday. Why don't you come over on Tuesday when she's alone and see what you can do?" When Trip's eyebrows shot up and his old confident grin appeared, Cheryl hugged herself. "Meanwhile, I'm sure she'll be happy to take care of Winston. Just leave him."

He gave her a wink and left with Cheryl slowly shaking her head, thinking how easy it was for someone with a rock-solid ego like Trip's to regain any momentarily lost confidence.

CHAPTER TWENTY-TWO

Walter Satterfield walked into the conference room and gave the board members the kind of enthusiastic greeting thirty years of backslapping had taught him made a strong impression. A hastily drawn site plan titled "Option II" hung on the wall, and a spreadsheet, showing what they would gain from dividing the ten acres on the peninsula into lots, sat at every place.

For the second time since he started down the hall, Walter checked to make sure his cell phone was turned off. The last thing he needed during the meeting was one of Billy's calls, which had become incessant from the moment they withdrew their condo proposal. And Walter hadn't dared not answer them for fear he might show up at the office, or worse yet, the house. But his next call would have to wait.

He went through the proposal, explaining that if the economy held out, they could probably get rid of the twenty half-acre sites for a million and a half each over the next two years.

But Walter would be out of there much sooner than that. And so would many of the board members. They'd already made millions developing this exclusive resort community and were now ready to move on.

Walter briefly sketched out how he planned to unload the various parcels they owned, and concluded that they should be able to dissolve the company within twenty-four months. Any properties left would be listed with the real estate firm they expected to sell their building to. This in itself would bring a good price, since it sat at the gateway to the development that would yield endless resale opportunities in the coming years.

The cheerful aura that filled the room made Walter feel even more dejected than when he entered. The stockholders were to enjoy the privileges of the rich while he was stuck with Billy. He hadn't slept nights for weeks trying to come up with a way to get rid of him. But every

208

scheme led to the same dead end—Billy wasn't going anywhere. He was a leech; and that's what they did—suck the blood out of their victims.

Between all the handshaking and back patting, Walter made up his mind that it was time to make a move no matter how desperate. He went back into his office, turned on his cell phone and placed it on the desk. For the first time since he got the gadget, he looked forward to getting a call.

Feeling unusually tired and dizzy, he told his secretary to cancel all his appointments. He reached over and picked up the picture of his wife from the credenza. This entire nightmare had brought him one consolation. She was enjoying his success to the hilt. She even looked at him in the way she did when they were first married, when he held so much promise. It had pained him deeply to see that look fade over the years, even though he had achieved more than most men.

A vision of her in a white turtleneck sweater and plaid skirt on the Smith College campus entered his mind. He'd been out of school and in business for four years and felt strange on the women's college campus, but he'd come to ask her to marry him. He knew then that it would be a challenge to please this vivacious girl, so full of dreams and high expectations, but it was those very virtues that excited him.

He leaned back in his chair and stared thoughtfully at her picture for a long moment. He knew how he could escape Billy once and for all, but he couldn't kill himself and leave her.

He put the picture down, slowly spun around, and sifted through the facts for the hundredth time. So far, no one could connect him to Billy except his maintenance supervisor and secretary. Nothing to worry about there. If Billy disappeared they wouldn't even notice.

Who else could Billy have told? A girl friend? Some other twisted individual he wanted to impress with his lurid exploits? That didn't worry Walter too much either. How believable would that sort of person be? Plus, in all likelihood, they'd probably be too well known in police circles to step forward in the first place.

Good thing he'd always given him cash and left no paper trail. But there still was the will. If Billy came up missing and someone found it among his things, wouldn't they figure it was stolen? Walter laughed bitterly to himself when he thought of all the explaining Tommy Warren would have to do, but dismissed that as something he could easily weasel his way out of, especially with his cadre of relatives who infiltrated every agency in the county. Besides, Mo's granddaughter would be so happy to get her hands on the property he doubted she'd press for an investigation.

Only one person worried him. Mac Moultrie. Walter could almost feel that Mac was on to him. He must have suspected something, or he wouldn't have questioned Tommy about Billy.

The cell phone rang. Walter was going to take one last stab at getting the will.

Walter's car rolled to a stop on the asphalt road behind the plaza and the car lights dissolved. The place was deserted except for two cats lurking around the trash bin. He checked his watch. One o'clock. His wife wouldn't miss him. By now she knew he couldn't sleep and expected him to roam the house all night.

The truck slowly appeared from around the building and crept up behind him. A small wiry figure jumped out and quickly occupied the front seat of Walter's car, bringing with him the rancid smell of cigarettes.

Walter could see Billy was in an agitated state and the thought crossed his mind that he could be in danger. He patted his side to make sure the Smith and Wesson he'd slipped in his pocket was still there.

"Did you bring it, Billy?"

"What kind of a no-count greeting is that?"

"All right, Billy. How are you?"

"I'll be a lot better if you git me that job."

"Billy, how many times do I have to tell you we don't have a head of security? All we've got is a gate with someone sitting in it twenty-four hours a day with their hands on a phone ready to call the police if there's any fuckin' trouble."

Walter buzzed his window down. The aura of stale cigarettes emanating from Billy was starting to nauseate him. "You promised you'd bring the will. Now where is it?"

"You promised me a job!"

"I'll get you one for Christ's sake!"

"What kind of job?"

"I don't know! Something! Just hand over the goddamn will!"

"Not so fast, Walter. With me as your partner you won't need it."

Walter slowly turned his head toward Billy. "What the hell are you talking about?" It wasn't bad enough Walter felt tired, now he wanted to puke and the pain in the middle of his chest was getting worse.

"Maybe you could get me a little office at your company. Where I'd be nearby in case you needed me."

"What in the hell would I need someone like you for!"

Hearing his own words, Walter immediately realized he was losing his grip. He had to get a hold of himself or he'd never get his hands on the will. He took out a handkerchief and, with a shaky hand, wiped the sweat pouring from his forehead.

"Billy, I've got your ten thousand; now where's the will?"

"You should have used my help to get rid of those two before they caused all that fuss over the turtles. It would have been easy to arrange a one-way trip to the bay for that boat of theirs."

Walter reached into his pocket and felt for the gun. "I want you to get off the island right now. Mac's been asking questions about the old man's drowning. He also wants to know who you are and what you're doing here. You better give me the will and take the money and go before he starts talking to the police."

Billy patted his leg agitatedly and looked out the window at the dimly lit loading dock. "You fucked up this whole damn deal! We were sittin' right pretty. All you had to do was let me take care of those two." He turned toward Walter. "I'm takin' charge now, Walter. And the first thing I'm going to do is git rid of that nosy fisherman. Now give me the money!"

Walter pulled out the gun. "You're out of your mind if you think I'm giving you another red cent without the will."

"Walter, you don't want to be pointing that at me unless it's loaded."

Walter's face twisted as if he were in pain. He waved the gun erratically. Billy's hand started toward the gun.

Walter got his bearings back and shoved it in his face. "I've got half a mind to blow your brains out of your head. Now where's the fuckin' will!"

Lightening fast, Billy grabbed the hand with the gun and twisted, but Walter's grip was strong. Their sweaty faces were close enough for Walter to inhale Billy's tobacco-laden breath, making him want to retch.

Suddenly the look in Walter's eyes went from hate to stark fear. He slowly released the gun and clutched his chest. His breathing came in short spurts. The heaving stopped as abruptly as it had started. He slowly sank back against the seat, eyes wide open, mouth agape.

Billy was stunned breathless, but only for a moment. He carefully took the gun from out of Walter's hand and tucked it under his belt, then reached into the dead man's breast pocket for the money. A truck backfiring on the highway startled him and he dropped the envelope. He felt around on the floor without taking his eyes off Walter's horror-stricken face until he retrieved it. He got out of the car and hastily wiped his prints from both door handles, looked around like a cagey animal, and took off.

🐚 *CHAPTER TWENTY-THREE*

Trip dropped his garment bag on the hotel bed, walked over to the window and pulled the drape aside. Reflections from the lowering sun danced on the Savannah River and glowed orange on the fleet of boats nestled in their moorings on the bay. The street down below was teeming with people out for dinner or an evening stroll. He glanced at his watch and wondered what Nicky might be doing and wished he were down there with her on his arm bustling off to an elegant restaurant.

He sat down on the bed and flipped open his briefcase. Nicky's notes lay on top. His eyes skimmed over the drawings, and he could hear her soft Boston brogue repeat the words. He ran a finger across the image of Loretta Caretta but his mind turned on the little girl who loved animals and the gentle way she held on to him as he carried her home that night. He swelled with desire remembering how willing she'd been. He pictured her once again standing on the beach offering herself to him, surf spray glimmering off her flesh.

He slowly cracked his knuckles. Ever since his college days, he'd fantasized about spending his honeymoon sailing in and out of the charming seaport towns along the coast of the Carolinas and had steadfastly reserved the experience so he could discover them with whomever he would spend the rest of his life.

The encouragement he got from Cheryl made him set everything in motion. Malcolm had agreed to lend him his sailboat. Now, all he had to do was talk Nicky into the trip. He was confident he could manage that. After all, didn't she say they had to get to know each other? What better way than a week together in his partner's Gulfstar? He smiled to himself as he turned the name over in his mind—*The Brown Pelican*.

His cell phone rang. As unlikely as the probability was, hope leapt into his heart that it might be Nicky.

212

"Hey, gorgeous. You still breakin' all those li'l ole Charleston belles' hearts?"

Trip fell back on the bed and laughed. He pictured Mary Beth standing erect with a hand on her hip. "I'm afraid all those sweet things have had about as much of Trippett Alston as they can rightly stand."

"Oh, Trippett, don't you be goin' and underestimating the endurance of Southern womanhood."

The whole time the two were engaged in teasing and bantering, Trip wondered why Mary Beth had called, until she finally got to the point.

"Trip, I need your help. It took forever to wrangle your number from your partner, but he finally gave in when I told him I was worried about my sister-in-law."

Trip jumped up. "Is anything wrong?"

"It's a long story, Trip, and I won't bore you with it, but Nicky's got another brother besides my husband. You might have seen him. He was down there for a couple of weeks. He wants her to come back to Boston, and I'm afraid she's fixin' to do just that."

"When?"

"Wednesday."

Trip wanted to kick himself. He should have insisted Cheryl get Nicky to come out and talk with him when he took Winston over. But the way Cheryl had suggested he come over on Tuesday after she left for Ohio convinced him everything was going to be all right.

Trip's thoughts shifted to Mary Beth. He wanted to know how much she knew. "I was talking with Cheryl Washington last night. She's staying there."

"Yes. We talked a few times when I called the house. It's a shame about old Mo's land."

"Cheryl told me she was leaving next week. Funny she didn't mention anything about Nicky."

"If I hadn't stopped by the gallery that handles her work this afternoon, I'd never have known either! Darn that Jack! I couldn't get a word out of him when he came back! And now he's gone and done this!"

The frustration in Mary Beth's words began to answer a lot of Trip's questions.

"That brother of hers has had a stranglehold on her for years and doesn't want to let go. He just about squeezed the life out of that girl. There I go again! I know it's not his fault; he's a schizophrenic, for Pete's sake. But now he's got the medicine he needs ... *and he's going to take it if I have to shove it down his throat myself.* He's a right maniac when he goes off it. Oh, Trip, if you have one ounce of pity for that girl, you'll help me

213

keep her right where she is. She seemed so happy before Jack showed up. If she comes back now, Jack's never going to let her go."

Trip walked over to the window and looked down at the throngs on the street. "I've met him."

"I'd love to know how his face got all busted up."

Trip kept silent.

"A lot of this is our fault. We left the poor thing to handle that crazy brother and her aged parents all by herself. But we had no way of knowin' how bad things were, bein' in Charleston and all. God, when I think of all the years she had to handle that mess with no help from anyone … bless her little heart. At any rate, I've just finished talking to her and she's hell-bent on coming home until next spring. My husband's at a conference in San Diego and I haven't been able to get through to him yet, but I'm prayin' he'll be able to get her to change her plans."

Trip quickly thought through his schedule. He had meetings set up for the next two days between a host of suppliers and the couple who were planning on buying his new project. However, if he got back Saturday night, that would still give him three days.

"I'm stuck here in Savannah until Saturday afternoon, but I'll do what I can." He shuffled through his briefcase for his schedule. "In the meantime, can you have your husband call me after he talks with her?"

He jotted down her phone number and hung up. Darn it! Why did I wait so long! Maybe he could get Malcolm to handle the next two days. No. He had a wedding to go to. Trip lay down on the bed, crossed his feet at the ankles and folded an arm under his head while he rearranged his schedule in his mind. Tomorrow he'd call the designer at the lighting center, and if he could move their Saturday appointment up an hour, he'd be back at the island before nightfall. He just had to stop in Charleston to get something from his mother.

Billy entered the beach house and yanked the string on the kitchen light hard enough to dislodge it from its base and leave it swinging by its wires. Damn! He'd pushed Walter too hard! And now he had to do something about the damn fisherman who was getting suspicious.

Billy was sure Walter's body hadn't been discovered yet, but he was already feeling the pressure to leave. First he had to do something about Mac. He took a beer out of the refrigerator and slammed the door shut; and after giving it a second thought, kicked the appliance hard enough to jam it against the wall.

He threw his head back and guzzled the beer until the bottle was drained, then hurled it through a window, exploding the glass into the night. How could this have happened! He was so close. He pulled out a chair and sat down. Suddenly, he swiped everything off the table and sent dishes and bottles crashing against the wall.

A vision of the little artist girl clouded his brain. It wouldn't take much to grab her, tie her up and take her to his place in the mountains. After he was through with her he could bury her in the woods like his father had done with that pretty little hitchhiker. She had started out feisty too, but he'd never forget the way she begged while he took off his pants as his father tied her to a tree. He was fourteen at the time, and she was the first girl he ever did. They split the thirty dollars they found in her wallet.

That memory reminded him of the envelope he took from Walter. He pulled it from his back pocket and counted the bills. Just like Walter had promised: ten thousand. Billy ran through his options. He had enough to live on for a while and with Walter and the nosy fisherman gone, there would be no way anyone could link him to the old man's drowning. But the fisherman's death had to look like an accident.

He sat staring ahead into the darkness as the plan took shape in his mind. He folded his arms, slouched back onto the chair and rocked on the back legs. After a long while, he rose and got a tool chest from under the cot in the corner and set it carefully on the table.

Billy ran his fingers around the box, over the worn paint, reflecting how it had served him in the years since his father had passed it on to him. He reached into his pocket for his keys and unlocked it.

He methodically took out a series of items and lined them up on the table. He went over to the bureau, got down on his knees and pulled out a second box from underneath, smaller than the first. He put it on the table, unlocked it and took out the tin of ammonium nitrate conveniently supplied by his cousin who worked at the fertilizer plant in Greenwood. He wiped the sweat from his forehead with the back of his hand and got out the C4 plastic explosive.

The whole time he made the bomb, the words of his Klansman uncle sounded in his brain. *Watch me closely, son. They don't call me Dynamite Bob for nothin'.* Billy had gone to live with him in Alabama after getting into trouble and had stayed until his uncle was arrested for blowing up the homes of two local black families. The man died in prison before Billy could brag on how he learned to detonate the fuses by remote. No "drip bucket" timers where a fishing bobber was placed in a container of water for him.

The finished bomb rested next to the detonator on the table as he tore through the shack stuffing his belongings into a duffel bag. All he had to do once he placed the bomb was set the fuse. He checked his watch. If those two were going fishing in the morning, the girl would probably pass by with the dog around eight and he'd have to blow them up together. But if the fisherman was going out by himself, he could take care of him first and then double back, kill the dog, grab the girl and take off with her to the mountains.

He made his way down the moonlit path to the creek and noted Mac's cabin was dark and the motorcycle gone. He'd already checked out Mac's boat a couple of times, and if his memory served him right, he stored a metal toolbox in the hold. It had to be just for emergencies since he'd seen Mac tote a big one down to the boat for repairs. It was the perfect place. When the bomb exploded, everything would fly upward and outward impaling the two with razor sharp shrapnel before the boat went down. There'd be enough metal flying through the air at three thousand feet per second to kill them both.

Mac's boat was afloat in the water—a definite sign he was planning on going out. Billy climbed aboard and carefully opened the hold. He flashed his small high-intensity light around and lifted a seat cushion, revealing a bright orange plastic box. He snapped it open and rifled through the dozen or so fuses resembling sticks of dynamite along with something that looked like a sawed-off shotgun. Better not put the bomb in there. If they got boarded by the Coast Guard, this flare kit would definitely be inspected.

He put the cushion back exactly as he found it and lifted another, exposing the toolbox. He gently lifted it out and placed it on the top of the hold. He held the flashlight between his teeth while he emptied it. His hands shook as he fastened the bomb securely to the bottom with putty and set the fuse. After carefully replacing everything and gingerly setting the box back, he wiped his face with his sleeve. His clothes were sopping wet from sweat, and the cool night air was beginning to give him the shivers. He was dying for a cigarette, but couldn't take a chance of being noticed. He double-checked to make sure he had put all his supplies back in his carryall, and jumped off the boat.

Nicky dragged herself out of bed, merely glancing at the coral line at the horizon that signaled the sunrise. She felt none of her usual ebullience at greeting the day as she spiritlessly packed lunch for herself and Mac. She went into the bedroom, stood at the mirror and brushed her hair back behind her ears before putting her whale watcher's cap firmly on her head and adjusting it.

216

She stared at herself a few moments and shook her head. Why had she promised Sean she'd call him back on Sunday? There was no point in it. Everything was settled. Jack wanted her to come home, and Mac wanted her to go. The other night, as she stood by her bedroom window and watched Trip leave, she wanted to run after him and stop everything from happening. But she held back when the thought entered her mind that if he really wanted her he would have stopped at nothing to get her to come out.

She slung her camera over her shoulder, went back into the living room and switched her thoughts to the happier prospect of a day on the ocean with Mac and their trip to the abandoned Cape Romaine lighthouse.

Cheryl rustled around in the other bedroom packing for her departure on Monday. She had said she couldn't go out with them because she had to finish, but Nicky knew better. Cheryl just wanted to let her spend the day alone with Mac.

Cheryl had been ecstatic when Deveroux withdrew their zoning application, until she phoned her parents and found out the company was going to go ahead with the purchase anyway.

The two girls avoided talking about the future, worried that if they voiced their concerns about where their lives were heading they might spiral into depression. Instead, they spent their evenings telling each other stories.

Nicky loved sitting out on the porch listening to Cheryl repeat her grandfather's yarns, and it healed her spirit to recall all the happy times she'd known at home in spite of Jack's illness. Some nights Cheryl sang spirituals, a perfect ending to the vignettes of her ancestors' experiences in the tidelands.

The way things now stood, the girls would be in touch in the spring. They made vague references to the possibility of Cheryl visiting again next summer, but since so much uncertainty existed, they were careful not to make firm plans. They did know, however, that they would be friends for life.

Cheryl came out of the bedroom.

Nicky picked up a drawing she'd done of her sitting on the beach. "I want you to have this, Cheryl. I'm only sorry I didn't do one of your grandfather's house before it got blown away." She looked around the room, and spotting the calendar with the pelican, went over and took it off the nail and set it on the table. "At least you can have this. Some of his notes are on it."

Nicky picked up her basket, and Winston, who had been watching her every move, jumped up wagging his tail. As the two made their way down

217

the road to Mac's house, Nicky felt like she was being torn in two. Mac had promised to keep taking Winston out on the boat, and Uta said she'd look after the animals on the porch until they could be released, but she still felt she was abandoning them.

The depressing thought of spending the winter working with Jack bounced around in her head, when an eerie feeling that someone was watching crept up on her. She slowly looked around the terrain but saw nothing unusual, and after noting that Winston didn't seem bothered, shook the feeling off.

Cheryl went out on the porch and looked out on the water for a while, then took a deep breath and sighed. She wondered if, after the family's struggle to keep a toehold on this beach for over one hundred years, she'd be the last Washington to set eyes on it. Discouraged, she folded her arms across her chest and strolled back into the bedroom. Most of her things were already packed and roped securely to the truck. She just had to throw a few personal items into a satchel and she'd be ready to take off on Monday.

What Nicky had said about her grandfather putting notes on the calendar picked her up a bit and she looked forward to examining it. But first, she was going to prepare a treat to make it feel more like an event. She went into the kitchen, poured herself a glass of milk and picked up a couple of cookies from a plate on the counter. She took them over to the table where the pelican's glassy brown eyes stared out from the calendar, pulled out a chair and sat down.

There were only three Ohio phone numbers in her grandfather's intricate but somewhat shaky script. It struck her as sad that the only people who he might ever want to talk with were hundreds of miles away. Funny, she never remembered getting a call from him. Instead, it was her dad who performed the family ritual of phoning him every Sunday night after supper.

She thumbed through the stained monthly pages attached to the bottom of the sheet, then casually flipped the calendar over. Her heart leapt when she saw her name carefully written across the center of a large manila envelope taped to its back.

Mac guided the boat across the bay and out onto the ocean toward Lighthouse Island. Nicky stared past his profile; she couldn't help thinking the glorious blue sky and crisp fall air held an exciting promise for someone other than herself. Different from the hopefulness in the air the first time Mac had taken her out.

218

The boat motored headlong into a cool but gentle wind and skipped over the waves, sending up a thumping rhythm during the seven-mile trip. A pod of bottlenose dolphins swam alongside for a while but eventually disappeared.

Nicky pointed as the island came into view. "Is that it?"

Mac grinned and nodded.

"How come there are two lighthouses?"

He leaned toward her and spoke loud enough to be heard over the sound of the engine. "The first tower was sixty-five feet." He pointed to the smaller one. "The short one over there that looks like red brick couldn't be seen good by boats coming around Cape Romaine so just before the War Between the States they built a new one a hundred and fifty feet tall."

"Does it still work?"

"That thing was never used as an entry light; it just marked the shoals so people would know they had to go round. When everyone got radar after the Second World War, the Coast Guard replaced it with lighted buoys. Now it's what they call a day marker."

"Can we get into it?"

He shook his head. "There's no dock. The only way to get to the island is if we beach the boat or anchor it and go in on a dinghy. We'll just get as close as we can."

Nicky looked past Mac and brushed a lock of hair from her face. She noticed another boat off in the distance coming toward them. Probably someone else wanting to take a look at the lighthouse. They neared the island and Mac cut the engine. As the boat bobbed in the water, Mac opened a beer and settled down across from her.

"Okay, gal. First, let me see a smile and then what you've got in that basket of yours."

"It's mostly everything we had left in the fridge." She reached in. "You've got your choice of tuna fish or egg salad."

"I'll try one of each."

"It's hardly a good enough lunch for the hero of Chertaw Island."

"Don't you be callin' me that."

"Oh, Mac. If you had sold them your land, it would have been a real tragedy. I'll always love you for it."

"I'll keep that in mind the next time I'm short on cash."

He crossed his legs and drank some beer. "If it weren't for that li'l ole book of yours helpin' to stir things up, we'd never have gotten all that public support to begin with."

Nicky all of a sudden felt ashamed she had contemplated the

possibility of Mac selling his land to Deveroux and considered herself lucky she hadn't said anything. If she had, their relationship would never have been the same. Her suspicions that he wanted her off the island so she wouldn't be around to see him sell were now quelled. But now she couldn't quite figure out why he was still so anxious for her to go back to Massachusetts, other than not being able to forgive Trip for walking away from her. After lunch she was just going to come out and ask him.

She handed him the sandwiches along with a cookie, then opened a plastic container of leftovers and set it on the floor for Winston.

"It's a shame Cheryl couldn't make it," said Mac. "We could be serenaded with one of her hymns right now"

Nicky raised a brow. "You've heard her?"

"Heck, yeah! Everybody has. When her grandfather was alive they'd go out to check the traps and her voice would carry all over the marsh." He was silent for a moment. "I can't imagine the island without a Washington."

They ate quietly until Mac asked, "What time you leaving Wednesday morning?"

"As early as I can." Her eyes watered. "Are you going to be home so I can say goodbye?"

"Don't fret. I'll be there to wave you off."

In fact, he couldn't wait to see her go so he could get to the bottom of Mo's drowning. Mac took a bite of his sandwich and looked out at the lighthouse for a while before asking, "Have you told Trip yet?"

She shook her head. "No. I've written him a letter." She let out a short cynical laugh. "Actually, a pelican with purple sandals and a baseball cap wrote him a letter."

She cast her eyes downward. Mac cupped her chin in his hand and raised her head.

"Don't you be cryin'. Everything's going to work out."

Nicky started to look at him, but something over his shoulder in the distance caught her eye. The boat that had been following them had stopped. She got a funny feeling in the pit of her stomach when she saw Billy Cleary standing in the bow staring at them with a grin on his face. Then, for a bizarre millisecond—almost as if time stood still—she saw a blurred image of twisted fragments frozen in mid-air; and then nothing.

Mac fought off shock as he tumbled underwater among thick debris. One thought shot into his head—find Nicky before she went out with the tide! Memories of that night thirty years ago when he swam desperately searching for Lucinda Johnson filled him with terror. He had no feeling in one of his legs, but knew it was still attached by the way he was able to thrust himself forward. Thank God they were in less than fifteen feet of water.

He fought his way to the surface. Torn remnants blanketed the water, some still on fire, but no sign of Nicky. In a panic, he shouted out her name through the smoke, but there was no answer. He sucked air into his lungs for what he knew would be the longest dive of his life and propelled himself back under. The water was so cloudy he couldn't find the large chunks of the hull lying on the bottom until he was almost upon them. He frantically flipped them over. Nothing! No Nicky.

He swam along the bottom with strong urgent strokes, ignoring the sensation that his lungs were about to burst. Gripped with fear and desperation, he jettisoned in another direction, when suddenly in front of him, Nicky's motionless body floated like seaweed. He reached out, grabbed her shirt with one hand and shot to the surface with powerful strokes with the other. They erupted into the open with Mac already trying to breathe air into her lungs. The instant she started coughing he swam for a large seat cushion floating in the water and heaved her on top of it. She was barely breathing and unconscious. He quickly checked to make sure she had all her limbs.

Seriously hurt himself and fearful of going into shock, he frantically looked around for something to tie Nicky to the cushion with. Through the smoky haze two glistening eyes skimmed the top of the water as they came toward him. "That' a boy!" Mac shouted, fiercely hoping Winston still had his leash on.

Mac gripped Nicky firmly so she wouldn't slip off the makeshift raft and traced his hand around Winston's collar until he grasped the leather cord. He managed to get it unhooked and quickly lashed Nicky to the cushion. She was still breathing, but faintly. A seat cushion that seconded as a life preserver floated near enough for him to reach and he quickly put his arms through the straps. He spotted a life jacket floating in a cluster of debris and paddled over toting Nicky with him, and wrestled it onto Winston.

Blood swirled to the surface of the water, and he realized he better do something about his leg. He could feel pain throughout his body but was able to distance himself from it. He pulled off his shirt and raised his knee. His upper leg was ripped open and he was losing a lot of blood, but he didn't think the artery was severed. One thing was certain; they both had to get to a hospital fast.

Many minutes had passed since the explosion, but this was the first moment Mac had to think about what might have happened. The only explanation he could come up with, as he tied the shirt around his leg, was that the gas tank had exploded. But that made no sense.

Faintness rolled over him; he took a deep breath and shook it off.

Racking his brain for a way to save them, he remembered the flare kit and paddled over to a large cluster of debris and pawed through it. He stopped for a moment to make sure Nicky was still breathing, when out of the corner of his eye he spotted the flare kit bobbing on the surface. He reached it with two giant strokes and pulled it up onto the cushion next to Nicky. Noticing her breathing had become even shallower, he felt her pulse again for reassurance.

He had to work fast if they were going to make it. He flipped open the box and started to take out the flare gun when he heard the motor of an approaching boat. It was barely visible in the smoky haze. Mac waved an arm and shouted for help, until it idled up beside him with the hull looming above. Mac held on to Nicky and reached up for a hand, when suddenly a man leaned over and slammed him in the head with a monkey wrench. Everything went black for a second. Only the image of Billy Cleary remained clear in Mac's mind.

By the time Mac got his bearings, Billy was nowhere in sight. Propping himself up with his elbows on the raft, Mac deftly took the flare gun out of the box, snapped the release button on the side and tilted the barrel down. He grabbed a cartridge, quickly loaded the gun and slammed the barrel shut. Suddenly Winston started flailing around in the water. Mac's eyes darted up to see an oar coming directly down on him.

Pain shot through his head as the oar landed above his eye. Through the stream of blood, he saw Billy lift the oar with both hands and start to heave it back down on him again. Mac wedged a foot against the boat and thrust himself away with a powerful kick, aimed the gun and pulled the trigger. A powder charge, forceful enough to shoot the projectile at least two hundred feet, instantly imbedded the flare into Billy's chest. Screaming and spewing fire and smoke, he staggered aimlessly until he tumbled into the water.

Blood-curdling screams filled the air for what seemed an eternity as the flare continued to burn. Mercifully, the screaming stopped and Billy slowly slipped into the ocean, leaving nothing but a pool of blackened foam floating on the surface.

Mac somehow found the strength to shoot off two more flares before pulling himself up onto the raft and collapsing across Nicky.

🐚 CHAPTER TWENTY-FOUR

Nicky's eyes roamed around the dimly lit room that had as much ambience as the inside of an empty refrigerator. Two more gurneys with patients were across the room. Cheryl, who was sitting on a plastic folding chair nearby, noticed her stir and came to her side.

"Where am I?"

"The hospital, honey."

"Mac!" Nicky dropped her aching head back down on the pillow.

"He's up in his room. They operated on him earlier."

"Operated?"

"Don't worry. He's going to be just fine. His leg's kind of a mess and he's got a bad gash on his head, but he should be getting out of here in a couple of days." Cheryl wanted to tell her about finding the will, but decided to wait until she was more coherent. "Mac woke up a couple of hours ago. I was there when the troopers talked with him."

The whole time Cheryl had listened to Mac tell his story, she couldn't help feeling that the will somehow had something to do with the man who wanted to hurt Mac and Nicky, but she had kept her thoughts to herself. After the troopers left, she had anxiously pulled the papers out of her bag and handed them to Mac. When she asked if this meant she would get the peninsula, Mac said he would study them while she went back down to the ER to check on Nicky.

Nicky put her hand on her forehead and moaned.

Cheryl took her hand. "They've already taken x-rays and think you've got a concussion."

Nicky voice was barely audible. "What happened?"

"That creepy guy who's been bothering us blew up the boat."

"Ohh ... where's Winston."

"He's fine. The troopers brought him over to the house. Your sister-in-law called, too. She told me to tell you to stay put until she gets down here."

Nicky let out a long weary groan.

Cheryl felt a pang of guilt. Nicky had sworn her to secrecy, but in the excitement of finding the will and hearing about the accident, she had poured out Trip and Nicky's story to Mary Beth.

Nicky raised an arm and studied her wounds.

"They gave you a tetanus shot and some stitches and said something about maybe letting you go home once you came around."

"How long have I been under?"

Cheryl glanced at the clock. "It's almost seven now."

Voices drew their attention toward the door. A trooper entered with a nurse. They walked over to Nicky and the nurse squeezed her hand.

"Honey, can you handle some questions from this officer?"

Nicky gave her a slight nod.

The trooper appeared oddly at ease in the setting as he proceeded with his questions. As he wrote, every once in a while his arm brushed against his jacket and exposed his holster. The interview was brief and he acted like he was more interested in getting another piece of paperwork out of the way than launching an investigation with a dazed victim.

A doctor came in to talk with Nicky and ordered x-rays for one of the other patients before the nurse finally rolled a wheelchair in and said she could go home; however it was impossible for Nicky to leave without seeing Mac.

They found him sitting up in bed. Except for the bandaged eye and IV tethered to his arm, he appeared hale, until the weariness showed in his voice.

"What kind of a First Mate are ya, gal. Passin' out on me like that."

Nicky squeezed his hand. "How's your leg?"

"They patched it up as good as they could. But it ain't gonna be pretty."

"What happened? The trooper said if it hadn't been for a shrimp boat passing nearby noticing your flares, we would have been goners."

"It looks like that guy staying in the shack didn't like turtles and decided to blow us to kingdom come," said Mac.

Nicky knew the story was a lot more complicated than he was letting on, but she was too weak to question him. Instead, she said, "Mary Beth doesn't want me to leave until she comes down to get me."

"What are you talkin' about, girl. There's no need for her to come. You're not goin' anywhere. What good are you going to be to your brother in that shape?"

"But what about the house being cold?"

Mac tossed the question aside with a wave of his hand. "Oh, with a little bit of fixin', I'll have you warm as toast."

This sudden turnaround convinced Nicky that Mac had been hiding something all along.

He reached under the pillow, pulled out some papers and handed them to Cheryl. "Plus, Cheryl here just might want to stay on, too. Looks like this gal owns the peninsula."

Cheryl jumped up, clasped her hands and cried out, "Thank you, Lord!"

A nurse came in with a cart and gave the girls a look that suggested they leave. Nicky meekly waved goodbye as Cheryl wheeled her out, with Mac yelling after them to bring him some cigars.

After the nurse finished giving Mac a shot and a lecture, he tried to put all the pieces together. He figured Walter must have hired Billy to get rid of Mo so he could get his hands on the peninsula, only to have Billy turn around and blackmail him. Surely Satterfield wouldn't have had that scumbag around voluntarily. They must have searched for the will, but old Mo had outsmarted them.

Mac had wondered what Billy was up to when he didn't show up at the Mole Hole last night. And then when the state trooper mentioned in passing that they found Walter Satterfield dead from an apparent heart attack that morning, Mac knew what had set Billy off.

He evidently had a clandestine meeting with Satterfield, got into a row, and Satterfield keeled over. But not before telling Billy that suspicions had been aroused about his coming to the island right after Mo's drowning. That must have set Billy thinking about getting rid of him next.

Mac was pumped with pain medication, but he couldn't let go. He shifted his thoughts to his old playmate. He had never been able to determine exactly where Tommy figured in this ugly little drama, but with his signature on Mo's will, he now knew. Yet he was convinced Tommy had nothing to do with Mo's murder. As the firm's lawyer, he must have been in touch with the Washington boys and gotten a tacit agreement that they'd sell to Deveroux once the land passed into their hands. When Mo came to him to draw up a will giving the peninsula to another party, Mac was betting he ran to Satterfield with the information and somehow got drawn into the fringes of the conspiracy.

Mac had been careful not to say anything about his suspicions to the troopers, especially since he figured the FBI would at least give the case a look. Luckily, since Satterfield death was from natural causes, no one was going to go around trying to link him up with Billy. And Mac had gathered in his visits to the Mole Hole that Billy kept his mouth shut and spent most of his time listening and watching, so there probably wasn't anyone else out there who knew what had been going on between the two of them. All of this bode well for Tommy.

His old playmate had protected him years ago when Lucinda Johnson went missing, and now Mac figured he owed him one. He picked up the phone, got a number from Information and dialed. A very nervous Tommy Warren answered.

"Sorry to hear about your accident, pal."

"Cut the shit, Tommy. We both know what happened."

Tommy's voice became grave. "What do you want, Mac?"

"I got the will."

"Shit!"

"Don't worry. No one's left to incriminate you."

There was silence on Tommy's end.

"That is, no one but the guy you tried to screw."

"You gotta forgive me, Mac. Once I got in, I couldn't get out. Believe me. I didn't have anything to do with the guy that blew up your boat."

"Oh, I'm sure your hands are lily white."

"Okay, I admit I was a little greedy."

"Well, here comes your big chance to redeem yourself."

"What ... ah ... what do you have in mind?"

"Cheryl. I want you to take good care of her."

"Is that *it*?"

"I mean *really* good care. I never want her to know what happened to her grandfather. And I want you to keep those Deveroux vultures off her back. Believe me, Tommy, as long as I'm alive, if I see you dicking her around, I'll cause trouble."

"It's a done deal."

They fell silent. Mac pictured Tommy wiping the sweat from his flushed face. Before he was going to be completely out of the woods, however, he might have to do a lot of explaining why he didn't come forth about the will earlier. Being at the funeral and all, he could hardly say he didn't know Mo was dead. Mac figured the best person for Tommy to do the explaining to, was Cheryl. If he were lucky, she'd settle for his eternal gratitude.

"I can't tell you how much I appreciate this, Mac."

"Now we're even."

Nicky sat on the bed while Cheryl helped her get her clothes off.

"You want to take a shower?"

"No," Nicky moaned. "I'd have to get there on my hands and knees. I just want to die."

"You can't be dyin' lookin' like that. Let me get a wash cloth and help you clean up a bit."

Cheryl carefully wiped around the stitches on Nicky's arms and then held her head steady with one hand while she gently dabbed at her face.

"There. Now let's get you into something clean."

Cheryl peeked at her watch before reaching under Nicky's pillow and pulling out her pajamas. As Nicky stiffly put a leg into the bottoms, Cheryl held the top so she could slip it on.

"Where's Winston?" asked Nicky weakly.

"He was here when I left. Trip must have come and gotten him when we were at the hospital."

Cheryl helped Nicky get under the covers and sat down beside her. She gently stroked a comb through her friend's hair and spoke in a melodious tone that promised to break out in song. "If you hadn't gone and brought back that calendar, the chain would have been broken and the peninsula lost forever." She looked off into the distance and rocked. "Lost for me. My kids. My kid's kids." Her soft voice broke into a hymn as she continued to comb Nicky's hair. "*We'll walk hand in hand, we'll walk hand in hand, we'll walk hand in hand some day ... ay ... ay ... ay ... ay.*"

She suddenly stopped singing. "Did you hear somethin'?"

There was a knock at the door, then Winston burst into the room. He rested his head on the bed and looked up at Nicky. She reached over to pet him and discovered a plastic baggie tucked under his collar. Out of the corner of her eye, she saw Trip appear in the doorway. He had his old confident grin back—like he'd come for something and wasn't going to leave until he got it.

Cheryl rose, winked at Trip and slipped out the door.

Careful not to raise her head so she wouldn't get nauseous again, Nicky opened the bag, and when she started to unfold the note inside, a ring fell out. It was small with an old-fashioned cut diamond surrounded by tiny rubies. Her throat tightened. She glanced up at Trip and stared into his eyes for a long moment, and then read the note. *My father gave this to my mother when he asked her to marry him.*

Nicky looked up at the handsome grinning face. "And what did she say?"

"Sho 'nough, Sweet Pea."

EPILOGUE

Nicky dug her toes into the warm sand and adjusted her hat. She glanced over at the twins playing in a pool of water left on the beach by the receding tide. Their grandmother knelt in the sand, ignoring what it did to her linen shift.

"Robin, don't you be pourin' water on your sister's head, now," Elizabeth Alston gently admonished. The girls were nearly two and had luminescent blue eyes and softly curled dark hair like their mother. They wore colorful disposable diapers and sun hats.

Elizabeth Alston sat back onto a blanket shaded by an umbrella, an ocean breeze ruffling her hair. She looked over at Nicky who had picked up her sketchpad. "Land's sake, girl. You've already got enough pictures of me to fill up one of your books."

Nicky smiled and kept on drawing.

A tall slender blond in shorts walked toward them holding a small boy. Mrs. Alston waved, and Nicky looked up and smiled. She hadn't been able to blame Kim for fighting so hard to get Trip and had forgiven her years ago.

"Hey, girl. How you doin'?" said Kim as she neared.

Nicky patted her stomach. "I feel like a hippo."

Kim sauntered up next to them. "How much longer before you deliver?"

"Trip says I better wait 'til after the oyster roast."

Kim sat her boy on the sand at the edge of the pool and gently splashed some water on his feet. "Who all's comin'?"

"Pretty much everybody. I talked to Dede yesterday. She says Cheryl will be here with her husband and they plan to stay for two weeks. Dede's

228

working like crazy on selling her last lot. Heavens! Where do these people get all this money?"

"Talk about money, Cheryl's got to be rolling in it," said Kim. "Although I was surprised at the small beach house she had Trip put up for her."

"I wasn't. It looks good all by itself at the end of the peninsula. She did the right thing with the rest of the land too, selling off only eight half-acre lots," said Nicky.

"Have you heard from Mac and Uta?" Elizabeth Alston asked.

Nicky was now sketching the twins at play with Kim's boy. "They'll be back from Costa Rica any day now. Mac's going to help Johnny with the oysters again."

Kim looked around. "Where's Trip?"

"Where do you think? He's out on the peninsula trying to get our new house finished before he has to start on the one Dede just sold."

"I hope you don't mind. My husband and I walked through it last Sunday," said Kim. "It's going to be beautiful. Two tiers of porches facing the ocean and another two the marsh." She glanced up at the Alston beach house. "I don't know how you ever got that man of yours to agree to move out of that ole place."

Nicky smiled inwardly. "The plan is almost an exact duplicate of a historic house in Charleston he had the plans for."

One of the twins fell in the water and started to cry. Nicky started to get up but Mrs. Alston motioned for her to stay put. She picked up the child and bounced her around in her arms. "Is Mary Beth going to make it to the oyster roast?" she asked.

"She's coming with my mother and the girls, and hopefully Sean can get away, too."

They all looked up as Winston ran toward them kicking up the sand. Trip wasn't far behind.

"It's a disgrace the way that dog looks. He's way too fat," complained Elizabeth Alston. "Trip spoiled him since he was a pup and you're just as bad."

"What about your other brother?" asked Kim. "Is he coming?"

"He's too busy with his antique shop."

Nicky put her sketch pad down and slipped her pencil behind her ear. All she could hear was the gentle splashing surf as she drifted back to her last conversation with Jack. *I'd love to come down to South Carolina and sweat with all you guys, but, hell, this is my peak season!* She had told him she loved him and he had said the same. She remembered the fight on the beach and the hundreds of humiliations of her youth and she felt proud. She had never let her brother slip away, and he had never let go and somehow, by some act of God and leap of faith, she and Jack had made it.

Elizabeth Alston's voice faded as Nicky fixed her eyes on Trip strolling toward her. She and Trip were from different worlds and that would always be the case, but nevertheless they had rescued each other. Trip neared and she could see the confident grin clearly now. Their eyes locked for a long enough moment for her to tell him in her mind that she loved him for just needing tenderness when that was all she had to give.

Meet the author:

Rose Senehi

A writer is basically a storyteller, and all my life I've loved hearing people's stories and retelling them. (With a little embellishment, of course.) They seem to rest in a special place in my mind and whenever I have a peaceful moment they drift into my consciousness.

Originally from Michigan, I landed in Syracuse, New York after attending Syracuse University. I worked as a reporter for several years before becoming the corporate marketing director of The Pyramid Companies for whom I opened shopping malls throughout the Northeast. I drew from this highly charged environment to write *Windfall*.

The whole time I was racing from town to town opening malls, I lived on a hundred acre farm outside the small village of Cazenovia, New York, where I raised my two children, Jessica and David. I tried to inject the unique and wonderful flavor of the people of this small farming community into the characters of *Shadows in the Grass*.

Welcome to books from
INGALLS PUBLISHING GROUP, INC

For more information on books and ordering and
links to authors' websites, visit our main websites at:
www.ingallspublishinggroup.com

For more information about
Rose Senehi
her other books and projects
visit her website at:

www.rosesenehi.com